The Man from

By

James J D

Graphics by Amanda Rose

For all my family whose story this is.

Acclaim for The man from the Ministry

Acknowledgements

For the people who lived through this tragic time in our not so distant past and who's story this is based on. And to my partner Rita who helped me find the elusive white walled cottage on the heathland, lost to my family for more than 50 years. It is where the Mitchell family, my family, lived during much of World War 2. Although in this book I have called them the Miller family they are the Mitchell family who I owe so much too.

I would also like to thank the many friends and family members who helped me share these wonderful memories and write them down so that they will never be forgotten.

Despite having changed some of the characters named in this book and also the names of many of the villages and towns mentioned, it is based on a real family's travelling during the war years from 1939 until 1945. It tells the tale of the lives of an ordinary and rather large farming family made to travel the south west of England in the service of the many grand estates who owned most of the farms all across the country.

This story really begins with the shortage of farmhands forcing the government to take control of the farms, giving the estate owners set targets to aim for and moving the farm hands where ever they deemed they were needed with the aid of the man from the ministry.

The man from the Ministry

Prologue

This is the remarkable tale of a family's travels through the dark years of 1939 and 1945. My name is Ruby Miller, second eldest daughter of Mr and Mrs Miller and this is our story from the beginning of WW2 to the end.

There was a lot of us, as I had eight siblings; four sisters and four brothers, some of whom were barely weaned, and all of them came under the care of my older sister Jane and myself, quite an undertaking, as we were but children ourselves. I didn't mind all the hard work though, it was the constant moving that I didn't like, of never having a place to call home. Of feeling like an outsider, a mere stranger everywhere we went! None of the others seemed to mind or if they did, they didn't say anything. But I hated it, hated the looks I got at school as if we were one of the new kids... one of the evacuees which we were not. We belonged here, we were Somerset born... it's just that we were made to move so often!

The problem was our dad was a Journeyman, who knew all there was to know about the land and about farming. And so, his talents were required here there and everywhere and so we moved wherever there was a farm in need of his skills. Little did we know just how far from our roots that would eventually take us or of the great tragedy that it would afford us along the way! But that was a long, long way down the road. In the beginning we had to deal with the locals, people who thought of us only as shiftless, no-goods, stealing their jobs and the food off their tables.

'They called us the moon gone, the locals did, saying that we always came with the break of day and left by the light of the moon... travellers in other words. Gypsies if you will with no place to call home and only lonely roads on ahead of us. But, of course none of that was true, well almost none of it. True we travelled, but that was not of our doing that was the fault of the Ministry... and of the bloody war.

As a family we were close, of course we children grumbled a bit about having to change schools so often and not being able to keep friends for long. But still, we were happy enough with our own company and ever ready to make our own fun. After all we were country children and well used to living on farms miles from anywhere, but always surrounded by beautiful countryside for us to explore.

It was when the Ministry became involved, dictating just where we should be. Moving us from place to place. That's when our world changed! Suddenly there was nowhere we could really call home, one day we'd arrive at a farm and before we had time to un-pack, we'd be on the move again. It became quite head spinning. For the most part one place was much like another and farm work after all was the same or so we thought in the beginning! Then we came here to Home Farm and fell in love with it, and suddenly we dreaded the thought of ever having to leave. But of course, we knew we'd have too. When that time came, along with the rest of my siblings I was heartbroken, thinking that we'd never find another place to call home, not if we travelled a lifetime! But I was wrong.

There was one place, a beautiful place where we would stay longer than a few weeks, longer even than a few months. For almost 2 years we would revel in our very own garden of Eden deep in the heart of Sandbourne's heathland. Looking back now I wonder how it was that we found such tranquillity in the midst of a war that raged all around us. For our new home was but a stones-throw from Poole harbour a very real target for the German bombers. And yet, somehow, we came to love it.

Strangely it was the nearest we'd ever been to the war and yet it was as if we were in a world apart, as if nothing could touch us in our new wonderful wilderness. I have to admit to not feeling the warmth of the place right away however. In fact, on first arriving at our new home; as the moving van pulled onto the unwelcoming gnarled heathland, it felt like a darkness had entered our lives, and I cursed the day when that man from the Ministry had paid us a visit.

Chapter 1

I awoke strangely excited?

Although it was just another Sunday morning, I felt a tingle run down my spine as if today something quite extraordinary was about to happen! I shook the thought away as I got out of the bed I share with my sister Jane, who was already up and no doubt preparing breakfast. Hurriedly I dressed and went through to the kitchen to give her a hand, but she wasn't there? Realising she must have gone out into the yard to feed the pigs, I went over to the range to check on the simmering caldron of porridge before cutting up chunks of bread and quickly buttering them, knowing the little-ones would be stirring soon and my big sister Jane would be angry if she came back to find me daydreaming... again!

I was always daydreaming; dad says I should be awarded a medal for it. I smiled as I thought about our father, he was special, not just to me and the family but to anyone who knows anything about farming... damn! I'm daydreaming again! I glanced at the old mantlepiece clock; 7am, time was flying by. Still my mind wandered as I thought about dad and how well he was thought of in the community; 'Oh! To those who didn't know any better he was just a farmhand, a journeyman if you like. But to the landowners, the Lords and Ladies of the grand estates that hired him, he was a must have, a man for all seasons. They fought over who he'd work for next? Or at least they did until the Government took charge. Now father has become their tool, going where ever they deem to send him, and we, his family of course are bound to go with him. No easy feat as there are so many of us.

It's already hard to remember the names of all the farms we've been sent to during this time of great unease and uncertainty... a time that feels fractured somehow.

Once again, I was at it, my mind drifting off into the great unknown... I think dad's right, I should get a medal for daydreaming! I smiled if I didn't get on with my chores our Janie would give me more than a medal, a thick ear would be more like it. Was it any wonder I was daydreaming so much today, it's so hot in the kitchen, with the range blasting out its heat and the Autumn morning sunshine streaming through the window of our little cottage down the lane? God how I love Home Farm, to my mind it's the best place we've been sent too and hopefully it will be our home for a long time to come.

'Ruby Miller!' I growled angrily to myself in the quiet of the hot kitchen, 'pull yourself together girl!' I looked again at the clock; time was getting on, but in spite of the good telling off I gave myself; I could not shake off the feeling of excitement that I'd felt ever since waking this morning! There was something about today that had my mind running every which way, like I was expecting something to happen, something momentous. I shook away the silly notion. Nothing much was likely to happen to us, not unless... well no, there was no, not unless, nothing ever happened here... unless?

At first, I tried to ignore the ominous knocking on the front door, hoping one of my siblings might stir themselves and answer it. But of course; they didn't and so reluctantly I went to see who it was for myself. Halfway along the hall whoever it was hammered on the door again, it was a seriously determined sort of knocking causing me to pause, what on earth could be so urgent.

It was a typical slow end of summer beginning of Autumn sort of day as I opened the door to the stranger. The sun seemed reluctant to give way to the beckoning Autumn clime and for a moment caused me to shield my eyes.

'Yes?' I asked abruptly. I tried to hide my impatience, but I had things to do...the washing to hang out, the hens to feed, the family breakfast to get ready!

'Mr Miller?' the man asked stiffly, taking off his spectacles and giving them a vigorous clean.

I sighed, 'No! Of course not!' I snapped. 'I'm his daughter Ruby.'

'I mean is he in?' he said, unamused by my answer.

I looked him up and down; he was tall and spindly, all arms and legs, and he had a pointy nose and sticky-out ears which I would have found quite funny had I been in a better mood! But I was not in a better mood and so could only think how ridiculous he seemed. And so out of place standing there in a yard full of cow shit dressed like a bloody undertaker! Although I knew he wasn't one of them, they were more, humble. This one stood there like an asshole looking at me as if I were the village idiot!

'Who are you then mister?' I asked, standing my ground. Then, even before he answered, it hit me; 'You frum the Ministry then?' I guessed. Having seen his like before. He took a deep breath, obviously annoyed that I was questioning him but I didn't care. I was in charge and so he could tell me or bugger off. Not that I'd ever dare say such a thing to his face. 'Yes, he said at length; I'm from the Ministry, now would you please answer my question... is your father at home?'

I frowned; this was not good! What did they want of us now? I felt like saying that he had the wrong address, as he stood there looking down his long pointy nose at me. I wished him away; he was so not of our world! Everything about him was shiny and black, from his funny bowler hat and impeccably neat clothes, down to his gleaming black shoes; although they at least were not as pristine as the rest of him having picked up some of the cow shit off the yard. I smiled; now if only the squirrels would start throwing their poo at him instead of the odd green hazel nuts, I'd be happy.

As if by request a white dollop of pigeon poo plopped onto his shoulder causing him to smear it across his beautiful black jacket. I couldn't help but giggle.

'That's nature for you, sir,' I said. 'I just needed the bramble bush to join in now and snag his sleeve on his way out and that would make my day.' He just stood there for a moment shaking his head in disbelief. I wanted to shout at him; 'get over it mate It's only a bit of shit for goodness' sake'. He took a deep breath; 'so is your father at home or not?' he asked again.

I felt an angry response coming and bit down on it, counting to ten as dad had taught me to do when I got angry, just to give myself the chance to calm down. 'He's out across the fields, mother too. Off that way, down the lane and over the stile.' I pointed, starting to shut the door on him.

'No, no, I can't go chasing across the fields, please give him this.' He pushed a letter into my hand then started back across the yard through the gate and up towards the main road. I watched him go, enjoying seeing him tiptoeing across the muddy yard in an effort to keep a little shine on his black shoes. I smiled, though I knew I shouldn't, when he trod in a pile of still steaming dung.

On my own again, I turned the letter over in my hands wondering if I should give it to my big sister Jane just in case it was important, but in the end, I decided that if it was important the stranger would have taken it to dad instead of leaving it with me. With that I put it on the mantelpiece next to the old clock and got about my chores knowing my big sister would be cross if she came home and found that I'd not finished them. She was a stickler when it came to doing our chores, that and seeing to the little-ones. Not that I needed telling, but she'd tell me anyway! I smiled, despite everything we got on well, when she wasn't being so bloody minded.

Later, when my sister Jane came in from feeding the pigs, I showed her the letter and watched the frown on her forehead deepen.
'This is frum they Ministry people,' she frowned. 'I bet it's an order fer us to move;' she sighed. 'Let's just hope, it's somewhere local so we can stay where we are and keep going to the same school.'

I saw the look of worry on her face and began to worry myself, but surely, they wouldn't move us again so soon, not when we were just beginning to settle into Home Farm? Well, Home farm was what we called our little tied cottage down the lane, although that was the name of the whole farm really. I'm not sure our place actually had a name of its own.

'Do we have to do what they say Sis, I thought dad worked for the farmer not they ministry people.' I grumbled.

'It's because of the war our Rube' it's about us doing our bit ta feed the nation,'

'Hah! I bet you heard that on the wireless!' I accused.

'So, what if I did, it's true enough and we could be sent anywhere.'

Now that was scary! 'Do you think they might send us a long way frum ere then, Sis? I worried.

Janie shrugged. 'I had hoped we'd not be hearing frum them yet for a while, it's only been a couple of months since we got here, but I've quite taken ta Home Farm, Rube, I really have.'

I nodded; 'Me too, Sis and I really don't want ta have ta find a new school or new friends again so soon, so let's keep our fingers crossed,' I added.

'What will be will be, little sister,' Janie sighed.

I suddenly felt angry; 'Why can't they leave us be, folk already think we're Gypsies 'cause we move so much,' I groaned.

Janie chuckled; 'they do not. I've never heard that kind of talk and I see more of the neighbours than you, our, Ruby.'

'But they do,' I insisted, 'the Gypsies down the lane, they call us! True, we live down a lane, but we ain't Didicoys,' I snapped angrily.

'Course we're not. You do know this farm is part of Lord Brympton's Estate, and not just anyone is chosen to work for him. So that makes father a bit special. Everybody knows that, an' if they don't then I'll soon remind 'um,' Jane barked.

Finally, I grinned, 'I bet you would too, Janie,' I said, giving her a warm hug.

The little ones started to trickle into the kitchen then wanting their breakfast, and so we concentrated on feeding them. Although neither of us were able to keep our eyes off of the letter on the mantlepiece.

'What do you think, Janie, another local farm, or...'

She got angry then; 'Well I don't know do I, we'll just have to wait and see,' she snapped.

With that mum and dad walked in to snatch a bite to eat before continuing with their work out across the farm. I dearly wanted to point out the letter to them, but as usual, breakfast for them was a quick stopover before continuing their work, and so, to my and to Janie's disappointment they didn't even see the letter and we didn't mention it, knowing how busy they were.

It was a long rest of the day for me, especially when Janie left to do her bit out across the farm and my other siblings went seeking adventure in the nearby woodlands, leaving me all alone with the little-ones, with the letter a constant in the corner of my eye. With a great effort I put it from my mind and concentrated on cleaning and tidying the house and playing games with the little-ones, until Janie returned and we prepared the tea for when mum and dad got home. The letter though was a torment and I couldn't stop myself from continuously looking at it, and caught our Janie doing the same.

When they finally got home it was our Janie who cracked first!

'There's a letter on the mantlepiece, I think it's from the Ministry' Jane said even before they'd taken their muddy boots off.

Mum looked tired and a little haggard, if truth be said, seeming much older than her 39 years, that she always boasted was a year younger than dad. I thought for a moment that she was going to leave opening the letter until after tea but instead she took it down and opened it right away.

'It's frum the Ministry sure enough father,' she said, 'we'll speak about it later.'

Janie and I exchanged disappointed glances. I could see by the look on her face that she was as eager as I was about what was in the letter. But it was obvious mum was going to save it until she and dad were on their own and so reluctantly, we concentrated on feeding the little ones whilst keeping our ears open to what mum and dad were chatting about at the other end of the kitchen table. However, it was impossible to hear what they were saying for the most part as mum was whispering and being super secretive, much to my annoyance.

'I don't like this, our Ruby,' Janie sighed, 'something's up!'

Finally, we were forced to get on with clearing the kitchen and so roped our Janet and Bella into helping what with them being the next eldest girls. Our Jack and Danny were older than them but claimed that it was women's work! Silly boys! They always got a clout from our Janie, but in the end, it was quicker to leave them out of it all together. I had to smile, for they always paid the price for their cheek, as my big sister would find them even more chores to do.

Later, with the little-ones tucked up in their cots and the rest of our siblings in bed, Janie and me stood by our bedroom door trying to do a little eavesdropping on mum and dad.

'I've been dreading this, father...' We heard mum say!

'Oh dear,' I whispered softly.

'Shh! She's still speaking,' Janie hissed.

'The maids won't like leavin yer mind mother what with the little ones ta see to,' we heard father grumble.

'Well, there's nothin ta be done about it, we're ta be on the road come Friday of next week, and that's that.' mother snapped.

'Next Friday! I gasped. 'As soon as that?'

'Tis not the when, ma, tis the distance,' dad grumbled. 'I make it a good 50 odd miles frum yer!'

'Did you hear that Sis, 50 miles, I can scarce believe it, why, we've only ever been as far as Yeovil Town which is just 5 miles away.'

Janie tugged my sleeve; 'we should go to bed,' she whispered, 'it's getting late.'

We settled down, but I couldn't sleep, my mind was in a whirl;

How could the, Ministry people be so cruel to ask us to go so very far away? Don't they realise how difficult It is for such a large family as ours to pack up everything at such short notice, and travel 50 odd miles across the country? Do they even care? I clenched my fists, trying to calm down, trying to understand their reasoning. Alright, so father was a journeyman, a man for all trades when it came to the land, and his skills are sought after every which way. But that don't mean they can just do as they please with us. We have rights... don't we? I felt my temper boiling up and bite down on it, but still the anger remained.

'How dare they send us so far away!' I grumbled to Janie. 'As if our lives aren't hard enough.'
'But that's how it is on a farm, Sis' Janie sighed, 'hard and dirty,' and the truth is we love every minute of it and you know it.
Oh, sure sometimes it would be nice to have electricity, instead of candlesticks, and having running water would be nice with so many siblings to keep clean, and we both hate having to go down to the well at the bottom of the garden, especially in the middle of winter.'

I had to admit to myself that our Janie was right, despite all the hardships I would not change a single day of our lives. Alright, so I might complain about the chickens invading the house now and then and about the mess they leave behind, but that's me! My big sister takes it all in her stride, dirt and all, while I kick up such a fuss! I know Janie thinks me a bit of a prima donna at times, but it's just because I like cleanliness not just around the house, but for myself too. And perhaps I do like to admire myself in the looking glass too much and brush my long, auburn, not ginger hair, as Janie calls it, a lot. So, what's wrong with that? I just like to look pretty... I am pretty, despite the spattering of freckles across my nose and cheeks! I'm the prettiest one in the family anyway, not that I'd ever boast or anything!

I could hear Janie's gentle snoring at my side and turned to look at her, she took after dad, had his dark brown hair and his unruly scruffy look, every inch of her countryfied. True I'm of the country too but not the same as her. I have more of mum in me, I like a pretty dress and nice shoes! I'm a Sunday best type of girl if truth be known.

Lying there next to Janie, I suddenly felt a little guilty! Being prettier than her didn't mean a thing. She was my big sister, my rock, solid and reliable and so very kind and caring, always putting everyone else's needs above her own. And even though she was only 13 and just a year or so older than me, she was so much stronger, not just physically but mentally too, nothing ever got the better of her, and that's why we all looked up to her.

The way she took such good care of us all while mum and dad were off across the fields was amazing. I smiled, if truth be known many of the little-ones thought of her as their mother, not that I'd ever tell her that. She'd give me a clout for sure! Just like she did when I threatened to tell our school friends how we often have to trudge across the yard in our wellie boots with our dresses tucked in our knickers. But that's only in the wet and windy days of winter mind, when the rain was running like a stream across the yard and down the lane.

It was when the winter rain turned to snow and the running stream to ice, that's when things got very hard! That's when father has to keep the fire burning the night long and still the icicles creep down the inside of the bedroom windows and the snow blows beneath the front door. I snuggled closer to Janie as memories of frozen fingers and toes chilled my bones. Even so, the harshness never really got us down, for we all knew in a few months we'd have the Spring to look forward too. A time of such beauty in the countryside, with an abundance of flowers along the awakening hedgerows, with wonderful displays of primroses and cowslips in the fields all around. All of which we'd pick for mum to put in vases and spread around the cottage so that it smelt like Spring inside as well as outside. And so, each morning, when I opened my eyes, my heart would sing.

At last, my body relaxed as the rigors of winter in my mind turned to thoughts of Spring. But then a naughty little voice whispered in my ear; 'That's how it is here, but will it be the same where we're going?' I felt a tear trickle down my face. 'It's not fair,' I muttered to myself; 'it's just not fair.' I felt Janie stir at my side, so I feigned that I was asleep, not wanting to worry her with my negative thoughts. But I could not stop them tumbling on.

Would the next place be as nice as this one? Here we have room to spread are wings, room to grow, able to run and play out across the estate, to make secret dens in ancient woodlands, and learn to swim in crystal clear streams and sun warmed mildewed ponds that only the deer and other animals know of, and later meander through orchards of apples and pears, and climb atop hayricks of golden straw and watch a multitude of birds making nests in the trees all around.

'And now we're moving fifty miles away!' I began to cry.
'You alright Sis'? Janie mumbled softly at my side.
'Just dreaming, go back to sleep,' I whispered.
I took a deep breath; I was going to miss Home Farm. It might be just a tumbledown old place in the back of beyond to many, but we'd only just gotten used to calling it home. I couldn't help but wonder once again, if we would ever find another place like it?

As I lay there, an image of father popped into my mind and I sighed. How silly was I. Home was not a particular place, it was where ever he and mum and my brothers and sisters were. Finally, now I could settle down, but before sleep claimed me, I thought about dad and how much I loved him and his silly pranks and practical jokes. Mum rarely saw the sense in all his horseplay, or Tom Foolery as she called it, but to us kids it took the edge off many a hard day.

Finally, I was ready for sleep, but no sooner had I closed my eyes than the dreaded sound of the air-raid siren screamed out its wailing warning. Leaping out of bed I helped Janie gather up the little-ones and make a mad dash across the yard to the bunker at the bottom of the garden. The little-ones were complaining bitterly about being dragged out into the cold, but dragged they were, like it or not.

The war was almost a year old now, not that we knew much about it living as we were out in the countryside, although father worried that the German planes might target the nearby town of Yeovil where there's an aircraft factory. But not this night, this night it would seem they had other targets in mind as they passed us by. Still, we stayed in our shelter and father told us of his time in the army back in 1918, of how, by luck, he had just missed the 1st great world war, it having finished before he was called up. He was sent to India though, where he caught Malaria, which as it happens is what has kept him from being called up this time around.

Some might say he's very lucky, and perhaps that's true, but I've seen him shivering and shaking unable to even stand upright when the disease returns, which it does quite often. And even without that worry, in this year of 1940, life is hard, rural life is hard. But then life has been hard for everyone for a long time now, before the beginning of the war we were still in the grip of, what most people called the great depression. A terrible time for the whole nation, although, thankfully, we ourselves have never experienced too much hardship. Oh, our shoes are a bit worn down and our clothes all come from the jumble sales, but we always have plenty to eat and father keeps a roof over our heads.

As I sat pondering with one of the little-ones fast asleep on my knee, I recalled my last visit to Yeovil town before the war, where I witnessed how desperate a time it was for many who were starving and begging for crumbs on the street corners.

Many of them were brave men and women who had fought for our country during what was known as the Great War... the War to end all Wars! And now here we were again!

My thoughts drifted to the photos of my two uncles on the mantlepiece, who both died in that Great war and I felt quite sad that I never got to know them.
How many other children after this war will be looking at fading old photos and thinking the same, I wondered?

Despite the cold of the shelter, I managed to fall asleep, and woke up to Janie taking the little one from me. 'Mum and dad want to talk to us before they go off to work... don't let on that we already know,' she hissed.
'Has the all clear sounded, then?' I asked rubbing sleep from my eyes.
She shook her head, 'You'd sleep through anything our Rube,' she chuckled.
'Not your snoring, Sis,' I grinned, struggling from my wooden cot.

With our siblings once more tucked up in their beds in the cottage, we joined mum and dad at the old kitchen table, where they were hurriedly finishing breakfast.
'No doubt... no doubt! You over heard your father and me talking last night, so I'll not waste my breath repeating what you already know,' mum said, pulling on her wellies.
'We heard some of what you said, but not where we're going?' Janie dared to say.
'Well, you heard all you need to know then,' mother sniffed. 'There'll be no school for any of you this week, the two of you will be in charge of the boxes and suitcases, and make sure you pack everything we'll be needing.'

As they went out the door, dad hung back and gave us a wink; 'Think of it as a great adventure,' he grinned. Janie and me had no time to talk about it, already the little-ones were filtering into the kitchen wanting their breakfast.

Now, it was never easy looking after so many on top of all the chores we had to do, but we had a system, Janie and me. To make it more manageable for ourselves, we'd split the children between us.

My group contains most of the little-ones; Violet, Morgan and Charley, all of whom are under four years old. Sometimes, I had to admit, I felt it a little unfair that I should have to look after all of the tots, who clung to me the day long and most of the night too! Although, if I'm being honest, I did have our Janet to help me, she being the third eldest behind Jane and me.

Whereas poor Janie had no help at all and she had amongst her lot, our brothers Jack and Danny! They were the two oldest boys in the family, and a more unruly pair would be hard to imagine. Our Bella might have done more to help her but she being as meek as a lamb, was, in truth no real help to anyone.

'Do you think mum might go into Yeovil before we head off next week?' Janie asked, as we served up the porridge to the kids clambered onto their seats around the table.
'Maybe! I know there's a jumble sale on tomorrow, but she's not said anything about us going,' I frowned.

Later when mum and dad came in for lunch, I dared to bring up about the jumble sale in Yeovil town and was surprised by mum's answer; 'I thought I'd said,' Yes, we are going to the jumble sale, it might be our last chance to buy clothes for the little-ones before we leave, if that's alright with you our Ruby,' she smiled, knowing how much I loved to go into Yeovil.

It was only about 5 miles into Yeovil town from our place, although with the roundabout route the bus took it seemed to take forever as it zig-zagged from one village to another, down narrow country lanes. Still, it was a day out and I love it, as did our mum. Catching the bus at the top of the lane the next morning I could hardly contain my excitement.

Although we arrived quite early there was already a sizable crowd gathered around the doors of the small-town hall, many of them glancing nervously back and forth, shuffling and inching forward ready to make a mad rush as soon as they opened for business. As well as town folk I saw the odd Gypsy here and there, all of them ahead of us unfortunately. I cursed that the bus had been so late... now it would be a free for all.

Mum was gripping my hand so hard that it hurt and I tried to pull away, but then the doors were thrown open and all hell broke loose! For the most part I stuck close to mum, grabbing for things she told me to grab for, ducking and diving here there and everywhere, pushing and shoving people aside if I had to, for there was no quarter given at the jumble sale and mum expected me to come back with what she'd asked me to get.

On returning home, once mum had left to join dad out on the farm, Janie demanded to know all about my daytrip into Yeovil. And so, with my siblings gathered around expectantly, I delighted in telling them of all that had occurred on our day at the infamous jumble sale. Recounting the action in all its glory, although I have to admit to exaggerating a little, which I consider fair enough as it gives my siblings a better tale to listen to!

They could scarce believe it when I told them of seeing old Mrs Green in a tug of war with Mrs Peabody over a moth eaten, ugly yellow jumper, which was stretching the truth a little, as seeing the amount of damage to it they both decided against it in the end. Although, Mother threatening to slap a rather posh looking woman as they both grabbed for the same pair of leather sandals was perfectly true. Mum won of course and I showed off the sandals on my feet, to prove it.

As nice as my stories of the jumble sale were, the, older children also wanted to hear of any news or gossip! All I could offer was that the air force base on the outskirts of town had taken several hits, but nothing serious, which was good, although not exciting enough for my siblings.

They did enjoy a bit of drama now and then. It was in Yeovil last year that I heard about the pending war with Germany! I recall that only too well! I remember rushing home to tell mum and dad, only to find that they weren't the least surprised, and all dad said was; 'war or no war, I still have the cows ta see to, and the bloody fields ta plough ' he'd sworn, as he stamped into his working boots. My brothers and sisters were excited by my news though, not that any of them truly understood the terrible truth of what war meant, not that I understood any better myself?

What happened after that was quite strange and one or two of my siblings thought I must have got it wrong, because for months nothing happened! People began to call it the phoney war and so it seemed to most of us. It wasn't until we had the first evacuees arrive in the area and were issued with gas masks, that I realised what I'd heard must have been true! And then, when I saw friends and neighbours, building bomb shelters at the bottom of their gardens and taping their windows in case of bomb blasts, I knew my world was about to change, perhaps forever.

It was a scary worrying time, and that's why when it happened and I heard it, I didn't tell the family of the news about our defeat at Dunkirk... and that the Germans were building an armada on the beaches of France just across the channel, so creeping ever closer to our shores! Hearing it made me realise the need for the wailing sirens and the enforced blackouts.

It was during the blackouts when our normally dark country nights became blacker still, that things began to seem weird! It was so strange not to have the lights of nearby Yeovil town glowing in the distance. Instead, we were blessed with a perfect night sky, lit only by the stars and the moon.

'A poachers dream;' Dad winked, as he found me standing at the back door looking out into the darkness.
'Tell your sister ta be ready an' we'll head on out tonight.'

I felt a surge of excitement as the country girl in me came to the fore. The fact that it was against the law did make me feel a little nervous however. Although at my side as we started on up the lane Janie was as calm as can be, with her arms full of deer traps. 'You got the rabbit snares Rube?' She whispered as we moved out of the lane up along the hedgerow at the top of the field. 'Yes,' was all I could manage, trying desperately to keep my knees from knocking.

'Over yer then maid,' dad called back to me. He shone his small torch along the ground being careful to shield it with his hand; 'See, this be the start o' the rabbit run, girls,' he whispered, 'we'll lay 'em along yer.'

One by one dad took the wire snares from me and then we moved on to the snares he'd laid the day before; four of those held rabbits, which dad seemed pleased with. 'That'll do us fer a day or so, he said. 'Now let's see if we have us a nice deer or two.'

As we entered the small coppice at the top of the field dad had Janie lay her deer snares among the trees, before checking on yesterday's traps, where we found one small deer. Strangely the thought of killing a deer didn't feel right somehow, rabbits yes, but deer, no. I blame mum for reading us the book of the lovable little deer, Bambi a little while ago. But dad had no such feelings and so we went home with four rabbits and one small deer.

'Should we be careful in case the gamekeepers are out and about.' I whispered juggling the rabbits in my cold hands.
'No, tis the farmers that 'ave the last say, an' they don't mind maid, as long as I share's it with 'em!' dad chuckled.
'Get a move on there, Sis,' Janie hissed, 'this deer's gettin' heavy,' she had it slung across her shoulders, not something I could have managed, I'm sure.

With that I stepped up the pace and we hurried on home. That was the last night for our poaching exploits, but it was a good haul to be taking with us on our long journey next week. Mum, I knew would be pleased with our catch.

I couldn't get excited, as good as our night had been; the news the Ministry man had given us was still haunting me... 50 miles! I shook the horrible thought away. It was breakfast time and I needed to get on.

Janie's gratingly loud voice brought me back to the present as she bellowed at our Danny who was up to mischief yet again.

'Take that,' I barked, clipping his ear on passing.

'Ouch! What was that for? You don't even know what I did wrong,' he protested.

'Don't care, and you'll get another one if you don't watch it my lad,' I growled.

'You worried about leaving, Janie?' I asked later, catching her alone in the kitchen.

'Aren't you, Sis, in just a few days we'll be moving 50 miles away... 50 miles!'

I shivered at the very thought of it; 'That's a long way Janie! Do you think we'll ever come back from such a distance?' I felt like crying but held it back with a giant snotty sniff.

'Let it all out Rube' better to shed a tear now rather than in front of the little ones.'

She squeezed my hand and we fell into a sloppy hug; 'Don't worry I'll keep it together Sis,' I promised.

'That's the spirit, who knows, we might be back in a few weeks, Rube', we never stay anywhere for very long,' she smiled.

She was right, that's why everyone called us gypsies... and for once I didn't mind!

For the rest of the week, it was all about packing cases and labelling everything, making sure we knew what every box contained. Although our Jack and Danny did their level best to confuse us by constantly switching the labels, for which they were duly punished, not that it stopped them getting into mischief whenever our backs were turned.

Despite their nonsense we were finally all packed up and ready to go, although we were still no wiser as to where we were going? With that in mind Janie and me decided on the Thursday night, the day before we were due to leave, that it was time mum told us!

'Alright... alright!' she sighed, I suppose you should know... we're heading for a place called Sandbourne, well not exactly for the village, but to a place nearby, to a farm out on the moor.'

'On a moor? What do you mean on a moor?' I asked.

'Well, not a moor... more like a Heath, I think!' she said, as we helped to load the removal van.

'A Heath!' Janie frowned.

'What the hell is a Heath? I asked.

I was too late to dodge her hand as it swung at me clipping me neatly on my right ear. 'Watch your mouth,' mum warned. Close by I heard our Danny snigger, and vowed to make him pay later.

'Sorry,' I apologised as Janie and I helped her load the little-ones into the back of the van ready for our long 50-mile journey into the back-of-beyond.

'A Heath is like wasteland... I think,' mum sighed, as I climbed in the back with everyone else and she clambered up beside dad and the driver.

'Wasteland! That doesn't sound very homely Sis?' Jane sighed softly in my ear.

I shook my head a feeling of dread bringing tears to my eyes.

As we drove out of the familiar old yard, I felt very sad, and as we pulled up onto the main road that would take us to our new destination, I couldn't help but wonder if we would ever again return to our beloved Home Farm.

Chapter 2

I have never been afraid to dream of new things, of new horizons that might better our lives, if I had we might never have enjoyed our time at Home Farm. But will this journeys end see us to a place of betterment or will it be as disastrous as it sounds? Wasteland! Mum had said we'd be living on wasteland, which seems a million miles from where any of us want to be. I fought back a shiver not wanting my siblings to see my fear of what lies ahead of us!

I watched Janie moving among the little-ones trying to keep them calm, assuring them that there was nothing to be afraid of, that we were just going to a new home, that's all, a better home... which was a great big lie of course, as we had no idea what sort of place we were going to. 'Sandbourne, now what sort of name is that for a farm?' I muttered to Janie as we began our journey. 'And out on some wasteland!' she whispered back; 'Could things get any worse?'

It was at least pleasing that we were in agreement on that, we both thought our new home was going to be a disaster, and now I could only hope that we wouldn't be there very long, that we would be called back to Somerset, and Home Farm.

Janie settled into the seat at my side and gently squeezed my hand in hers, letting me know that she understood my worry. 'Don't fret, Rube, whatever lies ahead we'll face together, you and me, and as you know, nothing ever gets the better of us', she grinned.

I smiled nervously, desperately wanting to believe her as we settled into our long journey, but it was difficult, we were not just going around the corner! We were heading for somewhere completely new! Up to now we'd only ever lived in down the lane cottages in the heart of Somerset, a county where our family had its roots, and was all we'd ever known. Old rickety places we may have lived in at times, but they were in a countryside that we all knew and loved.

I know many people say that travel is a good thing, that it broadens the mind and gives you new horizons to look upon, and while that may well be true, I cannot help but worry that what lies ahead might not be all we hope for. I sighed, none the less it was our journey to make, whether we liked it or not! A cold shiver ran down my spine reminding me that winter was but a whisper away as we headed on towards our new home. Only a day or so ago the weather still had a touch of Summer about it but now, a week or so into September it felt completely changed, now there was a definite autumn chill in the air. Strange? But then all of 1940 has been a little on the bleak side. Glancing out of the window I notice that the road was already slick from the previous evenings rain and I prayed that the threatening storm would hold its peace until we reach our destination.

The removal van carrying us on our journey into the unknown was old and rattled incessantly, and at times I put my fingers in my ears to drown out the noise. This made dad smile.

'It could a been worse, maid, they could o' sent a horse-n-cart fer us,' he chuckled.

'Don't be silly Fred,' mum grumbled; 'As if they would.'

'So, what do you think, maid? This old scrap of metal or a good old hoss-n-cart?' he asked.

I had my head down, busy changing our Charley... 'a good old hoss-n-cart,' I finally answered, much to mum's annoyance.

As nice as it was chatting with dad, I knew our chat was just a distraction! I could hear the ominous drone of aircraft. I had hoped the bad weather might have saved us from them for a day or two, but obviously not! As I turned back to the rest of the family all huddled together along the wooden planks at the side of the van, I saw the panic in their eyes, for we all fear the sound of aircraft until we know if they are ours or theirs!

'German bombers!' I heard dad mutter.

'Since we lost that battle of Dunkirk back in June, they've got free range, it seems ta me,' the driver said, glancing up at the sky.

I felt my legs go weak, thinking of all the rumour's I'd heard of an armada and an invasion while I was shopping with mum back in Yeovil town. Could this be the start of it? I gripped our Janie's hand so tight she dug me hard in the ribs in protest.

'Bastards!' Mum growled through gritted teeth.

Rubbing my sore side, I felt myself blushing, I'd never heard mum swear before. She'd always said that swearing was the language of the uneducated, those who had no words of wisdom to offer. She also said that if she heard any of us swear, we'd get the back of her hand, and be on chores for a week.

So, I was amazed when a few minutes later she repeated herself!

'Bloody Bastards!' she swore.

Some of my brothers and sisters sitting behind me sniggered and I turned to quieten them but my sister Jane was already banging heads together, so I left her to it.

Sitting as I was directly behind mum, dad and the driver I had a good view through the cracked and murky windscreen, although I wasn't pleased at what I saw; high in the sky I could make out dozens of planes, buzzing along like a swarm of angry black flies.

'They'll be goin' fer Poole Harbour,' dad growled. 'Same route as us!'

A little while later we heard the air-raid siren and the boom, boom of the anti-aircraft guns somewhere on ahead of us, followed by the dreaded sound of exploding bombs, and the nerve wrenching scream of the German fighter planes as they swooped down to make their kill!

I stuffed my fingers back in my ears and closed my eyes.

Meanwhile we journeyed on, all of us trembling with fear, the little ones sobbing and clinging to Janie and me for dear life; 'Open your eyes,' Janie growled in my ear; 'you're frightening the little ones,' she hissed.

Reluctantly I did as she asked, though I was still unable to look up towards the skies at the dog-fight being fought far above us.

'There goes another one... we got another of the buggers,' dad cried out triumphantly.

I forced myself to look up, and was in time to see a German plane in flames plummeting towards the ground. Strangely I found myself praying that the pilot had managed to escape! I shook the thought from my head, after all, he was a German!

Just how long the battle lasted I had no idea, but I was pleased when finally, the all clear sounded and the drone of the German bombers faded into the distance.

I was still shaking when dad reached back and squeezed my hand; 'Tis over now maid, well done,' he smiled. 'You did well.'

I felt so pleased with his praise I couldn't help the toothy smile I wore for the next few miles and would have worn longer had my big sister not brought me back to earth;

'See what you can do when you listen to me, our Ruby!' she grinned.

'I wasn't listening to you, I was just seeing to the little ones,' I protested.

'What, with your eyes closed?' she laughed.

Before I could reply, the driver spoke;

'Not far now?' he barked, grinding the gears of the old engine as we came to a slight incline. I put my fingers back in my ears and he gave me a toothy grin through his straw-like bushy beard.

Just then Janie tapped me on the shoulder; 'I think our Morgan needs seein' to," she said holding her nose as she passed our little brother towards me. I knew there was no point in arguing, I could smell the stink for myself, and he was one of my lot after all, but it wouldn't have hurt her to change him after all I'd just done Charley!

I was about to say as much, when mum said it for me.

'Janie, stop playing the big sister... and next time do the job yourself, it wouldn't kill you!' she snapped.

I tried to hide the delight of seeing my sister put in her place, but so obviously failed as mum turned her anger onto me.

'I don't know why you're smiling, young lady; he's your charge, you should have noticed he was in need of changing,' she accused.

I hung my head and got on with it, and I did it quietly, until he started wriggling! 'Oh! For goodness' sake hold still Morgan!' I raged, trying desperately to take off his dirty nappy without getting his shit all over myself

'Ugh! Keep that away from me,' Janet cried jumping to her feet.

'Sit down Jan', and don't be such a baby, it'll be your turn to do this soon,' I told her sternly.

'I don't think so. I'm not old enough, am I mum?' She sniffed.

'You're old enough if our Ruby says you are, young lady,' she's in charge of you.' mum told her.

I grinned and tossed her the fouled nappy; 'Put that in the bucket by the door,' I ordered.

'I don't know why our Jack or Danny can't do more... just because their boys,' Jan sniffed, as she scuttled to the back of the van on her hands and knees.

She had a point! I looked to see them snuggled together at the back of the van, sleeping soundly like two little angels! I frowned... Angels! More like little devils!

As if to prove my point Jack awoke and without any provocation pushed his brother Danny off the end of the bench, where he landed with a thud amongst our meagre possessions piled in the belly of the van, sending saucepans, frying pans and cups and saucers in all directions.

'Jane, Ruby!' Mum yelled 'What on earth's going on?'

'Don't ask me,' Janie replied with a grin, 'Ruby's in charge.'

I gave her such a look, that if looks could kill, my darling sister would already be dead. 'Don't worry mum it's nothing, just the boys messing around,' I called, through gritted teeth.

'Ouch! What was that for?' Jack moaned as I gave him a whack around the head.

'You know very well what it was for,' I said rubbing my hand which was still tingling from the slap I'd given him.

Out of the corner of my eye I saw Danny grinning and making faces at his brother's discomfort, so I leaned forward and clouted him too.

'Hey, cut that out!' he complained.

'I'll give you another one if you're not careful,' I warned, raising my hand.

'Tha's not fair... hey, mum, our Ruby's just hit me for nothing,' he cried.

'If I come back there, you'll not be able to sit down till next Sunday week, so think on tha' my boy,' mum warned him. I stifled a smile and watched my young brother go crimson as he clambered back onto his seat, suitably chastised.

A few minutes later I was almost thrown from my own seat as the van lurched savagely as we turned off the open road onto a deeply rutted, muddy, dirt track.

'Can ee' see ta the gate, Fred,' the driver asked bringing the van to a halt.

I watched dad jump out and open the big wooden gates, then close them behind us after we passed through, before returning to his seat next to mum... suddenly, for no apparent reason I had butterflies in my tummy and felt quite light-headed.

'You alright our Rube' Jane asked, quietly slipping her hand into mine, she could be lovely at times my big sister... when she wasn't being my big sister.

'Can't you feel it Janie, it's all a bit creepy, don't you think?' I shuddered.

We both looked out of the window at the dark tangled bridleway on ahead carving its way down through a coarse unkempt heathland, that seemed as dark as hades! I clung tighter to Janie's hand, as the boggy undergrowth either side of the track, seemed to try and draw us in! This was not farmland! Not the sort of farmland we were used to anyway, where were the green fields, where were the orchards? This was all just a tangled black mess, with no rhyme nor reason to it!

I was glad our siblings couldn't see this bleak place we were about to call home.

Janie whispered so that only I could hear; 'It does feel a bit strange, but it's just another farm, that's all,' she said reassuringly.

We both sat in silence then as the van trundled on down the beat-up, muddy track, rough tangled gorse dragging at the wheels as if in an effort to stop us. And for a moment I thought it had succeeded as with a sudden lurch we came to a halt.

'Are we there?' I asked stretching my neck to look ahead between mum and dad.

'Not yet, but just look at tha', mum gasped.

Sat on a small plateau of land I saw a white cottage, and it did look pretty, but we'd lived in better... so why was mum so excited?

'It's just a cottage!' Jane grunted coming to peer over my shoulder.

'No! Not the house, that,' mum said, pointing.

Jane and I both leaned forward together and saw the shimmering blue image mum was pointing at beyond the cottage. 'Is that a lake? Do we have a lake in our back garden?' I gasped.

'No, not a lake, daughter, it's the sea,' she smiled.

'The sea!' Jane and I repeated in unison.

'Yes, bring everyone forward, let them all see it.' Mum was smiling.

Before we knew it, our siblings were swarming all over us to get a better view, for none of us had ever seen the sea!

Mum and dad often spoke of taking us to the seaside one day, but that was as far as it went... and now... I stared again at the glimmering vista; and now here it is right on our doorstep! I hugged Janie and she hugged me back and our brothers and sisters all jumped for joy, though I doubt the younger of them actually knew what all the fuss was about.

'Alright, back to your seats now, the driver's going to take us to our new home... Janie, Ruby, see to them now, that's it, settle them down.' mum ordered.

With great difficulty we managed to get them all seated again and the driver started us rolling down the hill towards the old white-walled cottage in the heart of the rugged heathland. Suddenly, what had appeared at first glance a bit scary was in fact a little magical!

As we pulled into the cobblestoned yard, I was pleased to see that we had a strong railed fence all around it, so much easier when it came to corralling the kids, and the wooden gates that we passed through looked good and strong too. I glanced over towards Jane and she seemed equally pleased by what she saw.

'That'll keep the little beggars in,' she grinned.

With that we pulled up at the front door and all piled out.

'Start unloading the van,' dad ordered, before we had chance to run off and investigate.

I hesitated, not quite sure what to do about the younger ones. But I had no need to worry; 'I'll take Violet, Morgan and Charley with me,' mum said.

With a sigh of relief at not having to deal with the little ones Jane and I roped the rest into helping us unload the van. As usual Jack and Danny did their best to get out of doing anything, but we soon had them working alongside us, it took a bit of bullying and one or two threats, mind you. Thankfully it didn't take long to empty the van as there was precious little to unload, apart from our clothes the bedlinen and the kitchenware; cup, saucers, plates, saucepan's, etc. Most of our stuff we'd left behind with Grandma Miller in Yeovil, stored away in her spare room and in her attic. What with us being called upon to move so often it was the easiest thing to do, after all, sometimes we only stayed in one place a week or two at the best.

With the van unloaded dad headed off with the driver, to report to the farmer and receive his working orders for the following day.

'I've changed my mind Sis, this is going to be a great place to live, I just know it,' I beamed.

But there was little time to dwell on that thought as the younger ones were running riot, charging from room to room, with mum, a little-one under each arm screaming at them to stop.

'Thank goodness,' she cried as Janie and I came into the house.

'See to them will you Janie; and Ruby, go to the kitchen, the good farmers wife has left a cauldron of stew, feed the children will you, it might settle them,' she sighed wearily. Going through to the kitchen I quickly stoked up the range, but rather than see to the children first I put the kettle on... mum sounded as if she needed a nice cup of tea, the little monsters could wait.

Later, with mum content with her tea and the children fed and watered, I went with Jane to check out the rest of the cottage; although in truth it wasn't a cottage it was a house. Together we headed up the stairs that led to four good sized bedrooms.

In the first there was a large bed with a baby's cot in the corner; 'This must be for mum and dad and little Charley, Jane said as we stuck our heads around the corner. In the next room was a single bed and a large double, along with a sideboard.
'This can be Jack and Danny's room', I suggested.
Janie nodded, 'And our Morgan can have the single bed, although I do feel sorry for him, he's only 2, the poor lamb. I might have him in with me yet, I'm undecided,' she confessed.

I must admit I felt a little uneasy myself at the thought of little Morgan sharing a room with our troublesome brothers, although I didn't say as much to Janie. However, as we left the room, I linked arms with her. 'Maybe we could take turns having our Morgan in with us,' I suggested.
She dug me in the ribs with her elbow; 'You took your time, ginger!' she grinned.
'Hey! I was always going to offer, I just wanted you to suffer a little, that's all sis... and anyway I'm not ginger, I'm auburn, alright,' I protested.

Chuckling; we moved across the landing to check out the final 2 bedrooms, one had a large double, to be shared, this time, by Janet, Bella and Violet. The other room had two singles that would do nicely for Janie and me.

With the upstairs well and truly explored we made our way down to check out the rest of the house, both of us a little concerned by the lack of noise. We found most of the family in a well-furnished living-room, which included a large comfortable sofa, two armchairs, a rocking chair and two small stools. A big raggedy rug lay in front of a huge open fire that all the kids, except Jack and Danny were snuggled down in front of.

'Have you seen your brothers?' mum asked as we came into the room.

We both shook our heads.

'Now where do you suppose those two monkeys have gone,' mum worried.

'Should we check the yard?' I asked.

Mum nodded, so I stepped out to check. But they were nowhere in sight!

'I'll wager they've wandered off, the little devils,' mum muttered.

'Do you want Ruby and me to go out and find them,' Jane offered.

'No, I'll go myself,' mum replied, moving through to the kitchen to put on her coat and shoes.

'You two just see to the kids,' she called as she went out the door.

She'd barely left before she was back again; 'Your father has them,' she called.

With that they came through the door, or rather they were shoved through the door by a very angry father, in fact I'd never seen him so angry.

'I caught these two down by the backwaters, trying to launch Farmer Drakes old rowing boat.'

'They stole a boat?' mum growled, catching them both by the scruff of the neck.

'No, I caught um, afor they 'ad the chance, the little beggars. Still, they've got their punishment, Farmer Drake's goin' ta ave um cleanin' 'is pigsty's fer a day or two,' dad grinned.

'That's not fair, we only sat in the old boat, we didn't even get it into the water,' Danny whined.

'Still, you sat in a boat, that's exciting, Bella sighed. 'I wish I'd been there.'

'Then you'd be cleaning out pigsty's along with your brothers,' mum snapped.

33

Bella, who was ever the quiet one blushed and slipped back to the shelter of her siblings, all gathered to hear their brother's latest escapade... and resulting punishment.

Later, as things quietened, Bella approached her brother again; 'Did you really sail a boat'? She asked in awe.
Jack bent down to whisper in her ear, 'No, we got caught didn't we, but there's always another day,' he winked, lifting her up and twirling her around.
'Can I come next time... oh please let me,' Bella pleaded.
Jack ruffled her blonde curly hair... 'You might end up cleaning out the pigs you know sis,' he laughed.
Bella stood tall, well as tall as she could, which brought her up to her brother's shoulder; 'It would be worth it for an adventure like that,' she sighed.
Danny who was listening nearby decided to butt in; 'We're not taking any girls sailing,' he growled, 'they'll only get in the way.'

By now all the children were listening and little Violet started to cry, although at 3 years old she was too young for anything, still she didn't like being left out.
'Cry all you like,' Danny snapped, 'You can't come, none of you can! It's a boy's thing and as Morgan and Charlie are too young, that just leaves Jack and me, so there!'
Now it was Janet who got angry; 'Watch it Danny, I'm a year older than you and there is no way you can say what I can or can't do,' she shouted angrily.
'But, I'm older than you Jan, and I agree with Dan, this is a boys thing,' Jack insisted.

Before anyone could say anything else, to our surprise, dad intervened.
'I've something ta say on this,' he barked.
Suddenly you could hear a pin drop, this wasn't like dad at all!
'I 'ad a word with Mr Drake and ee agrees that as we live so near the water, one or two of you need ta learn to row, so as ta keep you all safe.'

Out of the corner of my eye I could see Jack and Danny grinning like a couple of excited monkeys, and I suddenly felt very angry, this wasn't fair, it wasn't fair at all, and I could tell by her expression that Janie didn't think it was either!' But before we could protest dad held a hand up to silence the room; 'So,' he continued; 'I've decided tha' the two who'll train on the rowin' boat are... Jane and Ruby!'

There was a moment of stunned silence, and then everyone started speaking at once, the girls out of excitement, the boys full of anger, but I noticed a smile on dad's face as he turned away and winked to mum, who choked back a laugh as she went to join him in the kitchen. I guess that was the day I realised what a wise man father really was, he had no education to speak of, but sometimes, I've learned over the years, common sense far outweighs academia, and this was one of those days. I felt so proud of him and so pleased for me and our Janie; we were going to be sailors!

Sadly, though, later, dad said that it would not be for a good while yet, not until the weather softened and the waters calmed. In the meantime, mum suggested that as we had a week to settle into our new home before starting school, we should go out and explore the area. And so, the next day we did just that, checking out the garden which was vast and at the end of which was a path that led into a small woodland. Some of the little ones wanted us to make them a little den, which to Janie and my surprise, our troublesome brothers, Jack and Danny offered to do! Leaving us to help mum with the unpacking and the never-ending housework.

It was Saturday, dad had already started his new job down on the farm that nestled along the sea. And although I'm sure it was nothing to him, just another job, to us it was as if he'd gone off to work in Fairyland! And when he got home that evening and we tried to question him on the wonders he must have seen, he just chuckled and shook his head, promising he would take us down to the farm so that we might see our wonderland for ourselves.

On Sunday, after dad had left for work, mum took us down to investigate the bomb shelter at the bottom of the yard, although I couldn't think why we would need one out here in the middle of nowhere? Still mum insisted that we check it out and make sure it was in the best possible state. Later, after Sunday roast of poached rabbit, baked potatoes and greens, we had a visitor! Much to our surprise the local vicar came to welcome us to his parish and to invite us to worship at his church the following weekend. It was most unexpected, but mum thanked him and agreed that we would all be there, which seemed to please him no end.

The following day I felt quite excited, it was Monday, a day none of us particularly liked as normally we'd be going off to school, but not today, we had the day to ourselves. With dad gone off to work and mum busy doing the washing, Janie and me dressed the young ones and made the breakfast, hoping that if we cleared all our chores quickly, we might be able to go down to have a look at the boat that we were going to learn to row. But just as quickly as they'd formed, all my hopes were blown away, when mum called Janie and me out to the kitchen where she was busy with the weekly washing.

'Today I want you to take the older children and find your way to the main road, as you'll need to know how long it takes to get there. That's where you'll catch the bus to school,' mum explained. 'The bus stop itself is a few yards down the road as you come off the heath...
'Ruby! Are you listening?'
I felt my cheeks reddening; 'Sorry mum I was day dreaming,' I apologised.
'Well, you'd best take heed young lady, should you miss the bus it's a long walk to Sandbourne village' she warned.
I nodded, hiding my blushes as we went out the kitchen door.
'And keep your eye on those two,' mum called after us as we crossed the yard with Janet and Bella in tow. I didn't bother to respond as I knew she meant Jack and Danny; who else? Already they chose to run on ahead taking not a blind bit of notice of Janie or me as we tried in vain to call them back.

Thank goodness, the bridleway, although it twisted and turned led in only one direction, up and off the heathland. And that's where the two little devils were waiting for us. On reaching them Janie grabbed them and tweaked both boy's ears so hard they cried out in pain. Still, it wasn't a lasting injury as a few minutes later they were laughing and shouting and pointing down the road!

'Look at that... will you look at that!' Jack cried, as we all stepped from the heathland.

Down the road, heading right for us were two tanks and an army lorry full to overflowing with soldiers. 'Come on you lot, give um a wave, give our lads a wave.' Danny yelled, removing his woolly scarf and swirling it around in the air. Instead, I put my fingers in my ears as the vehicles trundled noisily on by.

'Why do you always do that, sis?' Jack sighed, shaking his head.

'Cause she's afraid of a little noise,' Danny jeered.

'No, it's because it hurts my ears, if you must know,' little brother,' I snorted angrily.

'Huh! Bet it doesn't hurt as much as when our Janie tweaks it,' Jack grumbled.

'And I'll tweak it again, if you don't mind your manners, ' Janie warned.

Ignoring the boy's, I asked Janie how long it had taken us to get to the bus stop.
She shrugged, 'mum will be able to tell us when we get back,' she said.

With that she started us back along the bridleway towards home and it seemed no time at all before we were back in the yard, shouting for mum to check the time by the mantlepiece clock.

'You've been gone less than an hour,' mum said, coming through the door with a tub full of wet clothes to put through the old mangle that stood alongside the wall in the back yard. 'So, let's say a half an hour each way,' she estimated. 'Just to be on the safe side.'

'What time does the bus reach the stop in the morning?' I asked, going over to help her with the washing.

'8:00 o'clock,' mum grunted, straining to put a pair of dads working trousers through the mangle... 'So, you'll need to leave here no later than 7:30', she panted.

Wiping her brow, she turned to us. 'Jane, Ruby, you stay here, Jack, Danny, go in and give the little one's a drink of water, and have one yourselves you must be thirsty after your little trek,' mum ordered.

I exchanged looks with Janie; 'Wouldn't you rather one of us did that, mum?' I asked, watching how rough my brothers were, pushing and prodding the little ones towards the kitchen.
'No, I want you both to go down to Mr Drakes farm, find father, he'll let you know what's, what,' she smiled.
I felt a surge of excitement shoot through me... were we going to be sailors today after all? I couldn't believe it.
'Did you see mum?' Janie frowned. She actually smiled? She hates, doing the washing, and she smiled? Can you believe it, Rube?' Janie said, shaking her head.

I was so excited I couldn't even speak, was it possible that we were going to go out on the water? I looked up to the heavens, the sky was cloudy and grey and the wind was picking up, not an ideal day to go sailing! But dad knows best.

We were over the backyard by this time, opening the gate, and heading down across the ragged heathland, far below we spied a red bricked Victorian farmhouse, which we guessed belonged to farmer Drake. A little way beyond the house I spied the sparkling water of the bay. For a moment we stood transfixed by the beauty of it all.
'It's lovely,' I gasped... like something out of a fairy tale!'
Jane tugged my sleeve; 'Come on, dad will be waiting,' she urged.

Tearing my eyes away from the scenic view I followed on behind Janie my head in quite a spin. Then I heard dad shout! He was sat atop an old tractor waving like mad at us, then with a rattling roar he gunned the engine into life and trundled over to where we stood.
'Ups you comes then girls,' he said as he drew alongside us.

Scrambling up onto the seat next to him we held on tight as the old tractor took off again heading straight for the glittering water; and as we drew closer, I could see that there was at least two men waiting there for us.

'Hi Fred,' the older of the two, hailed, as we came to a halt. 'This must be yer two, oldest maids.' he said, coming to meet us. 'Hello, girls, nice ta meet ee', he greeted amicably.

Janie and I dipped our heads in return and accepted his hand to help us down from the tractor.

'I'm Farmer Drake an' this be my boy Robbo,' he said, gesturing for the young man to step forward.

'Pleased ta meet ee, ladies, I'm sure,' the young man grinned.

'Ladies!' We both blushed, and did a little curtsey, not quite knowing the best form of greeting... father laughed, and we blushed anew!

'Robbo, will teach ee about the rowin' boat', and you'd best, mind 'I'm well girls, this yer bay can be a grievous place', farmer Drake warned.

Robbo nodded, underlining his father's words.

'Right Fred, we'd best leave um to it and get back ta work, the farmer grunted turning on his heels. 'Good sailin' girls,' he chuckled as he walked away.

'You take heed o' the lad mind,' father said, as he started the tractor and set it rumbling back up the field. 'And be sure ta be 'ome fer tea,' he shouted above the roar of the engine.

For the next few hours, Robbo taught us about rowing boats; from getting in to it safely, to disembarking without ending up in the water, and finally, what we were both waiting for, how to row properly without capsizing. It wasn't as easy as either of us thought it would be, but it was a lot of fun, much more so than looking after the kids or doing endless chores!

'Either of you old enough ta work?' Robbo asked quite out of the blue.

'I'm nearly old enough,' Janie said.

I gave her a look, she was lying, she was nowhere near old enough.

'Why?' I asked, curiosity getting the better of me.

'Cause Lady Seymour's back in her Manor at Sandbourne and seekin a maid,' he sniffed. 'Should you be wantin ta apply I'll be goin ta the village one day this week,' he offered.

'Thanks Robbo, I'll go in with you and see what's what,' Janie grinned.

I was stunned, but be it on her head, Janie was her own boss.

Later, when we arrived back home, exhausted but happy, we were bombarded by a hundred and one different questions by our excited siblings, all eager to hear about our adventure, even Jack and Danny couldn't help but ask about it, as jealous as they were.

'Do you think dad will let us all go and try it out tomorrow?' Jack asked as we washed our hands ready for tea.

'Not a chance, besides, Ruby and me have to practice more before any of you lot can come on the boat,' Janie told him.

'But that's not fair... your girls, it should be us,' Jack growled angrily.

'Huh! After what the two of you did, you'll be lucky to get on the boat this side of Christmas,' I snapped. '

'Besides,' Janie interrupted, 'You've an awful lot of pigsties to muck out first.'

Everyone laughed at this as Jack and Danny stomped off out into the yard in a huff.

That week; the week before we started school, Janie and me practised every day on the boat. A couple of times I saw Jack and Danny cleaning out the pigsties as we passed on by. They didn't look very happy, but then they only had themselves to blame.

Sunday morning saw us all clambering into the back of Farmer Drakes rickety van again, the one that had brought us here, only now it was taking us to our first service at the old Episcopal, St Nicholas church in Sandbourne Village.

'Look, there's the school over there,' I said.

But our Janie wasn't looking at the school; 'That must be the Manor House, Robbo was talkin of,' she pointed off down the road. I still couldn't believe that she meant to try for a job there, mum would be furious.

The church was packed, mostly with people wearing black. Mourners, I guessed, for the two local young men the preacher spoke of in his sermon, both killed in the line of duty on foreign soil. It was all so very sad, and I was close to tears as I listened to the stories of loss and suffering going on not so very far away, across the English Channel.

For the first time, as I sat quietly on my pew holding tight to my sister Bella's hand, with little Violet on my knee I began to realise the horror of war! Beside me, Janie drew in a deep breath and hugged our Morgan and Charlie tight, as if to keep them safe from it all, whilst even Jack and Danny seemed moved by the sermon too, as they sat silently taking it all in, side by side with mum and dad and our Janet.

I think what shocked us all was the age of the young men that had died, for neither of them had passed their teen years... and now never would. It was a sad, sombre drive back to our house on the heath, not a single word was spoken by anyone the entire journey, not even by the little-ones, which just added to the strangeness of the occasion.

The following day came at us in one mad rush! It was to be our first day of school. For Janie and me that meant rising extra early; washing and feeding our siblings to have them ready to go out the door on time. Dad had left for work, and for mum it was washing day as usual and she was already busy stoking the boiler readying it for the first load. I didn't envy her, what with there being so many of us there was always a lot for her to do, although she never complained, she just got on with it.

By the old clock on the mantlepiece it was 7:30 am, and time for us to go, my legs were trembling as we waved mum goodbye. Just why I felt so nervous I couldn't say, we'd done this so many times of late, and one school was very much like another. So, I should be used to it! But still, something was nagging at me.

Gritting my teeth, I forced the silly thoughts from my head and set off with my siblings across the heath to catch the bus on the other-side. Me and our Jane set to our task in earnest, herding the others on ahead of us like a flock of sheep. For the most part it was easy going, although Jack and Danny did their level best to make us miss the bus by dragging their heels and fooling about. But a couple of whacks from Janie soon put them in their place, and we reached the bus stop with time to spare. There were six of us on our way to school; Janie had the two rascals in her charge, while I looked after Janet and Bella, both of whom were nervous but well behaved.

'Why do we have to catch the bus? We could walk... it can't be that far to the village... I bet Dan and me could run it in ten minutes,' Jack whined as we stepped from the heath onto the road.
'Just stand still and wait!' Janie fumed, 'Unless you want another sore ear each,' she threatened.
I shook my head, I didn't envy her at all, those two were simply the worst!

Thankfully we didn't have long to wait as the bus came around the corner and trundled to a halt at our side and we all clambered aboard. In truth it wasn't the cleanest bus I'd ever seen, the red tartan seat covers were threadbare and faded, while the floor was little more than a waste bin. I'd hate to think what mum would have said had she been with us, she would probably have ordered the driver to clean up the mess himself. I smiled, that was mum alright, she hated untidiness, she had 9 children to see to, and yet our home was always spotless and so she expected the same from everyone else.

However as much as I agreed with her, riding in an untidy bus did not upset me as it did her, especially as it was only going to be for a short trip, although the chewing gum that stuck to my shoe did make me angry.

Despite the state of the bus, I hoped for quiet ride into the village, but sadly it rattled like a tin can full of pebbles, and then, if that wasn't bad enough, the dreaded wail of the air-raid siren started up! 'Bloody hell! Surely not,' I heard the driver swear. I turned to our Janie; 'I didn't think they bombed during the day anymore?' I cried.

Suddenly there was a mad panic; kids were screaming and clinging to each other and the driver was shouting at us all to get off the bus, ordering us into the ditch alongside the road, which we all did as the deep boom, boom, boom of the anti-aircraft guns over Poole harbour and along the coast echoed across the heath and down the long winding road that led to the village.

For what seemed like hours we lay in the cold damp ditch shivering, too afraid to even shed a tear. I held my sisters; Janet and Bella close to me, lying across them to keep them from harm, desperately waiting to hear the all clear, as the bombs continued to explode in the distance. It was strange, although I'd heard many nights of bombing up and down the coast this seemed more real, more personal somehow! I shook the thought from my head and glanced over to where Janie lay, like me she had her charges close, keeping our Jack and Danny in the ditch whether they liked it or not.

Then just as quickly as it started the bombing ceased and the huge bombers turned for home casting big black shadows over our heads, causing us to sink deeper into the ditch. Daring to glance up I saw them, they were monstrous! Like something out of an H. G. Wells novel! Then came the worst of all as smaller more agile planes, came swooping down wailing like demented demons, shooting at anything and anyone in their path.

Janet and Bella started screaming and it was all I could do to stop myself from joining in as we lay there listening to the sharp, zing, zing, zing of the bullets, snapping at the ground like angry wasps, some of them making holes in the empty bus and along the new tarmac road. Then my heart skipped a beat as I heard Janie scream! I looked over to where she lay and saw her beating on Jack for all she was worth!

'What's wrong?' I called to her.
She slapped our brother again not caring for the bruises that he would surely wear; 'The stupid little bugger tried to catch the bullets,' she said, hauling him back down into the ditch. 'One of them missed his fingers by only inches,' She struck him again. 'Now you stay there till I say so,' she commanded.

I stroked Bella's real ginger, not auburn hair, as she lay perfectly still beneath me and held tight to Janet's hand, who at 7 years old knew how to behave, unlike her silly elder brothers. We stayed where we were until the all clear was sounded and then climbed frightened and shaking back onto the bus, finally resuming our journey on to the village and to our new school. Although we were late, we were still some of the first to arrive and Jane and me decided to sit together, even if it meant our Jack and Danny would be free to create more mayhem, but then, that was the teacher's problem not ours, we'd had enough of them.

Soon the other kids came trickling in, some of them looked a bit scruffy and in need of a good bath. They were the evacuees from the big cities, we found out later, but they were nice enough, and our Janet and Bella were soon making friends with one or two of the quieter kids. Unlike our dear brothers who were getting to know two of the more, rowdy boys, although judging by their accents they weren't evacuees, they were locals, and right from the start I could see that they were as full of mischief as our Jack and Danny!

Still, it was good to have them off our hands for a while, and the teacher; Mrs Harrington as soon as she arrived had the measure of all four of them. 'You! You! You! And You! Stand up, she ordered, pointing towards the four of them. They got to their feet shuffling nervously as she approached them. 'Now! Your names are?' she asked our brothers.
'Jack Miller.'
'Danny Miller.'
They replied sheepishly.
'And where do you live?'
Our Jack hesitated, 'On the Heath,' he said.

'Oh, I see... well the Heath is a big place...' she began.

I put my hand up, as it was obvious neither of my brothers had the slightest idea of the name of the house where we were staying; I only knew it because the farmer's son Robbo told me.

'Yes?' Mrs Harington said, turning to me.

'He's my brother and we live at Newton Cottage,' I said.

She nodded; 'And your name is?' she asked.

'Ruby Miller... and this is my sister, Jane,' I said, placing my hand on her shoulder.

'Um! And are there any more of you?' Mrs Harrington asked, with a frown.

Janet and Bella stood up, both blushing profusely as they introduced themselves.

She waved them back to their seats; 'So there are six of you then?' she said.

'Six of us of school age,' Janie replied. 'And three more at home.'

Mrs Harrington raised her eyebrows; 'Well six is enough to be going on with,' she smiled.

I felt relieved, she seemed nice, I glanced across at my two brothers, already huddled down with their two new buddies; who I learned later were the Davis twins; and as devilish as our Danny and Jack. I felt sure it wouldn't be long before they got up to mischief, it was written all over them. Thankfully, this time though my fears were without foundation, as the day passed without any sign of trouble from my brothers and their new friends, or from the bloody Germans; and we spent our time doing every day, school lessons... and although I wasn't much of a scholar, it was nice to have a few hours of normality.

At the end of our first school day, we caught the bus back to our stop, accompanied by the Davis boys whose father owned a small holding on the other side of the Heath, only about a mile or so up the track from us... I wasn't sure if that was a good thing or not, they had the look of trouble about them and my brothers needed no help on that score.

But as the days rolled on, I had to admit that my first impression of the twins proved to be wholly wrong; Oh! They could be boisterous and loud at times and just a little naughty, but in truth they were no worse than my siblings, and a sight less troublesome than most of them. And what's more, they seemed to have a calming effect on our, Jack and Danny, and that was a miracle in itself!

In the week or so that followed we began to notice the village of Sandbourne filling up with more and more troops and sailors, and equipment. Rumours of invasion was rife, and all along the coast the beaches were off limits, strung with barbed wire, and heavy tank traps and landmines.

Why on earth would the Ministry people send us here? I wondered. Did they have it in for us?

But then, one day after school as we reached the summit of the heath on our way home, I stood looking down at the sparkling water far below. It was simply breath-taking and to my surprise our Jack and Danny came to join me and I'd never seen them looking so peaceful, or so at ease with themselves. It was as if they truly belonged here.

Yes, I decided, there is something about this place that sings to me, something that obviously sings to my troublesome brothers too, I could see it in their faces? Who knows, Sandbourne, might be just perfect for us all.

Chapter 3

As Lady Seymour, the wife of Lord Seymour, Laird of Kirriemuir Castle, in the heart of Scotland it is up to me to be the face of tranquility. To stand strong at my husband's side and hold myself up tall and to never ever show the world the anxieties that I feel. At least, that is what they tell me, all the wise old men of the authority, who counsel my husband in his duties. But I am not him, nor am I made of granite, how can I not worry when my husband is about to go off to war? Wouldn't the people expect me to show concern, just, as they do when their own loved ones go off to fight? It is inhuman not to show any emotion, and I will not be the stone statue they expect me to be... I will not!

Sometimes, well-meaning people, who have only your best interests at heart, can get things entirely wrong and without intending to, steer you in a direction, that left alone you wouldn't dream of taking. They mean no harm of course, but they tend to lead with their heads, when at times common sense dictates another path, one that is often heart led!

A rather dangerous route to take sometimes and I'm afraid, perhaps more often than is wise, it is the route that I choose to follow, especially where my husband and my children are concerned and I offer no apologise for that.

'Sandbourne Manor will be ready for you and the children by the time we get there my love, however you will need to hire some staff I'm afraid' Rory said, interrupting my thoughts, his soft voice tinged with the beautiful Scottish accent that I knew so well bringing a smile to my lips.

Standing by the French windows looking out across the wild Scottish highland, I wiped a tear from my eye, and turned to face him, 'thank you Rory, I'm sure I can manage that.' I felt so disappointed, what with our home here being so far from everything I thought we'd be left alone, that my husband Rory, Lord of Kirriemuir, would stay here, training the men of the highlands, getting them ready for combat.

'It had to come, my dear, after the battle of Dunkirk, I was expecting it.' He managed a smile, 'after all I'm a commander and so it is only right that I should be the one to lead my men into battle.'

I nodded that I understood. Being his wife, I went where he led me and didn't argue, for he was a good husband. Still, all this order and duty, that's a man thing, as a woman I care more about the children, about family, rather than duty!'

His voice interrupted my thoughts once again. 'I will be travelling down with you, my love, it's a long way and I will see you arrive safe before anything else.' he smiled. I reached for his hand; 'The children will like that, as it might be a while before we see you again. Will you have leave do you think, before... well before... you know?'

'Before I go off to war, do you mean,' he smiled. 'To tell you the truth, my dear, I don't know, not until I report in to my unit, but at least we'll have this time together.'

He hugged me then and I held him close, the thought of him being at war a frightening image in my head that I couldn't get rid of for a while.

'As we're starting our journey on Friday, we should tell the children tonight, I'll ring for Nannie West,' I suggested finally, 'I'm sure they'll still be awake.'

'No don't ring, let me go up and tell them myself, I expect they're waiting for me to read them a story anyway.' Rory smiled.

You don't mind if I come with you, do you, I quite like your stories myself,' I chuckled.

'Do join us,' he laughed. 'Who knows when we might do this again?'

As we got to the top of the stairs, we heard Nannie West doing her best to quieten them, but they seemed to be unusually restless and on seeing us they let out a squeal and rushed to the door... and right away I knew that they suspected something was up!

'So, what's happening, you might as well tell us, we know something is going on!' Crispen demanded. I sighed, Crispen! It was ever him who came with the questions, even though he was not the first born, but then, his elder sister Grace was ever the quiet one. As for little Florence she simply went along with whatever the other two said.

'Sandbourne! We just love Sandbourne!' Crispen whooped.' As they got the news.

'It's so close to the sea, why wouldn't we,' Grace clapped.

Florence stayed quiet for a moment and then giggled and started clapping along with her siblings... 'So, who wants a story then?' Their Father asked.

'Me! Me! Me!' They all cried out... 'And me please, I laughed, snuggling up with the children on Crispens bed with them all around me.

Friday came around quickly and as we passed through the great iron gates at the end of the driveway I wondered when we'd be back... if we'd be back, for war can ask a terrible price from each and every one of us! The fading photographs on the walls and on the mantlepiece of loved-ones lost in the last great conflict are there for all to see. I felt a shiver run through me; 'Pray to God this war will not add to that tally.'

'Is Nannie's car following?' my husband called from his seat next to the chauffer, it seemed so unnatural not to have him back here with us, but even our new Bentley wasn't big enough to take the five of us on its back seat. Still, it seemed right that he should be in the front, he was the head of the family after all.

In answer to his question, I stole a glance out of the back window to the other vehicle following on behind; 'Yes everything's fine,' I called.

With that we all relaxed and looked out across the great expanse of tumbling heather and gorse, and over the wild highlands, where great Stags ruled their domain with pride, a place so very far from the rigors of manmade war. Up here it was a simple thing, it was natures thing; there were no guns or bombs, just the clashing of antlers, with one winner and one loser.

I sighed and settled back to my seat alongside the children.

'I wish Nannie could have travelled with us,' Grace sighed, looking over her shoulder to where the other car followed on behind.

I smiled, 'Are you tired of our company already then child?'

'Oh no, it's just that we're usually with her this time of the day, either walking through the grounds or doing lessons in the great hall, it's about that time, that's all.'

It was clear that they were already bored and the journey had only just begun, luckily, I had the solution in my handbag and I pulled it out with a flourish.

'The Beano comic book!' Crispen squealed with delight.

I passed it to Grace as she was the storyteller.

'But where did you get it mother?' she asked.

'Nannie got it for me,' I had to confess. 'She had to go to Dundee to visit family and I believe that's where it's printed.' I explained. 'Now, she's told me how much you all enjoy the characters in it, and so there you are,' I said, sitting back.

'So why haven't I heard of this... this... what is it called?' Rory frowned.

'Beano comic book,' I smiled. 'But don't fret, it's new, it's only been going for a year or so and I'd not heard of it either.'

With the children finally settled I managed to relax, we had a very long way to go, and the plan was not to rush, but to do the journey in stages over the next two days. Our first thought had been to go by rail but that would have meant a long drive to the nearest train station then transferring our luggage from cars to train! Too much unloading and reloading and so by road it was, all the way. Still, it was a long tiring journey and even with my little surprise, time dragged terribly slowly and even myself and Rory were beginning to suffer the rigors of sitting in one place for so long a time. So much so that we ordered the driver to pull into a country lane and all got out to stretch are legs and unpack the lunch pack Nannie had put together for us.

It was a cold but sunny day and it was nice to watch the children running and playing in the nearby green field for an hour or so, before continuing on our way. Manchester was our first stop off, and we arrived at our destination late at night. Curfew was well underway by this time and everything was as black as black could be. The air-raid sirens were wailing even as we pulled into the forecourt of the grand hotel, and several porters ushered us from the car, I quickly looked to be sure that Nannie was also being taken care of in the second car. Just then the sky was suddenly lit by an array of searchlights, seeking out the bombers. Head down with Nannie and Rory's help we ran, shepherding the children on ahead of us, down into the dark underbelly of the hotel.

The children huddled together and the look of fear in their dear little eyes is something I'll never forget. Neither Rory or myself had realised just how alien this would be for them, goodness, it was frightening enough for me! Living as we did in the middle of nowhere, deep in Scotland's beautiful highlands, had not schooled any of us to face anything like this! I took a deep breath, but sadly this was our future! Where we were going; Sandbourne, may not be as big a target, as cities like this one, but it was on the coast and so would be a target none the less.

Once the raid was over and the all-clear siren sounded, we were taken up to the foyer and then to the dining room, where a quickly prepared supper was already waiting. None of us could sleep when we finally got to our rooms and I was pleased that Nannie was with us, she took the children off our hands and that gave us the chance to talk. Although we were both tired, there was a question that I had to ask my husband, although I knew he'd be reluctant to answer, for fear of upsetting me, but I just had to know.

'When we reach Sandbourne Manor, how long will it be before you are sent for,' I asked my husband bluntly.

He pulled me to him, holding me close. 'The truth is,' he sighed, 'I have no idea, I wasn't expecting this to happen so soon! What with our Scottish Estate being so remote, I concentrated only on training the men, nothing more,' he sighed. 'But I should have known better, war seldom stands still for long, my dear, and I knew this moment would come. Rory confessed. 'Many of the men I trained went off to Europe, God help them. While others have gone as far afield as Egypt. As for myself, I serve and obey and so await my orders.'

With that we retired to our bed knowing that come morning we had another long day on the road to face before arriving in our next halfway house in Oxford.

After all the drama in Manchester the children were very quiet as we headed out of the great northern city on our way South. On this occasion however, the good news was we'd have more time to relax as we'd be arriving in Oxford in the afternoon, giving us much longer to rest up before taking to the road again.

I think the children wondered what was wrong with their father and me as we drove into Oxford, we were both grinning like idiots and I just had to reach forward and put my hand on his shoulder! What they didn't know was that Oxford University was where we'd first met! It was fifteen years ago when we were both doing law degrees, we met at one of the lectures and fell in love, and that, as they say, was that. I felt Rory squeeze my fingers and knew he was remembering too... 'God how I love him'.

'Oh! Stop it you two, for goodness, sake,' Crispen groaned.

I felt myself blush a little and removed my hand from my husband's shoulder. We both chuckled and the children laughed too.

The hotel wasn't far from the University, which was a bit of a worry in case the German's decided to target one of the country's leading schools of learning.

Nothing happened that night though, nor the following morning, as with permission from the Dean, we took the children on a tour of our old haunt, and they were, I'm pleased to say, delighted by what they saw... 'You mean, you came here?' Grace questioned in disbelief, as we strolled around the wonderful ancient rooms and corridors. I blushed and Rory chuckled; 'Your mother is very clever I'll have you know, lass, her grades were better by far than my own,' he confessed. I shook my head; 'We were on a par, if truth be known... not one of us better than the other, and I hope that's how people here remember us.' I insisted.

It was nice to be part of that great old place again, if only for a brief spell, and it was with regret that we, once more took to the road the next day, starting on the final part of our journey down towards the west country and the village of Sandbourne. It was a long haul across the country, and the change in scenery from one county to another was stark indeed. Already the change in the land was apparent, as we drove ever deeper into the southwest. I took a deep breath, the air felt so much cleaner, somehow. I sighed; I'd forgotten just how beautiful this part of the country was! Everything was so much greener and vivacious, just bursting with life. Even the men at work across the fields gave us a cheery wave and wished us a good day.

It was a pick-me-up I sorely needed, for I was at odds with myself for bringing my children from the safety of our highland retreat, where the war was not on our doorstep as it would be here. But despite my worries, it was too late now for such negativity for we were nearing the end of our long journey, and I readied myself for what lay ahead!

'Get ready children,' I said, excitedly, stretching forward to get a better view.

As we came over the brough of the hill with old thatched and tiled, cottages of Sandbourne village splayed out below us, and beyond them, the sparkling blue sea, despite being ready for it, I still gaped in wonder, as I always did. Reiterating that surely, there couldn't be a more beautiful view in all the land.

To my surprise, people were gathering to greet us as we made our way down the hill and into the village, although I couldn't imagine how our coming had spread so quickly, but then, that's how it is in a small community. I shook my head, with such rife gossip it's a wonder the Germans needed spies. They waved and cheered and we waved back as we drove past, before going through the gates of our estate on the other side of the village.

I wondered as we continued slowly through the grounds just how well Grace and Crispen would remember the old manor house as we hadn't been here for a while? And as we rumbled through the gate house and came to a halt by the front door, I was struggling myself to remember exactly how long ago it was since any of us had last been here! It was before Florence was born; I can remember that much... so, perhaps five years? Rory had come down a few times on his own though, just to check on the estate and the skeleton staff we kept here, but he'd never found anything amiss in all that time, and all seemed well now.

I need not have worried about the children. As soon as the car stopped, they were out of it and running, shouting, up the steps and along the hall, to find their old bedrooms. Nannie, as soon as her car pulled up hurrying to catch up.

As the driver helped to unpack the two cars and set about moving things to the right rooms, the telephone in the hall rang, for a second, I waited for our butler Wilson to answer it, but then remembered that he'd left us to join the navy 6 months ago. Now usually in his absence the maid would answer it; but at the moment we didn't have one of those either! And so being nearest I answered it myself. It was for Rory!

As I handed him the phone, he mouthed, silently; 'Sorry!' then took the call.
A few minutes later he came to find me; 'I'm sorry, darling, but I have to report in, it sounds rather urgent... I'm so sorry!' he apologised again.

I kissed him on the cheek, in reply. 'When are they expecting you?' I asked.

'Now, today, I'm to catch the next ferry across to Poole, where a car will be waiting to take me to headquarters. I'll just say goodbye to the children, then I'll be on my way.'

I was disappointed, but not overly surprised that my husband was called away so soon. The country was on invasion alert and if the Germans came, this part of the country would probably be where they'd head for first. A shiver ran through me and once again I regretted the decision to bring the children into such a dangerous area. But if it turned out that their father wasn't sent abroad, it was more than likely he'd be based in this area. Of course, we could have remained safe hiding away on the Scottish Highlands, waiting with trepidation for a phone call or a dreaded telegram! I shivered at the thought. Much better, I decided, to be where he was, or where he might be! As tired as we were, it was decided that we'd go to the ferry terminal to see Rory off. I wasn't surprised as the children had used the terminal before, and it was something they loved to do.

When we arrived, like myself, Grace and Crispin, were surprised at how busy it was, it certainly hadn't been like this before! There were soldiers and sailors milling about everywhere, all waiting to be taken across to Poole Harbour. It was just crazy! There were even two ferries in operation, one going out and the other coming in. But neither of them was for Rory, as we pulled up two navy officers greeted us; 'Commander, Sir, will you come with us please,' then whisked him away to a waiting motor boat, giving us barely time to wave him goodbye!

'So, when will Father be back?' Crispen asked on our journey back to Sandbourne.

I couldn't lie to them; 'The truth is I don't know, we will just have to wait,' I sighed. Grace, I could see was close to tears; 'They won't send him away before we get the chance to tell him goodbye, will they? she sniffed.

'No! Of course not, he'll be back later today,' I smiled, doing my best to hide my own doubts.

It was gone ten o'clock when he returned and I could tell by his face, it wasn't good news that he brought back with him. I was only pleased that the children were in bed, and fast asleep thanks to their rather busy last few days.

'So, out with it, where will you be going and when?' I asked rather abruptly.

He took me in his arms and whispered softly; 'Egypt, but you never heard that from me! And I leave on Tuesday.'

I had to stifle a gasp... so far and so soon... I could hardly stop myself from crying, but it wasn't crying that he or I needed now it was comfort, and so we went to bed and made love as if he'd never be coming back... although I prayed to God that he would.

Breakfast was a sombre affair, although little Florence wasn't aware of it, laughing and playing with her food as if all was well, but both Grace and Crispen knew something was wrong.

'So, are you going to tell us?' Grace asked finally.

It was not like her to take the lead, but on this occasion her brother remained silent as if not wanting to know the truth of what was going on. Rory looked to me, as if to say, tell them please, but I looked away, knowing that it was his place to explain what was going on... and tell them he did, although he left out the destination, telling them only that he'd been ordered to report to his unit at once.

On the Tuesday, we didn't go down to the ferry to see him off this time, we said our goodbyes instead at the front door, watching as he climbed into the car that they'd sent for him. The children all ran behind it, waving as it disappeared up the long drive and out of sight. As they returned to my side even little Florence was in tears and I gathered them all about me to comfort them, until Nannie came to lead them away, back into the Manor House, where it was time for them to attend their home schooling in the playroom.

Usually, I would tutor them myself but today I had other things to attend to, we needed more staff and a cook and a maid were top of the list if we were to keep house properly. And so, I had people to interview for the jobs... well, for one job actually, as our old local cook, Mrs Brown was ready to come to work for us again, and so with her it was just a matter of shaking hands and welcoming her back. The position as maid however was less simple, there were three applicants for it and I knew not which to choose. Fortunately, Mrs Brown came to my rescue, warning me off two of them, saying one was lazy and the other untrustworthy, and so that just left the one.

'Can you tell me your name please I asked her... she hesitated... not a good start I thought to myself; 'Don't be nervous, I won't bite,' I smiled.

She blushed and half curtsied; 'I'm sorry, um! Your Ladyship, only I'm not really old enough... I was going ta lie about my age, but I can't.'

I moved closer, intrigued; 'Well that's honest of you, what's your name?' I asked.

'Jane your Grace... Jane Miller.'

'And how old are you Jane if you don't mind me asking?'

'Thirteen... just thirteen... um, your... um!'

I held my hand up to stop her, then I smiled, she made me smile, and then I put on my stern look! 'Yes, thirteen is too young, when do you turn fourteen?'

'Not till next year,' she said.

'Well come back then and I'll find you a job, I like your honesty Jane Miller,' I told her.

As she left, I had a feeling that I'd be seeing her again, that she would indeed return on her next birthday and I was surprisingly pleased about that.

In the meantime, I turned to Mrs Brown's local knowledge to find us the help we needed to keep the house running smoothly, and she soon found us someone and all was well again... Although I did miss my husband so.

As the weather took a turn for the worse and the winds blew in bitter cold off the broiling sea, crashing against the manmade barricades along the beaches, threatening to tear them asunder, I waited for any news of Rory. Already nearly a month had crept by without a single word from him and I was getting worried. To make matters worse I was running out of excuses to tell the children and they too were becoming anxious. I tried calling his unit twice, but no one admitted to knowing his whereabouts! Although surely someone must have heard from him?

In desperation I decided to try one more time, but again the phone kept ringing and ringing, and I knew no one was going to answer yet again. I was almost reduced to tears but I held myself together as I heard the children coming along the hallway... and they seemed very boisterous indeed!

'Mummy, Mummy,' Crispen shouted; 'It's Daddy, he's here... he's here!'

As I turned, the children came bursting through the door, their arms wrapped tight about their father's waist and I burst out crying and joined them, almost causing all of us to collapse down onto the tiled floor.

'Why didn't you call, let us at least know that you were alright,' I cried into his shoulder.

Nannie came then to usher the children away, and I promised them, that after we'd spoken, we would all have tea together, that sent them off happy.

Together and alone, we talked, not that he was allowed to tell me much; 'I've been locked away, training, I can't tell you for what purpose, and I'm sorry, I know you must have been worrying about me... all I can say is that the training is over and I can spend a little time at home before my posting.'

'You're on leave then?' I felt quite excited; 'How long will you be staying, a few days, a week or what?'

'A few days... maybe a week, we'll see,' he smiled.

He seemed fit enough and his face was lean and strong, as was his body, and I wondered just what they were training him for. I would not ask him though for I knew it would hurt him not to tell me or to have to tell me a lie and so I simply held him in my arms and said no more.

He was with us just four days before they came for him and it was all I could do not to shed a tear in front of the children as he was driven away. 'Daddy will be back soon,' I promised them and myself as we watched him disappear up the drive. But in my heart and in my head, I knew it wasn't true, but I needed something to hang onto, we all did.

In the days that followed, with Nannie doing most of the children's schooling I had very little to occupy my time and so found myself on many occasions just sitting playing the piano all alone in the parlour the sound of it reverberating throughout the house.

'That's very pretty your grace.'

I looked up to see Nannie standing in the hall on her way to tutoring the children and I smiled; 'It helps when I'm feeling a little down,' I sighed. 'It's going to be a long winter without my husband, and I'm not sure what to do to pass the time... oh I have the children, and you, nannie, but I miss my Rory deeply,' I said sadly.

'The Reverent Clancy is seeking someone to play the church organ, what with Christmas just around the corner, also some of the women in the village have formed a committee to help the war effort, and I know they are looking for others to join them. Perhaps you could choose to help one or both of them, my Lady?' she suggested.

I smiled, 'Nannie you're a gem, I'll speak with Reverent Clancy this very day and if you could make enquires for me regarding the women of the village, I'd be grateful. Things were looking up, already I was beginning to feel useful again and I hadn't spoken to anyone yet, but I intended to remedy that right away.

I found Reverent Clancy alone in his church practicing his sermon for next Sunday, so I sat quietly on a pew at the back until he was done, and so absorbed was he that my presence went unnoticed.

'Lady Seymour!' He finally acknowledged. 'How very nice to meet you, I had planned to pay you a visit when you'd had time to settle in, to welcome you back to the village.'

I rose to shake his hand as he came to greet me; 'You're new here aren't you Reverent, I believe it was a Reverent Blake that was here the last time we came down, although I do believe he told us of his plans to retire.'

'Yes, my Lady and he was true to his word, he retired some three years ago, and I was fortunate enough to be given this wonderful parish as my own, Reverent Clancy smiled.

I congratulated him warmly and then came straight to the point of my visit; 'I find myself at a loose end now that my husband is away, and need to find a way to occupy myself. I am informed that you might be in need of an organist, what with Christmas being but a month or so away?' I hesitated waiting for him to respond.

To my surprise he came down the aisle in such haste he almost tripped up. 'I do indeed, oh yes indeed, your Ladyship,' he beamed.

'So perhaps we could get together and you could run me through the dates and so on... oh and also would you happen to know who it is in the village that I should ask about joining the committee to help the war effort? I asked.

'Ah! That would be Mrs Jennings, I'll introduce you if you're here for Sunday Mass,' he said; 'You know it's rare that we have new families join our congregation,' my lady, but yours will be the second new family to join us this month. 'A Mr and Mrs Miller along with their children came into the parish around the same time as you yourself,' he smiled.

I was intrigued; 'Tell me Reverent, this Miller family, do they have a daughter by the name of Jane?' I asked.

He shrugged; 'I'm sorry my Lady, but there seemed to be rather a lot of children and I didn't catch all their names, one of them could have been called Jane... in fact... yes, there was a Jane, I'm nearly sure of it... why, have you met her?' he asked.

I shook my head and changed the subject; 'Are there many women on this committee of Mrs Jennings, only I don't want to put anyone's nose out of joint,' I said nervously.

He dispelled my worries out of hand; 'Having such an eminent person as yourself on board can only enhance them, I'm sure,' he assured me.

I laughed; 'Believe me Reverent I'm only a Lady because of my husband's title, true, my father is a landowner in Scotland but he is by no means a Laird. I met Lord Seymour whilst studying at Oxford University, we fell in love and that was that.'

He smiled; 'Then you know our world too, my Lady, which makes you the perfect fit for our Mrs Jennings committee, don't you think? That's if she'll have you of course,' he chuckled.

I felt myself blushing, it would be just awful to be turned down, why, I wouldn't be able to show my face in the village for fear of being laughed at! Perhaps, I thought on my way home, I should just help the Reverent out with his organ music and leave it at that. My head was in a whirl as I sat by the fire contemplating what to do... could they turn me down... would they? So, absorbed was I in my thoughts that I didn't hear Grace come into the room and snuggle up to me; 'You look sad mummy, would you like me to read you a story?' she offered.

I smiled, 'Yes, read me a story from your Beano comic book,' I sighed.

A little while later Nannie came with my other children and Grace read to us all until it was their bedtime and I was alone with my thoughts once more, but not for long, as Nannie returned to sit with me. She looked angry and I wondered what the children had done to upset her?

'It's not the children my Lady, it's you, fretting over such nonsense, wondering if you're good enough for this silly committee, of course you are, and you jolly well know it,' she said angrily.

I smiled, this was so unlike Nannie, but she was right, in the scale of things going on in the world, my worrying about whether I'd be turned down for a committee was just silly.

Sunday came around much too soon and as I walked across to the church my stomach was full of butterflies, even though the Reverent and I had been practicing the hymns he wanted me to play every night since I offered him my help. We'd agreed to begin with something nice and cheerful as it was much needed at this time, and so as the congregation settled in their seats; I began with; All things bright and beautiful, one of my children's favourites. Out of the corner of my eye I could see them sat alongside Nannie, singing their little hearts out.

After that the Reverent began his well, practiced sermon, while I took the opportunity to look over the huddle of parishioners, trying to guess which one was our, Mrs Jennings? My gaze fell on a tall, stern looking woman, who was busy wagging a finger at one of her neighbours, yes, I decided, she was the one. So, when Reverent Clancy introduced me to her later, I was not surprised. She was very elegant indeed and curtsied low, causing me to blush not wanting such formalities in this place of God. 'Please sit, Mrs Jennings,' I said taking a pew myself.

Not wanting to hang this thing out I came right to the point; 'I understand from Reverent Clancy that you are the one to see about joining the committee to help the war effort, if so, I would be interested in coming on board... if you'll have me?' I added hastily.
She smiled; 'I am the one to see, and will we have you... why of course we will be proud to have you, welcome to the committee my Lady,' she beamed.
Still, I hesitated, 'don't you have to ask the others?' I asked.
She laughed; 'Not when it's so obviously the right thing to do, Lady Seymour, it's not as if you're one of the heath people!' she cast an evil eye towards little Jane and her family.
'Are you acquainted with that family?' I asked as I watched them file out.
Mrs Jennings shook her head; 'I believe they're new to the district, they arrived around the same time that you yourself got here... 'I'm not sure but they could be Gypsies,' she said shaking her head in disgust.

I made no comment to that, but arranged to meet with her and the rest of the committee the following Wednesday evening in the village hall, despite my misgiving at her tone towards the Miller family. My mind was made up, I needed something to do whilst my husband was away.

It was a damp murky night as I made my way through the village to the small green wooden hall, it was passed curfew time so all the lights were out and I just had my own little torch to guide me. It was quite a struggle and I lost my way more than once, but finally I made it, even if I was the last to arrive.

'Sorry if I've kept you waiting,' I apologised.

Mrs Jennings waved my apology away with a warm smile. 'We don't mind, really we don't,' here let me take your coat, please Lady Seymour, come sit here next to me,' she offered.

I hesitated, the seat was already taken, but the occupant quickly moved as Mrs Jennings shooed her away!

'That's it, now let me introduce you to my little band,' she smiled.

I looked around, little was right! There were but three others, five in all including Mrs Jennings and myself! 'I thought there would be more?' I confessed openly.

'Believe me, my Lady, we are more than enough when it comes to arranging fund raising,' Mrs Jennings smiled. 'Why, last month alone we organised the local hunt ball, and the month prior to that the army and navy officers' dinner and dance, and made a good £50 for our charities.'

The others looked exceedingly pleased with themselves, but I was not, for as good as it was, I expected something different, something that included the local people.

'What about the village and the many farms, have you done anything to involve them?' I asked, realising I was treading on thin ice judging by the committee's lack of reference to them thus far.

For what seemed an age there was a stunned silence until a red-faced Mrs Jennings spoke, 'um, well we never thought of including them, thinking that they simply wouldn't have the funds to contribute much... and what could they bring to the event anyway?' She shrugged. I got to my feet; my face no doubt red with the anger I was feeling; 'Well let me tell you, ladies, in Scotland we have a thing called; The Highland Games, where people come from miles around, and it's the volume that brings in the coin, not how much each of them has,' I said.

One of the others timidly raised her hand; 'We used to hold a Gala every year back in Dorchester, I guess that's the sort of thing you mean, my Lady?'

'Yes, that is exactly what I'm talking about, um...'

'Mrs Anderson... Amber,' she blushed.

'Thank you, Amber,' I smiled. Before turning again to Mrs Jennings; 'May I continue,' I asked.

She nodded, although I could see she was not pleased, not pleased at all.

'Now I know it's not my place to say, being new to the group, but in my position as Lady of the Manor, I would be remiss in my duties if I did not engage the whole village in any enterprise we decide to do in the future. But ladies, that takes nothing away from all you are doing for the war effort, and I'm in awe of all that you have achieved in the past, and if you decide to continue without me, I wish you well with all my heart.' I added.

The air raid siren sounded then... and I thought, 'Saved by the bell', as we hurried to the nearest shelter to wait it out.

It was late by the time I finally made it back home and the children were fast asleep deep down in the cellar so I didn't disturb them, I spoke with Nannie instead, telling her of all I'd said at the meeting. To my surprise she laughed aloud her eyes sparkling with glee.

'It never hurts to throw a spanner in the works now and then, my Lady,' she said.

I frowned as I went off to bed; was that what I'd done, thrown a spanner in the works? I hadn't intended too, I just thought it would be better to involve everyone, we were all in the same war after all, rich and poor fighting side by side, there was no discrimination on the battlefields and so there should be none here either. If this committee didn't agree with that then it was not for me. As it turned out that was the last meeting of the month, or it was supposed to be, but I had a bee in my bonnet now and asked for another one, which to my surprise was granted. This time I asked that it be held in the warmth of my home, so that I might welcome them with a glass of warm punch and a roaring fire, so much better, I thought than a draughty old hall.

There were no objections to my suggestion not even from Mrs Jennings, although I wasn't sure if any of them were really keen on another committee meeting, or simply eager to see inside the Manor House, so that they could tell their friends. Whatever their reasons they all arrived on time and in good spirit, although they were surprised that I'd also invited Reverent Clancy along as he wasn't part of our committee! However, he was a part of my cunning little plan!

With everyone seated and enjoying a glass of punch, to the surprise of the rest of the committee I invited Reverent Clancy to open the meeting.

'Ladies,' he smiled getting to his feet. 'I would very much like your help in putting together a Christmas nativity scene along with a Christmas eve carol service. The children of the village school will be at your service, as will be Lady Seymour who has offered to play the organ, doing whatever carols you choose for the night.' He paused letting it sink in. 'As you know,' he continued; 'The Nativity Service was cancelled last year due to the war, but with your help we will not let them cancel it this year.'

'No, we bloody-well won't!' Mrs Jennings swore, quickly putting a hand over her mouth and apologising for her bad language. We all laughed and I was pleased they were all in the right mood because I had something else that I wanted their help with, and I really wasn't sure if they'd go for it.

'Ladies,' I said getting to my feet. 'I do hope you have all had enough punch.'

'Oh dear, I don't like the sound of that,' Amber giggled.

I smiled and continued; 'As well as organising the Nativity I want us to put on a Christmas Pantomime!' for a moment they just looked at one another, lost for words.

'When you say put on… you mean organise, of course?' Mrs Jennings said, finally finding her voice. I could see Amber, Betty, and Stella on the edge of their seat, awaiting my answer.

'I'm not sure how to put this, ladies…but no! I mean as part of the cast..all of us!'

Again, the silence; which was broken my Reverent Clancy chuckling.

'I don't know why you're laughing Reverent, the Panto we'll be putting on is Aladdin, and you will play the part of Widow Twankey, as traditionally, Widow Twankey is played by a man. I smiled. Everyone laughed then, as I went around topping up their glasses of punch, silently cursing myself for the lack of a maid, cook had found me one but I still had to interview her!

As we broke up for the evening, I was pleased to note that all the stiff haughtiness I'd witnessed at our first meeting was gone. Although Mrs Jennings did turn at the front door; 'We really can't let the Reverent take part in the Pantomime you know, he'll lose face in front of his parishioners,' she said.

I smiled; 'And what of you and me? I believe your husband is an Admiral, and me, well I am what I am, should we not worry about losing face too?' I asked.

She simply stared at me and then smiled; 'You really are different my Lady, but in a good way.' She left then shaking her head, and I closed the door, wondering what ever it was that I'd started here.

But did I regret it? No, what with this damn war there was so little left for people to celebrate. Let them take Halloween and Guy-Fawkes day, but we would have our Christmas, we would not let them take that away, the people needed something to give them cheer at such a terrible time.

Chapter 4

In spite of my doubts and my conviction that my big sister Janie is up to something, we are settling nicely into our white-walled cottage out on the heath. It's early days yet of course, but its growing on me and I'm prepared to give it a fair chance. Although I have to admit, I still hanker for Home Farm, back in Somerset, and pray every day for a quick return there. But this place has its good points, especially for Janie and me, what with us learning to be sailors when the weather allows. That is a huge plus of course, but is it enough?

My big sister Jane calls me a worry-wart, and accuses me of always having a bee in my bonnet, about one thing or another, although until now I certainly would have argued with that notion. I glanced across the kitchen, watching her feed the little-ones, she smiled and winked at me! I noticed she had that mischievous look in her eye, the one that says; I'm up to something, and you know it but you'll never guess what. But I'm convinced that this time I do know. Something is going on between our Janie and Lady Seymour.

'Ruby, are you daydreaming again?' mum called across the kitchen.

Ignoring her, I continued with my line of thought, for I pride myself on being aware of the things going on around me. Being curious, dad calls it, prying, mum says, while according to our Janie I'm just plain, nosy! I smiled, all that means is that I rarely miss much. And that is why I'm certain our Janie is up to something, although I don't know what?

'Ruby!' mum called again, sounding a little annoyed now.

'I'm just thinking,' I finally called back to her.

And I was! I couldn't be sure, but had that Lady Seymour been looking at our Janie during the church service? I tried to catch my big sister's attention again as we sat at the table during breakfast but this time, she refused to hold my gaze, then finally when at last she did, it was with a brazen grin that told me everything! She'd done it, she'd gone for the job Robbo had told us about.

I didn't like it, not one little bit and I couldn't help but worry what mum would say? She'd be angry for sure and rightly so, we were so busy helping dad around the farm, what with the fruit orchards being full to overflowing with apples, pears and plums and the fields full of enough pumpkins to feed an army, all in need of picking.

'Don't worry sis,' Janie whispered across at me, before I'd as much as opened my mouth; 'I didn't get the job, as I confessed to being too young,' she sighed.

'You did... but why?' I asked.

'Because I felt guilty and because I like her... she did say for me to go back when I turn 14, that's something I suppose,' she sighed.

How I admire my big sister, she's so brave, I would never have the nerve to do such a thing, in fact I'm not sure I would even be able to speak to someone like Lady Seymour.

There was little time to ponder such matters however as October raced by and with the coming of November, we were still so very busy and now even the weather was worsening.

We'd lived on many farms before and endured cold, wet and stormy days, and it was all much of a muchness. The wind and the rain sweeping across the land, then the coming of the snow and ice when the ponds and the streams freeze over and the hedgerows and the trees go to sleep, in fact everything shuts down including us, saving strength for the return of better times.

It's not the same here though. Out on the heath, the shutdown is more complete? Whereas back in Somerset, despite the weather we'd always managed to stay in touch with all that was going on around us, and with the war, with a quick trip into Yeovil town. Here it was different... it felt so odd, as if we were isolated from the whole world! Out here, on this piece of wasteland, the bitter cold days and nights seem colder still, the hoary old grass of the heath crackling and crunching beneath our boots in a language all its own, as we go about our daily chores, or venture off to school across the crisp, white, wintery way.

It's all so very weird and eerie that I can't find the words to describe it, but I feel the oddity of this place just the same! It's as if we've stepped into a different place, like someone has flicked a switch disconnecting us from the real world completely, it reminds me of a tale I'd heard about a road that's seldom used. The strangeness that I felt on the very first day when we'd turned onto the heath from the main road, still abounds, leaving me with a feeling both of dread and of wonder and I still have no idea which will win the day!

It is all so very bizarre; we can hear the bombing and the anti-aircraft guns booming out, and we can even see the searchlights arcing across the night sky, and bear witness to the burning buildings, and sometimes, when the wind is in the right direction, we can hear people screaming! But none of it touches us, it's as if we are living in a world apart from everyone else.

It makes me feel a little like Robinson Crusoe, but without my man Friday, instead I am marooned with my family, on this strange island somewhere beyond the reach of normality. It's an odd existence being so isolated and yet so close to it all, and yet that's how it is and our lives rumble on. Here we are in November of 1940 and instead of news of the war, we are hearing very different news being whispered. All across the heath and around the village they are talking of a Pantomime and a Nativity, both to be held in the Sandbourne church. It was the Reverent himself who brought us the news, along with invitations for us to take part in both; the little-ones, he suggested could be part of the Nativity whilst us older ones could be in the Pantomime.

The room simply exploded at his news, I've never heard such excitement from my siblings, or from mum either, who immediately volunteered her services to make costumes and to do anything else that was needed, whilst Janie and me offered to help her, hoping that would save us from having to take part in the Panto itself; But mum saw through us straight away; 'You'll not only help me with the costumes, girls, you will also take part along with your brothers and sisters,' she ordered.

'Oh, and you will be in the Nativity too,' she added, 'someone has to look after the little-ones.'

'But that's not fair,' I protested, 'Our Janet and Bella can do that... and what about Jack and Danny, they should be doing something to help!'

Mum gave me one of her; 'for goodness, sake, stop moaning, stares,' and I took a deep breath and quietened down, not wanting to sour the atmosphere, which was still on a very lovely high.

'Don't you worry my girl, you will all be involved, your brothers too,' mum reassured me. 'I've a meeting with Reverent Clancy this afternoon and will be putting you all up for whatever he might need. 'Now; Jack and Danny, you are coming with me, so get your coats on,' she ordered, her voice brooking no argument.

Janie and I looked at one another, wondering why she'd take those two little monkeys with her, rather than the two of us, knowing that they'd be Lording it over us for sure on their return.

'If they as much as grin in my direction I'll clout them for sure,' Janie vowed, reading my thoughts. Both on edge, we were primed and ready on their return, but to our surprise they were remarkably quiet and when we looked towards mum as she came through the door, she smiled.

I waited until mum had gone out into the kitchen to prepare the evening meal and then I pounced, or rather Janie and me pounced on our brothers, demanding to know what parts if any they'd been given. Despite our threats, at first, they were reluctant to say, until I said I'd just go and ask mum if they didn't tell us, and realising there was no escaping the subject Danny opened up.

'Alright,' he sighed. 'I'm the front of the horse... and he,' he pointed to his brother...

'No! Don't tell them,' Jack warned... 'Is the horses ass!'

Janie and I just couldn't help it and both burst out laughing, whilst our darling brothers were busy rolling around the floor hitting each other.

'Ruby! Jane! Whatever is going on?' Mum called from the kitchen.

Dragging our brothers apart, we called back; 'Nothing mum... nothing... 'just a bit of horse play,' I added with a giggle. Janie laughed, but our Jack and Danny failed to see the joke and stomped out into the yard to continue their rough and tumble. In the meantime, Janie and me went to play with the little-ones keeping them amused and their minds off the increasingly cold weather.

With November came a quiet spell, a time of lent, Reverent Clancy called it, giving us time to trek back and forth across the wintery heath to practice our rolls for the much- anticipated Pantomime. From the get go, my sister Janie and me had issues; as my part in the Panto was better than hers. I was to play Wishee Washee, the brother of Aladdin, the main character, whilst she was just one of my unnamed assistants, and she didn't like that one little bit. Still, as I reminded her, it was better than being the ass end of a horse! That made us both lighten up and giggle.

We were so excited when at last the day for the Pantomime came, as we were well-rehearsed and raring to go. Although we were more than a little nervous when we snuck a peep through the curtains to see that the hall was packed with all manner of people, from all across the neighbourhood, including soldiers and sailors from nearby military bases.

Despite being nervous, I have to say we put on quite a show, especially our Jack and Danny as the Panto horse that tripped and stumbled its way hilariously around the stage and into people's hearts, bringing cheers and laughter every time it appeared. Janie and me could scarce believe that it was our impish brothers bringing such joy to everyone! Not even our characters could better that, and even if I say so myself neither Janie or myself put a foot wrong. But even our brothers were eclipsed in the end, by none other than Reverent Clancy in his role as Widow Twanky, he was simply magnificent, although I could tell by the faces of those people unfamiliar with our Pantomimes, like many of the Canadian soldiers, that they found the idea of a man dressing as a woman quite strange.

Still, it was a huge success and he received a standing ovation... so much for Mrs Jennings worrying that he would diminish his standing in the eyes of his parishioners. As for her own reputation and that of the committee and Lady Seymour, if anything it had been enhanced, as the locals watched them join in the fun, laughing and singing along with everyone else.

The people simply cheered and cheered and cheered, I'd never known anything like it. It was a memory that stayed with us as we made our way back across the heath, laughing and chattering our way through the gathering darkness. Instead of making for the house we went straight to the air raid shelter, as it was about that time, and a few minutes later we were proved right as the siren gave out its high-pitched scream. Once inside the bunker we talked of the Panto, whilst the sound of the bombing echoed all around, and there we remained for most of the night, until the all clear sounded.

Janie and me were the last to leave, my head filled with the strangeness of it all?
'Can you believe it, Sis?' I muttered, as we came out into the starlit night, 'Aladdin and bombing all in the one night!'
'Living out here, I think I believe anything is possible,' Janie smiled, taking my arm.
I looked up at the starry sky, now, once more, a picture of beauty, that just a few minutes ago spewed death and destruction upon us; 'I agree sis, how strange is this new life of ours, how very strange.'

Although the Panto was behind us, we still had the Nativity to come and incredibly our Morgan was chosen to be the baby in the manger... yes, Jesus Christ himself would you believe! And of course, it was going to be mine and Janie's job to make sure he was clean and ready for his role as the son of God! Even now, days after mum gave us the news, it's all we can do to keep a straight face; Our Morgan, Jesus Christ, who'd have thought it. Still as funny as it is to my sister and me, mum and dad are proud of it and so we don't want to let them down, as tiresome as the little-ones can be at times.

Fingers crossed, I thought, as we left the house on the way to the church and the Nativity, that today would not be a day when the little-ones, our Morgan in particular would misbehave! Mum, spotting my stress and took me aside; 'Stop fretting child, you'll only make matters worse,' she warned.

I took a deep breath and glanced over at dad walking at her side, he gave me a reassuring wink and from somewhere I found a smile and started on across the yard, but our Morgan was already restless and whimpering and that was not a good sign, it was not like him, he was usually a quiet little soul. That's why he was chosen for the role. I could only hope that he would settle down! But then, halfway across the heath he had to go and soil his nappy, forcing us to stop and change him, I was not pleased at all, and said as much, bringing the wrath of mother down on my head, telling me to stop complaining and to get on with it, saying that I should remember that he was the main attraction... Jesus Christ, and because of that we couldn't be late.

Our Jane chirped in then; 'He's not you know, mum, not really, he's just our little brother, doing what he always does, shitting himself at the wrong time,'
'Ouch!' Janie cried out as mum swiped her across the back of the head. I laughed, and then got the same. 'Now get on with it,' she hissed. At her side dad stifled a chuckle as mum gave him a dirty look, which brooked no more nonsense. Despite the delay we made it on time and managed to lay our Morgan in the manger without too much fuss, where to my surprise he closed his eyes and went to sleep. Now that was truly a miracle!

Like the Pantomime the Nativity was a huge success, giving us all for a brief moment a reminder of normality, not that there was much in the way of normality for many of the poor people attending, what with loved-ones away fighting in the war.

I stole a glance towards Lady Seymour, knowing her husband was one of those gone off to fight. Although, like the rest of us she seemed to be enjoying the Nativity, I spied a faraway look in her eyes and I knew she was thinking of him, wishing him here.

All through the afternoon my attention kept turning to her, she was not at all what I'd expected, not the great, grand aloof lady of the manor at all. I'd not realised that at the Panto, but in truth that had all been a little frantic, and I had my own lines to remember, and anyway she'd mostly been part of the music scene. Now I'm able to take a closer look at her; She is certainly very beautiful there's no doubting that, with her long raven black tresses gathered about her shoulders, and her, surprisingly ocean blue eyes, dancing every which way around the room, and not afraid to return a smile. To my surprise I find myself envying our Janie for having the courage to meet her, oh why, oh why, couldn't I be so brave?

After yet another successful project we made our way back across the heath full of good spirits, even mum and dad, especially dad, he was a man whose pride for his family shone bright in his eyes, and I could have hugged him to bits! It was nice to see him happy, he had a hard life for the most part. These last couple of months, with first the Panto and now this, was the only times he'd managed to show his usual smiley self.

I don't think any of us realise just how hard he has to work out there on the farm, in truth most of the time we very rarely see him, as he's gone long before we get up in the morning and doesn't return home, until after our bed time. That's why it was so nice to have him with us today, although in truth he did look so very tired, even mum was looking at him in that worried way of hers, causing me some concern. Still, I know my seasons well, and I know that as we move deeper into December, the picking seasons will be over and life will be a little easier for him. Now perhaps he'll be more relaxed and be his usual, funny, humorous self again, rid himself of all those worry lines, after all he'd only just turned 40.

As dad's life started to get easier though, mum became busier as we started to get ready for the festive season. Usually, us kids would be excited by the thought of Christmas, but us older ones knew not to expect much this year, what with the war and everything.

Although rationing was still only a threat, there was very little to be had in the shops. Fortunately, as we lived on a farm and Janie and me along with dad still did a bit of poaching, we were well stocked up. We'd even managed to barter some illegal game for some sweet stuff, of which there was little to be had anywhere. Therefore, I was pleased to see our favourite Christmas pudding steaming away in the old boiler. After all, what would Christmas be without its pudding?

On Christmas eve we went to a carol service at St Nicholas church in Sandbourne village, along with farmer Drake and his family, squeezing into the back of his old van, with the Davis twins and their folks who we picked up along the way. We were all pleased that for once there was no air raid sirens or searchlights scanning the sky, only twinkling stars and a big yellow moon to show us the way.

It was just the perfect start to the Christmas festivities; the church looked serene with the Nativity laid out before the alter, just as we'd left it, minus our Morgan of course, he having been replaced by a rather expensive looking wax doll, that so obviously must have come from the Manor House. I glanced around looking for Lady Seymour, and spotted her at the back of the church seated at the organ, which she began to play, accompanied by the choir singing all of our favourite Christmas hymns, with the Reverent Clancy smiling down from his pulpit. I felt so overwhelmed by the beauty of it all that I thought I might cry!

Everything was just perfect, and later when we got home, farmer Drake, his good wife and his son, our friend Robbo, and the Davis twins stayed for supper, although Mr and Mrs Davis had to return home to see to their animals, but they returned later in time for a Christmas drink of homemade mulled wine and a minced pie.

It was all quite magical really, especially when the snow began to fall lightly across the heath and we gathered, family and friends together, in the yard to sing Christmas carols and make merry; even if we did feel a little guilty for doing so, what with all that was going on in the world. And yet, for once I didn't allow myself to dwell on that, tonight was about joy and laughter and sharing Christmas with friends and family; for once we had food a plenty and enough homemade mead and lemonade to drown in.

It was gone ten o'clock in the evening before our guests bade us good night and wished us a merry Christmas, before returning home to bed down their animals. Both Janie and me agreed that today had been the best day ever, as we settled the little-ones and reminded the others that Santa was on his way, and saw the look of joy on their faces. As I stood over them, I realised that it was a long time since I'd seen them so happy and excited. Before Janie and I could retire to our beds however, we still had things to do! Mum needed help to prepare the food for Christmas day and dad was waiting for one of us to help him wrap our siblings Christmas presents and to fill their stockings ready for them to wake up to. We both wanted that job, but I beat our Janie to it by tripping her up; ignoring her threats of revenge, and to my surprise, mums whole-hearted chuckles, I made it to dads' side and began filling stockings at the kitchen table.

Looking around, it was all just perfect, the homemade Christmas decorations that we'd all helped to make, hanging around the house, and the Christmas tree in the corner of the living-room cut from the woods out across the way, along with the Yule log resting in the fireplace... It was all just so wonderful that I thought I must be dreaming!

The weeks had simply flown by since we'd arrived, and now here we are, still strangers in this wild unruly place, preparing to celebrate The day of days! I felt like dancing a jig!

'Ruby... Ruby! Stop daydreaming, you can leave father to finish that, go and start plucking the chickens,' mum called across to me, as I stood with my head in the clouds... again!

Out of the corner of my eye I saw our Janie smirking and poked my tongue out at her only for mum to clip my ear; 'I swear the two of you are more trouble than the little-ones, at times,' she sighed.

'But, mum!' I tried to protest.

'The chickens, girl, the chickens!' she growled. 'At this rate we'll never find our beds.'

Without another word I got on with the task.

'And no more nonsense from you Jane, go and help her, or we'll never be done,' mum sighed.

'In trouble again, maid?' Dad chuckled, 'trouble seems ta be your middle name.'

He had that twinkle of mischief in his soft brown eyes, that we were all so used to and loved so much, but seeing it now; for the first time I realised that it was probably from him that our Jack and Danny got their cheekiness!

Shaking it all from my head I concentrated on plucking the chickens, it was already well past our bedtime and I was very tired, and we still had plum puddings to see to and cakes to decorate, and breakfast to set out ready for the morning. But finally, it was done and Janie and me stood back to admire the feast of food laid out across the kitchen, if nothing else we would eat heartily over the Christmas festival. It was a testimony of how hard mum and dad had worked to make this time so special, even if our stockings were full of second-hand toys and books, mostly from jumble sales. In truth we were over joyed to have even that. And when the little-ones awoke, they had no care about whether or not their presents were old or new, as they raced from room to room, screaming with glee, showing off what Santa had left them.

The house was filled with so much laughter and sheer joy that for a while we were able to put the thought of the war from our heads, as we celebrated our fortune at having found this beautiful sanctuary to call our home.

A few days after Christmas with the return of the bombing, the weather, as if in protest, also, turned nasty. The light snowfall across the heath gave way to blizzards and freezing conditions, the like of which no-one in this part of the country had seen in many a long year. The paths all across the heath became treacherous, as day upon day the snow deepened. Father just about made it down to the farm, now locked solid in its winter coat, alongside a bay now completely frozen and beyond our world. As for school, that was out of the question, as we were now marooned, only able to go as far as the front yard!

To my surprise mum started to teach us at home, in truth I didn't know she was capable until Janie reminded me that she'd stood in at our school in Halsey, teaching Maths and English when one of the staff was sick. So, like it or not mum was now our teacher!

It was a bad start to the new year of 1941 as we welcomed it alone, unable to wish even our closest neighbours well. And so, it was for all of January and much of February, although somehow, after the first week or so, the Davis twins managed to call on us, by toboggan, they said. What a shock it was to them though when mum roped them into her maths and English classes, to see them so speechless was quite a treat. But saying that, it didn't put them off coming, in fact they began turning up early, much to our surprise.

It was the beginning of March before we were able to finally make it off the heath, and even then, what with the snow melting, turning the ground into a quagmire, it was a struggle. Still, we made it to school, although with the change of weather came the German planes to bombard us, but not always with bombs and bullets this time but with propaganda, dropping thousands of leaflets, telling us that we should surrender, that we had no chance of winning and our government was simply sending our young men off to die needlessly.

Mum said for us to collect the leaflets as they'd do for lighting the fire!

Although we were officially back to school, it was such a struggle through the boggy heath that we only went three times a week, so mum continued her lessons at home and still the Davis twins came to take part.

By the end of March things were back too normal. The Germans were back to dropping real bombs again and we were back to our proper school days. The weather now seemed to be on the turn, with a definite feel of Spring in the air; and the heath, quietened by the snowfall was beginning to blossom again, throwing off winter's shackles. The heather and gorse turning yellow and purple all across the way, and the once ice-bound boggy ponds, thawed and alive with all manner of creatures; from toads and lizards to hypnotic dancing dragonflies. It all seemed so very beautiful and I had the feeling that despite the bad start to this year, it was going to be a better year for all of us... and who knows the war might soon be over!

With the weather getting ever better, Janie and me had some good news, we were told that we could start practicing on the rowing boat again.

'Hah! I'd rather play in the yard!' our Danny said when I teased him about it.

'Really! You'd rather play in the yard than go rowing?' Janie said joining in teasing them.

'Yes, Jack snapped, 'If it means we can get away from bossy sisters!' he growled dragging his brother with him into the yard.

'Well, what do you make of that, Sis?' I grinned.

'I think so much the better for us, now we can learn to row in peace,' Janie smiled.

The backwater was calm as we met up with Robbo by the small wooden jetty; 'Hi girl's' he waved, 'Tis just the perfect day ta row ta yonder island,' he grinned.

Janie and me looked at one another; 'Row to the island! Do you think we're ready for that?' Janie asked, beating me to it, for I had my doubts too! After all we hadn't used the boat for quite a few months and we were out of practice.

Robbo simply grinned; 'All you have ta do is what I taught 'ee, and you'll be fine,' he said. 'Besides, you did say you can both swim; so, at the very worse you'll only get a soakin'. 'Mind you girls, it'll be mighty cold,' he chuckled. Without another word he climbed in and gestured for us to do the same, regardless of his confidence though, I almost tripped and fell in the water, but Robbo caught me and steadied the rocking boat for Janie to climb in.

Thankfully, as soon as Robbo pushed off from the key, all the training he'd given us came flooding back and we set off for the island in the middle of the bay. To our surprise it took no time at all and we made it without mishap and without any help from our instructor, who sat there grinning like Lewis Carroll's, Cheshire cat. 'I knew you could do it, I taught you well' he bragged. Neither of us answered as we were trying desperately to clamber ashore without falling nose first into the water as we climbed off the boat. 'That's right girls, now tie 'un off and that's that!' He ordered, climbing ashore himself.

We weren't listening anymore, as we had our minds on exploring!

It was a small island but not as small as it seemed from the mainland; there was a flat parcel of grass land that dipped down to the brackish water, along the edge of which was a small stand of trees, where I spied several red squirrels giving us the eye.

'This would make a lovely picnic spot,' I suggested, striding across the flat piece of land.

'Yes, we could build a shelter, and stay overnight in the summer,' Janie enthused. She grabbed my hands then and we did a jig, much to Robbo's amusement.

I'd never seen her so enthusiastic about anything before; but then just as quickly her mood changed and I could see something was bothering her!

'What's wrong sis?' I asked.

'Well, I'll be 14 soon and old enough to start work, and even if I don't get to work at the Manor House for Lady Seymour, mum will insist that I work somewhere... so I'll not be able to do any of this with you,' she said sadly.

We were growing up fast my sister and me; I put a consoling arm around her shoulder; 'Don't worry Janie whatever happens we'll find a way to have our picnic, I promise,' I assured her.

She dug me in the ribs; 'It's not as if I'm leaving home or anything, so who knows, as you say, we might find a way, now come on let's explore some more,' she said marching on ahead.

It didn't take long to walk around our island and we were soon back in the boat, both a little subdued now causing Robbo to ask why? He laughed when I told him; 'It's not the end of the world, girls, we all as ta grow up and start work! That's just the way of things.'

'Well, I refuse to grow up until I've had a picnic on the island with my brothers and sisters!' Janie snapped angrily, pulling so hard on her oar that the boat wobbled badly.

As we came alongside the key Robbo jumped ashore and tied the boat to its mooring and then turned to us; 'Well you two are ready to go it alone from now on,' he grinned. Janie and I looked at one another in disbelief. 'I'm not so sure about that, Robbo,' I said, 'did you see how we both nearly fell in the water when we set off, and how our Janie nearly capsized us on the way back?'

'I did no such thing,' Janie snapped angrily.

'You did too,' I argued... 'just because you have to start work and so might miss the picnic.'

'Miss the picnic! You do know that without me there will be no picnic, unless you think you can row to the island alone,' she snapped.

Before I could answer Robbo spoke; 'If you're going to act like babies then I'll tell your father that you're not ready yet,' he warned.

I felt so ashamed and I could tell my sister did too. 'Sorry sis,' I apologised.

'No, you're right Rube, I did nearly sink us with my silliness,' Janie admitted.

We hugged then and Robbo laughed and turned away, 'well done,' he called over his shoulder, 'I reckon you're ready now, girls!'

That heralded the end of our lessons with Robbo; and both Janie and I were a bit sad about that. He was a nice young man and not bad on the eye either. As I watched him walking away, I wondered if Janie, like me, was a little in love with him? It was going to be strange not having him here anymore when we come down to use the boat! But the more I thought about it the more I agreed with his decision, Janie and I were ready to go it alone.

A couple of days later we gained the confidence to ask father if we could make a solo trip to our island, our very first unsupervised journey. To our delight, he said yes and even came down to the key to see us off. I could see him standing anxiously on the jetty as we made our final strokes to bring us safely to our destination and even though it was too far for me to see, I knew he'd be grinning ear to ear. His two little maids had done it... he'd be so very proud of us.

The next stumbling block in our quest to picnic on the island was mum, for I knew she had her reservations, mostly concerning our dear brothers; Jack and Danny, although in truth they'd changed somewhat of late, but could we convince her of that? Strangely it was the Davis Twins we had to thank for their better behaviour, and I never expected that! In truth I had thought they'd have the very opposite effect on our Jack and Danny, making them even naughtier... if that were possible!

But I have to admit the truth, our devilish brothers are rarely in trouble anymore, spending most of their time out across the heathland and down towards the beach, finding rocks and curios for their collection. The only time of late that they'd found themselves in hot water was when they'd crossed the heath while the red flags were flying, which meant live munitions were being used. We only found out because they were brought home in an army jeep and lectured about crossing the heath, when the red flags were flying, something we'd all been warned about.

Although father was rightly angry with his sons, he had something to say to the soldiers too, declaring, once again, that it was not right for the military to use the heath as a live firing zone, while families like his lived there. And if they continued to do so, then it needed to be better protected than just flying red flags! Mum nodded her agreement before slamming the door on them. With her in such a mood, both Janie and me worried that it might lead to her saying no to our picnic adventure on the island as she could be a worry wart at times. Still, it was now or never, and so after supper, when our siblings were all in bed, we dared to ask her!

To our surprise she didn't say no... although she didn't say yes either! 'I'll think about it,' was what she said, and so we left it at that, knowing there was no point in pushing the matter further, as mum would not be rushed, so we'd just have to wait. Time passed slowly for Janie and me as we waited for mum's approval to sail to our island, but at least we could temper our frustration by practicing our rowing, but for the rest of our siblings the wait must have been agony, making me wish we'd never told them.

However, a week or so before Janie turned 14 on the 16th of May 1941, mum finally gave her permission for us to row to our island and hold a party for her there. For a good hour or more the house was in uproar, with everyone shouting and running around in sheer excitement and it was all we could do to calm them down and settle them in their rooms.

'Hey Rube!' Janie whispered that night as we sat on the edge of the bed looking out of the window; 'I told mum today about Lady Seymour saying for me to go back after my 14th birthday, and would you believe it; she said, I could try for it... isn't that great?'

I nodded and smiled; I was pleased for her of course, but at the same time I was a little bit jealous; working at the manor house was something I would love to do.

'You know, I never thought mum was ever going to make up her mind about us spending a night on our island?' Janie sighed, changing the subject.

I peered out of our bedroom window onto the silent heathland; it was a warm night, the crickets were chirping and the frogs were croaking and everything was just perfect... perfect for a moonlight picnic, I thought, as I drifted off to sleep.

That night however fate took a hand, and threatened to rip our well laid plans asunder, and we didn't even know until we awoke the next morning to a landscape completely changed! The Germans unbeknown to us had dropped incendiary devices all across the heath, we'd only been saved from being roasted by a troop of soldiers digging a trench around our house. That we'd not known how close we'd come to dying made me tremble as I went with Janie to help mum, who was busy taking mugs of tea and plates of toast out into the yard for the tired and dirty faced soldiers who had saved our lives.

'Now 'ere's a pair o' sleepin' beauties and no mistake... hey girls, did nasty old, Mr Hitler wake you up?' someone called to us. I blushed and Janie giggled.

'Naw! I spec' you was talkin' too loud, Bert, that's what woke em!' Someone else laughed.

Ignoring the soldier's silly banter, we hurried to do our bit, both amazed by the fact that we'd very nearly been burnt to death without knowing anything about it! All thoughts of going on a picnic were lost by the events of that day, and the following days were much the same as the Germans increased bombing all along the coast... it seemed to me a personal thing, that Mr Hitler was determined to stop us going on our picnic, but I was equally determined that we would go, just as soon as we could.

I have to admit to growing doubts however as night after night they came and we watched the dark skies turn red with the burning glow of fires; as ships and dockyards exploded and towns and villages burnt, until we thought it would never end.

One night Janie and me stole out of our beds to go and stand high up on the heath, watching the big heavy bombers; the screeching fighter planes and our own darting Spitfires, as arcing searchlights scanned the night sky for the noisy Ack, Ack guns, to pick out their targets. It was like being in a great arena, with the war unfolding before our very eyes, it was mad, it was scary... it was real! Just then two planes collided, one of ours and one of theirs, exploding into a million pieces... I saw no parachutes, and said a silent prayer for both pilots, knowing that I shouldn't be praying for the German as he was the enemy, but something inside of me said that I should!

As we watched the dog fights continuing overhead, my ears were ringing with the sound of war, and I was tired of witnessing the destruction all around. I couldn't help but wonder if things would ever return to, how they once had been. Would there be beaches again without barbed wire, without tank traps... without land mines? Would we ever again play on the sand, build castles of delight? Suddenly I found myself crying, because right now, I couldn't see it ever happening, the old days, I feared were gone forever.

Two days before Janie's birthday however things calmed down, the German planes failed to come?
'Turned to the big cities, is my reckonin' dad said over breakfast.
As sorry as I felt for those big cities, I could not help but be pleased that they were leaving us alone. Now, perhaps we could once more look forward to our picnic to celebrate our sister's birthday, and to camping out on our island. Goodness knows we deserved a little lightness after such a bombardment.

On May, 16th 1941, everyone was full of excitement, it was a bright, warm and sunny day, and it was Janie's birthday and at breakfast everyone seemed to be talking at once, until mum banged her serving ladle down with a clang, drawing our attention to her. As one, we fell silent, all tingling with excitement?

'As you know it's our Janie's big day, today she's no longer a school girl, she's now a young lady,' mum smiled. Our Jack and Danny muttered something about their sister, being no lady the way she treats them, only to get the back of my hand each, bringing a yelp from them, and a giggle from the rest of us.

Mum ignored their cries of indignity; 'I've decided that you can celebrate her big day by rowing over to your island as planned, just promise you'll behave,' she looked directly at our brothers; 'and listen to Ruby and Jane, as they'll be in charge.'

There was a moment of quiet and then the room erupted with cries of sheer joy, with siblings running and dancing around the kitchen table, upsetting the little-ones who had no idea what all the fuss was about, but mum quickly quietened them down with a crust of buttered bread each.

I hugged my big sister, 'You see, Janie you will get to go to the ball!' I chuckled.

She dug me in the ribs; 'I'm not Cinderella, Sis,' she laughed.

Together we jigged around the room with our siblings, overjoyed that our dream was about to come true, that we were going to celebrate Janie's birthday on our island.

'Thank you, mum;' Janie said, beating me to giving her a hug, but I was close on her heels, throwing my arms about her and almost bursting into tears.

'None of that now Ruby, I know how desperate you and your sister are to go on your picnic and so today that is exactly what's going to happen... if you still want too of course?' she added with a smile.

'Oh! Yes, we do, we really do,' I answered for the both of us.   'Well then, now is the time, 'I've packed up some food and drink, and dad is waiting down at the key with everything else you'll be needing... so off you go now... oh and be careful!' mum added with a smile.

For a moment no-one moved, all of us a little stunned, I looked over at Janie, who was gaping, like a fish, and like myself, unable to find the words to describe the joy we felt, it took our brothers to break the spell as they leapt to their feet.

'Can we ask the Davis twins along?' Jack whooped.

Mum hesitated looking towards Janie and me; 'I suppose it'll be alright as long as they understand that Ruby and me are in charge,' Janie said. It was all our brothers waited to hear as they rushed out the door to ask their friends on our great adventure, returning in less than half an hour, with not only the Davis twins but also their mother, who wanted to know what was going on?

Once mum had assured her that all was well, she gave them leave to join us and we set off down across the heath with our supplies of food and drink packed away in two canvas rucksacks, carried by the grateful twins. On reaching the jetty we found dad waiting, but also, to our surprise Robbo was there too, standing by the rowing boat… or rather, the two rowing boats?

'We got the loan of a second boat,' Robbo explained. 'We thought it might be quicker that way, as I expect you'll be needin' help with the tents and that,' he grinned. Janie and me looked at one another and blushed… we'd both forgotten all about having something to sleep in?

Dad chuckled; 'You do want to sleep over, dunee, girls?'

I nodded feeling like a complete idiot; 'Yes, of course, dad,' was all I could say.

'Alright then Robbo, they're all yours,' dad said, stepping aside.

Robbo took control then; 'Jane, you and Ruby will take your sisters, Janet and Bella along with one of the Davis twins, and I'll bring your brothers and the other twin, if that's okay,' he asked.

'After I've dropped them off, I'll come back for the tents and the rest of the gear,' he explained.

I watched as Janie nodded her agreement, she looked as scared as I felt, after all neither of us had ever taken passengers before, only Robbo, but he didn't count, what with him being our instructor.

We waited nervously for everyone to climb aboard and then we set off, both of us scared to death that we might capsize and see our loved ones splashing about in the water. I cursed myself silently for thinking like a fool and stroked out strongly towards our goal. Mooring the boat safely and helping everyone ashore, I felt so proud of myself, you'd have thought I'd crossed the Atlantic Ocean.

Thankfully, it was a nice balmy day and the water was so quiet and still that it might have been taken for a sheet of mildewed glass. Everyone was so excited as we stood waiting for Robbo to arrive with the second load, consisting of our brothers and the remaining Davis twin. After dropping them off Robbo returned to get the tents and our gear, leaving Janie and me to try and contain everyone's excitement as they whooped and hollered around the little island, only stopping when the rowing boat returned with our camping gear.

Janie and me led the way to the piece of flat land in the middle of the island, where we wanted the tents erected, leaving Robbo and the boys to get it done. They were not the best of tents but being ex-military, they would afford us good shelter for the night. Whilst the boys were busy with that us girls set about gathering wood for the fire. It was important to have the fire going as soon as possible, so that we could cook our supper before curfew. None of us feared that the Germans would target such a tiny speck of fire on such a small island, but I agreed with Janie, that we should abide by the law on this occasion.

As soon as the tents were up, Robbo set off back to the mainland, leaving us all alone to do exactly what we wanted. One or two said we should go for a swim, but Janie and me vetoed that, after all this wasn't the small stream, we'd learned to swim in back in Somerset, this was the sea, and who knew the strength of the currents here. Swimming or not, I felt a tingle run down my spine, this was so exciting! To be left all alone on an island, how many kids got to do such a thing... none, I'm thinking! Only us! I wanted to shout out at the top of my lungs... 'Look at us... just look at us... Whoopie... Whoopie!'

Instead, I lay down on the grass, feeling it cool and tickly on my skin as I looked up at the cloudless sky; 'Is this real?' I whispered to myself. Strangely, despite my own excitement there was an odd lack of talking, which was surprising as most of us could talk till the cows came home... as mum would say! Instead, everyone was busy; the boys, making the fire and gathering logs for us all to sit on, while the girls were breaking out the food and drink ready for our supper. Getting up, I went to help them.

I knew the silence was not bound to last, and I was right as our Jack got to his feet and ran a circle around us all screeching like a banshee!

'We're free,' he screamed; we're free, no grown-ups to tell us what to do, to make us do chores, we're free... we're free;' he roared. Running around in a circle, like a lunatic!

On his second circuit Janie tackled him down to the ground then sat on him! 'Just remember little brother, we are all free... to enjoy ourselves, not just you, understand,' she said threateningly.

'Ok, I get it, now will you get off, Sis, you're hurting me,' he grumbled.

Giving me a wink, she let him up; 'Just making sure everyone knows who's in charge Sis,' she whispered in my ear.

I smiled; as if any of our lot needed telling who was in charge, the Davis twins, maybe, but not our siblings, they all knew how strong she was. We'd all witnessed her striding across the fields at dad's side with a brace or two of wild ducks strung about her neck and a string of rabbits too, even a young deer at times. But it's her other strength we admire her for, the strength to lead and give advice.

Although I envied the closeness, she had with our dad out across the field, I was close to him as well, but in a different way; with our Janie it was hunting, with me it was story telling!

That was one of his things! He just loved to tell stories... ghost stories mostly! And I, unlike most of my siblings, including Janie, loved to hear them.

Thinking of dad and his ghost stories gave me an idea, I decided to tell one of my own as we huddled around the fire eating our supper of baked beans and sausages and powdered eggs. The story I chose was one that dad had told me one night when I couldn't sleep for all the noise of the bombing going on across the bay, it was a story that none of my siblings had heard.

'Someone douse the fire,' I said as we settled down in our little circle, with darkening sky casting shadows across the campsite it was just perfect conditions for a ghost story, and so I began!

'One night, as dad was walking up across the heath after finishing his work on the farm, he heard the footfall of someone coming towards him, whoever it was however was not walking normally, they were sort of shuffling along and they were whistling a low tuneless, birdsong, like nothing he'd ever heard in his life. He stopped to listen, unsure if it were real or simply a trick of his imagination, but as he stopped, so too did the tuneless whistling and shuffling! But the moment he started on, so did it, getting closer and closer… nearer and nearer!

I paused to look around at the circle of siblings and friends gathered about the now dead fire, all of them hunched up close, some clinging to the ones sat next to them, all wide-eyed and trembling, even the boys. I glanced toward my sister, Janie, who, I knew just hated ghost stories more than anything else, she stared back at me trying to keep a brave face, but I could see that I had her, she was scared too. Taking a deep breathe I continued with my ghostly tale.

'Dad tried to put it out of his head as he plodded on up the pitch-black path, after all there was nothing to be done, he simply had to carry on and meet whoever it was coming down the track! He patted his trusty old shotgun, at least he could protect himself with that, even though he had no cartridges left.

With that thought in mind he continued on, every step taking him closer to the strange sounds on ahead, which were getting ever louder... until finally, out of the darkness a huge man; a soldier, appeared! His uniform was bloodstained and in tatters, hanging off him, revealing a nasty gash across his left knee, no doubt causing him to limp and shuffle?

They were on the same path and about to collide when dad hurriedly stepped aside; but if the soldier saw him, he paid him no mind, passing on by as if father wasn't there, and then, just as quickly as he'd come, he was gone, disappearing into the darkness, leaving behind only the ghostly echo of his tuneless whistling!'

I paused again and put a hand to my ear for effect; 'Listen, do you hear something? Is that whistling, oh my God! It is... it really is!' I cried into the gathering dusk. Almost as one the circle gathered closer together all wide eyed with fear, our Janie too, and I couldn't hold back a little laugh at the sight of their faces.

'Right, get her,' Janie yelled, as she pounced on top of me with the rest close behind her.

'Try to frighten us would you, sis, well two can play at that game; Jack, Danny, the rest of you, grab her, I think she deserves a wet bath, come on, to the sea with her,' Janie cried.

Suddenly I was lifted and carried to the shoreline; the sea looked very dark and murky as they swung me back and forward over the water... 'No! No! I screamed, 'it'll be freezing!'

Janie laughed, 'Now who's scared little sister?'

'Throw her in... Throw her in!' I heard Jack and Danny, shouting.

'No, please,' I screamed. 'Don't do it.'

'Okay, let her down, I think she's learnt her lesson,' Janie chuckled.

Reluctantly I was lowered to the grass on the edge of the water, although I could still hear my charming brothers begging to be allowed to throw me in the sea. I made a mental note to deal with them at a later date, the little monsters.

By the time everything settled down again it was nearly time for bed, but not before we had a good old sing-song and sang happy birthday to our Janie, and danced and romped around the island for a while. But with the coming of darkness, most were yawning and stretching and ready to call it a day. I did wonder if we'd have trouble getting the boys to go to their tents, but apart from the odd rowdy outburst, they went quietly enough, and we heard nothing more of them, unlike our sisters, Janet and Bella! I'm sure they would have talked the night away had not Janie threatened to get me to tell another of my ghost stories, that finally shut them up. Once they'd gone to bed, leaving me and Janie at last on our own, we went to sit on the edge of the sea and look up into the black night sky, lit by sparkling stars and a beautiful full moon.

'Do you suppose they'll come tonight, sis?' I asked.

Janie gave me one of our dad's favourited winks; 'Perhaps they know what a lovely time we're having and don't want to spoil it,' she grinned.

I laughed; 'Or perhaps Mr Hitler is afraid of upsetting you, Janie.'

We both had a good old giggle at our silliness, and held hands as we looked up into the heavens. 'It's so beautiful' I sighed.

Janie didn't answer for a moment, then said; 'Do you know what they call this kind of moon, sis?'

I shrugged; 'A poachers moon?' I guessed.

'Well, that's what dad and most of the farmers call it, but the Germans have another name for it; they call it a bombers moon! They say it highlights their targets perfectly.'

Suddenly the magic was gone, taken away once more by the enemy; Quietly we stole back to our tents beneath the broken beauty of the night.

The following evening before the German planes returned, dad and Robbo came to take us back to the mainland, and away from any bombing out across the bay, aimed at the ships at anchor and Poole harbour itself, which was but a stone throw from where we were.

In an act of defiance Janie and I refused to go down to the air-raid shelter when we reached home, but settled our siblings there just the same, leaving our Bella and Janet in charge. Mum went with dad out across the farm helping him catch up on his work after he'd stopped to get us home. Throwing caution aside, and with no one to stop us, Janie and me went up to the highest point of the heath to watch the deadly moonlit dog fights, as our own Spitfires joined the action.

The raid lasted what seemed to be hours as we watched wave upon wave of enemy planes pass overhead, the smaller fighter planes swooping down to shoot up anything that moved. It was like having our very own arena, a place of blood and death, like they do in Spain, or so I'd heard, where people go to witness the tormenting and killing of bulls, just for the fun of it! Seeing this, I wonder how anyone can enjoy such a spectacle, to be part of the killing of a fellow creature is nothing short of barbaric. Suddenly I was crying, and Janie dug me in the ribs; 'Get a hold of yourself, Ruby,' she barked.

We heard mum calling then... so she was back... and we were in trouble for not going to the shelter and for not looking after our siblings, turning together we started down toward the yard.

Just then two planes dived down so low, both locked in mortal combat, that we were actually able to see the pilots faces as they passed above us, it brought the war home to us like nothing else had. Suddenly we realised that we hadn't simply been watching one piece of metal high in the sky verse another piece of metal, but one human trying to kill another! It was quite eye-opening. And what's more the German pilot was not the monster, all the papers painted him to be, and that we thought him to be, in truth, he'd looked just like us, which was even more disturbing.

It was all me and Janie could talk about for the next few days, even telling the kids at school and having our teacher explain that of course the Germans were like us, after all our own Royal family were part German.
Now I didn't know that!

Just how much like us the Germans were, however, we were about to find out.

A week or so after the aerial fight, a platoon of soldiers paid a call at the house to warn us that they suspected two Germen fliers who'd been shot down were hiding out on the heath.

For days the soldiers combed the area in vain, in the end deciding that they must have moved on, perhaps towards the coast in the hopes of stealing a boat to get them home.

'Why don't we try to find them ourselves,' our Jack said, one day out in the yard.

Our Janie beat me to giving him a slap; 'Don't be so silly, Jack,' she growled.

Later in bed however we revisited the idea; 'It makes more sense than waiting to be murdered in our beds, mind,' Janie admitted.

It was an idea that festered and grew throughout the night and when we awoke in the morning and talked it over, we both agreed that it was something we needed to do.

'We can't tell mum though,' I said.

'No definitely not mum... or dad come to that, he'd not let us do it either.'

It was still early, about 6am. 'Alright, go and fetch our brothers, Rub, we'll tell them now,' Janie said.

Jack and Danny were most upset at being dragged out of their beds so early, but once we told them the reason they soon calmed down, although it was hard not to give them a smack for the smug; 'we told you so,' look on their faces. After breakfast, once we'd finished our chores and the little-ones had been seen too, we sent our brothers off to fetch the Davis twins, figuring the more of us there was, the safer we'd be, although we decided not to tell the rest of our siblings, for fear of it getting back to mum and dad.

Once mum and dad had gone off to work on the farm and the little-ones were being looked after by our Janet and Bella, we armed ourselves with kitchen knives and heavy iron pokers and started our search for the German airmen.

It was quite eerie creeping stealthy through the woods down by the farm, the place, we thought they'd most likely be. Our Janie led the way, followed by Jack and Danny, then myself, with the Davis twins bringing up the rear. Even though Janie and I knew our way around these woods, from our hours of poaching with dad, today was different... rabbits and small deer, didn't fight back, these Germans though would!

That was a scary thought and one that wouldn't go away as we crept through the undergrowth, jumping at every single sound, whether it be a crocking frog or a chirping bird. It was a thing of nightmares and of dad's ghostly tales... only this was real!

'I'm scared Janie,' I whispered, making my way to her side, as we crept through a stand of gnarled old oak trees, that reached down to the edge of the backwater.
'Me too, Rube, but I'm pretty sure they're not in the wood, we've checked all the places they might be hiding; It's my guess that they're long gone,' Janie said, with a sigh of relief.
'We should check on the rowing boat while we're here,' our Jack suggested. 'They may have stolen it and rowed over to your island and be hiding out there.'
'Good idea,' Janie conceded, leading the way down to the small jetty where the rowing boat was moored, and to where her and me had shared so many good times. But the boat was still there, and it was getting late and so we decided to call it a day and head for home. I felt both disappointed and not a little relieved, to be honest, not that I was going to admit to the latter in front of my brothers although judging by the fear on their faces they felt the same.

'And where have you lot been?' Mum demanded as we trooped into the kitchen.
Stealthily our Jack returned the knives to their drawer, while Danny put the pokers back to their resting place in front of the living-room fire.
'Just playing in the wood,' Janie answered, taking the lead as was her place.
'Right, but from now on I want you all to stay close to the house,' mum insisted.

She was worried, I could tell, and that wasn't like mum! Something was wrong?

Suddenly I felt even more nervous than I had creeping through the wood, and I had goosebumps running down my spine again.

'Do you think they're still out there?' I asked Janie later. We were perched on the window-seat in our bedroom looking out into the dark, listening to the wind whispering through the heather.

'No! We had a good look around. I believe what the soldier said, that they're more than likely to be somewhere along the coast, trying to get a boat to take them across the channel,' she sighed easing off her perch and climbing into bed.

Her answer made sense and made me feel a lot better, after all why hang around a boggy old heath when you could be sailing for home! The thought softened my nerves and I made to return to my own bed, but then mum came bustling in, and the look on her face scared me!

'They're out there... and I know exactly where they are?' she blurted out.

'What!' Janie and I exclaimed in alarm.

'I said, I know where the Germans are hiding,' mum insisted.

'Then why haven't you told the soldiers?' I asked trembling with fear.

Her answer was incredible! 'I wanted to be sure, the army has enough to do,' she said.

'And you're sure, are you,' Janie asked nervously.

She nodded; then blew out the candle she was carrying before beckoning us to her side; 'See that patch of shrubs to the left of the gate...' Janie and I strained to see.

'Over there, near the largest bush, just off the pathway,' mum pointed.

As hard as we looked, we could see nothing unusual; 'but how can you possibly be sure?' Janie dared to ask.

For a moment I thought mum was going to blow her top; but she remained calm; 'I've been watching old Gypsy, farmer Drake's dog, he's been sniffing at that bush most of the day, but what clinched it for me; not more than an hour ago I spied a tiny light, like the glow of a cigarette... oh, they're, there alright girls I'd bet my life on it,' she insisted.

Mum seemed absolutely certain, and that was scary. It was no wonder we didn't find them out in the woods today... they were right here all the time, on our doorstep!

'Is dad home yet?' I asked nervously, praying that he was.

'No, and he'll not be back for a couple of hours yet,' mum said.

'Then what are we going to do?' Janie asked, looking as frightened as I felt.

Mum walked slowly to the door; 'Look after the little ones Jane! Ruby, you come with me,' she ordered, already making for the stairs. Janie and I stood there for a moment, just looking at one another, perplexed, and then we hurried after her down the stairs and into the kitchen, where we found her loading father's shotgun!

'Mum! What are you planning to do?' Janie asked in alarm.

'Well, first I'm going to check that they're out there, and if they are, I'm going to capture them,' she said stuffing extra cartridges in her coat pocket.

'No, no, mum,' I cried, 'let the army deal with them'.

'Well, I would but they're not here are they, and to get to father we'd have to go right past where they're hiding, and so the only solution is for me to go out there and get them myself, and you my girl are coming with me,' she said putting a hand on my shoulder.

I thought I was going to be sick; 'but mum, this is crazy,' I protested.

'I agree with our Ruby, it's madness, mum, let's wait, at least until dad gets back!' Janie pleaded.

Mum held her hand up to silence us; 'As I said, Ruby you're coming with me... and Jane you see to your brothers and sisters and to the little-ones, and be sure to lock the door behind us and only open it if I ask you to,' she ordered.

'Alright then, Ruby, grab the torch and let's go,' she commanded.

Reluctantly I did as she asked, and we slipped out into the darkness. My heart was in my mouth as we crept across the yard, jumping at the slightest little sound or movement. Although it was but a short distance, just over the yard and a little way down the heath, it felt a lot further and my insides were churning so that I thought at any moment I would be violently sick.

'Make sure you shine the torch into the bushes as soon as I tell you to,' mum ordered... and stay out of the line of fire,' she growled softly as we came off the yard onto the heath.

That was one thing I didn't need to be told, what with my trips out poaching with father!

'Get ready child!' mum hissed, making me quiver with fear, knowing that we were almost there.

I thought for a moment that I was going to collapse with fear and mum must have thought I would too, as she stopped to let me calm down, but only for a moment, soon we were on the move again, until the bushes we thought they were hiding in were right in front of us!

Mum gestured for me to be ready with the torch and then she tore the foliage aside and I shone a light in, and there they were, crouched together, two of them, shaking with the cold or with fear, I wasn't sure which, but I held them with my torch beam and neither of them moved a muscle.

'Do either of you understand English?' mum asked

The older of the two nodded and mum ordered them out of their hideaway, telling them to crawl on their bellies and lay flat on the ground.

I was impressed, I knew how good mum was at giving orders to us, her family, but to German's, wow! That was something else again.

'Ruby... Ruby!' I blinked and shook my head clear; mum was speaking!

'Yes, what should I do now?' I asked, finally listening.

'Take the torch and run down to the farm and fetch father and some of the men, I can manage to take these two back to the house on my own,' she insisted. 'You did a good job tonight, well done child, well done,' she smiled.

Mother capturing Germans!

I couldn't get it out of my head as I ran down through the heath; 'how brave she was... how brave I was. Hah! Our Janie would never believe that. But in truth all I'd actually done was hold the torch, mum had done the rest... God! She was fearless our mother... what if they'd had guns and attacked us. I had a bit of a panic attack then, but it soon passed, had they fought back, there was no doubt in my mind that mum would still have captured them... or shot them down! I felt a surge of pride as I increased my pace, tripping and stumbling my way down through the dark heath towards the farm.

'Is she alright?' was the first thing dad asked, worrying, as always about his 'Old Dutch!' As I told him what had happened.

'Yes, mum's fine,' I assured him, watching him, farmer Drake, Robbo and the other hands grabbing up guns and pitchforks. 'The silly mare could've got herself killed,' he muttered angrily as he led the charge up through the heath.

As we reached the front door, dad had us all stop and entered slowly on his own, his gun at the ready; 'Iris... are you alright?' he called hesitantly.

'Yes... we're in the kitchen Fred,' mum called back, much to everyone's relief.

We found her perched on a stool, her shotgun in her lap watching over her prisoners, who were sat on the tiled floor gulping down mugs of hot tea, although the younger one on seeing them, spat his out in front of them... 'Hey now, we'll have none of that my lad;' mum barked.

'Sorry for him, he has no manners,' the older one said, shaking his head.

'I am a Nazi, a true blood,' the young German said in broken English; he saluted by throwing his arm out in front of himself; 'Heil Hitler,' he shouted.

'And we'll have none of that nonsense either boy, now sit down before one of these brave lads knock you down,' mum warned him, seeing the look on dad's face.

With that he slumped back to the tiled floor, and for a moment I thought he was going to burst into tears, I hadn't noticed out there in the dark just how young he looked, now seeing him in the light of the kitchen, he didn't seem much older than Janie and me. I felt a bit sorry for him.

'Has anyone gone for the home guard?' Mum asked after a while.

'It's all-in hand mother,' dad assured her with a smile.

'Here, you can give that up now Iris,' farmer Drake said tapping the barrel of the shot gun still nestled in her lap, smiling she passed it to dad.

'Ruby!' mum called. For a moment I just stood there, paying her no mind... until... 'Ruby, for goodness' sake! What's wrong with you girl? Go up and see if Jane needs any help with the little ones, she must be worried about what's going on down here.'

Finally, I dragged my gaze off the young German and did as she asked, taking the stairs two at a time in my eagerness to tell my sister all that had happened, and was still happening. I found them all in one room, huddled down on the big double bed, with Janie guarding them with one of dads spare shot-guns.

'Should you have that?' I questioned on seeing her.

'Never mind that, what's going on, have they gone yet?'

I shook my head; 'Not yet, but dad and farmer Drake along with Robbo and some of the farm hands are here now, so there's nothing to worry about,' I assured her. There was a buzz of excitement among my siblings and then Janet asked; 'So what are they like, these Germans?

I shrugged; 'Didn't our Janie tell you? She saw them for herself earlier?'

'Well, the thing is, sis, I didn't get a good look at them. Mum asked me to make a pot of tea and then ordered me up here,' she sighed. 'So, what are they like, Rube?' Janie insisted. Bella must have seen the glint in my eye, and she pounced on it! 'Our Ruby fancies one of them,' she accused.

I felt myself blushing; 'don't be so daft, Bel, they're the enemy!' I blustered.

'Then why are you going so red in the face?' Bella accused.

'You'll be going red in the face when I give you a good smack, now shut up, foolish little girls should be seen but not heard,' I said using another of mum's favourite sayings. If I thought that was the end of the matter, I was wrong, now our Janie of all people joined in. 'So, Rube, they're good looking, are they?' she grinned, with her most mischievous face on.

'Well, one of them is,' I made the mistake of admitting.

Suddenly I was surrounded by siblings bombarding me with questions... 'which one... which one is handsome?' Bella demanded.

Finally, I gave in; 'The young one, I swear he can't be much older than Janie and me, and he has the blondest hair and the bluest eyes I've ever seen, and when he's not scowling, he's just perfect.' Janie got to her feet; 'Right I'm going down to see for myself, so take charge Ruby, and he'd better be all you say, sister, or else,' she laughed.

As she went out the door, and before I could stop them; Janet and Bella shot passed me closely followed by our Jack and Danny, leaving me feeling pretty useless! In the end I was left with only the little ones; just, Violet, Morgan and Charlie.

A few minutes later I heard mum on the stairs, herding my brothers and sisters on ahead of her; I was expecting a tongue lashing for letting them out of my charge, but instead, as my siblings trooped in, heads hung low, mum followed them in with a smile on her face?

'It's easier to guard Germans than look after this lot, don't you think, Ruby?'
Before I could answer, she said; 'Especially if they're good looking, right.' She chuckled. Everyone laughed and all I could do was keep quiet and soak it up, knowing them to be right.

The next morning, as we got ready to go off to school, it was all anyone of us could talk about and I was forced into telling what had happened over and over.

The two Germans had been taken into custody sometime in the early hours, by the home guard, both of them in the end praising mother for her bravery and for her kindness. Thankfully there was no mention of my own role in all of it, and I was glad, after all, I'd only carried the torch.

At school the atmosphere was buzzing, somehow it would seem the whole village had heard about the incident and were queuing up to find out more, and our Jack and Danny were only too happy to oblige, even if they didn't have the full story of that night. By the end of the day, mum was being heralded as a hero, and plans were being made to throw a celebration party in her honour... something I just knew she'd hate.

Suddenly, what with all the commotion I was glad that my part in capturing the Germans was being over looked, although mum did her best to let everyone know how brave I'd been. Not that I recalled feeling brave, just very scared mostly. Dad did say how proud he was of me, but he added a warning, that I should never, ever do anything like it again... as if I would?

My siblings, were all dying to know all that had happened that night, but I told only Janie, and that was the following day, as she was rinsing my hair in the kitchen.
'Come on Rube, tell the truth you nearly pooed your knickers, didn't you?' she laughed.
'Do you have to be so crude Janie?' I tutted. 'But it's true I nearly did, but then I thought of how you'd tease me forever if I did.'

'Forever and a day sis, forever and a day,' she chuckled.

Then she got serious; 'tell me the truth Rube, it must have been very scary, they are the dreaded Hun after all, the scourge of Europe and all that. You couldn't have known that they were just men and not the Demons that we all heard them to be.'

'To tell you the truth, sis, it was a lot scarier when we were searching for them in the wood on our own... we must have been mad to do that! Just you and me with the Davis twins and our brothers, armed with pokers and kitchen knives... I shuddered, 'at least mum had a shotgun.'

'As for me thinking they were Demons, I did have a good idea of what they looked like. If you remember, Janie, we saw them up close out on the heath that night when they were flying low. But to tell you the truth, Sis, it's a lot easier hating them and picturing them as demons... rather than handsome buggers like that young one.' I sighed.

Janie frowned; 'I know Rube, and he surely is a good-looking boy, but the enemy is the enemy no matter how handsome they might be, and if ordered, I'm sure that young one would kill any or all of us in the blink of an eye. We all need to remember that.'

I decided to change the subject; 'What do you think of this idea of throwing a party for mum?'

Janie shrugged; 'Well, we both know she'll hate it, but a party is always a good idea, don't you think, sis, people need cheering up what with all that's going on. But in truth, it should be a party in your honour too, sis, you helped capture those Germans, and it's no good denying it,' Janie insisted.

I sighed; 'No, we've spoken of this, I only held the torch, now leave it sis, please... but I do agree, people need cheering up and a party would be just the thing, but for mum... just for mum,' I insisted.

Chapter 5

I'm sure that most people imagine that being the Lady of the Manor is easy and I'm sure it is for a lot of my counterparts who are more used to their roles. But for myself right now it is a burden, especially without my husband to share the load.

It's true what they say; life moves on and we have to always follow in its wake come what may, putting all that the world throws at us aside. My darling Rory has gone off to do his duty, and it is the way of things in these crazy days of war. And now I must continue along the road he bade us take, if not always with a glad heart, but with the knowledge that it is where he will expect to find us on his return. I am only thankful for the activities I have ventured into of late and the remarkable success of the Pantomime and Nativity, I was lucky enough to be a part of.

Still, I feel miserable! A bit like old Scrooge out of Charles Dickens a Christmas Carol; I want to cry out to the world; 'Bah! Humbug!' For I am sad and feeling so terribly alone even with Nannie and the children by my side. In truth all I pine for is to be once more at Kirriemuir and have my old life back, for Sandbourne feels nothing like home without Rory. I fear that it's not really about where we are, anywhere without my darling husband will be hard for us. Mainly because we don't know where he is and what danger he might be in. I thank goodness once again for the new friends I've been able to make here, without whom I'm not sure I would have coped. I call them friends, but of that I'm not really sure anymore for I have seen nothing of them these past few months. My fear is that they find me not the grand Lady they believe I should be, or that they are used to.

It's a shame because I was hoping we might go on to do many other things to aid the war effort together, but as yet no other meeting of the committee has been called, and already Spring is here, with the promise of new beginnings, although sadly as yet, not for me.

A gentle knock on the door disturbed my troubled thoughts and I crossed the room to see who it might be, as through the window, I can clearly see Nannie and the children walking in the garden.

'My Lady, you have a visitor,' the new maid announced as I opened the door.

I frowned, for I was expecting no-one.

As the maid stood aside, the merest glimpse of my latest visitor's unruly brown hair told me exactly who it was and brought a smile to my lips, as even before I saw her strong angular face, I knew her to be the leader of the Miller children, part of the family who had helped with the Nativity and the Pantomime, at Christmas... and who had applied here for a job even though she was under age.

'Miss Miller, don't tell me, you have now turned 14, how delightful,' I smiled with genuine pleasure, for I liked this plucky young girl, for her honesty if nothing else. After all she need not have admitted to being under age when she'd applied to work for me, I'd not have known any better.

She looked towards my new maid... whose name I really should try and remember, instead of continuingly referring to her as the new maid... 'Wendy... that was it... Wendy!'

'Clearly my Lady I'm too late, as the job's gone,' she sighed.

'Well, we are still in need of a kitchen maid, would that suit you, um! Jane isn't it, how nice it is to see you again,' I smiled.

It was clear that she didn't know whether to curtsy or bow or what, but that was something she would learn in time, and I was willing to give her all the time she needed, for she had already won a place in my heart, and so giving her a place on my staff was a forgone conclusion.

'Are you sayin' you'll give me a job, my Lady?' she said, eyes wide in disbelief.

'Well, I did give you my word, that if you returned when you turned 14, I would give you a place on my staff, and so, yes, the role of kitchen maid is yours if you want it, Jane.' I told her, loving the look of disbelief on her young face.

For a moment I thought she was going to burst into tears; 'I can't believe it,' she said, 'I turned 14 only a week ago and already I have a job, a real job. I'm not a school girl any more, I'm a young woman... what will mum and dad say... what will my brothers and sisters say? Oh, thank you, thank you, my Lady,' she said wiping away a tear.

'Well, a belated Happy Birthday, Jane, my, you certainly don't waste any time,' I smiled. So, when can you start,' I asked, smiling at her look of complete disbelief?

'Monday week, if that suits you, my Lady, that will give mum time to put one of the others on my chores, not that they'll be very pleased about it of course,' she grinned.

'Do you think your mother will be alright with you working here?' I asked.

'Oh yes, mum will be very pleased, dad too, they both like you, they say that you are not a bit like a Lady! Oh! Sorry, I shouldn't have said that... of course they think you a Lady, um, just not... well you know, posh, if you know what I mean?'

It was all I could do to stop myself from laughing aloud, but I simply nodded that I understood and left it at that. 'So, we will see you a week on Monday then,' I said, walking to shake her hand. 'I will inform cook, she will be pleased to finally have some help in the kitchen,' I smiled, ringing the bell for the... for Wendy, our new maid to show Jane, our new kitchen maid out. Looking through the window I watched her all the way up the winding drive, noting with pleasure her jaunty gait, satisfied that she was going to be a perfect fit in our household.

An hour later, after weeks of seeing hardly anyone, I had another visitor, and it was none other than Mrs Jennings, head of the committee, whom I hadn't seen since Christmas. At first, I was pleased to see her, but then I noticed her widow black dress and alarm bells went off in my head! She half stumbled as she crossed to the chair opposite me, and I reached out to steady her; 'Tell me my dear,' I said, helping her to sit down.

'It's my husband, the Admiral... he's gone... he's dead,' she sobbed.

'Oh my! Was it his ship, was it sunk?' I asked softly.

She shook her head, fighting back her tears, 'No my Lady, he died at home in his bed, of a heart attack! I thought I should tell you as I will be moving away, closer to my children's school in Cambridge, so you will need someone else to take my place on the committee.'

I patted her hand; 'Now, don't you worry about that, you just do whatever you need to do, and if you need us at all, just ring and we'll be there, no matter where you are in the country,' I said sincerely.

'Thank you, my Lady,' she sobbed, dapping at her eyes with her pretty handkerchief. 'Will you please inform the rest of our friends, I've just been too busy to contact them,'

'Of course, I will, my dear, now, will you share a pot of tea?' I offered reaching to ring the bell to summon the maid, halfway there however she stopped me.

'I'm sorry my Lady but I really can't stay, the children... I must get back... you understand!'
With that she stood and I moved to give her a hug; 'We'll meet again, I'm sure of it, my dear,' I said kissing her lightly on the cheek.

'Oh! I, almost forgot, you must have this?' She took a small notebook from her purse and pressed it into my hands; 'It's my address book, you'll find all the committee members numbers in there, along with their home addresses.'

Thank you was all I could manage, my mind full of the irony of life, that a man like her husband in the midst of this bloody war should die peacefully at home in his bed! There were tears in her eyes as the maid came to escort her out and my thoughts turned to my own husband Rory, and I said a silent prayer for him, wherever he might be.

The following day I decided that it would be a good Idea to contact the remaining members of the committee to see about renewing our endeavours to raise funds for the war effort. And so, one by one I called them on the telephone; Amber Anderson, Betty Troy and Stella Smith. They were all very sad to hear about the death of Mrs Jennings husband, but like myself they were eager to continue doing our bit for the war effort. With that in mind we agreed that there should be another meeting, with the view of, firstly finding a replacement for Mrs Jennings, and secondly coming up with a new idea to raise funds. It was also agreed that we should meet at my manor house the following week to discuss the best way forward. I was more than pleased at their enthusiasm and now paced the floor of the lounge in search of a fund-raising idea to put before them... that is until there was a knock on the door to disturbed my line of thought.

'Yes, what is it?' I barked rather irritably.

Sheepishly, Mrs Brown, my cook poked her head around the door... 'um! I just wondered if you'd heard, my Lady?' she stammered nervously.

'Heard? Heard what? No, don't tell me... we've been invaded!' I gasped, my legs going weak.

'No... no, my Lady, I'm sorry, but I thought she might have mentioned it yesterday during her interview?'

'Do you mean Jane Miller, our new kitchen maid? What on earth might she have to tell me that brings you here in such a lather?' I frowned.

'Well, my Lady, I thought she might have mentioned about how her mother captured two Germans who were hiding out on the heath... went out with her husband's shotgun she did, just as brave as you like, and held them captive in her kitchen until the home guard came for them.'

I could scarce trust my ears; 'are you sure you have the rights of it, Mrs Brown? It sounds a little like something out of a Hollywood movie to me,' I said shaking my head in disbelief.

'It's all across the village, my Lady, and our head gardener, Mr Hodge, is in the home guard and it was he and his unit who went to take the Germans into custody.'

'Our Mr Hodge, you say, well he's a trustworthy soul, so it must be true, but I can scarce believe that our new kitchen maid didn't mention it. Well, well, what an interesting family,' I muttered as cook backed out of the door.

In the days that followed there was much commotion about the brave woman who had captured the two Germans, and I heard that arrangements were being made to honour her with a party up at her home on the heath, and I was pleased when I received my invite, for I longed to meet her. I had of course seen her before, but that was only across the length of the church during the Nativity and the Panto. Now I was anxious to meet her up close and to find out more about her. Clearly, she was someone worth knowing, although I wasn't sure my ladies on the committee would agree. However, if I was going to play a role in any future fundraising ideas, things would have to change, I wanted more of the local people involved. Mrs Jennings, I'm sure would not have agreed, but she was gone now and so it was up to the rest of us, we'd either move forward together, or perhaps I'd have to rethink my role with them.

My thinking was that as our Christmas Nativity and the Pantomime had been so hugely successful, we should continue on that path, and not go back to upper-crust Officers Balls, and all that. That was all so old hat, for the privileged few, while this war united everyone, or was supposed to. Now that we'd taken such a bold step forward with our ventures over Christmas, we should not even think of taking a backward step.

On the day of our agreed meeting, as usual they all arrived together in Amber's car, and were all as pleased as I was myself to be getting back to committee business. Although all were saddened by the departure of our dear Mrs Jennings, and raised a glass of Sherry to her before the meeting began. I did detect a little excitement as the meeting got under way and it wasn't long until I found out the source of it; 'We have all been invited to the home of our newest heroin, and just can't wait to meet her… can you imagine, she captured two Germans single handed!' Amber enthused.

I smiled; 'Yes, it was our Mrs Miller, you remember her, it was her baby boy in the manger for our Christmas Nativity. As a matter of fact, I have only recently taken on her daughter as my kitchen maid, how's that for a coincident Ladies?'

There was a brief intake of breath, obviously they had not expected our heroin to be so lowly born, as if only the better classes could have performed such an act of bravery.

'I have also been invited to her party and I'm only too happy to accept, particularly now that I know that you will all be there,' I smiled.

That softened things and we began to discuss what we'd gathered here for, to renew our efforts for our war targets, now all we needed was an idea, but to my delight, they already had one. Amber rose and cleared her throat; 'We have been mulling over an idea our dear friend Mrs Jennings had, before her dear, husband passed,' she sighed sadly. 'She had this idea of us organising a village fete... a village fete, can you believe her coming up with that, my Lady?'

It made me feel wonderful, obviously my idea of including everyone had stuck with her, and now she had come up with this, it made me feel positively proud.

'I think it is a splendid idea, but what do the rest of you think, we are a committee after all,' I encouraged. 'But before we get into that, we should talk, we haven't seen each other for months and I'd like to know how you all are, and how your husband is Amber and how yours is Betty?' I asked.

Poor Stella who was the oldest of our group at the age of 42 and a widow, having lost her husband in the first great war at just 19, spoke up as well; 'I'd like for us to catchup too, it feels like an age since we all had a good gossip together,' she smiled.

Amber was the first one to speak; 'Well, as you all know, my husband David, thank God, survived Dunkirk, and I had a letter from him two days ago, he's still with his unit and not been sent out yet... but no doubt that will be soon,' she sighed with a tear in her eye.

Betty took a long drink of Sherry before declaring nervously; 'My Barry came through Dunkirk safely too but is back out there now, I don't know where, of course,' she said sadly.

We had a break then as the maid brought us in a pot of tea and a tray of cooks best homemade scones, which was just the ticket to get us past this moment of sadness.

For the next hour or so we tried to put the war from our minds, as hard as that was, to concentrate on this idea of a village fete which we all agreed was a very good idea indeed.

'And should we hold it on the village green?' I asked. 'Although it is a little on the small side!'

They looked at one another rather sheepishly, then Amber, whom I noted seemed to be the new head of the committee, cleared her throat, in rather a nervous sort of way!

'Well, we were sort of hoping you might allow us to hold it here, on the manor grounds, my Lady?' she said hesitantly.

That took me rather by surprise and I had to think about it for a minute as I considered my children and what Rory, my husband might think of it. Deciding in the end that my children would love the idea of a fete on their doorstep and Rory would sanction whatever I thought best for us all.

'Of course,' I said at last, putting them out of their misery. 'There is one other thing we should think about while we're here, and that is a replacement for Mrs Jennings... any ideas, ladies?'

There was disappointingly a general shaking of heads.

'Oh, well, never mind, I'm afraid it will have to wait until after our celebration out on the heath,' I sighed, ringing for the maid to take the tray away.

'You know, I'm sure I must have seen this Mrs Miller at the Pantomime or the Nativity, but I just can't put a face to her, isn't that awful?' Betty said.

Amber nodded her agreement, and I could tell by the look on her face that she felt as guilty as her friend, and so I did my best to reassure them that it was nothing to get upset about.

'Our Mrs Miller is not a show off, ladies, she tends to keep herself to herself according to her daughter Jane who is about to start working for me, she also tells me that this party is not something her mother cares for, and would willingly call it off if she could.'

'So, it seems that none of us are acquainted with this mysterious Mrs Miller, but soon, hopefully we can remedy that, ladies,' I smiled, genuinely pleased at the notion.

Amber got to her feet; 'Well, I for one can't wait to meet her after what she did,' she said.

Stella shivered; 'Can you imagine it, marching out into the heath with a shotgun, knowing that there are Germans out there? I'm sure I would never have been so brave,'

The talk then turned to the dilemma she'd been faced with and what any of us might have done faced by such a predicament? We all confessed that perhaps we'd have locked the doors and waited for our husband to come home and deal with the problem.

'I have it!' Amber suddenly squealed jumping to her feet.

We all chuckled; 'What is it that you think you have, my dear,' Betty asked finally.

'Our new committee member, we should ask her, this Mrs Miller, what do you think ladies, to having a real hero on board?' she asked triumphantly.

I was a little jealous, if I'm being honest, and a little annoyed with myself, of course we should ask Mrs Miller to be our new Mrs Jennings. It was obvious, and I should have been the one to see it first. But I hadn't and it was out there now. All that remained was for us to vote on it, and we did, and it was unanimous, Mrs Miller would be our new committee member, if she chose to accept the post. Now all that remained was the when and where to approach her on the subject.

Amber thought we should just jump straight in as soon as we could, but I disagreed, after all we couldn't hijack a celebration party that was for her, it would be stealing her moment. No! We needed to choose the right time, even if that meant waiting a week or two. That is what I said and what, in the end was agreed to, we would bide our time for now.

'And now ladies, I suggest we concentrate on the idea of putting on a fete, so that when we do get to asking Mrs Miller, we will have something to put before her.' I suggested.

Everyone agreed, but then we realised that we didn't actually know what a fete consisted of, or exactly what went into the making of one.

All the ladies started talking at once then, and someone said something about, lions and tigers and clowns and I burst out laughing, I just couldn't help myself. 'No, no, ladies, that's a circus, think smaller,' I giggled. 'Wait, I believe one of my children's books might have the answer?' I suggested.

Going to the library wall, I took one of the books down and opened it; 'Ah! Here we are, village fetes,' I said. Triumphantly I began to read it aloud.

'We will need;
Coconut shies,
Bat-a-rat stall, whatever that is?
Tombola
White elephant stalls
Raffles
And a home-made cake stall.'

'There, how is that to be getting on with,' I offered.

Amber giggled; 'That sounds more like it, forget I said any of the other stuff, like lions and tigers and all that.' We all joined in her laughter and studied the list. I dearly hoped that one or two of the others understood what most of the things I'd uncovered were, because I had no idea, for instance what a, White- elephant stall was. But judging by the look on the faces around me neither did they! But it really doesn't matter, I told myself, as I watched them climb into their car and head off up the drive, we have time to find out and will be seeing one another soon at the party on the heath. All we needed now was for Mrs Miller to agree to come on board with us, I prayed that she would because I had a feeling that she would be a great asset to our cause.

Thinking of her and of the party being thrown to pay tribute to her bravery, I had a plan how I might show my own deference to her, although I was a little worried, she might think it a little over the top. I hoped not for I simply wanted it to be something she and her family would treasure forever. I smiled to myself, it had come to me one particularly sleepless night, when the German bombers were giving us hell, it was a show of defiance to let them know that even our women were better than them... so there!

To that end I decided to use my families Barouche and two beautiful white stallions to show off our hero in the best of light. They had only ever been used once before and that was at a Royal wedding. It was not just a message to the Germans, to let them know that we will not be easy to take should they invade. It was also a beacon of light to the locals, a show of the old British splendour that our nation is built on. I did hesitate, just for a minute, wondering if my husband Rory would approve of me doing this, after all such grandeur was a tradition of his family not mine! I smiled; 'He'd be fine with this!'

On the morning of the event; Amber, Betty and Stella arrived together in a large black Bentley, followed by a host of other vehicles, some old, some new. Just how far the story had spread I had no idea, but I did know that the mayor of Dorchester was coming to award our heroin some kind of medal. Which to my mind was only fair, after all had it been a soldier on the field of battle, he'd have been given a medal of valour. So why not a housewife defending her home and family from the very same enemy, shouldn't she be awarded the very same honour?

I knew the answer to that and looking up the drive at the long line of cars, so too did a lot of other people, all waiting patiently for me to lead the way across the heath to meet our heroin. I felt so very proud for her as I ordered the Barouche to be prepared and the stallions to be made ready for the journey. I hadn't told the children of my plans to use, what my son Crispen called, 'the posh carriage,' and as I expected he sighed and declared that in his opinion it was all a bit too posh!

I smiled; 'Well then, let me tell you why I'm doing this;' And told them the whole story of the Germans on the heath, and of her bravery in capturing them.

'Now if ever a bit of pomp was called for then this is the moment, don't you agree Crispen?' I smiled, ruffling his hair.

'Fair enough, mother,' he conceded.

'Oh wow!' Grace sighed, listening to every word. 'I can't wait to meet them, I really can't... and one of them is coming to work here you say, that's wonderful.'

'Well yes, but she'll be in the kitchen mostly, but if Nannie West allows, I'll see if she might agree to talk to you, perhaps tell you about her family and of her life out on the heath. However, for tonight please don't pester them, children,' I begged.

'Now, are we ready? Alright then, it's time to go... Nannie can you make sure they are clean and tidy, please,' I asked. As she checked them over, I couldn't help but wish she was coming with us, but I knew that it wouldn't look good having a Nannie in such a humble home, and so we were on our own.

We climbed aboard the Barouche and the driver calmed the prancing horses and started them up the long driveway. Although I was looking forward to the evening, I held a small ridiculous pocket of fear in my breast, that sometime tonight, I would have to give a speech, something I simply hated doing. Shaking the thought from my head I sat back to enjoy the pleasant clip clop of the horse's hooves on the old concrete road, the sound softening as we came onto the grassy track across the heath.

'Wow! Have you ever seen anything like that before?' Crispen gasped looking back.

I glanced back myself, and was alarmed at just how long the precession was following us...

Suddenly I was concerned, as I hadn't expected so many people, how on earth were the poor family going to cope? As if reading my thoughts, my daughter, Grace piped up; 'The Reverent Clancy has been up to see the family, to warn them just how many to expect,' she said.

I smiled and relaxed a little, at least they wouldn't be taken completely by surprise! Directly behind us were my three committee members; Amber, Betty and Stella and I hoped and prayed that they would not turn their noses up at the little homely, house on the heath.

On my lap, little Florence was getting restless, she'd never ridden in a horse drawn carriage before and I saw that the constant clip-clop of the horse's hooves was making her nervous.

'Here, let me have her, mother,' Grace offered. 'From here you can see the white-walled cottage out on the heath... look Florrie, see that house, that's where we're going,' she told her young sister as I handed her over.

I switched seats so that I could see for myself and had to admit it was a beautiful sight, this white walled cottage, like something from a story book, a suitable home for a true heroin! I thought.

Behind us Amber in her big black Bentley honked her horn loudly, obviously excited and anticipating meeting our, would be newest committee member. I just hoped that she and the others would remember what we'd agreed, that we wouldn't approach her on the subject today!

With a shake of my head, I put my negative thoughts aside and concentrated on the view up ahead, the white walled cottage was a picture, set as it was amongst the vibrant yellow gorse and shades of bright purple Heather.

As we drew closer, I could see figures in the yard awaiting our arrival and stretched the sinews in my neck in an effort to recognise our hostess, but quickly realised that she wasn't there, I could see Jane though and pointed her out to the children as the one coming to work at our manor house. This caused a stir of excitement and I quickly had to quieten them, and I silently gave myself a telling off for stirring them up so. It was now that I missed not having Nannie with us, she'd settle them quickly enough! I tried, I really did, but as we grew ever nearer so their excitement threatened to get out of control!

Chapter 6

As I stood in the yard waiting for our guests to arrive it was all I could do to prevent my knees from knocking, I was that nervous; a Lady, a real honest to goodness Lady was coming here, to our home, I could scarce believe it. I'd heard about her from our Janie and seen her for myself, at a distance, but, wow! She was actually coming to our home. It just didn't seem possible! With a huge effort I reined in my emotions; 'For goodness' sake,' I told myself; 'This is not for you, mum's the heroine.' I glanced over my shoulder to where she was hurrying this way and that making sure we were ready. She didn't look any different... she was still just our mum!

I prayed that people weren't expecting too much. Sometimes when meeting ones Hero or Heroine they can be a huge let down, as they don't live up to your expectation! I hoped with all my heart that these guests would not be disappointed with mum! If they were, I think I might cry! I shook the thought away and turned my mind to her Ladyship; having only seen this Lady Seymour, across a crowded church, and only having our Jane's version of her to go by, I really wasn't expecting too much, for she had not seemed much at a distance, and my big sister was easily pleased.

'Ruby, no daydreaming now, keep an eye out, they'll be along anytime soon,' mum called to me from the kitchen as I stood in the yard looking out across the wild beautiful heathland, waiting.

Summer was on its way and lately I'd spent most of my spare time out and about discovering the heath in all its beauty. Although it was clear it had not yet reached full bloom, the heather was already vibrant in bright splashes all across the heath and I couldn't wait to see it reach full blossom as we moved further into Summer.

It was all a pleasant surprise for I had not imagined this wild place could possibly compete with our old haunt back on Home Farm, with all its lovely wild flowers out across the fields and along the way. But I was surprised, this Sandbourne Heath had a magic all its own! Until now, I realised, I'd not really appreciated this new place, we'd come to call home! But it held promise, it really did, all I had to do was to open my eyes and my mind to see it.

'So; no more mooning over our Somerset!' I told myself. 'This is a new beginning, get used to it!'

'Ruby, are you daydreaming again?' mum called, bringing a snigger from our Janie, on passing.

'No mum,' I replied, a little red faced, having been caught out once again.

The sunshine was just starting to wane, casting a soft reddish hue across the heather and the down, when I spied our visitors, a whole host of them. I shielded my eyes to get a better view and saw a stream of cars stretched in a long line across the heath, all led by something, quite magical, almost as if it had been torn out of a storybook! It was a beautiful carriage drawn by two magnificent white horses.

'They're coming mum!' I called over my shoulder, and a second later she was there at my side. She didn't look very happy, as I suspected, she was never one to be the centre of attraction, but there was nothing to be done about it and so all she could do was smile and accept it.

Many of them I recognised, as they drew closer, as being from the village of Sandbourne, but there were many I didn't know at all, some of them representing the army and a few from the home guard. Even our teacher, Mrs Hardington was among the guests, along with Reverent Clancy, both arriving together in an old ford car that made quite a racket as it trundled across our cobblestoned yard. But the guest who stole the limelight was of course the Lady of the Manor, who gave me the warmest of smiles as she stepped from her magnificent carriage, her three elegant, well-dressed children in her wake all of them looking a little nervous and out of place among the grown-ups.

Although we'd invited her, its true to say that none of us really expected her to come. On first seeing her and her children as they stepped from her beautiful carriage, which mum later told me was called a Barouche. I could only stop and stare, as I'd never seen the likes of them, not in all my lifetime. Oh! I'd had glimpses of her and them too before, in the church and in the village hall, but seeing them this close, just left me speechless. The only word to describe her Ladyship was elegant, I decided, as I watched her glide across our cobblestone yard as if she were on a dance floor, wearing such a warm smile on her pretty face as she was introduced to mum. It was a genuine smile too not one made out of duty.

'Mrs Miller,' she beamed. 'How very brave you are, my dear, and what an honour it is to meet you and your family, you are a welcome addition to our little community. Indeed, we could do with more families like yours, and I hope we become good friends as well as good neighbours,' she smiled.

I could tell mum was uncomfortable by the way she, half curtsied, half bowed in return, before turning bright red and almost tripping up the step into the house. But if Lady Seymour noticed, she hid it well as she took mum's arm and walked in alongside her as if nothing had happened, leaving her children to follow on behind, which they most gracefully and obediently did. I turned to Janie who was at my side; 'Wow, what a lovely person she is, you are so lucky to be going to work for her, Sis... do you think you could ask for a job for me?'

We were just about to step from the yard into the house ourselves, but Janie stopped me in my tracks, a sour look on her face that told me she was not pleased with me.

'No, I won't ask for a job for you Ruby, you're not old enough, be patient, you're only 12, you've another 2 years of going to school ahead of you yet,' Janie reminded me.

'You could at least ask!' I pouted. 'Never mind, perhaps I'll ask her myself while she's here,' I said.

She turned on me like an angry Tigress, 'No, don't you dare Rube, this is mum's time, I'll not have you stealing her place in the spotlight; do you understand?' she threatened, standing over me.

She was angry and I knew her well enough to know that if I tried any nonsense, she would come down on me hard... and anyway she was right, this was mums party!

I would just have to wait... but there was no way I was going to wait 2 more years, I decided, as we entered the house, now overflowing with people.

'Make sure the little-ones and the others are alright,' Janie whispered as we came through the front door.

I quickly made my way up the stairs to the biggest bedroom where I found our Janet sat on the bed telling the rest of them stories, and not ghost stories, I was pleased to note, while on the floor our Jack and Danny knelt playing marbles, as quiet as mice! I could only think that mum had either bribed or threatened them, either way suited me as long as it kept them quiet. It was good to see our Janet taking a turn looking after the little-ones for a change, leaving Janie and me to help mum down at the party, serving drinks and food to our guests.

Mum and Lady Seymour had been joined by three other women and they were all looking out of the window, staring out across the yard.

'So, just where were the Germans hiding?' I overheard Lady Seymour ask, as I came back down the stairs and into the living-room.

'Over yonder, just the other side of the gate, my Lady,' mum said, pointing, as one they all stretched forward to get a better view.

'Really, they were that close! You must have been very fearful for the safety of your children, my dear,' Lady Seymour, said, the other's nodded in agreement.

'Aye, I surely was, my Lady, nothing else would have given me the courage to try such foolishness,' mum assured her.

I stayed where I was, hovering, fascinated by the tall elegant aristocrat. I didn't even notice one of the other ladies come over to stand with me, not until she spoke.

'Hello, you must be one of Mrs Millers children, how do you do. My name is Amber, a friend of Lady Seymour, or rather not so much a friend but a member of the committee she is a part of... tell me, um... sorry, what is your name my dear?' she asked.

'Ruby... Ruby Miller, my lady,' I said, rather surprised that such a posh lady should bother to speak to me, but she was insistent, leaning in close as if she had something very important to say.

'Tell me Ruby what does your mother think about committees?' she asked, quite out of the blue.

Before I could answer, Lady Seymour came over and literally shooed the woman away, muttering a soft apology in passing, leaving me to wonder what it was all about. A few minutes later the woman who spoke to me and a couple of others left, all of them apologising profusely to Lady Seymour, although I had no idea why. The one who had spoken to me seemed quite upset?

'She's lovely, isn't she, Rube?' our Janie said coming to stand on the stairs with me.

Still confused by what had just happened all I could say was; 'Yes, she's beautiful!'

Unaware of what had happened my big sister nodded, and continued on; 'I'm betting she has a fine nature too, sis, and I can't wait to begin working for her, and I promise when the time comes, I will ask her about employing you, Rube.' She assured me with a smile.

As Janie moved off to fetch more drinks and food for our guests, I remained where I was, a little confused and so lost in thought that I didn't see her Ladyship return across the room and so was quite taken aback when I heard her voice say my name, and was even more surprised to find her standing right in front of me!

'So, Ruby, isn't it? 'I'm sorry if my friend confused you by her behaviour, she was not meant to do that, I can't explain now but I do owe you an explanation, and you'll get one soon,' she promised as mum came to join us.

'So then, are you enjoying this?' Lady Seymour asked, changing the subject with a smile.

I turned awkwardly to face her but could find no words to speak, 'um! Yes, my Lady,' I said, once I'd unravelled my tonsils.

She and mum both chuckled; 'She's not usually so tongue-tied,' mum assured her.

'I hear that you are very good at telling stories?' Lady Seymour smiled.

'Well, the little-ones like them, the others too, I think, my Lady,' I blushed.

'I wonder? I have to make a silly speech soon, do you think you could look after my children, perhaps take them up and introduce them to your siblings, or read them a story,' she suggested.

Her children were standing a little behind her and looking very bored. 'Yes of course my Lady, if they'd like to follow me, I'm sure my brothers and sisters would love to meet them,' I offered, noting the look of delight on her children's faces, no doubt only to pleased, to be away from the grown-ups for a while. I was glad that our Janie came up too just in case I had any problems with our two rascally brothers.

Thankfully the little-ones were all sleeping peacefully, and my brothers and sisters were more than happy to have new friends to play with, all be it posh ones!

'Hi, I'm Bella, and this is my sister Janet, and our Ruby and Janie you already know, and over there in the corner are the little-ones,' she said pointing to our sleeping siblings... and those two playing marbles are my brothers Jack and Danny,' she introduced solemnly. Janie and me looked at each other in complete disbelief, our Bella never so much as said a word to anyone, let alone strangers? Now here she was talking as if she were the leader of us all. I stole a look at my big sister, who was the leader of us all, thinking she might be annoyed, but she was just standing there open mouthed, and then she burst out laughing and all was well.

After her introductions, Grace stepped forward; 'Thank you Bella, I'm Grace and this is my brother Crispen and our sister Florence, it's nice to meet you,' she smiled.

'Want to play marbles, Crispen?' Jack asked.

'Yes, come on, you can take my place,' Danny offered getting to his feet.

Crispen grinned and sank to his knees to join in the game.

'Will you tell us a story, Rube,' our Bella asked, making room for us on the bed. 'No ghost stories though,' she pleaded.

I agreed, and told them the story of my trip into Yeovil town to the jumble sale, where mum almost came to blows with someone, and a couple of women fought over clothes not fit to wear.

Grace frowned, 'what's a jumble sale?' she asked innocently.

Janie and I giggled and left our sister Janet to explain as little Florence climbed up on her lap.

Lady Seymour had just finished her speech and I could tell by how much mum was blushing that it had been all about her and her amazing exploits out on the heath, of which I had played my part. On seeing me her Ladyship came to speak with me as I came off the stairs back into the living room; 'Thank you,' she said, as Janie hurried away to help mum with the food and drink. 'I've been thinking, if your mother can spare you, you might think about coming to the Manor house now and then, to read to my children?'

I could scarce believe what I was hearing, was Lady Seymour offering me a job?

'I can't offer you permanent employment, of course,' she said bursting my bubble.

But it was something, I would be in the manor house and who knows where that might lead.

'I understand, my Lady, but I would love to read to your children, they are very nice.' I said, holding my excitement down, afraid I might holler it to the rooftops else.

She smiled her loveliest smile; 'If you have a miniscule of the courage that your mother has, it will be my pleasure to welcome you to our home, Ruby… an absolute pleasure.' Wow! The way she spoke about mum made me feel like I was living with a heroine from one of our Danny's comic books, and not our mother! Who would have believed it?

Things got busy then, and Janie came to hassle me about helping her, taking my mind away from the prospects of working at the manor house, even if it wasn't a real job. Instead, I was forced to concentrate on filling glasses and fetching food from the kitchen to keep our guests happy. During my many visits to and from the kitchen I noted with interest, mum and her Ladyship in a close conversation and worried that mother was saying no to me working at the manor house and when a few minutes later Lady Seymour sought me out, I guessed I was right and mum had said no!

'I have just had some startling news from your mother...

Here we go, I thought, no Manor House for yours truly!

'Please, let's speak outside in the yard, my dear,' Lady Seymour suggested.

I followed her out, and she shut the door, then turned, placing a delicate hand on my arm!

'Why didn't you tell me that you helped your mother capture those two Germans, Ruby, that's amazing, it truly is, you should be so proud of yourself. I know your mother is proud of you, and so am I. 'Oh, I understand you not wanting to tell people, but as far as I am concerned, this party is for you too, young lady, however I will honour your wish and I'll not even tell the children if you don't want me to,' she smiled.

'Thank you, my Lady, I would prefer no one else knew, after all I only held the torch, as I told my siblings, nothing more than that!'

She smiled; 'The very fact that you ventured out at her side, to face such danger, is testament to your bravery, young lady, and echo's your mother's courage. Ruby Miller, I will deem it a privilege to welcome you into my home should you agree to come and entertain my children,' she said.

I was quite taken aback; 'You mean, it's alright, that mum said yes to me coming to the manor house, well that's great, thank you my Lady... thank you so much.'

She smiled; 'So, it is settled then, Ruby, your mother has agreed for you to come twice a week, starting on Monday next. She has also agreed that you may stay over should the weather be inclement.'

I must have looked a complete fool standing there with my mouth agape, but I could scarce believe what I was hearing... mum had agreed all this?

Lady Seymour's voice brought me back to myself; 'to have you come over and tell stories to my children will be just wonderful, you have no idea how much they miss their father, and how much in need of entertaining they are. You will be, God sent, my dear, just the perfect remedy.'

Thanking her I went to find mother; 'It's not a job mind!' was the first thing she said.

'But you're okay with me going?' I questioned, still unable to believe my luck.

'I've no complaints on that score, as long as you still do your share of the chores here,' she insisted.

I felt like jumping for joy, me, little me, staying at the Manor house, I could scarce believe it, and with our Janie yet to start there, what on earth would she think?

I knew I should seek her out and tell her my news, but just then dad arrived home from work and I rushed to head him off, as did my big sister, both of us with the same idea, that he'd be filthy and we'd need to keep him from the guests, by shepherding him into the kitchen and keeping him there! As we reach his side however, he laughed and did a little twirl in the doorway, he was spotless, dressed in his Sunday go to church best! 'I knew it would be a posh do, so I changed down at the farm,' he chuckled. 'Now where's this 'ere Lady... where you hidin' her girls? I hope she's worth all this dressen up business?'

'Sh! Quiet dad, she'll hear you,' I pleaded, trying to spot where Lady Seymour was, hoping in fact that she was upstairs with her children or out in the yard.

'Ah! That must be 'er, well come on girls, introduce I then,' he insisted playfully.

Desperately trying not to, we, steered him over to where her Ladyship was speaking with Reverent Clancy.

'Um! This my Lady, is our father,' I introduced half-heartedly.

She gave me such a sharp look that I immediately felt guilty! How could I be ashamed of my dear, wonderful dad… how could I? I felt so embarrassed as I walked away, leaving them to chat. From across the room, I was surprised at how well they seemed to be getting on, even laughing together. That will teach me to be such a little snob, I thought later.

Slowly our guests drifted away, until only her Ladyship and her children remained, and it turned out that there was a reason for her staying behind, she wanted a word with mother?

'Mrs Miller, the reason I am still here is because I have a proposition to put to you… now please feel free to say no, I will understand completely,' she smiled. 'I'll not beat about the bush; I belong to a committee… the same committee that organised the Pantomime and Nativity.

We do it all to raise money for the war effort, and recently one of our number had cause to leave us, and we are all in agreement that you would be her perfect replacement… so what do you say?'

'Can I think on it,' my Lady,' mum asked, to our surprise and embarrassment.

I looked at Janie and she looked at me, with the same look of incredibility on our faces, was mum mad, this was Lady Seymour, for goodness-sake; she should just say yes at once.

'Of, course you must think on it, talk it over with your husband and let me know your decision when you've decided, send a message with Ruby or Jane, if you like!'

'Just so you know, we are toying with the idea of putting on a village fete, Mrs Miller,' she smiled.

I watched her climb into her Barouche, where the children were snuggled, waiting to be driven back to their Manor home. Where, I thought, soon to be going to read to them for an hour or two, and perhaps sleep over should the weather turn nasty, although sadly that didn't look likely.

'A village Fete! I can't believe mum didn't just say yes instead of asking if she could think about it,' I grumbled to Janie, later in our bedroom. 'What is there to think about? It's for a good cause, and she was quick enough to help with the Panto and Nativity at Christmas! 'She should have just said yes!' I pouted.

My mood was not all bad though, as I said goodnight to my sister and climbed into bed; my head full of dreams of becoming a lady in waiting! My thoughts turned to mum, and the celebration that had been throw for her by the villagers and the wealthy land owners... and of the gold certificate of bravery on the mantle-piece, given to her by the Mayor of Dorchester himself. All of which she absolutely deserved. When, finally I did fall asleep it was with mum front and foremost in my thoughts, wondering how it was that I was blessed with such an amazing person in my life?

The days dragged slowly that week but finally the following Monday after school, instead of catching the bus back home, I walked down the winding drive to the Manor House, tucked away on the edge of Sandbourne village. As I arrived at the huge wooden doors and tugged on the bell rope, I thought of our Janie, wondering how her first day here was going?

I had little time to dwell on my thoughts of her however as the old wooden door swung open and I was greeted by a rather nervous looking young girl, whom I took to be the new maid, Janie had mentioned. But before either of us could speak there was a squeal of voices and I was being tugged inside by the three very well-dressed children, that I'd met a few days before, at our house on the heath.

'No... No! This will not do,' Lady Seymour scolded, coming to my rescue. 'Nannie... Nannie, will you please take them back to the playroom... I'll not have this!'

A rather kindly looking older woman came bustling in and shepherded them away... but not before the smallest of them came tugging at my skirt; 'Your name is Ruby, isn't it?' she asked politely.

I smiled down to her, 'Yes, we met last week at my home,' I called after her as she was led away.

'Ruby!' I heard her say softly to herself... 'I like that name!'

'I'm sorry Ruby, they're not normally so rude, but they are so very excited to have you here, in fact I've never known them take to anyone so quickly? It must have been the stories you told them, when we visited you,' she surmised.

I felt a little guilty, as I'd only told them one story before handing them on to my sister Janet, if anyone deserved praise then it was her. I would have done more for them that night but there was just too much for Janie and me to do helping mum with the guests and the food and drink. But obviously, somehow, I'd made an impact on them without realising it. Now that was new, it was usually my big sister Janie who made people sit up and take notice.

With the children gone back to their playroom, where ever that was, Lady Seymour gave me a little tour of the Manor House; It was the most amazing place I'd ever seen in my life, looking from the front door, there was a long beautifully tiled hall, lined with portraits of well-dressed people from bygone eras, people I didn't know, who were, no doubt ancestors of the family. But there was one that I recognised... 'Wow!' I gasped, 'Queen Victoria!' I stopped spellbound to read the writing beneath the portrait; 'On the occasion of her majesty Queen Victoria's visit to Kirriemuir Castle in the year 1892.'

'You met Queen Victoria, my Lady, how wonderful,' I said in awe.

She chuckled; 'It's true she came to Kirriemuir Castle, but it was a little before my time, unless you think me that old, Ruby... or perhaps, being kinder, you think I have weathered well.'

Blushing I reread the date 1892, what a fool I was, but thankfully she saw the funny side and was still smiling as she led me on the tour of the Manor House.

At the end of the hall was a sweeping, marble staircase, like something out of a fairy story and I half expected a Princess to come down to greet us! But none did, as Lady Seymour led me beyond the staircase to a huge ballroom, it's dark hardwood floor polished and gleaming as she turned on the beautiful hanging glass chandeliers high overhead, it was the most wonderful room I'd ever seen! All around the outside of the dance floor were tables and chairs and at one end there was a band stand, where no doubt a magnificent orchestra would play… it was all quite magical.

There were other rooms on the ground floor; like the Lounge and the Drawing room and of course the kitchen where our Janie worked, but Lady Seymour led me up the marble staircase next, to another corridor; 'We call this the Long Gallery, it's where more of my husband's family portraits hang, 'none of my family though, I prefer them to hang on the walls of Kirriemuir castle,' she smiled.

'Now I'll show you some of the bedrooms… but not all of them for we have 28 not counting the servants wing, where there are another 12, and I would not want to bore you.' By the time we returned downstairs my mind was racing, how on earth was the house managed, after all I knew she only had one full time maid and one cook… it seemed an impossible task? As if reading my mind, she said; 'Of course we couldn't possibly look after so many rooms, what with the shortage of staff at the moment, and so all the rooms except the children's, mine and Nannie West's are shut off for now, until we resume having guests, although I've no idea of that happening for a very long time yet,' she said sadly.

With still one or two rooms to show me, she walked me through the Parlour, where she and the family usually congregated, and then into the drawing room, where guests were received, and then finally we visited the kitchen, where I was hoping to bump into our Janie, but she had already left.

'Oh, and we must not forget the playroom,' Lady Seymour, said leading me on. 'it's where the children spend a lot of their time, either playing or being home taught by, Nannie or myself, and if I'm not mistaken, its where they are now, awaiting your company,' she smiled, opening the door.

'Ruby!' a small voice cried... 'Look, it's Ruby.' With that Florence came running over to greet me as I entered behind her mother, she was quickly followed by her brother and sister, who also greeted me warmly, although I really hadn't done anything to deserve such a show of friendship.

Lady Seymour smiled; 'Come along Nannie, I think we'll leave them to get better acquainted,' she said, and they left.

For a few minutes I couldn't move, not even when the children came swarming around me. My mind was whirling? Was this real, was I actually standing in the Manor House or was it all a dream? I closed my eyes and shook my head thinking it might help restore me to reality, but when I opened them, the children were still here, and so was I... so it was all real! Not in all my wildest fantasies did I ever picture myself here, in this magnificent place, I only wish my siblings were here with me to share my beautiful dream... but who knows one day they might?

Little Florence brought me over a book, and I proceeded to read to them, sitting where I supposed their mother or Nannie west would normally sit, on the chair, with them sat on the carpet in front of me in the middle of the room. For the next hour or so I either read to them or told them stories of my own making, thrilling them with my family's adventures on the many farms we'd stayed at and of our life on the heath. A knock on the door interrupted us as Nannie West came to say that a car was waiting at the front door to take me home, the children moaned, begging me to stay, but still I left, a little disappointed at not being asked to stay for tea if I'm being honest.

Lady Seymour was waiting at the door to see me off, a brilliant smile lighting her beautiful face; 'Thank you Ruby you did well, I believe my children have really taken to you,' she said warmly. I felt myself blushing a little as I went out the door, but I was pleased just the same that her children and me had got on so well... 'Oh, by the way, has your mother said anything about coming to see me?' she asked.

I shook my head; 'If it's about your committee, I think she's waiting until she's talked it over with dad, my Lady,' I said, having eavesdropped as much.

She laughed; 'I doubt much gets past you or your sister Jane, does it Ruby. I'll just have to be patient until she's ready to tell me;' Lady Seymour sighed. With that I climbed into the back of the big black car and set off for home, with a hundred and one tales to tell my siblings, who I knew would be just full of questions.

Our Janie, I guessed would begin by teasing me; and she did! 'They could at least have invited you to tea Sis!' she started with. Before I could find a suitable reply... one that I could say in front of the others, mum chimed in.

'If you must know Jane, I asked Lady Seymour not to ask your sister to tea, deeming that it wouldn't be fair on the rest of you, now go to the kitchen and set the table,' she ordered.

It wasn't often our Janie was shown up in front of all the family, but I guess mum was making a point, not just to Janie but to me too... her point being that, we might work for her Ladyship, but that we were her children and so subject to her rules and to her timetable. After tea mum and dad went back out across the fields, and I was cross examined by one and all, particularly our Janet and Bella, both of whom, dreamt of going to such places as the Manor House and so they wanted to know everything about it, and about the expansive gardens? Not that I'd explored them. But even so I spend the next hour describing in detail all I'd seen during my tour; from the magnificent ballroom, with its beautiful glass chandeliers, to the grand marble staircase and the long Gallery, with portraits stretching off into the distance, and of all the bedrooms, mostly shut and out of use for the time being.

My siblings sat listening in sheer disbelief that such a place could be real, convinced that I surely must be stretching the truth of it, and when finally, I convinced them I was telling the truth, they said that I was so very lucky to have seen such wonders for myself.

'I'd give anything to see the place,' Janet sighed.

'Me too,' Bella chimed in.

'Well, maybe you will one day, you never know,' I smiled going to sit on the edge of their bed.

'Oh, do you really think so?' Janet enthused softly.

'Anything is possible, sis,' I smiled, getting up to leave them to dream on it.

I found Janie in the kitchen washing her hair over the sink and so went to help her rinse it. 'Hard day, sis?' I asked, pouring a jug of warm water over her short rather tufty brown hair.

'A lot harder than reading stories, I expect, don't you?' She sniffed.

She seemed upset! 'Is anything wrong, sis, have I said something out of place?' I asked. Reaching back, she touched my hand, 'no, I'm just tired, being a scullery maid is not all I thought it would be, sis, it's just none stop work, from the moment I arrive until it's time to leave,' she sighed.

'A bit like here then,' I grinned.

She poked me in the ribs and I doused her with cold water, and we both giggled.

Later as we were sat in the living-room in front of the fire, drying Janie's hair, we talked about Lady Seymour and her children and I brought up the subject of her husband.

I don't know much about him,' Janie admitted. I only know that he is abroad somewhere, fighting in the war... somewhere in the desert, I think, although no-one really knows for certain.'

'It must be horrible, knowing your loved one might never come back,' I sighed.

'Oh, Rube' you shouldn't say such things, just be sure that you never do in front of Lady Seymour or her children,' Janie warned.

I gave her hair an extra hard tug as I was drying it with a towel; 'Well of course not, I'm not that silly... all the same it must be awful for them, not knowing if he's safe or not... imagine if it were our own dad!' I shivered.

'Ruby, now you stop that kind of talk! Change the subject... Do you know yet if mum is going to join this committee of Lady Seymour's?' Janie asked.

I shrugged, a little irritated by her; 'All I know is, her Ladyship is still waiting for a reply and that she'll be a bit upset if mum turns her down.'

With that mum came into the kitchen, followed closely by dad, both looking very weary from their day out on the land.

'Ah good, I was hoping you'd both be here,' she said.

Janie and me stood there with bated breath... waiting and waiting, while she took off her boot's, then her long work socks, shrugged out of her coat poured both her and father a glass of water and then sat down and took a long swallow, before turning back to us.

Father chuckled; 'come on now mother don't tease the maids!'

Mum smiled across at him and gave him one of his own favourite winks; 'Right then girls, tomorrow, you, Ruby, will take this letter to Lady Seymour, it's the answer to her question... which, I'm sure you're both itching to know, well, it's yes. I will join her committee... and thanks to your father might have an idea to improve her fundraising.'

'What idea?' I asked excitedly.

'Never you mind girl, you just give her the letter.' Mum said, following dad into the living-room where he was enjoying a rare read of his favourite newspaper. 'Did you tell 'um?' we heard him ask.

'No, they'll know when it's time for them to know and not before... are you listening girls? Mum called, making us back away from the door.

Dad laughed; 'You are a one, Iris,' he chuckled.

'Never mind them Fred, are you sure about what you told me yesterday, and if you are, when can we take a ride out to see for ourselves?' We heard mum say.

It was a mystery? What on earth was mum talking about? Was dad sure about what? And what was it, mum wanted him to take her to see for themselves?

'I might try and get dad on his own later, he might let it slip without mum about,' I said.

'You watch yourself Rube, mum will skin you alive if she catches you,' Janie warned me.

I knew the risk, but I was determined to find out what was going on, I was my mother's daughter after all... and so after tea, while mum was taking a bath and Janie was seeing to our siblings, I cornered dad alone in the kitchen, on the pretext of him telling me a story that I might use to entertain Lady Seymour's children... but it didn't work!

'I know yore game, maid,' he chuckled, an' I'm not playin' it, I'd rather it be yore ear that gets clipped than mine, girl.' Beyond the door I could hear my sister Janie giggling... damn, her.

'At least I tried,' I grunted, later to Janie, as we sat on the bed. 'But seriously sis, what do you think is going on?' I puzzled.

'I'm sure we'll get to know when they're ready to tell us, Rube, so stop fretting so much and go to sleep, it'll be time to get up before you know it?' Janie sighed, sleepily.

She was right, it seemed I'd only closed my eyes for a few minutes, before mum was shaking me awake; 'up you get sleepy head, the little-ones will be stirring soon,' she said. 'I'm on my way out to help father at the farm, just don't you forget to give Lady Seymour my note,' she called back, as I struggled out of bed.

'Can't our Janie take it with her?' I shouted after her, 'she'll be there much earlier than me?'

'Your sister would forget her head if it wasn't attached to her shoulders,' mum insisted, as she went out the door. 'That's why I've given it to you.'

After getting dressed I made sure to pick up the note and put in my pocket, all I had to do now was to remember to give it to her Ladyship, later, after school.

'Don't worry Rube, I'll wait after my shift and make sure you deliver the note, I'm not quite as forgetful as mum says,' she sniffed.

She was, but I was not about to tell her that and so I simply smiled and nodded. Before Janie set off, she helped me to get the little-ones up, and dress and feed them, which took the best part of an hour, leaving little time for me to worry about anything else. But as I waved my big sister goodbye, I could not take my mind off, what-ever it was mum and dad were planning.

'Stop fretting, Ruby Miller,' I told myself as I watched Janie go off to work. 'You're making a big thing about nothing!'

'You're quiet,' Bella said as we walked with our Janet, Danny and Jack to catch the bus to take us to school, all the while my fingers teased nervously at the note in my pocket to be sure it was still there.

As usual these days the bus was late and despite my telling them not to, our Jack and Danny set off to walk to the village and school, we passed them about halfway, laughing and fooling about; 'You're going ta be late!' I shouted from the bus window. They simply laughed. It was still a little odd not having our Janie with us anymore, but she'd left school now, and although it was hard for me to get used to, at least our Janet was stepping up to the mark and helping me with our siblings. Not that she had any sway over our Jack and Danny, who recognised that she was certainly no Janie and neither was I come to that, but I at least could bang their heads together when it was needed, and so our Janet left it up to me to keep them in line!

'You alright, sis?' Janet asked as we stepped from the bus in the village.

'I've got something on my mind,' I sighed, fumbling again with the note in my pocket, wishing I knew what it said.

'Look! There's Becky over the road, she'll cheer you up,' Janet smiled.

I waved as our friend crossed over to join us; Rebecca or Becky as she prefers to be called was my new, desk mate, having taken the seat next to me when our Janie had left school. She was fast becoming my closest friend and a much needed, assistant when it came to handling my brothers, for Becks was as tough as my big sister, and our Jack and Danny knew that.

My two brothers were still not in sight as Becks came across to join us, and I guessed that they'd deliberately chosen not to catch the bus so that they could meet up with the Davis twins.

I was a little concerned as it was my job to get them to school and mum would blame me if they played truant! But just as I started worrying, they came over the brow of the hill, and they were, as I thought with their friends. On seeing me they started to cross over to walk the rest of the way to school with me, but then they spotted Becky, and they don't much like my new friend as she's too much like our Janie and brooks no nonsense from them or from anyone, come to that. Perhaps that's why Becky and I get on so well, she is my big sister revisited, which is good for me and not so good for my two mischievous brothers and what's more she is faster than our Janie, so there is no getting away from her... I smiled, recalling the day she had chased down my brothers and their friends when they had skipped school, herding them back up through the village for all to see their shame at being caught by a mere girl! Much to my surprise school went well, the Germans stayed away and my siblings apart from our Jack and Danny behaved themselves.

Before heading off to the Manor house after school, I stood in the village with Becks and watched our Jack and Danny clamber aboard the bus, and I was glad to see the back of them. They'd been nothing but trouble all day long, in the end even Mrs Hardington had enough of them, sending them and the Davis twins to stand in the corner, which was quite funny to have all four corners occupied at once.

With them gone I walked Becky back to her home in the village, before making my way down to the Manor House to give Lady Seymour the letter from mum. The mystery of what it contained still giving me a headache. No doubt mum and dad had a good laugh about my dilemma as they went about their work today, knowing the nature of my curiosity... or nosiness as mum would put it!

Chapter 7

Although I was the Lady of the manor, Ruby was late and that made me smile at how at ease with me these Miller children were. I reined in my impatience, she was young and so had young things to do, just as I once had. She had a right to be a little tardy, especially with everything that was going on in the world. Perhaps she has a boyfriend or a group of school mates that she likes to hang about with, who can blame her if she has, life is for living, isn't it?

'Take your pleasurers where you can,' that is the maxim that we all live by at the moment, a selfish one maybe, but one that is ever relevant with each passing minute of this damned war. To miss a chance to do something or to see someone you love might be the last chance you get. I felt my eyes welling up with tears; Would I still have that special moment with my Rory, or had it passed me by.

I bit down on my bottom lip! 'No! I will see him again... I will!' I affirmed quietly to myself as I watched Ruby finally come over the brow of the drive, making her way down to the house.

I was so pleased to welcome her back to our home, the children having taken to her so well. The, little dears were so desperately in need of a distraction from all that was going on... from the bombing and burning... and the terrible loss of life. And although a few stories might seem like nothing at all to most people, to us, now, with Rory away, they would serve my children well.

Despite me asking them not too, my youngest daughter Florence and even her elder brother and sister, disgraced me once again, by rushing to greet our guest, swarming about her like bees around honey! It was all so embarrassing, that I was forced to call for Nannie to take them away, while I spoke with her, for I was desperate for news from Mrs Miller. To add to the confusion, Jane came up from the kitchen asking my permission to speak to her sister, which I granted, despite being eager to know of their mother's decision. In fact, I could wait no longer.

'Ruby, did your mother give you anything for me... a message perhaps, or...'

'Yes, sorry my Lady, a note, she gave me a note for you,' she said, handing me a rather crumpled letter, that had so obviously spent the day in a school girls pocket!

Taking the note, I waved permission for the sisters to speak with one another, while I read with satisfaction that their mother would indeed join our committee.

As the girls moved apart and Jane started to retreat back to the kitchen to take her leave of Mrs Brown, my cook, I stopped her. 'I would like to pay a call on your mother today, Jane, when might be a good time for me to do so?' I asked, as she hovered by the steps leading down to the kitchen.

'7 o'clock would be as good a time as any, my Lady,' Jane replied.

'Excellent, then will you please let her know that I am coming,' I smiled warmly.

I watched her through the window as she made her way up the drive, and then I went to find Ruby to tell her that I'd be giving her a ride home this evening.

My next task was to ring the ladies of the committee and let them know the good news and arrange for them to come here the following day to discuss our plans. Despite still being rather annoyed at Amber for pestering Ruby the night of the party, everything had turned out well in the end and so all was forgiven. I did have a few words with my colleague just the same. But that was behind us now and thankfully no damage had been done as Mrs Miller was indeed prepared to join our committee. As I hoped the ladies agreed to come when I phoned them and were all pleased that Mrs Miller would be joining us. Now we could get on with our fundraising for the war effort. Neither Ruby or I had much to say as I drove her home after she'd spent some time reading to the children, both of us lost in our own thoughts.

Mrs Miller was waiting for us, and as Ruby went to check on her siblings, her mother and I sat in the kitchen over a pot of tea.

I couldn't help but smile, despite our obvious different status she was not in the least overawed, in fact she looked perfectly at ease, which was a joy to see. She raised an eyebrow when I told her that the idea of a village fete, had come from Mrs Jennings, after all it was not exactly her thing, but it was a wonderful idea just the same. And one that I thought we should run with... I only hoped our new committee member agreed.

'Now there's a strange thing... a strange thing indeed,' Mrs Miller, exclaimed, 'I might know of something to enhance that idea of Mrs Jennings, but I can't say yet... not yet!' she said mysteriously.

'But can't you at least give me a hint?' I pleaded.

She shook her head; 'Not yet, my Lady, I 'ave to make more enquires,' she insisted.

Mysterious indeed. But she promised to reveal all at the committee meeting the next day. It was obvious that she would tell me no more and so we enjoyed our tea and spoke of other matters. Leaving me to stew on it on my drive home and for all of the rest of the day.

Amber, Stella and Betty were the first to come the following day, arriving together in one car, and they were all eager to meet our new member, our heroine of the heath, who, much to their annoyance I had not allowed them to mingle with at the party. When Amber had ignored my request and I had asked them all to leave I thought it might spoil our relationship but they took it in their stride and put the blame firmly where it belonged, on Amber. But that was in the past now, today they would meet Mrs Miller properly, although she was running a little late and I hoped nothing had happened to prevent her coming!

Finally, though, she arrived, apologising for keeping us waiting, her excuse being that she'd had to wait for her husband to get back to her with some news, and he'd been held up!

'Well, I do hope it was good news that your husband brought you,' Amber dared to say.

Mrs Miller smiled, 'You might say so, in so many words, but then again, you might not. It'll help with your idea of a village fete, but it'll add ta the workload no end, mind?' she warned.

We were all intrigued... what on earth did she have in mind?

We sat with bated breath waiting for her to enlighten us, while she sipped her tea and nibbled on a biscuit, with a mischievous glint in her eye, until Betty could stand it no longer; 'Please put us out of our misery, Mrs Miller,' she pleaded.

'It's Iris, my dear, and the idea came from my husband Fred. He was speaking to a farmer from a village this side of Dorchester, who told him of a fair that was stranded there, and we both wondered, Fred and me, if we might be able to use it alongside of the village fete idea... combine the two, maybe, what do you think?'

Stella jumped to her feet; 'A fete and a fair both, what a wonderful idea... what about it, ladies,' she asked, standing in the middle of the room, with her arm flung wide. 'We can do it; I know we can.'

I rose to my feet to take the floor; 'Yes, I think we can too, but as Iris said it will be an enormous task to take on... but oh my, the people would just love it, wouldn't they?' I sighed.

'God knows people need a little something good in their lives right now, so let's give it to them, ladies,' Amber agreed wholeheartedly.

'So then, ladies, it's settled, Mrs Miller... um! Iris, can your Fred arrange for us to go and see this fair and find out if they will be willing to travel down the road to us?' I asked.

Her face lit up; 'Already asked and they're more than willin' my Lady,' they just need a date and to know where it is, you, want's em to bring the fair to,' she said.

'Right then, ladies, I take it you won't object to it being on my estate, so that just leaves the when, and I think it should be sooner rather than later... so why don't we aim for the 28th of July! Now I know that will only give us about 5 weeks or so, but I'm sure we can do it?' 'And besides, it will be the week after the schools break up for the summer holidays and so that will make it easier for all of us... especially you Iris, you'll not have to worry about getting your children off to school... and you'll have the older children to help with the little-ones,' I said. But even as I returned to my seat I wondered if we could do it, there really was an awful lot to do and so little time to do it all, but as I looked around the room, there was not one face of doubt among them.

'Alright then, ladies, who wants to go and see a fair, right now?' Amber said getting to her feet.

Everyone put their hands up and I laughed, 'So we are all up for going then, but do you know the way Iris or should we find your husband and ask him the way?'

'Don't worry, my Lady, I know's the way, Fred took me there a day or so ago, tis but 20 minutes up the road,' she said.

'So then, if there are no objections, we'll go now,' Amber said, getting to her feet. 'Come on ladies, we can all squeeze into my car, it's big enough,' she assured us.

I hesitated, it was all happening very quickly and there was a lot to think about... a lot to do! Still, it was exciting, and we all hurried out to climb into Ambers big black Bentley, not a car that I could ever imagine myself driving, but she handled it well... even if she did drive a little too fast, for my liking!

'How's that!' she bragged as we pulled into the field where the fair was parked. '15 minutes, not bad hey ladies?' she bragged.

All a little dishevelled we climbed from the car and went to greet a gaggle of people in the middle of a circle of brightly painted caravans, who didn't seem in the least surprised to see us. They had travellers written all over them; the men wearing trilbies and patterned cotton shirts, with handkerchiefs tied about their necks and the women, looking every inch of the fairground in their long colourful calico dresses and beautiful floral headscarves. As we came together a man stepped forward and doffed his hat; 'Hello again, Iris,' he beamed. 'So, this be yore committee ladies then,' he surmised.

Iris nodded, 'Aye this is them,' she said, introducing us one by one; as she got to me, she stopped: 'And this is Lady Seymour, who's land we plan to take your fair to, should you agree,' she said.

'Pleased at meet ee' my Lady... ladies,' he smiled, through a light whiskery beard; 'I'm Jake and I be the one lucky enough to own this fair, not that I can do much with it without my friends and family, who are all away somewhere, doin' their duty... I'd be with um but for this!' He held up his left hand on the end which there was a pirate like hook! I got this bugger in the last war,' he sighed.

'Anyway, enough of that, of course you must have my fair, just tell us where and when and we'll be there, although being shorthanded...' he chuckled and held up his hook! 'Sorry ladies, just my little joke,' he apologised. 'But seriously, we will need help, firstly to bring the fair to you and secondly to find enough people to help us run the rides and that,' he said.

Iris stepped forward; 'Don't you worry Jake, I've spoken with my Fred and he has tractors and vans ready to tow whatever is needed to the site, and as for people to man the rides and the stalls, you can leave that to us, right ladies,' Iris volunteered. I moved to stand at our new committee members side, 'That's right... um! Jake, we'll either do it ourselves or find others to do it for us,' I smiled.

To my delight the rest of the committee nodded in agreement, and so it was settled and we thanked the friendly travellers, climbed in the car and returned back to my estate, with Jake, in his battered old van following on behind. His wish being to get a feel of the land where his fair would be put and to decide the site for each ride.

Amber drove slower going back, with Jake struggling to keep up and so I was able to see more of the countryside as we drove along the winding road, past remnants of old Corfe Castle up on the hill, another casualty of man's foolishness, proof, if it were needed that we have learnt nothing at all from our past. That war, leaves only ruins in its wake, whether by cannon balls or Slingshots, hundreds of years ago or by German Bombers today. It was a sober thought that stayed with me until we drove onto my estate, where my thoughts took on a much happier theme, the planning of a fair and fete!

We left the cars at the top of the drive and walked out across the first plateau of land, looking down at the two other plateau's that made up my estate, just the perfect site for something like we had in mind. I was pleased that our new friend Jake was of the same mind as he came to join us.

'This be perfect, my Lady,' he grinned. 'Flat ground is just what we need, specially, for the likes of the Ferris wheel, the Helter-skelter, and the bumping-cars, they can be a bit noisy too, best up 'ere away frum the grand house, I'm thinking,' he suggested.

'I think that's a very good idea, Jake, then we can put the fete down below close to the house and the main gate, and use the back lawn for afternoon tea's and anything else we decide upon,' I gave Iris a gentle hug... 'this is all thanks to you, my dear,' I told her.

She shook away my praise; 'It's down to my Fred, really,' she said... 'but it belongs to all of us now, my Lady, we're the ones who 'ave to pull it off!'

Amber, Stella and Betty came over then with ideas of their own and pretty soon the whole thing was planned, now we just had to make it work.

'What should we say we are raising money for?' Stella asked. 'People usually like to know.'

She was right, people always gave more freely if they knew what it was their money was going towards. There was a general nod of agreement but still no-one came up with an idea, until I plucked something out of the blue... A Spitfire!' I suggested... we say it's for helping to build one!'

'That's a good idea,' Iris agreed; 'we can always do with one o' they bugger's,' she swore, making us all laugh.

'Right then, ladies, back to planning the event,' I said sharply, time was marching on and we needed to end the day with a complete plan in place.

'Now, is there any project that you would prefer to do... any part of the event you'd feel more comfortable taking care of?' I asked.

Iris was the first to step up; 'Well, I'd rather see ta the fair than look after the garden party on the back lawn,' if I 'ave a choice,' my Lady,' she offered.

'That sounds reasonable, is that alright with everyone?' I asked.

They all agreed that it was, although I had something else to add, if Iris was willing. 'As the fete is just below the fair could you and your family manage that too?' I asked.

It was a lot of work for her, but although I barely knew her, I had a lot of faith in her, and there was no one I trusted more to keep a strong hold on things. And besides, I feared, myself and the rest of the committee would be busy trying to keep everyone fed and watered.

As I watched Iris making her way over to speak to our friendly pirate, I was surprised at how pleased I was at having met her and her family... although we are virtual strangers, there is a definite bond forming between us that I am at odds to explain. After all, they are not the sort of people I am used to; not the wealthy, shooting hunting set, nor the worldly intellects from our days at Oxford. I smiled, wondering what my husband Rory, would make of them... deciding in the end that he'd like them, they were honest and direct, traits that we both appreciated greatly.

'My Lady!' It was pirate Jake; 'If you please; I would suggest putting the bumping cars right here, where it's nice and flat, with the helter-skelter, over yonder,' he pointed. 'That way whoever is looking after one can also see to tuther,' he suggested.

I smiled warmly, this man was going to be a boon, to us, although I had the feeling, we would need to keep a watchful eye on him, he had a twinkle of mischief in his eyes.

'You may place them where you see fit, Jake, I trust you know what's best, and should you have any problems then ask; Mrs Miller... er! Iris, as she will be overseeing both the fair and the fete... with your help of course, along with any of your people you see fit to use,' I added.

And so it began; for the next few weeks things were frantic, with Mr Miller and many of the local farmhands helping the fair people to move and assemble everything, until soon my grounds were unrecognisable, full of finished and half-finished fairground rides.

'Well, that's the helter-skelter almost complete and the floor for the bumping cars done,' my Lady, Fred sighed, wiping his brow, as I walked by; 'Next week, we'll be ready to add the cars, and it'll be finished,' he assured me, thinking perhaps I was checking up on him!

'Um! I'm just looking for your wife, Fred, have you seen her?' I asked a little sheepishly.

'Ah I see!' he grinned; looking a little relieved, 'I think she's down seein' to the fete, my Lady? At least tha's where she was headin', last I saw of 'er!' he said doffing his trilby hat.

Taking my leave of him I found Iris mapping out the site of the coconut-shies, the tombola and white elephant stalls, whilst also organising the raffle tickets.

'Would you like any help, Iris?' I offered, stopping at her side.

'No! But thank you for asking, my Lady, my Jane and Ruby should be along any time now, so we're all good here. How are things going on the back lawn? Is everything set up for the tea parties?'

'Um! Yes… yes, Iris, everything is going smoothly,' I assured her.

It was quite bewildering, the speed in which it was all being put together and I had to remind myself that it was only a few short weeks ago that we'd come up with idea and now look at all this? I stood looking out across my once pristine grounds, now strewn with fair rides and fete stalls, some finished, most not!

As I started to walk again up through the site, I saw Fred and Pirate Jake putting together, one of my own children's favourite games; The Hook-a-duck stand, it made me stop and smile; oh, how we all loved to have a try at that; Grace, Crispen and little Florence, even Rory and myself! Whenever the fair came to town, it was the first thing we headed for.

Just remembering those good times brought a tear to my eye… and brought my husband to mind; 'Oh, Rory, please, please, stay safe,' I murmured, softy.

How he'd love what we were doing; to see his children so excited at having such things as a fete and a fair right here, on their doorstep… I'd give anything for him to have shared the look on their little faces as they peered out of the windows and witnessed the Helter-skelter being built and the bumping cars and everything else being put up! All before their very eyes! They'd known about the village fete of course, but the fair was something else, something that not even I could have envisaged?

Once everything was almost ready, Nannie and I took the children on a tour of the site, explaining everything to them, I was so happy at the look on their faces, I thought they were going to burst with sheer joy, especially when I told them about the owner of the fair!

'Are you saying we have a pirate, a real live pirate on our estate?' Crispen gasped, seemingly forgetting everything else.

I laughed; 'Yes, my dear, a live pirate called Jake, and he's even got a hook for a hand! Just like captain Hook, in the Peter Pan book,' I explained.

'He won't hurt us, will he?' Little Florence asked nervously.

'No, he's a tame pirate, my darling,' I assured her, with a cuddle.

'So, where is he then, this pirate?' Grace demanded.

I had the feeling we were getting away from the main business, of the fete and the fair and so I brought us back to that; 'Jake is the owner of the fair and is here with his friends to put it up for us so that we can raise some money for the war effort,' I told them.

'Our friend Ruby will be here to help, along with all her family, so that will be nice, we all like Ruby, don't we?' I said; 'It's going to be a big, big day, for all of us, and lots of fun too.'

'Will we be allowed to help too mother?' Grace asked. 'After all, if the Miller children are doing their bit, shouldn't we be doing ours? Father is away fighting in the war, so we'd be helping him!'

Crispen and even little Florence nodded, following her siblings lead.

'Leave it with me and I'll see what I can do,' I promised. 'I'll make sure you all have something to do, so that when you next see your father, you'll be able to tell him how you helped with the war effort, and make him so very proud of you all.'

With that I made a mental note to have a word with one of the Miller girls to ask them to find something for my children to do, and also ask them to introduce, Grace, Crispen and Florence to our friendly pirate, which I just knew would make their day.

The following week as I gathered in the grounds with the rest of the committee to oversee the finishing touches being put in place by a growing number of volunteers, I was pleased to see, Ruby and Jane taking my two daughters on a tour of the almost finished fairground. In the meanwhile, Crispen was busy carrying turnips, the replacements for coconuts, to the coconut shies... and helping Iris set up her White- Elephant- stall, wearing a smile that said he was enjoying himself.

'No, no! Florence, you can't climb in there, you'll break it!' I heard Ruby cry out, and I hurried to see what was going on?

I was in time to see Ruby preventing my youngest daughter from falling head first in the hook-a-duck pond, in her eagerness to have a go... 'No, Florence, you'll just have to wait till we've set it all up,' she said, trying to sort the plastic fishing rods out.

Now, if I'd have spoken to her like that she'd be in tears by now, but to my surprise she simply giggled and held her arms out for Ruby to pick her up. But Ruby was still entangled in fishing rods and so didn't respond, and I thought... oh dear, here we go! Expecting Florence to kick off, but before she did, Jane grabbed her up and slung her up onto her shoulders; 'Alright then, Florence, let's you and me catch us a duck,' she laughed. With my little girl chuckling away, I left them to it, going back to the house, to check on cook, to see how she was planning to cope with the added pressure of catering for a tea party out on the lawn when the time came? Not that she'd have to manage alone, I'd hired some of the women from the village to help her, as Jane would be working on the stalls and helping with the fairground rides.

As I walked around the site, everything seemed quite hectic and a bit crazy, with people either laughing or cursing their way through their problems, struggling to complete all that had to be done, and I began to worry that we wouldn't be ready on time... and now I began to fret, wondering if I'd forgotten something... like, who was seeing to the bumping-cars, the helter-skelter, the Waltzer... and...

I felt a gentle hand on my shoulder; it was Iris; 'Now don't you worry, so, my Lady, we got this under control, you go and see to your tea party,' she smiled. I took one last look around, she was right, everything here was fine, and I should be concentrating on my own job, making sure we had enough tables and chairs set out on the back lawn. But when I arrived there, it seemed that I wasn't needed there either, as my fellow committee members; Amber, Stella and Betty, had it well in hand; sorting what tables went where and what food would be on the serving tables, and making sure there were enough chairs to each of the tables people would be sitting around.

After a brief chat with them I returned to the kitchen, to catch up with cook and was surprised to find Pirate Jake working alongside her! But it was the concerned look on cook's face that worried me!

'He's making toffee apples!' my Lady! Only, I don't think that's legal, and I hate to think where he got the apples, or more worryingly, where all the sugar came from,' she whispered to me.

I crossed the kitchen to where Jake was busy working away, seemingly without a care in the world, as innocent as I myself and cook was; 'Should you be making those?' I asked him directly.

He looked up from the stove; 'I'm also makin' Fairy Floss, my Lady,' he grinned.

'Fairy Floss?' I queried.

'Most folk call's it, Candy Floss,' my Lady,' he said.

'Candy Floss... Fairy Floss, it makes no difference, Jake, most people are struggling to come by enough sugar to sweeten their tea and so it might cause a little friction, and we don't want that now do we, so no toffee apples and no Candy Floss, if you please,' I insisted.

I thought he might argue, but he simply grinned and tipped his hat to me; 'Right you are my Lady, I gets your point. Perhaps I'll give the children those I've already made; how does that sound?'

'I'm sure they'll love it,' I said warmly, as I walked away...'Oh, but save one for me,' I smiled.

Everything was going so fast I needed a moment for myself... we were almost there, almost finished and even if we wished to change anything it was too late, there was just a few days to go!

As I wandered alone in the back garden checking for about the hundredth time the progress of the tea party area, Iris came to see me, looking a little troubled and straight away I was concerned that something had gone wrong with our great plan.

But she soon assured me that all was well; 'It's just that, apart from Ruby and Jane I haven't yet given any of my other children their roles,' she worried.

I sighed with relief that it was nothing more serious; 'Well, why don't we run through things now, while we have a moment to ourselves, Iris,' I smiled.

'Yes, yes, lets!' Iris agreed.

'Alright then, lets me and you go through all the jobs that need filling and you can decide who best to fill them,' I smiled.

I could see already that our little chat was taking a load off her mind and by the time we'd finished talking, all of her children had a role to play and Iris was pleased.

'Right then now that we've settled that, you need to go home and tell them right away, my dear, this very moment, in fact I'll drive you,' I insisted.

'Thank you, my Lady,' Iris called back to me as she stepped from the car outside of her cottage out on the heath, the frown she'd been wearing earlier replaced by a smile. I gave her a wave and started back across the heath, my mind already running through the list of things still left to do before we'd be ready to open up the gates to the public. But at least now the list was shorter, and things were slipping nicely into place.

Chapter 8

'A penny for them Ruby,' our Janie called across the kitchen table, I smiled but didn't reply, my mind a little troubled by something that I didn't care to speak of, not now! As mum came through the door turning to wave to Lady Seymour who had given her a ride home, I couldn't hide my anger. I have never believed in secrets, especially unnecessary secrets, as they are seldom kept and almost always the cause of resentment. So why was mum keeping the roles that my brothers and sisters were to play down at the fair and fete from them? I understood that she might be still deciding which of them should do what, but she must have a plan in mind, and keeping it a secret this near to the big day was wrong! If it was to stop the younger ones getting too excited it wasn't working as they are beside themselves with the thrill of it all. And what's worse is that they think Janie and me are the ones keeping secrets from them, and it's putting a barrier between us, and it's not a nice feeling.

The truth is, that although Janie and me know our roles we have no idea of the roles our siblings will be asked to perform, it has all yet to be confirmed and laid out as a plan to be followed. That's down to mum and Lady Seymour, and I'm convinced that even dad has no idea of their plans for us, and that makes me angry, we all should know by now. With that in mind, Janie and me tackled mum even before she had time to take off her coat. Determined to find out exactly what was going on. It was time our siblings all knew just what was going to be expected of them.

'So, mum, when are you going to tell us all the full plan?' Janie dared to ask as we confronted her in the kitchen.

'Although Janie and me know what's expected of us, our brothers and sisters have no idea what roles you have chosen for them, mum,' I said backing my sister up. She gave me a hard stare and picked up her serving spoon and banged it noisily against the stove, bringing the room to an expectant whisper.

'As you all know we have almost finished putting everything together down at the Manor House, thanks mainly to your father and the other farmhands,' mum informed us. There was a general nodding of heads, indicating that they'd already heard as much... 'and is it true our Janie and Ruby, will be helping with the rides?' Janet asked aggressively.

There was a chorus of angry mutterings. Mum banged on the stove again bringing order once more.

'Alright... alright, yes they will, with the help of our newest friend; Pirate Jake, and his fairground people' she announced.

Janie and I looked at one another, none of our siblings knew anything about Jake and I saw the look of excitement on my two brothers faces at the mention of Pirate Jake and waited for them to explode with questions, which they duly did.

'Pirate Jake? Who's Pirate Jake?' Danny demanded.

Janie leaned towards him; 'Like mum said, he's our new friend and he owns the fair.'

'Wait... he owns the fair and he's a Pirate!' Jack interjected with a snort of disbelief.

'Why haven't we heard of him before?' Danny demanded, getting to his feet.

'Sit down my lad... I'm sure I must have mentioned him before,' mum said.

'No, never,' Jack accused angrily.

'Oh well, never mind you know now don't you,' mum sighed.

'But is it true, is he really a pirate?' Danny asked from across the table.

'Oh, he's real alright, not only that, but he has a hook for a hand!' I added for devilment.

'Hah! Now you're just making things up!' Danny accused, turning to mum for the truth.

She laughed; 'It's all true, his name is Jake, he has a hook for a hand, just as your sister says, and they call him Pirate Jake,' she confirmed.

For a moment no-one spoke and then they all started speaking at once; all wanting to know when they were going to meet this Pirate, our Jack and Danny jumping up and down with glee.

'Alright, settle down,' mum ordered, taking charge again; 'You are all going to be a part of it. Over the next few days Jane and Ruby will be instructing you all in the roles you're to play in the running of the fair and fete, if you behave yourselves that is,' she growled, her gaze resting on Jack and Danny.

'Alright, you two, come with me,' she ordered, leaning over them.

I watched as sheepishly they followed her into the living room, wondering just what devilment my two brothers had been up to now? Janie came to stand beside me; 'What do you make of that, sis?' she muttered.

I shrugged, trying to recall any mischief they'd been up to lately, but in truth could think of none, of late they had even been, dare I say it… good!

A few minutes later they were back, both wearing enormous grins; 'We're to be in charge of the coconut shies,' they whooped, dancing a circle around Janie and me. We looked at one another in disbelief; that our demonic brothers should be put in charge of anything was beyond belief.

'It keeps them where I can keep an eye on them, as I'll be in the Tombola and White Elephant stalls right opposite,' mum winked.

Now it made sense, and Janie and me had a little chuckle together.

'That's good, that means they'll be well away from us, Rube,' my big sister sighed.

As we were to be in charge of one or more of the big rides up across the fair site, our devilish brothers would indeed be well away from us, and I threw Janie a smile of satisfaction. If mum noticed at all she let it slide, turning instead to our Janet and Bella; 'Lady Seymour has asked if the two of you can help her and the other ladies of the committee out on the back lawn with the tea party,' she told them. I suddenly felt very envious as they hugged each other gleefully and danced a jig together.

Finally, she turned back to myself and Janie; 'As the oldest I would like you, as well as helping to run the fairground rides; the Helter-skelter, bumping cars and all that, to also sell some raffle tickets.'

I don't know about Janie, but I was disappointed with our lot, I had hoped to take a turn out on the back lawn, to work alongside Lady Seymour and her committee ladies.'

On seeing the look of disappointment on my face mum smiled; 'It could have been worse, girls, you could be stuck on the White Elephant stall along with me... and why do they call it that anyway, where's the white elephant girls? She frowned.

I was angry with what Janie and me had been assigned and I wasn't really listening to mum, so what if she didn't know what a White Elephant stall was? It was her own fault, wasn't it? Not that I'd ever say so, not to her face. I could see that Janie was as upset as I was, she'd obviously, like myself, hoped to be out on the back lawn, at some time, serving tea and cakes to grand Ladies and Gentlemen, not looking after great big fair rides, all the day long! If anything, it was worse for her, she was already part of the kitchen staff and so rightly had the expectations of being involved in the tea party! To make matters worse we learnt that our younger sisters would be wearing their Sunday best dresses with pretty ribbon in their hair.

'What about the twins,' our Jack shouted, breaking into my thoughts.

'What about the twins,' I sighed, not in the least interested.

'They'll want to help too,' Jack insisted;

'They could always wash up the tea things?' I suggested, sarcastically.

'What! No, that's a woman's job,' Danny whined.

'Don't worry I have a job for them,' mum interrupted, 'how do you think they might feel about running a tug of war?' she asked our brothers.

'They would have to be in charge of everything to do with it mind, organise and run the whole event themselves. It could be between the Village men, Reverent Clancy could put a team of them together, and the farmhands, your father could find a team of them, I'm sure,' she suggested.

For a few moments there was silence, until mum spoke again; 'Well, what do you think, boys, can they do it?' She asked.

Before they even answered I was shaking my head at the very thought of such silly boys having anything to do with such a project, but mum seeing my doubt, gave me the evil eye daring me to object.

Jack and Danny loved the idea and set off at once to tell their buddies the news… returning to inform mum that the twins were thrilled with idea and already making plans to catch up with both dad and with Reverent Clancy. Which pleased mum no end… had she forgotten how naughty they could be?

'May it be on mums own head,' I thought later that night curled up in my bed.

Both Janie and me were tired and ready for a good night's sleep until our two brothers snuck into our rooms, pestering us some more about Pirate Jake, demanding to know if it was true that he really did have a hook for a hand. Their feet barely touched the floor as we grabbed them like bags of potatoes and ran them back to their own rooms, leaving them both with a bruise or two.

The next morning was manic, everyone was excited, not just because it was Friday and the end of the school week, but because it was also the end of term, and tomorrow was the big event! Such was our excitement about the up-coming event that the end of term had all but passed us by, when usually the beginning of our school summer holidays was a time of jubilation. But right now, we had so much still to do down at the fairground that there was no time to think of holidays! Although it will be nice for me and our Janie not to have to rush our breakfast before seeing to the little-ones and hurrying our siblings off to school, it meant more work for me though now that our Janie was working. But nothing was going to spoil what was on the horizon, our huge fair, stroke fete, something that our whole family was going to be a part of, was tomorrow… tomorrow! I reminded myself for about the hundredth's time as I saw to the little-ones and made the breakfast and roped our Janet and Bella into doing their bit, all with one thing in mind… we were almost there.

However, as usual when you're looking forward to something, the day dragged so slowly, the lessons all bleeding into one, none of it sinking into my brain, not even the history lesson which was my favourite... but today 1066 and all that took second place to Saturday 28th July, 1941. I smiled, it's almost here...

'Ruby Miller... hello is anyone at home?'

'Uh!' I grunted looking up to find Mrs Hardington glaring at me.

The other children started laughing led by my own siblings; Janet, Bella, Jack and Danny and even my friend Becky at my side was chuckling.

'Sorry Mrs Hardington,' I apologised, my face burning with embarrassment.

She leaned in close; 'I know you have a lot on your mind, my dear, but do try and forget it for a few hours won't you, it might help to ease your worries to do a little learning,' she smiled.

'But first, who among you is looking forward to tomorrow and our Fete and Fair,' she asked.

Our Jack was the first one to stick his hand up; 'I am, unless the Germans invade us that is,' he grinned, looking directly at me, knowing how I feared that very thing happening on our big day. Now that was a terrifying thought! An impending invasion... I shuddered and our Jack chuckled.

'You alright, Ruby?' I smiled at Becky as she plonked herself down in Janie's old seat next to me.

'I sighed, yes, just my brother scaring me with thoughts of the bloody Germans choosing tomorrow to invade us, Beck's. It would be just like them to spoil everything,' I groaned. 'They could you know, ever since Dunkirk, people have been expecting it. They say they're gathered on the shores of France in their thousands!'

Becky shook her head; 'best not to dwell on that, Rube,' she said, giving my brother the evil eye. 'Just focus on the fair and the fete coming up tomorrow... I'll be there, you know, lending a helping hand,' Becks assured me. 'I volunteered to work on the fairground... although I don't know what I'll be doing yet, they did say that I might be needed in the kitchen,' she half grimaced. 'But I really don't mind, as long as I get to have a go on one or two of the rides,' she grinned.

I felt a lot better knowing that my friend would be there, and yet I still said a silent prayer; 'Please don't let the invasion be tomorrow... please!' I prayed. Out of the corner of my eye, across the class room, I saw my two brothers giggling at my obvious discomfort, the Davis twins too... 'You want me to sort them out for you Rube,' Becky offered waving a fist in their direction.

I shook my head; 'thanks all the same but I'll see to them myself, when I get them home, they are going to have so many chores to do they won't know what hit them,' I smiled.

I hated the fact that both Jack and Danny knew my fear of loud noises and how frightened I got when the bombs were falling, even if they were miles from us. The only saving grace was that of late the Germans seemed to have changed tact, concentrating more on the big cities, leaving us along the coast alone. The threat was still there though, born out by the increase in soldiers and heavy armoury on the roads and the strengthening of the defences on the beaches and along the clifftop, with huge pillboxes armed with Lewis, machineguns, and anti-tank traps being laid everywhere. I shuddered then got a grip of myself, this was no good, I needed to be more positive, tomorrow was going to be fun!

I glanced at Becky again and felt so grateful that it had been her who took my big sisters place, she was, like our Janie, in so many ways, strong, resourceful and so very calm. She oozed confidence, I felt it, as I'd always felt it from my sister... and not only that, looking around the class I noticed my younger siblings looking towards her too, our Jack and Danny rather warily, after their first encounter with her, the memory of which made me smile as it always does, the image of them being dragged through the village by her, makes me so pleased to have her as a stand in for our Janie.

Leaning towards me she whispered; 'Let the bloody Germans come, we'll see 'em off, should they dare interfere with our big event tomorrow,' she grinned.

It was good to know that she'd be there, even if it did end up with her being in the kitchen, at least her and our Janie would spend some time together. Oh, to be a fly on the wall there!

'Perhaps we'll get the chance to catchup at some time and enjoy a ride together,' I said.

'No perhaps about it, Rube,' she grinned. 'After all it's because of your family that we're having the fair and the fete at all, so I think you're owed a few perks... you should all be very proud of yourselves,' she said, sincerely.

Across the room I could see our Janet and Bella sitting tall in their seats, while my brothers, Jack and Danny, now seemed a little nervous, wondering no doubt what Becks and me were talking about, I gave them a knowing nod just to keep them guessing. As I looked around at all my siblings, I realised just how well we fitted into this tight little community, and that it wasn't anything the Germans could do that really frightened me, it was getting another visit from the man from the Ministry, telling us that it was time for us to move on! I shook the nasty thought away, that was all out of our hands, the thing to do was to enjoy what we had now and only worry about that when it happened, which it would, I knew, one day!

After school, the Davis twins and my brothers, along with Janet and Bella, too, walked with Becky and me through the village and down to the estate now changed into a full-blown Fair and Fete! It was simply amazing and had my brothers and the twins running around in circles trying to see everything, closely followed by my young sisters, while Becky and me stood and laughed at their antics. Mum came walking up through the site then, much to our surprise and she had the little-ones with her, she looked tired and a little out of sorts, which was not good, and usually meant someone was going to catch an earful!

'Janet, Bella, you already know your roles for tomorrow, so instead of hanging around doing nothing, you can take the little-one's home,' she ordered brusquely. 'Look sharp now, and see to it that they are fed and changed by the time I get back,' she snapped, passing the pram to them.

I could tell by their faces that my sisters were not at all happy, that they'd wanted to stay and soak up the atmosphere of the fairground, which is, I have to admit, quite breath-taking. Even the people putting the finishing touches to the rides and the stalls were humming and singing cheerfully as they got everything ready for tomorrow morning.

As I watched my sisters walking downheartedly up the drive, I did feel a bit sorry for them having to miss out, but in truth, it really was about time they took on their share of seeing to the little-ones. Becky and me turned back to mum, expecting her to give us our orders, tell us what it was she wanted us to do next, but to my surprise she simply smiled; 'Have a look around,' she said, 'I'll call if I need you. Oh! And you boys behave yourselves, or there'll be no Fete or Fair for you, understand?' she said firmly, the four boys nodded. With that she left us and made her way towards the big house. We all just stood there for a moment not quite knowing what to do, then our Danny gave a whoop of delight, almost making me jump. 'Will you look at this... come on, let's have a go on the bumping cars,' he yelled.

In truth I'd forgotten my brothers were still with us until then.

'Oh, oh, better not, look who's coming,' Jack warned.

Following his gaze, I saw our Janie making her way towards us; punching him on the arm, for his cheek, I went with Becky to meet her.

'Hey, what was that for?' My younger brother objected.

'You know very well what it was for,' I scowled, tempted to hit him again for his cheek.

'Having trouble?' Janie asked as she stopped in front of us.

'Are we having trouble, boys?' I asked my brothers.

They both shook their heads and walked away sulking.

'You know Becky don't you sis?' I asked her.

'Of course, how are you Becks?' she grinned.

My new bench mate smiled; 'How's work treating you, Jane? Never thought I'd ever see you at a posh place like this, what's it like?' she asked.

Janie laughed; 'Neither did I, girl, but a job's a job and Lady Seymour is nice enough.'

At that moment I spotted her Ladyship chatting with mum and watched as they disappeared into the manor house together, no doubt to go over the plans for the morning again, leaving us to explore some more.

'Just look at the bumper cars, aren't they great? Come on Danny let's get in one!' our Jack laughed.

Our Danny hesitated and looked towards Janie and me; 'Well don't look at us, boys,' Janie laughed, 'Try asking one of the workmen if it's alright,' Janie suggested.

One of the crew nearby must have heard our Janie as he waved us on to try them out. We could only sit in them of course as they were still out on the grass, but it was fun all the same and gave us a feel for what it was going to be like.

After that we checked out the rest of the rides, nothing was quite finished yet, although the big wheel was being put up as we watched and the Helter-Skelter too. It was all so very exciting and we dearly would have loved to hang around and watch them all being completed but mum came to shepherd us home. As we left the estate, leaving Becky at her home in the village, it was clear by the volume of tanks and other armoured vehicles that passed us on the roads that our bus would not be running and so we had to walk... and as mum had reminded me once, it was indeed a long way. We reached home, only minutes before the air-raid sirens went off, warning us of another attack, looking up we could just make them out, moving like a great black shadow across the sky, no doubt their targets being Poole harbour and the ships at anchor.

We ran for the shelter, across the cobbled yard as the bombs began to fall and the big coastal guns barked out their noisy defiant reply, turning the tranquil day once more into a nightmare. As worried as I was about the big ships and people's homes being bombed, I was equally concerned that a stray bomb might hit our fairground, all be it some miles from their targets!

For the next hour we stayed in the shelter, until finally the all clear sounded and we crawled out, all of our earlier good humour dampened by this sombre taste of reality... Fair and Fete aside, we were still in the middle of a war! Tea was a quiet affair, with no one wanting to talk much; until our Jack opened his big mouth that is; Do you suppose they'll come again tomorrow?' he asked of mum.

'Do I think who will come tomorrow?' Mum sighed, obviously annoyed by the question.

'You know... them!' Jack repeated.

'Who, them... Father Christmas and his Reindeers?' she teased.

'No, of course not... the Germans... will they invade us tomorrow?' he persisted.

Mum looked daggers at him; 'Well how should I know, boy, no one can answer that question, not even Winston Churchill himself,' she snapped.

Jack knew she was on the edge of her temper and so went back to finishing his tea, but to all our surprise that was not the end of the subject as our Bella found her voice; 'If they do come, I hope it's after we've had the fair and the fete; as I'm really looking forward to that,' she sighed.

Although she hadn't meant too, she lifted everyone's spirits, sending all of us into fits of laughter, at the thought of the German high command arranging their invasion to suit her little timetable? Even mum had to chuckle at that, although Bella didn't think what she'd said funny at all! I don't think I had a wink of sleep that night, what with all the talk of stray bombs, and invasions and the like, that everyone had talked about most of the day.

Despite my lack of sleep, Janie and me were up early as there was a lot to do, as, regardless of the fair and the fete, we still had our chores around the yard and the house to do, before we could even think about getting ready for our big day.

As Janie and me went about our daily tasks I noticed that there was a strange atmosphere abroad, everyone was of course very excited about what the day had in store, although no-one was actually saying much, and so we ate breakfast in relevant silence. Even the little-ones were strangely quiet for a change, which was very odd indeed. In fact, everything was like that... odd I mean! It was Saturday for goodness' sake, and even if we hadn't had the event to go too, on Saturdays we were all usually bouncing with joy, as there was no school... which made this silence, odder still.

Thankfully though, we had two noisy brothers and our Danny suddenly let out an unexpected whoop of joy, before leaping to his feet and dancing a jig around the kitchen table. That broke the strange spell or whatever it was as the house returned to its normal noisy self, as everyone, including myself and even Janie joined in. Our crazy antics lasted until mum came in off the fields and gave us one of her... 'what the hell do you think you're doing? Stares.

'I hope you realise, girls,' she said looking towards Janie and me; 'that in less than 2 hours farmer Drake will be here to take you down to the estate?'

I glanced at the clock on the mantlepiece and saw that it was coming up to 6:30 am, still early, but not when you took into account that the fair and the fete would be open to the public by 10am! That gave us little time to make sure everything was ready.

Dad walked in then, and I thought for a moment he was going to hurry us along too, but instead he caught mum by the hand and danced her around the kitchen, inviting us all to join in. It was just like our dad to do something so unexpected and so lovely, so Janie and me caught up the little-ones and twirled them around, not wanting them to miss all the fun.

A loud clang on the stove and mum shouting for us to stop now and get ourselves ready, ended the fun, sending us all hurrying to wash and change, to be ready for farmer Drake's arrival. I had butterflies in my tummy as we all piled into the back of the old van, mother and father too, as they both had things to finish before the event opened.

Despite our early start the fair people were already hard at work when we arrived and I was amazed at how much more they'd done since last night. Pirate Jake grinned as we piled out of the van.
'Better ta come late, than not come at all, I suppose,' he called to us… 'And with the young'un's too, just what's needed ta try out the rides… if they want's to of course,' he laughed.

As one, we hit the ground running, my siblings to the rides, while I raced for the grand house, thinking that Lady Seymour's children should join us. Although they were fresh from their beds and finishing breakfast; Grace, Crispen and Florence, screamed with delight when I said what it was my sibling and me were going to do, and asked, did they want to join us? Lady Seymour flinched a little; 'Is it safe?' she asked.
'Mum's there and Jake, my Lady, and Janie and me will go on the rides with them,' I assured her.
'Thank you for thinking of my children, Ruby,' she said, wiping a tear from her eye, it's very much appreciated… may I come and watch? Perhaps I'll have a ride on something too,' she smiled.

For the next half an hour Janie and me led the rest of the children all across the site; from the Ferris wheel, which was scary fun, onto the Helter-skelter and then the Carousel, but my favourite was the Roller-coaster, although I did like the bumping cars, which gave us all a lot of fun, except our Janie who just hated me crashing into her… which made me do it all the more.

However, it was time for us to get back to work, there was still some snagging to finish and already people were beginning to arrive; I could see a queue starting to form at the top of the long drive. I felt suddenly nervous, soon they'll be paying their money and heading on down; I took a deep breath and went to my station by the Bumping cars... across from me, at the helter-skelter, I could see our Janie pacing back and forth, looking as nervous as me. And then suddenly they came... hordes of them streaming down across the site, all making for their favourite ride, and my bumping cars was one of them, and for the next hour or so I barely had time to think, collecting money and keeping the people happy. Thankfully, taking care of the Roller Coaster and the Carousel, I left to the fair people, who knew more about them. Still, I had plenty enough to do, as did Janie at the Helter-skelter, who like myself had one of the fair people assisting her.

There were people everywhere now making it impossible for me to leave my post, and I longed to know how mum was getting on down at the fete, hoping that she was managing to keep an eye on my troublesome brothers. When a few minutes later Grace came by looking for something to do, I asked her to take over for me while I went to find out for myself how mum was doing. Before going I called across to Janie just to let her know what I was doing, to my surprise she said she'd come with me as Crispen was relieving her for a while. Even as she told me, Crispen on seeing me, waved, looking so proud to be helping out. On reaching mum, it was a shock for both of us to see our brothers still behaving and running the coconut shies as if they were born to it... even if it was now, turnip shies? Whatever it was the crowd didn't seem to mind, queuing up to take their turn.

Like them, mum was equally busy on her White Elephant and Tombola stalls, but not too busy, I was pleased to note, that she couldn't keep a watchful eye on our Jack and Danny, as they were in the habit of changing from good too bad in an instant.

I noticed for the first time that she had alongside her no other than Pirate Jake and that there were a lot of people queueing up for his latest idea of; Palm and Crystal ball readings!

'Now I didn't see that coming,' I whispered softly in mum's ear, trying hard not to laugh.

She shook her head; 'No, child, and that makes the two of us,' she chuckled.

Janie and me couldn't stop laughing as we made our way back up to relieve Grace and Crispen, relating to them our friendly Pirate's newest venture.

They both laughed, Grace saying, to my surprise, that they had never had such fun before meeting us, even our Janie was delighted on hearing that.

'We can be troublesome too, mind,' Janie warned with a wink.

'But fun!' Crispen repeated, as they took their leave of us, going to speak with some of the fair people, seeking more work from them... the last we saw of them, they were cheerfully gathering up hessian sacks for the Helter-skelter rides. By the middle of the morning, we were being overrun even with the fair people helping out. I realised that I had to go and find more help, both for myself and Janie.

Thankfully our dilemma had already been noticed and a handful of fairground people came to our rescue, relieving us from our stations, stating that by rights we were not experienced enough to run such heavy rides, and we didn't argue.

Free of our responsibilities we went to check on our Janet and Bella, and to see how tea on the back lawn was going... and perhaps even get ourselves a bite to eat. When we got there, all the tables were full and there was a queue waiting for any to come free, meanwhile some of the less fussy were taking their tea sat on rugs on the lawn and it would seem, thoroughly enjoying the experience. I felt so proud of my younger sisters, when we finally found them, they both looked a picture in their black maids serving dresses, so much so that I barely recognised them.

'Can you take this out to mum and our brothers, they'll be starving,' Janet said, passing me a tray of sandwiches and a pot of tea, when you come back, we'll have some for you too,' Bella smiled.

We took the food and drink to mum and our brothers and watched as they shared it with Pirate Jake, which had me silently cursing for not having thought of him myself.

'So how are things back there?' Mum asked.

'Busy... very busy, I've never seen so many people before, I think most of the village must be here, and there's lots of soldiers and sailors and airmen... and just about everyone else!' I sighed.

Mum rubbed her hands together; 'the more there is the better it is for our cause, girl,' she smiled.

I nodded; then changed the subject; 'I think me and our Janie should check up on Grace and Crispen, they were up helping out at the fair the last we saw of them, near the big rides,' we should make sure they're alright,' I worried. Hurrying away, we found Crispen and Grace working together now, still on the Helter-skelter, but well supervised by two fair-grounders; 'Go down and get yourselves some food and drink,' I ordered. Grace smiled, then turned to the two young women supervising them; 'Would you like us to bring you something?' she asked. They shook their heads but thanked her anyway. As we watched them disappear among the jostling crowds, I spotted their mother, Lady Seymour over by the hook-a-duck stall, giving little Florence a chance to play.

'Have you seen anything of Grace and Crispen?' she asked on seeing us.

I said that we had and that they were fine and had gone in search of something to eat out on the back lawn, which seemed to relax her a little, although why she needed relaxing, I couldn't say, everything was going really well... still she did seem worried about something.

'Would you be a dear, and look after Florence for a while, Ruby?' she asked, quite unexpectedly.

'Of course, my Lady,' I said taking Florence in my arms.

'And Jane, would you come with me, in case cook is in need of assistance with the food,' she asked my sister.

'Yes, of course Lady Seymour,' Janie replied, following her down through the fairground.

I bumped Florence up onto my shoulders as she continued happily to try to hook a duck, until, with a little squeal, she cried out... 'Look... Look... I'm caught one... I'm doing my bit... look!'

We moved on then with Florence holding on firmly to the little soft toy bear she'd won for hooking the duck. I was feeling hungry now and realised I hadn't had anything to eat, and wondered if in fact, Lady Seymour had fed Florence yet. Deciding that it was the back lawn for us, I made my way back down through the fair and the fete, making a stop at my brother's turnip shies, which was still busy, as was mums Tombola Booth although her White Elephant stall was already sold out.

Pirate Jake was still in business though with his fakery, and he gave me a sly wink in passing that brought a smile to my face... the rogue... palm and Crystal ball readings indeed! I laughed aloud and mum, shushed me; She had the little-ones tucked away below her counter, and they were being so good, and were still sleeping, and that's the way we needed them to stay for a while longer yet.

'Jake, as punishment for all your nonsense, I would like you to see to the little-ones for a while, what do you say?' mum suddenly asked.

Our Pirate chuckled; 'It would be an honour, Iris, I'll look to em, my dear,' he agreed.

'I won't be long,' mum promised, 'I just want to check on the tea party, and see how my other daughters are. If the little-ones stir, perhaps you could give em a taste of one of the toffee apples you've got under the counter!' she grinned.

He laughed, 'Aye that I can, ta be sure,' Jake said, in his best Pirate voice. 'But how did you know I still had any?' he asked.

Mum chuckled; 'Not much gets past me my lad, you ask any of my girls. But not this one, Ruby, you're with me, look sharp now child,' she ordered.

I hurried to keep up as she started away, leaving poor Jake to see to the little-ones all by himself, and our Janie to see to the Tombola Booth and sell what was left of the raffle tickets, as well as keeping an eye on our brothers across the way from them. My brothers, I noticed, as we passed by, were still doing well on their turnip shies and I don't think I've ever seen them so happy... or so well behaved.

As we moved onto the back lawn a troop of Morris Dancers appeared as if from no-where and a brass band too, it made me appreciate the hours of planning mum and her committee had put into this whole event. Looking around at all the happy faces everywhere it made me a little sad; the sun was shining, the sky was blue, and thankfully, for once, bereft of German planes... but then, why on earth would anyone want to wage a war on such a beautiful day?

'For goodness, sake, girl, stop daydreaming, look there's your sisters, go and catch-up with them while I speak with Lady Seymour and the rest of our committee,' mum ordered, moving away.

I found my sisters, Janet and Bella busy serving tea and cakes out across the array of dainty little tables scattered across the lawn. They were now in full uniforms and looking so lovely in their black pinafore dresses and little white aprons along with their small white mop hats. To see them like this made me feel quite proud. And so, I went to speak with them. As I did, Becky came out of the kitchen area with a trolly full of fresh sandwiches and tea urns and we all came together at one of the big serving tables where we helped her lay out her wares, ready for them to be served to the customers.

'Here, grab a few for yourself,' Becky said, passing me a plate, just then Janie came to join us cheekily snatching away the plate meant for me. 'Jake said he could manage by himself and so sent me off to fetch some more food,' she grinned.

Finding another plate, I piled it up with sandwiches and scones and passed it to her; 'here, that should be enough for our pirate friend,' I grinned. Then watched, as Janie, to my surprise, only added a couple of small, finger sandwiches to the plate she'd stolen from me. Surely, she must be hungry after all our hard work today, I thought. But then I saw something sticking out of her apron pocket… it was a toffee apple… a toffee apple! She must have seen me looking as she quickly covered it with her hand; I smiled, so that's why she wasn't very hungry then.

'Can you believe that mum helped to organise all of this, Rube? She sighed, looking out across the garden, at the dozens and dozens of people, either sat eating or queuing for tables.

I smiled. 'Yes! I think mum can do just about anything she puts her mind too, Sis, and she doesn't miss much either,' I said letting my eyes fall on her ill-gotten gains!

She gave me her big sister, 'don't mess with me', stare.

'I do hope that you've a toffee apple for me tucked away somewhere sis!' I grinned. 'Or I might have to tell mum!'

'Don't worry, I've saved you one, unless I finish mine and decide to eat yours too!' she threatened, with a laugh.

Our Janet came back then; 'It's crazy in the kitchen Janie, I think cook is looking for you to go and help them out,' she said.

'I'll pop this plate out to Jake and then go and see what I can do to help in the kitchen,' Janie sighed.

As Janie was saying goodbye, Janet turned to me; 'Is it still this bad out front?' she asked, wiping her brow.

'Worse,' I confirmed. 'There's three or four times as many people out there, Sis.'

'Then I'm glad I'm where I am, Rube, I couldn't stand that.' Janet said, shaking her head.

'No, but don't you see Sis, it's wonderful, all these hundreds of people have come here because they, like the rest of us, are in need of a break from this bloody war, they're here in search of a little lightness in their lives.' I sighed.

Just then Lady Seymour came over to us, her children with her and also to my surprise our Janie who had only just left. 'Ah! Good, I've found you; Now, girls, gather up all of your siblings, your father will be taking part in the tug of war shortly and you should all be there to cheer him on.'

'I really should get back to the kitchen,' Janie blushed. 'Cook is...

'Cook is doing just fine, now run along... in fact I think I'll join you if you don't mind,' she smiled.

Janie and me looked at one another, surprised that the Lady of the Manor, would ask us if we minded her company... now that was really something. As we started towards the side lawn where the tug of war was being put on, the Seymour children came to join us; Grace and Crispen taking the lead, with little Florence already hanging onto my hand. 'Thank you for today, for helping us to be a part of it all,' Crispen said, sincerely.

Before I could say that it wasn't really down to us, that this was, in fact their home; Grace spoke up; 'Our mother would never have let us do half the things we did today if it wasn't for the fact that she trusts you and your family so much.' She seemed most certain of that, and I felt so pleased.

By the time we'd made our way around to the side garden the tug of war had already begun with the Davis twins leading the cheering; and it was all very noisy and boisterous. Our Jack and Danny and mother too were already there and we joined them adding our voices to theirs in cheering our dad on. Despite the noise of the crowd, I could hear father shouting and urging his team on, and that was not like him at all, but it was nice to see him so relaxed and enjoying himself.

'Come on Dad!' I yelled, almost in her Ladyships ear... she simply smiled though.

'Pull dad... Pull!' Janie screamed at my side... 'Drag 'em through the mud!' she hollered.

I felt my cheeks redden, that was just typical of our Janie, never content with a simple victory, oh no, she wanted to see dad's opponents dragged through the dirt.

'My, your sister is very aggressive, isn't she?' Lady Seymour chuckled. 'Perhaps we should send her off to fight the Germans... what do you think Ruby? Would your sister make a good soldier?'

Before I could answer a rather sour looking gentleman standing next to us spoke. 'Humph! If you must know; there are many who believe that we shouldn't be fighting the Germans at all;' he snorted.

Lady Seymour turned on him and I'd never seen her so angry; 'Lord Cartwright, if you feel like that then this is not the place for you, please leave, and take those of a like mind with you... Go sir, now! She raged, angrily.

'I was just saying madam... he started to protest.

'I don't care what you are just saying, sir... and it's, Lady Seymour, not madam... now leave and take those awful people with you,' she said waving towards a group of mostly old men all dressed in black. 'And if you are not swift about it, I will have you all ejected.' She warned him. Even as she finished speaking, a mixture of servicemen all who had overheard the Lords words came to stand with her, ready to do her bidding.

Seeing how hopelessly out numbered they were, he and his cohorts slunk away like whipped dogs; 'Don't even look at them my dears,' Lady Seymour advised turning our attention back to the tug of war and our father. The teams seemed to be evenly matched and both holding their own, producing a bit of a stalemate for the minute.

'Who are they?' I asked, staring after the nasty group.

'They call themselves; Black Shirts! They are Fascists and supporters of one, Sir Oswald Mosely, who is nothing more than a traitor,' she raged.

'And you know this man?' our Janie asked, tactlessly.

Lady Seymour looked quite flushed; 'To my eternal shame he was once a friend of my family, he and my husband met during the Parliament elections of 1926 when Sir Oswald was elected member of Parliament for Smethwick. He seemed a perfectly nice, amiable man back then,' she sighed.

'So, what changed him, my Lady?' I asked.

Lady Seymour shrugged, 'politics perhaps,' she offered. 'But never mind him, look, your father's team is winning,' she cried, turning our attention back to what mattered.

We were just in time to see dad's team of farmhands drag the villagers to their knees and then across the finish line to win. There was a roar of approval as Twin Marty was lifted shoulder high and paraded around the garden in triumph as the winning captain, whilst his brother slumped dejected among his beaten team mates. But their spirits were soon revived when they were brought refreshments, and it was good to see the twins united in harmony again, being on opposite sides just didn't suit them.

'Could you look after my children?' Lady Seymour asked, as I was about to go over and congratulate father... 'Only I really would like a private word with your mother and thank her for the wonderful job she's done here today. I have already thanked the other committee members, but I haven't had the chance to speak with Iris alone yet. I really don't know what I would have done without her... oh! And without you and the rest of your siblings, she added hastily. 'So, would you mind if I stole her away for a few minutes?' she begged.

I was properly impressed, she was some Lady, taking the time to ask me would I mind leaving her alone with mother, this was her Manor, she could do as she pleased! As I walked away, I glanced back to see her and mother in conversation and she had her arm around mum's shoulder, it was so lovely and mind blowing, what on earth did her Ladyship see in us?

I went to stand with Amber, Stella and Betty, the committee members, and they all looked as tired as I felt; 'My, what a day, girls,' Amber sighed, 'what a tiring but wonderful day!' She sat down on the grass, where we joined her; 'I knew from the beginning that asking your mother to join our committee was the right thing to do,' Amber sighed.

Stella smiled. 'I'll give you that, girl, it was your idea in the first place, and a great one it was.'

Amber blushed; 'In fairness, we all had the same thought really, certainly Lady Seymour did, it just happened to be me who voiced it first, that's all.'

The other committee ladies laughed then and got to their feet; 'In fairness Amber, my dear, you have never been shy to put it out there, and long may you do so.'

With that they said their goodbyes and went strolling arm in arm up across the site, a committee to the end. Our Janie also left then, going back to the kitchen to help cook clear up, which was disappointing. I had hoped we might have some time to ourselves, as a family, enjoying perhaps a go on some of the rides after the crowds had all gone. I looked out at the fairground to see the diminishing crowds, all heading for their homes, before curfew no doubt. But it wasn't them I was really looking at! It was the rides, just waiting there for us to take advantage of. It's not as if we don't deserve it, I told myself. But not without our Janie! As if in answer to my thoughts, she returned, along with our mutual friend Becky, whom I confess to have clean forgotten about what with all we'd had to do.

Pirate Jake and some of his people stayed behind after the dwindling crowds finally disappeared; to run the rides for us. Lady Seymour was a little dubious about her children safety on some of the bigger rides. But Janie and me assured her that we'd look out for them and so she agreed for them to join us. And so, we took them with us, even on the monstrous Helter-Skelter!

Later, as the light began to fade, we said goodbye to Lady Seymour and her children before helping the fair people shut down all the rides and give a hand in clearing the tables off the back lawn. Finally, it was time for me to go, along with mum and dad and the rest of the family. We walked with Becky back to her home in the village first, before making our weary way across the gloomy heath to our own home, all of us half expecting the sirens to sound, as they often did at this time of the day, but for once, the, bombers didn't come. The mood in our house that night was one of jubilation, our great gamble had paid off, we'd put on our fair and fete, in spite of the Germans and it had been a huge success.

In the days that followed, no one talked about anything else, from the butcher's shop to the bakery, to the village store, there was but one subject on everyone's lips; our fair and fete! And once more mother was the hero, although she was quick to deny it.

'This is a victory for everyone and I'll not take the credit for myself, that just wouldn't be right,' she said angrily. 'After all, it was our former committee member, Mrs Jennings who came up with idea of throwing a village fete,' she argued.

'But combining the two, that was your idea mum,' Janie insisted, as we sat in the kitchen after tea, going over the event and all that had happened.

'No, it wasn't, that was your father's idea, if I'm being honest,' mum admitted.

All eyes turned toward dad!

'All I said was that I knowed of a fair that was stranded close by,' he said, reaching for a roast potato, ''an mother put two an' two ta gether, and that was that!'

'Look, it's not important who found what first, the important thing is, that we, all of us, you lot included put it all together and made it work,' mum insisted.

'Well said Iris,' dad grinned.

'Well done to us all, Fred,' mum smiled.

Later, when Janie and me were alone, I confessed to not seeing mum and dad so happy for a long time. 'She seems to have changed since we got here, Janie... happier even than when we were back in Somerset on Home Farm!' I added.

Janie shrugged; 'Could it be the sea air? My sister suggested; 'Or perhaps because our troublesome brothers are not so bad anymore? Although I don't think that's down to the sea air. More like down to the Davis Twins if you ask me!' Janie said.

I nodded in agreement; 'I have to confess, Sis that I had those twins down to reinforce our brother's naughtiness, but in truth they seem to have calmed them down,' I admitted.

Janie smiled, 'with things going so well, I really hope we don't hear from that man from the Ministry ever again, Sis, as I would hate to leave here. I really feel as if we've finally found a place that is a perfect fit for us, don't you?'

'If they do force us to go, I hope it's not until after my birthday on the 12th of September,' I sighed, longing to have Her Ladyship and her children around to help me celebrate it.

'I still can't believe that you're nearly 13 Rube, almost old enough to leave school and get a proper job,' Janie said, 'I bet you're hoping Lady Seymour will take you onto her staff; now wouldn't that be the best birthday present of all. But I'm afraid there's no chance of that happening, not for at least another year, anyway Sis, mores the pity.' Janie teased. I was used to Janie teasing me, but I also knew how desperate she was to see me happy, and doing the job that I would love to do, working for her Ladyship. That thought made me feel a little down in the dumps, for neither Janie or myself could alter the fact that I was still a year too young, more's the pity.

Life returned to normal after all the excitement of our fair and fete, with us doing what we usually do during the school holidays, besides helping around the farm and around the house. And that meant, mainly, running wild out across the heath. With no more school for six whole weeks we took to building dens out in the woods and house trees up in the branches of mighty oaks, whilst swimming in cold glistening streams that bled down into the sea. When the weather allowed, we took the rowing boat out to our island, camping out as we had before. Even Nannie came with us now and then, sporting a tent of her own for herself and Lady Seymour's children, keeping a watchful eye on them as they ran and played across the island. One day, Lady Seymour herself came out to the island whilst we were there, rowed over by Robbo, it was heart-warming to see the pleasure on her face as she watched her children so happy in our company. But she had another reason for her visit, she came to tell us that thanks to all of our efforts at the fair and fete, altogether we'd raised £250 towards a new Spitfire, a sum that I found quite staggering, as did everyone else, who began clapping and slapping each other on the backs.

Her Ladyship, I noticed had tears in her eyes as she watched her children celebrating alongside us for their part in the event, she was as proud of them as we all were, but I could tell that she was wishing her husband were here to enjoy this moment with his family. The look of sadness on her pretty face almost brought tears to my eyes, and I prayed that he was alive and well, even though I'd never met the man.

Chapter 9

I didn't stay long on the Miller girls island, but I was pleased that Nannie was there to take the children off my hands for a few days. Just how they had persuaded her to go camping with them though, I'll never know and I might even have laughed about it if I wasn't feeling so angry and foolish. The reason I was in no mood for laughing, was that I had allowed myself to be duped, and made a fool of, and by some of my own people too! My husband Rory would be so annoyed with me now if he were here, for letting myself be out manoeuvred by a few stiff-necked old men, as he was prone to calling his senior military colleagues. I blushed with the shame of my mishandling of the situation; I was Lady Seymour and should have done better and not allowed a few crusty old men to dictate terms to me!

Sometimes however even people you have come to rely on can let you down, whether by mistake or by design, but the thing to do is not to cry over spilled milk, as they say. You just have to pick yourself up and get on with it. And that is just what I intend to do after falling into a trap of my own making and agreeing to hold a ball in my manor house! But there is one person I know who will not like it, and I dread to tell her. Thank goodness then that she isn't here at present, but will be returning later today and so I have until then to find the courage to tell her just what it is I have done!

It was the children who came running in to find me first, all talking as one about their adventure with the Millers out on their island, Nannie came in behind them, and at first glance I could see that she knew something was wrong.

'My Lady?' she questioned, sending the children to the play-room so that we might be alone.

It took me a few minutes to pluck up the courage to tell her, 'Nannie, I am going to put on a general dance here at my Manor house.'

She made to reply but I held my hand up to stop her.

'It is what I agreed to do, to get permission for the fete and fairground, as all the armed forces were against the idea, saying that it was too much of a risk as we are so close to Poole Harbour'.

'However, they said; if they allowed us to continue with our planned event, then they would want something in return...' I took a deep breath, waiting for her to reply!

'But that's scandalous, my Lady, it's nothing short of blackmail!' Nannie protested... 'How dare they... would they have presumed to force this upon you if his Lordship were here... I don't think so!' she said, shaking her head in anger. In truth, in all the years I've known her I have never seen her so furious, and it was all I could do to calm her before the children came to see what all the fuss was about.

'And the ladies of the committee, what is their view, my Lady?' She asked, crossing the room to sit with me on the sofa.

I hesitated; 'I haven't told them yet, Nannie, but I fear, their opinion will be the same as your own, and that is why I'm wondering whether or not to ask for their help?'

She rose angrily to her feet; 'Oh! My Lady, after all you've accomplished together, how can you even think of not asking for their help. How would you feel if they kept something like this from you?' she said, pushing her point home.

I sighed, she was right, of course, and anyway, what was I thinking. I couldn't do this alone; I wouldn't know where to begin. Thanking her for her forthright words of wisdom, I let her get back to the children while I made some phone calls. I invited my ladies to our first Committee meeting since our great success, just a week ago. Despite it being August and the beginning of the school summer holidays the weather was changeable. Yesterday when Nannie and the children had been camping out on the island it had been fine and sunny, today, just like my demeanor, it was cloudy and grey, with a hint of rain in the air... Oh how foolish I felt as I waited for my friends to arrive, what on earth would they think of me allowing myself to be caught in a trap like a helpless little mouse?

As usual Amber was first to arrive along with Stella and Betty all intrigued as to why I'd called the meeting so close to our last success. The maid showed them in and I asked them to sit, but I would say nothing until we were all there and that meant waiting for Iris, who was running a little late, which was no surprise. Still, it did nothing to settle my nerves, knowing that they were not going to like the fact that I had gone behind their backs.

Finally, Iris arrived and I got straight into my reason for asking them here; When I had finished telling them what had occurred, at first there was no reaction, all of them seemingly stunned, even angry, but not at me, but with the people who had forced me into holding the dance.

'You should have refused point-blank, my Lady,' Amber railed... getting to her feet, 'they had no business forcing it on you, no business at all... An Officers Ball, indeed! How dare they'.

I quickly put her right; 'No, not an Officers Ball... my dear, that's what they asked me to put on, but I insisted on a general dance, for all ranks and even civilians, thinking that we might invite everyone, villagers and farmers too!' I corrected.

Standing at my side, Iris chuckled; 'A general dance! Really, my Lady? And they went for that? I think they took on the wrong one when they decided to tangle with you, Lady Seymour,' she said.

I smiled; 'Although, I really have no idea about such things and so called you together hoping that we might come up with some idea's ladies,' I pleaded.

I saw Amber and Stella look at one another and smile; 'As Betty got to her feet, to claim the floor; 'don't worry, my Lady,' she said, 'we three have helped to put on many a jolly dance in our time, you can leave that part of things to us,' she beamed, embracing her partners in crime; Amber and Stella.

'We have the addresses of a few good bands, although the drink and the catering might be a little trickier,' my Lady,' she pointed out.

'We still have the names of the village women who helped us with the food on the back lawn, we could always ask them to help us out again?' I suggested.

'Yes, and old Mr Briggs, the village pub, landlord, I'm sure he'd be willin' ta do us a deal on the drinks side of things;' Iris offered up. 'On leaving here today I'll go and ask him, or get my Fred to have a word with him as they're good friends... but either way, I'm confident we'll sort the drinks problem.' She insisted.

'Thank you, Iris. Next comes the when? Shall we say, next weekend, ladies, Saturday the 11th of August, after all we have contacts in the military bases so we should be able to spread the word quickly enough, and I'm sure we can get a few posters done in just a few hours, to put up around the village as well as the camps.'

Stella, burst out laughing; 'My word, you do like to do things in a hurry, my Lady, just four weeks or so to put on a Fair and a Fete, and a mere week to put on a dance... wonderful!' she giggled.

I blushed; 'Is it too soon, do you think?' I asked.

'No! No! She insisted, 'I just love the faith that you have in us... and I'm sure we can do it to!' Stella assured me.

'Well, maybe, but right now I would like you all to come with me on a tour of the manor house, to decide where we should put things, where the bar should go, for instance, and the cloakroom, and a place for the food tables. The ballroom and the bandstand of course are already in place.'

We checked out one room at a time; designating each a purpose on the night of the dance; The Drawing room and the Lounge for the food, while the library and the long hall could house the bar, and we could use the children's play room as the cloakroom, much to their dismay. Although they were fine with it when I explained that once again, they'd be doing their bit for the war effort.

For the next hour we busied ourselves making plans, coming up with ways to increase our coppers for our good causes, everyone chipping in with ideas.

'Back in Dorchester,' Amber, mused; 'There is a drawing on the pavement of a Spitfire and as they walk by people toss coins into it, to be collected up every evening.' Also, as you know, women have to pay to use the public toilets, well now, so do men... we could do that too!' she suggested.

I screwed my nose up at that last idea... 'and who would ask the men for their pennies?' I frowned. 'No, I don't think so, my dear,' I smiled. 'But I like the Spitfire idea... if we can get someone to draw it for us, that is!' I added.

'Well now, my Jane is good at that sort of thing, why not get her to do it, she could also do the posters, with a bit of help,' Iris suggested.

'What a lovely idea, and perhaps my own children could lend a hand,' I proposed. 'I also think we should run a raffle, as people are always up for one of those,' I smiled. That was our final decision of the long day, agreeing to meet up the next morning to hammer home the fine details, and so once again I had a restless night's sleep.

For a change Iris was the first to arrive the next day; with the exciting news that old Mr Briggs, the village pub landlord was prepared to provide all the drinks for our dance, at cost price, which was just perfect, he also offered his service as a barman and his daughter to serve as barmaid. With the drinks sorted I went to see how preparations were going in the kitchen and found cook poring over a list of names, most of whom had helped us out before; 'I've chosen eight, my Lady, I think that should be enough, given that I'll be running the kitchen,' she growled.

I had every faith in cook and so I simply accepted that she knew best and moved on, taking Jane along with me, as I wanted to speak with her.

'Has your mother spoken to you about the dance next weekend?' I asked.

She nodded, the excitement in her eyes clear to see; 'So you like to dance?' I smiled.

She blushed; 'When I get the chance, my Lady... which isn't often these days.'

'Well, perhaps you will soon, my dear. But first, did your mother say anything to you about posters and a drawing of a Spitfire?' I asked her.

She nodded and pulled a piece of paper from her pocket; it was a little untidy but it was a poster advertising our dance; I read her crumpled first effort;

WELCOME TO A DANCE, AT SANDBOURNE MANOR,
ON SATURDAY Next, FROM 12:00 NOON
RAISING MONEY FOR THE WAR EFFORT
ALL DONATIONS WELCOME AT THE DOOR
FOOD AND DRINK AVAILABLE TO PURCHASE ON SITE

It wasn't terribly well written but given the time we had it was good enough and so I ventured into my husband's office and found twenty or so sheets of blank paper for Jane and Ruby to use.

With my children looking on the two girls set about their task, finishing to my delight, only two hours later. In time for Stella, Amber and Betty to pick up, and deliver to the military camps in the area and also to the shops, the church and the pub in the village. Although, I could see that both Ruby and Jane were tired after finishing the posters, there was another task I wished them to do, but first I let them rest with an assortment of biscuits and a glass of lemonade each, while I sent my children off to collect as many stones as they could find.

Once they had a good pile, I explained what they were for; 'First... Jane! Can you draw the outline of a Spitfire, right here, beside the front door... it doesn't need to be a full size one, about six feet long should do the trick,' I explained?

She looked a little nonplussed, as did the rest of the children, but she took the chalk I offered and started to draw the miniature Spitfire just the same; after about a half an hour she stood back, and there on the floor was a perfect replica, if a lot smaller, of a Spitfire;

'Perfect,' I smiled; 'now children, I want you to put the stones all the way around the drawing?'

'But what are we making?' my daughter Grace queried.

'A bank, my dear... a Spitfire bank! Hopefully people will toss coins into it as they pass... the stones will stop the coins from rolling out, then at the end of the day we'll collect up the money and add it to our coffers,' I told them.

'Shouldn't we have some kind of sign to let everyone know what it's there for?' Crispen asked.

I was so pleased that my children were all taking part in this idea; 'I think that should be something that I myself undertake, after all I should do my bit too.' I smiled. So, it was decided, and while the children laid the stones around our Spitfire, I retired back into the house to add my contribution to all their hard work, in the form of a sign post, which cook helped me place at the foot of the wonderful sculpture. Finally, when it was all done, Nannie came to toss two pennies into our little bank, followed closely by the children, all of whom I gave a six-penny piece to throw in, Jane and Ruby too; and then I followed suite with a half-a-crown, and declared our bank, well and truly open.

But the bank was just the beginning; there was so much more for us to do, but thanks to cook we had more than enough people to help us prepare for the upcoming dance; as she not only recruited most of the women from the village who had helped us before, she also got them to bring their husbands along to help with the heavy furniture that we needed to move so that we could turn the Lounge and the Drawing room into food halls, where people could buy a bite to eat and drink, as Mr Briggs, the pub landlord set up his bar along the walls of both rooms, insisting he'd need all of that space, at least, as there was always a mad rush for food and drink at these events. Along the hall, the children's playroom, now with their willing consent, was a cloakroom, where people could leave their big coats, while they enjoyed themselves on the dance floor.

Amber and the rest of the committee came to stand with me all wearing the same look of satisfaction that I myself now wore.

From the front door to halfway up the drive the band could be heard warming up, adding to the atmosphere of the ballroom that was looking quite beautiful, its crystal glass chandeliers, sparkling and shimmering across the sleek shiny dancefloor.

To my delight, finally it was done, everything was finally ready; all the helpers were in place, and the kitchen was fully staffed, now all we needed was the people! I checked the time on the grandfather clock in the hallway; on my way up to the children's bedrooms, to make sure they were ready. 11:30am, thirty minutes to go, people would be arriving at any moment! Grace, Crispen and little Florence, looked immaculate as they sat patiently on the edge of their beds with Nannie, and I was pleased to see, Ruby, putting the finishing touches to them.

'So, are we all ready?' I asked, going to glance out of the window, in time to see the first of our guests coming over the brow of the drive, although, on second glance I saw that it was Iris and her husband, now that was a surprise, as I knew Fred had said that he'd be too busy to come! Leaving my children with Nannie and Ruby I went to meet them at the front door.

'Thought we'd see if there's anything you need help with, my Lady?' Iris said as the maid showed them in.

'No! On this occasion, Iris, everything is in hand; thanks, I should add, to your two eldest daughters; both of whom are here should you want them!' I smiled.

'There is one thing you needs us fer my Lady,' I turned to find Fred holding his arms out to me... when you need's ta take the first dance,' he grinned... 'Well, I'll be at your service,' he chuckled.

For a moment I almost blushed especially when Iris tweeked his ear and told him off, but then I saw all the people making their way towards the ballroom... I decided that perhaps Fred was right, being the Lady of the Manor, I should lead the dancing. With that in mind I called my maid Wendy over to show everyone where to put their coats, while I let Fred escort me to the ballroom to take the first dance... it made me smile the look of surprise on his cheeky face and the faces of many others too.

To be honest he was a very good dancer, well he was once the shock of my accepting his offer to share the first dance with him wore off. Out of the corner of my eye I could see Iris and my committee ladies trying to hide their mirth behind their hands. I tried not to blush or to laugh out loud; Ruby was so right about her father, he was quite the rascal, but I had a sense of humour too. Stifling a chuckle, I led him back to Iris and pointed them in the direction of the bar, where I left them with Mr Briggs, before moving on to ensure that there was someone stationed at the front door to welcome guests on their arrival.

I knew that some of the rich and wealthy land owners and some of the high- ranking men of the Military, would be just waiting to find fault with something if they could. Not thinking it prudent for someone like myself to be hosting this all on my own, without my husband being here to supervise. Well, they might think it, but I doubted any of them would have the courage to voice such thoughts, and I didn't care anyway. I had worried that hosting the dance so early in the day, when normally it would be an evening event might prove to be a bad idea, but at least now we wouldn't have to worry about the curfew, or half drunken people getting lost in the blackout. Despite my fears of no one turning up, they started to arrive, some in big cars, even some in pony and traps, but mostly they came on foot; the posh and the working classes alike, shoulder to shoulder, just as they are in this war.

One by one they stopped before our spitfire bank and smiling tossed in a penny or two. I hoped my children were watching from their bedroom window, and feeling proud. Ruby brought them down then and they stood at the side of their sculpture, explaining to any who cared to know what it was for, and that they had helped to make it, which brought a coin or two extra from approving guests, particularly the military ones.

Everything was going wonderfully well, better than any of us could have imagined, especially with so many people, all from different back grounds. All of us had expected some trouble, particularly when the men started drinking, and to that end I had arranged with the forces, that they each provide members of their own military police in case of trouble.

As it happened though, I should have asked for the local policeman to attend as it was two of the village men that had to be asked to leave for fighting each other in the Lounge. They went peacefully enough though and things soon returned to normal, the band playing everything from the Waltz and the Tango, to the new American Jive and Jitterbug! It was a chance for us all to join in the fun and so I had Ruby fetch her sister Jane from the kitchen and their friend Becky too. It felt so good to see them enjoying a dance or two, especially when they were joined by my own children who were over the moon, to be dancing with the grownups.

The only thing missing was my Rory and I had to bite back a tear, refusing to be sad seeing the joy on my children's faces. Their turn on the dance floor was sadly brief however as there was a queue of people waiting their turn to dance. Still as they trooped off, they all wore a look of joy. All told there must have been close to three hundred people crammed into the rooms and out on the dance floor. Some were even spilling out across the lawns, and by the time it came close to curfew, no-one wanted to leave, not even the military people who knew the rules only too well. Still, it was them who led the mass exodus, when the time came for us to close the manor house. Thankfully everyone else following their lead, all of them saying what a grand day they'd had, and thanking us warmly. As the last of the stragglers finally left and the band packed up their instruments and made ready to follow, I felt a tap on my shoulder; 'Hope you've not forgot our dance, my Lady?'

I turned... it was the Brigadier, one of the stuff shirts who forced me to hold the dance, he looked so smug that I wanted to slap him, instead I allowed myself to be steered around the dance floor under his gloating face...

but thankfully it wasn't for long! 'Um excuse me squire, this be my dance...' it was Fred again... I could have kissed him. For a minute the Brigadier hesitated and I thought there might be trouble, but then with a throaty growl he turned on his heel and gave way to my hero.

'See I told ee I could be useful, my new partner chuckled as he whirled me around and around.

Then he let out a yelp, and we all laughed, as Iris led him away by his ear just as Jane and Ruby came red-faced to offer their own apologies for their father's behaviour... 'is it any wonder our brothers Jack and Danny are so naughty,' Ruby sighed, at her side, Jane nodded.

'And is it any wonder he has such a remarkable family,' I added. 'It's clearly not all from your mother's side... I see a lot of him in you Jane, with your strength and straight talking, and he's in you too Ruby, with your playfulness and all your wonderful stories.'

'Would you like us to stay behind and help you clear away, my Lady,' Iris asked as she and Fred prepared to leave.

'No, but thank you for asking Iris,' however, the women from the village have already volunteered.' 'But, listen, why don't I run you home, it's been a long day,' I offered.

Iris nodded a tired looking thank you, but then said;

'Before we go don't you think we should all collect up the spitfire bank as it might prove to be a little tempting for anyone that's a bit hard up,' she said.

I agreed and called the children out who were saying their goodbyes to Jane and Ruby.

'Shall we collect up our spitfire bank?' I suggested.

'And me!' Florence insisted.

'Not you little sister, you can't count,' Crispen tutted.

Before little Florence burst into tears, Ruby swept her up in her arms; 'Why don't we count them together, Florence, I'm not very good at counting either,' she soothed.

'First we'll need some jars to put all the coins in,' I insisted... 'Jane, please go to the kitchen and ask cook if she has any, Grace go with her,' I ordered.

I took a nervous glance towards Iris and Fred, hoping that they didn't mind me telling their daughter what to do, but they seemed just fine, and joined in with the rest of us, scooping all the cash up into the jars; to be counted tomorrow, it was decided, much to little Florence's annoyance, who now, started to cry. Nannie came then to whisk her and my other two away, leaving me free to drive the Miller family home, before returning for a well-deserved, glass of red wine and a nice hot bath.

The next morning after the Sunday service in the village church, Jane and Ruby came as promised to help my children sort and count the coins; 'What are these little ones?' Florence asked holding up a tiny farthing. Her brother Crispen told her, but she ignored him, insisting on Ruby telling her, it was the same with the sixpenny pieces and the pennies and half-pennies, it seemed she hadn't forgiven him for telling everyone that she couldn't count! I found it all quite funny, and a lessen to my son for mocking his little sister last night, for clearly, she was not going to let him get away with it... as young as she was!

It took us most of the afternoon to separate and count all the coins, but finally it was done and we had an amount to announce to everyone; even Mr Briggs and his barmaid daughter here to collect his beer kegs and empty bottles.

'In the spitfire bank', we made,'£26.12s.8p', Ruby announced, much to everyone's surprise.

'Wow! That's amazing, Mr Briggs daughter, gasped.

'It's all they rich people, maid,' Mr Briggs, assured her, 'more money than sense,' he said, shaking his head, no doubt forgetting for the moment who's house he was in?

I saw Jane look towards me, wondering, no doubt, if I minded such talk, but I just smiled, Mr Briggs was a good man, and everyone was entitled to their own opinions.

The following day when Ruby arrived at the manor house to read for the children, I called her sister up from the kitchen, wanting to speak to the both of them.

'Jane, Ruby, I would like you to take a message to your mother and father, tell them that I would like to invite, all of your family, little-ones included to tea, next Sunday, if possible,' I smiled, much to their surprise. It was something I'd been thinking of doing ever since the Fair and Fete, as a thank you for all their help, and now with another success under our belts, there was no better time.

I was so tired of eating alone with just my children for company, as lovely as they are. Besides, the Miller family are interesting people, the sort of people that my Rory would have simply loved to get to know and he'd be pleased that they are part of my life. Standing by the window looking out across the estate, I felt a tear trickle down my cheek, Sandbourne Manor was just the most beautiful of places, but it was lacking just one thing, my husband Rory. It didn't take long for the children to hear about my plans and they came roaring into the room, so excited that you would have thought I'd invited the King himself to Sunday lunch!

'Is it true? Grace demanded; 'Are the Millers coming to Sunday tea?' Crispen and little Florence waited for me to answer, hardly able to contain their excitement.

'Yes,' I finally responded, amidst shouts of sheer joy, never would I have believed that such a strong bond could have been fashioned so quickly by my children and indeed by myself, and towards a family so distant from our own way of living.

Chapter 10

'Ruby Miller, are you daydreaming again?' Mum called from the kitchen.

I couldn't deny it, but who could blame me? It was just like something out of a storybook and I struggled to get my head around it; Lady Seymour has invited us... our whole family to Sunday tea! Who would believe such a thing was possible? It was simply amazing, so much so that I had Janie pinch me, every hour on the hour, to be sure I wasn't dreaming, which she did with gusto, causing me to yelp a lot, much to my brothers Jack and Danny's delight. But I didn't care, this was momentous, the best thing ever!

All the way home from the Manor House after Lady Seymour had sent us with the invite to give to mum and dad, neither Janie or I could quite believe it. It was quite the most ridiculous thing! Who would have thought anything like this could possibly happen to us? We were just an everyday family; we had no airs or graces. I got Janie to pinch me again! None of us had ever met the likes of her Ladyship before coming here. How strange life can be sometimes; although some people call it fate! Or serendipity, a chance meeting of like-minded people! And thinking about it, they had a point! For, if our Janie hadn't applied for a job with Lady Seymour, none of this would have happened. However, who would have guessed that our family of all people would be, as they say; sympatico, if that's the word, with the likes of her?

But from the very beginning each one of us on meeting her have been at our ease around her, even mum and dad seem perfectly calm in her vicinity. Maybe that's why Lady Seymour finds them such good company too. She certainly seems very comfortable with them. I still find it hard to imagine how such a thing can happen, after all, our worlds are so very different.

In truth I suppose, it's a bit like this war in the way that it brings people together from all walks of life, working as one to defeat a common enemy. Just thinking of the Germans makes my skin crawl with fear. Despite the success of the fete, the fair, and now the dance, all the talk I hear around the village and the farms is that there could be an invasion at any time!

Many of the people who came to the dance seemed nervous and spoke of the unyielding flow of war machines on the roads and the ever- increasing growth of troops, airmen and sailors all out along the coastline, every one of them expecting the Hun to arrive at any time... on any day soon. As for getting to school, the bus and other local modes of transport hardly ever use the highway any more, forcing most of us to walk across the heath to school and to the village when we need supplies. Regardless of this though there is little sign of panic and no-one complains, we all know the score and are preparing for the worst! And if it comes to that I have no doubt that this wonderful community we are a part of will all stick together and do its best. But for now, all thoughts of war, are secondary; 'Are you certain, that's what her Ladyship said;' mum asked for about the tenth time in a row... 'that we could all go, the little-ones too?'

For about the tenth time I answered her the same; 'Yes mum, she said all of us, the little-ones too,' I sighed. Then every time it was spoken of, bedlam, with everyone trying to speak at once, the thrill of being asked to the grand manor house, unbelievable to each and every one of my siblings, all of whom, after digesting the news erupted into a frenzy of joyous screaming as they danced around the kitchen table.

When I'd first told mum of Lady Seymours offer, the first thing she'd said was; 'let's hope your father is alright with it.' So, we had to wait until dad came in from his busy day on the farm, and wait again, with baited breath as mum told him. At first, I thought for sure that he was going to say, no, that we couldn't go, his face was so stern and sombre looking, but then he winked, and I knew he was fooling about.

Oh my! we were going to the manor house for Sunday tea; 'Whoopee!' I yelled... 'whoopee', everyone else repeated. Dad laughed and mum gave him a hug and then we all gave him a hug; 'thank you dad,' we all cried out, in unison.

The days seemed to dribble by very slowly that week and everyone was excited and bubbly, even the little-ones, who of course had no idea what all the fuss was about! We did though and so, as we set off on Sunday afternoon to go for tea at the Manor just bursting with excitement, for a while we put the war to one side.

'What a beautiful day,' mum sighed, as we made our way along the winding pathway across the heath. It was indeed a lovely day, in fact it was a perfect day, the sun was shining the sky was cloudless, the birds were tweeting and everywhere was full of life. I looked up, shading my eyes with my hand; the sky was as blue as the sparkling sea beyond the sandy dunes of Sandbourne Bay. I stopped for a moment; the view was stunning. 'If ever there is a day to remind us of our stay here, it is this one.' I muttered quietly to myself. Even the heath was more vibrant than I'd ever seen it, a swath of green, yellow and purple, and alive with all manner of creatures, like, lizards, snakes and rabbits all scampering and slithering cross our path as we made are way up to the small slip road that would take us to the big house.

Lady Seymour had offered to send her carriage to pick us up from home but mum had declined, saying that we'd make our own way, to save her the trouble. I was a little disappointed at first, but the walk over the heath was turning out to be a joy. It wasn't often all of the family went out together, it was especially nice walking hand in hand with dad. It was very rare for him to have time off work, but oh how lovely it felt to be by his side, to feel his leathery, warm fingers wrapped around my own...

Despite mum insisting that we walk all the way to the Manor, when we reached the slip road on the other side of the heath Lady Seymour's carriage was waiting to take us the rest of the way, I didn't hear our mum complain. With a little sigh, she waved us aboard. It was a tight squeeze to get us all in but we made it, although I had to sit on dad's lap with Bella on my lap, holding little Violet! It wasn't that I minded having my siblings on my lap, it was the fact that they were, creasing my party frock that annoyed me. Thankfully it was only a mile or so to the Manor so I could put up with it, even allowing for our Janie's teasing, as she only had one of the little-ones on her lap, and her dress was wrinkle free!

I was starving by the time we got there, and hoped we'd be going directly in for tea, but to my annoyance there was a delay as one of the guests; our own Reverend Clancy was late.

'He's been held up by a Christening,' Lady Seymour apologised. Ruby, would you be a dear and entertain the children with one of your stories?' Lady Seymour pleaded, taking me to one side.

I smiled, 'Of course, are they in the nursery, my Lady?' I asked.

She nodded.

'Can we hear a story too?' Little Violet pleaded.

Her Ladyship laughed; 'Of course, if your sister allows... what do you say Ruby?'

All of the younger of my siblings waited anxiously to hear my reply, although just why they wanted to hear one of my stories I couldn't think, as they'd heard them all before.

'Fine! Just be sure you behave,' I threatened.

I was pleased that Jack, Danny and the Davis twins, who had also been invited were being taken on a tour of the Manor by the new maid, so I didn't have to worry over them. I did feel sorry for the maid in charge of them though, as my brothers were beginning to slip back into their old mischievous selves. Still, it had been nice while it lasted, as mum would say!

It was a good hour before the Reverend turned up and we were all famished; even so, much to our annoyance, we were forced to sit through grace! But in the end, it was well worth the wait as we were treated to a variety of beautifully made ham and salmon finger sandwiches, followed by an assortment of homemade cakes, including, macaroons, butter and lemon tarts and shortbread ginger cookies; none of which any of us had ever had before; not forgetting the homemade lemonade for us, and tea for the adults. It was just about the most perfect day I can remember having in all my life and I just never wanted it to end, but sadly all things come to an end eventually. As we were leaving, to my surprise, and delight, her Ladyship asked mum if it would be possible for me to sleep over, as her youngest daughter, Florence was having restless nights, and she hoped that perhaps I'd be able to help.

Mum agreed, and so I stayed.
It did seem to help little Florence having me there as she fell asleep almost at once. I however did not find sleep so easy to come by and when I did, I was awakened in the early hours of the morning by a loud banging on the front door. Thankfully it didn't wake the children. I quickly dressed and went to find out what was going on, after all no one has visitors this early. I was just in time to see the back of a young boy as the door closed behind him; 'It's a telegram, it can only mean bad news,' the maid said as she swept passed. I had no idea what she was talking about, but a few seconds later; her Ladyship let out a wail of anguish, and I ran to see what was wrong? I didn't get far as Nannie stopped me in my tracks. 'See to the children, in case they're frightened,' she ordered, standing in front of me.

'But... Lady Seymour... is she unwell?' I asked.

She didn't reply and so I did as she suggested, going to look after the children, who were all awake by this time, standing, ghostly white in the doorway of their rooms, visibly shaking as they waited to be told what was going on.

'It's alright,' I tried to reassure them... 'It's nothing, your mother will tell you all about it in the morning; come now, back to bed with you.'

'Can we sleep in your room?' Florence asked softly, tugging at my nightdress.

'Oh yes please let us,' Grace pleaded.

Crispin didn't ask but I could tell that he thought it a good idea; 'Alright, but just for one story, then it's back to your own rooms;' I insisted.

The one story bled into two others before I managed to get them all settled and by that time the light was beginning to creep through the blinds, heralding the start of a new day, although I had a terrible feeling that it would be a day like no other! I rose early, and as I walked down the long hall, it was obvious that something serious was happening; it was so eerily quiet, there was not a whisper to be heard. Then I caught sight of the maid, her eyes were full of tears, and she shook her head at me, confusing me all the more; 'wait, please, wait,' I implored trying to make some sense of it all? She shook her head and continued on her way... now I was beginning to get scared, wondering just what might have happened that she should be acting so very strange. I was about to chase after her when Nannie came to take me aside; 'It's the master; Lord Seymour, he's dead... no one knows quite what happened, we only know that he was killed in action. It's such a terrible shame, he was a wonderful master and a very good man,' she sighed.

I fought back my tears, after all I never knew the man; but I did know his family, my thoughts flowed to them; My God! They were going to be so sad now; poor Lady Seymour, Crispin, Grace and Florence... Oh! Poor Florence, poor, poor little Florence. I began to cry then, hiding my eyes behind my apron as I ran out the door and up the drive.

Mother was shocked when I arrived back at the cottage and told her what had happened; she asked me over and over if, I was sure? When at last she believed me, she set off for the Manor House to give her condolences and to see if there was anything she could do to help. It was going on towards nightfall when at last mum returned, and we were waiting anxious to know all the details, but on her return all she would say was that Lord Seymour's death had been confirmed, and that the family were leaving for their estate in Scotland come morning.

The news not only shocked the rest of our family when we broke it to them over breakfast, it shocked the village of Sandbourne too, for the Seymour's were well liked. I felt so sad. It was going to be odd not having them around anymore, they had been a large part of the community. Our family, perhaps, more than most were going to miss them, the locals would miss them too of course but they were used to them coming and going between their estate here in Sandbourne and the other in Scotland, although sadly, this time they wouldn't be coming back. Which would of course mean that there would be a loss of many jobs as the estate employed quite a lot of local men and women, including our Janie and me. Although I was never officially employed by the estate, only by Lady Seymour herself as a companion to her children.

Our Janie was now employed by her, however, and this would be a blow to her! As for myself, I had hoped that come my 13th birthday on the 12th of September, Lady Seymour and her family might celebrate it with me, but that would never happen now. I felt a tear trickle down my cheek for the lovely family I would probably never see again. But I prayed that one day they might find their way back to Sandbourne, so we might resume our friendship.

Everything was suddenly different, where we had been so cheery just a little while ago, now we were in the depths of despair and the sunshine of this bright summer day was gone, as if winter had come early to steal it away. I don't think I have ever felt so sad, my thoughts were all about Lady Seymour and her children, knowing how very sad they must be, and wishing there was something I could do to help them.

'So, what would you like for your birthday,' Janie asked, breaking into my thoughts, in an effort to cheer me up, as we sat together on the great ragged rug in front of the hearth.

The question quite took me by surprise; 'I think I'd like a pony!' I said quite unenthusiastically. At least it made our Janie laugh; 'A pony? Oh, yes, my Lady... wouldn't we all.

I think you've been spending far too much time at the Manor, sis!' she teased. I blushed, I'd been joking, after all I couldn't even ride, but it sounded nice to have a pony.

Mum came in then with the rest of our siblings; 'I've been thinking about your birthday,' she said. 'Why don't we go out to your island and have your birthday party there,' she suggested. There was a moments silence then everyone started speaking at once, until mum held up her hand and quietened the room; 'I think after what happened down at the manor, we all need cheering up, so I suggest we use your birthday as a means to bring a little joy back to everyone.' There was a murmur of excitement and I felt a tingle run down my spine; 'Will we all be going over to the island then... you and dad too?' I asked.

She smiled... which was something she'd not done for a while now; 'Not just your father and me, but everyone?'

Janie looked at me in wonder; 'What do you mean, by everyone, mum?' she asked quizzically.

'I mean everyone, everyone... all of our friends and neighbours... the whole village,' mum said.

I leapt to my feet along with the rest of the siblings old enough to understand; 'The whole village... the whole village!' I gasped.

'Yes, everyone,' mum repeated.

'Wow! Can we do that, I mean, really, can we... how on earth would we get them all over to the island, it would mean an awful lot of rowing?' I said, in disbelief.

'Ah! Your fathers got a plan for that, perhaps you should ask him,' she suggested.

'But dad won't be home for hours yet,' Bella, groaned. 'Can't you tell us mum,' she pleaded.

Before she could reply, as if it were planned, dad came whistling across the yard, and we all rushed to greet him, everyone throwing questions at him before he was even through the door.

'What's this, a party? I know nothing about a party... who told you I did?' he barked.

We parted to let him enter, all of us looking totally confused. Why would mum say such a thing if it wasn't so? Then I saw dad wink at her and I knew he was just teasing us.

'Ah! I saw that,' I said wagging a finger at him.

'Saw what maid?' dad asking scratching his head; 'I said, I didn't know about any party!'

'Ha! but I saw you wink at mum,' I accused. 'So; it's true, we're having a party... a party on the Island.' Despite my sorrow for our friends down at the big house, I thought this a wise move by our mother, for the whole community needed something to raise their spirits now.

'What about getting everyone there, mum said that you have a plan?' Janie asked, as practical as ever.

'That I do maid... that I do,' he grinned, moving to the kitchen to take his work boots off.

Like a small train we all followed in his wake, eager to hear the big plan, but he looked fatigued, as he eased his boots off and had a good long stretch. No-one hurried him though, knowing like the rest of us he was upset by the sad news coming up from the manor house. Finally, though Janie went to sit at his feet; 'So, come on dad tell us the great plan,' Janie insisted, handing him his slippers.

He sighed, 'It's quite simple really, maid, as you all know there are a number of boats moored down at the jetty, the ones that were used at Dunkirk and left here by their owners. Well, I've had them checked and there's enough sea-worthy ones ta do the job.'

'But who will sail them... can Robbo?' I asked.

He hesitated, 'No, not Robbo, he's not here anymore.'

Janie and I looked at one another; 'Why... why isn't Robbo here, dad,' Janie asked.

'Don't you fret girls, he's joined up, that's all, he's a sailor now,' dad reassured us.

'Then who will sail the boats?' I asked again.

'One or two of the older villagers know a bit about boats and they've volunteered to take us over to the island, all we have to do is organise the party and tell them when.' dad smiled.

'So that's it settled then,' mum said; 'Janie, Ruby, set the table, its teatime,' she ordered, and just like that we were back to normal.

Well, the others were back to normal, but not me, I felt torn between excitement and sadness, not even our Janie had been thrown a birthday party like this; My God! The whole village was coming... but then there was that sadness of not having Lady Seymour, Grace, Crispen and Florence there! It just wouldn't be the same without them, it really wouldn't, not that I needed to say as much, I could see it written on the faces of the rest of my family, mum in particular. Seeing that I was close to tears mum came to put an arm about my shoulders; 'This is a difficult time for all of us Ruby, my dear and a sad time too, we have all come to think very highly of her Ladyship and her children, but we must leave them to grieve for now and be there for them should they need us,' mum said wisely.

I sniffed back a tear; 'I just can't stop wondering how they are and where they are now?' I sighed sadly, before going to help Janie lay the table for tea. Mum followed me into the kitchen where we found my sister red-eyed and still wiping away her tears, and we all came together in our grief, sobbing on each-other's shoulders, mum in the middle.

'They will be alright you know; war has a way of pulling people apart, of making widows and sometimes even orphans of many, but we survive and carry on, it's the only way,' mum sighed.

'But poor Lady Seymour, she loved her husband so very much!' I insisted.

'So did thousands of others, like the wives of the Dunkirk soldiers, and sailors and all the others who lost loved ones at sea or in the air, or during the blitz, in this insane, ruthless, bloody war.' Mum swore, taking me in her arms and giving me a hug. I could see that mum was close to tears, although her face was twisted with anger; 'bloody, bloody, bloody, war!' she cursed, clenching her fists. 'I wish I could shoot Heir Hitler dead!'

Dad came then to lead her away out onto the back yard, and I wrapped my arms around my big sister and we hugged, both sniffing away our tears, before returning to our chores. Neither of us had ever seen our mother so upset before, it was a testimony to how much she thought of Lady Seymour, and both Janie and me could relate to that.

'Do you think they've reached where ever it is that they're going?' I asked Janie.

She shrugged, 'Mum says that Scotland is a very long way from here, so I doubt it,' she replied.

The little-ones started playing up then and so we got on with the tea and tried to shut out the pain of the last few days, although that was an impossible task! Our friends were gone and we had no idea if they would ever again return from this Kirriemuir place!

Chapter 11

I hoped we'd packed enough for our long journey, I'd left most of it to the maid and Mrs Brown our cook who had offered to help, while Nannie and I saw to the children who were beside themselves with grief. We were no better though, but we dared not show it in front of them, for fear of making matters worse. I never thought to know such sorrow, for surely, we were such a happy family that nothing could possibly put a canker in our lives. But then, none of us fully understood the full-blown misery that grieving a loved one brought. But now I know what a savage stab to the heart it is and wonder if any of us will truly get over it. For my children's sake I can only pray that they will one day recover from losing their father so early in their lives... As for myself, I was sure that I never would.

The children were all so very sad as we travelled towards our home in Scotland. The news of their father's death had devastated them. Looking back... I don't know how I'd managed to tell them knowing how it would break theirs hearts. But tell them I did, because I had to, although the look of despair on their little faces was almost more than I could take. I was glad that I had Nannie to help with the children, although she was heartbroken too, for she had nursed Rory from a baby, what with his own mother dying so young. He had always been like a son to her and so her grief was more like that of a mother, than a nannie, and I accepted that. She was sleeping now, with my children snuggled all around her, and so now I could cry my own tears; tears that I've bottled up for days, not wanting to add to their sorrow.

Looking out of the car window I could see we were just arriving in Oxford, a place that holds so many wonderful memories it being where Rory and I first met. Unlike on the way down, we were not going to stop unless it was for a toilet break. We have two drivers this time, our aim being to stay on the road until we arrive at Kirriemuir, giving the children as little stress as possible.

On the other side of Oxford, I woke Nannie and the children at a garage so they might stretch their legs, use the toilet and then have something to eat from the hamper in the boot. As we travelled on, my mind started to wander, as much as I tried to keep it under control!'

It seemed like a lifetime ago now since we were travelling along this same road on our way down to Sandbourne. But, oh! How fickle life can be, we were so happy then, but of course Rory was still with us and we were all looking to the future with hope, even though he was going off to war! I recall the feeling of certainty I felt that he would be alright, after all he was my darling husband. With yet more tears I recalled what my darling husband had once said to me; 'War is war, my love, it has no favourites, death can take one man and leave the one standing at his side unharmed!'

The second driver turned as I sniffed back a tear; 'Are you alright, my Lady?' he asked. I waved away his concern and closed my eyes feigning sleep, not ready yet to answer him true. Taking a quick look at my children, my heart felt like breaking all over again, they had been so happy back at the Manor house, but now, everything has changed! Even when awake, no-one is speaking, or reading, nor even looking at the passing scenery, they are just sitting with their heads down, in a world of sorrow, even Nannie. But at least in sleep they find some solace, but there is none for me, I fear.

We drove through the city of Manchester and out the other side, with not a hint of German bombers, although a few miles beyond the city we were forced to stop and pull into a layby as there was a heavy raid, but nowhere near us, thank goodness and soon we were travelling again. Thanks to having two drivers who took it in turns, we were able to do the journey in a single day, pulling into the grounds of Kirriemuir Castle late in the evening. As I watched Nannie shepherd the children into the castle, I couldn't help but fear the worst, for now, this place did not feel the same to me, it did not feel like, home anymore! And if I felt like this, then so, I knew would the children... once this might have been Rory's home. But now that he was gone, I realised, it could never be my children's or mine.

Once Nannie had taken them up to their bedrooms, I sank onto the chaise longue and cried and cried; this was to have been our forever home; Rory's, mine and the children's. But now that would never be. Not for us, or for my Rory, for he would be buried in the far-off country where he fell, not under the soil of his beloved Scotland... I cried more bitter tears and cursed the bloodiness of war! Nannie came then to say that the children were all in their beds, and to remind me to let Rory's father, Andrew, the old Laird Seymour, know that we had arrived safely.

Thanking her; while she went to find us a pot of tea, I went to the telephone in the hall and called my father-in-law; the grand Lord Seymour, a man so like his son I thought I might break down on hearing his familiar brogue. His butler answered when I rang and so I had a moment to compose myself; still my knees went weak when I heard his voice; 'Hello, lassie, are you well... how are the wee-ones?' he asked in my Rory's voice. I almost collapsed, and couldn't answer for a moment.

'I'm holding up, Lord Andrew, although I fear my children are not and would be all the better for a visit from their grandfather,' I suggested.

'Of course, but I can'ee come, tomorrow, as I've the memorial ta arrange, although I could perhaps come over in the afternoon, for tea,' he suggested.

'The afternoon will be just fine, as the children will still be tired from our long journey and in need of a lie-in, so I'll tell them you're coming... they will be so excited, and God knows they can use some good news, we all can,' I sighed.

'Aye, that's true enough, lass, and I can'ee wait ta see you all again, now you have yourself a good night's sleep, and I'll see you tomorrow,' he said, before hanging up the phone.

I slept well that night, perhaps for the first time since the news of my husband's death. I put it down to hearing the Lairds familiar voice; like his son, he was such a good man, and I couldn't wait to meet him again, even under such sad circumstances.

For once the children seemed not quite so troubled as we waited for their grandfather to come; he was the most tactile of men, just like their dear father, demonstrating a genuine warmth, and always prepared to sit long hours with them; telling them of their Scottish heritage; of Bonny Prince Charlie and all the myths and legends of the highlands! Sometimes, I have to admit, whenever I'd heard Rory telling such tales I felt a little left out being English... but they were wonderful stories just the same.

As his car pulled up at the castle gates the children rushed out to greet him before I had time to stop them, but I couldn't scold them, they were in need of company such as his, as was I, and I all but joined them in their mould of greeting, throwing my arms around him before he'd hardly stepped from the car, trying desperately not to cry. We shared a pleasant, if sober tea together, before Nannie came to take the children off our hands, allowing the Laird and myself the chance to discuss the coming events of the next couple of days.

'It's all arranged, Lass, so there's nought to concern yourself with... the ceremony will be held in the village of Kirriemuir, from there, the coffin... empty of course, will be brought back here, to lay in state overnight, where a wake will take place, with family and friends and villagers too; for our boy was well liked by the locals,' he said proudly.

'So, the wake! How many will be coming, do you think, my Lord? Only...'

He put a hand up to stop me; 'If you're worried on the catering, fear not, my bonnie lass, for that is already in hand, with staff enough hired to see that it all goes smoothly,' he assured me. That was a relief, for we barely had enough staff to cope with our own family, let alone a host of strangers, and I really didn't want to take on any more as I wasn't sure that we'd be staying.

We were all ready when the cars came for us the next morning, although I could see by the look on the faces of my children that they really didn't want to do this, that they didn't see the point as their father wasn't actually here. Still, we all followed solemnly along behind the hearse and the empty coffin, all of us knowing that our Rory was not really in it but that we all carried him with us, in our thoughts and in our hearts. I hoped the children understood that, for it was the whole point of today.

The church was full when we arrived, with friends from the military and the local community. Sadly, though my mother and father couldn't come as both being scientists, they were shut away somewhere doing secret work and neither of them had siblings so there were not even any aunts or uncles, and being an only child myself, there was no-one else. I did notice one or two of Rory's family, from his mother's side, who were Irish, although I'd never met them myself, as strangely, none of them had come to our wedding even though they were invited. I remembered Rory once telling me that apart from his mother, whom he'd worshiped, the rest of his Irish kin were, anti, anything to do with the English, and so he had very little contact with them. As I looked them over, I noticed an elderly woman staring in my direction, I smiled, hoping for a positive response but she quickly looked away!

The Laird, who was seated behind us tapped me on the shoulder and nodded towards the lady I'd been trying to have eye contact with.

'That's, Rory's aunt Clodagh, his mother's sister, a very spiteful woman, who broke my dear wife's heart by refusing to come to our wedding, her reason being that, we Scots mingled too easily with the English,' he said, shaking his head.

'Since my dear wife passed, things have worsened between us, they refused the invite to your own wedding to Rory, and don't want any contact with your children,' the Laird declared.

'They called my son a traitor because he fought in the war on the side of the English, who they claim to be the real enemy, not Hitler.'

'Then why are they here?' I asked, a little angry and confused.

'For nothing good, lass, I'll wager on that, but I'll be keeping an eye on them, don't you worry.' The Laird assured me.

The service went off without a hitch and a choice selection of the mourners were invited back to the Castle for the wake, of whom, to my surprise the Irish congregation were part of. On reaching the Castle I warned Nannie to keep an eye on the children, not wanting them to have any more stress in their lives, and fearing that their father's, in-laws, were trouble waiting to erupt. Wisely after about 15 minutes, Nannie ushered the children away, taking them up to their playroom on the 2nd flour, and so thwarting any plans Rory's aunt Clodagh had of upsetting them.
Still, it didn't stop her and her companions from trying to disrupt the wake by arguing with Rory's soldier friends, calling them fools and worse for joining in, what they called; The English War!

As well as Aunt Clodagh there was a big burly man; her son, I learned later. He was already becoming boisterous, pushing and shoving people aside, until the Laird stepped forward.

'Clodagh!' He called, going nose to nose with her; 'Leave now, and take your son with you, or I will have you both ejected. How dare you disrespect my son Rory this way, and his good wife and children, who are your kin too, damn it!' he swore.

Although she went a little red in the face it was clear she wasn't about to back down and neither was her son, until two towering men stepped forward and physically lifted him and her off their feet and half carried them to the front door, before pushing them outside, then seeing them all the way off the property, forcing them to have to walk all the way back to the village. After they'd gone the Laird introduced me to the two giants who he'd called upon to help him;

'Lass, this, is Ralph and Barry, part of my staff and who I wouldn't be without.'

'Gentlemen, this is my son's wife, Lady Katherine Seymour,' he smiled.

They both bowed clumsily before backing away, returning to their duties of policing the room, not that it needed policing now, in fact it was peaceful enough for my children to join us and so I sent a maid up to fetch them and Nannie down.

The rest of the evening continued without a hitch until it was time for our guests to go, all promising to return the following day for the laying of the memorial headstone in the family graveyard beyond the big house. Typically, it was overcast and a little drizzly the next day as the headstone was put in its place, and the old vicar said a lament over it, praying that one day, Rory might be returned here to his final resting place, which brought a tear to all our eyes, the children as well. Later, alone with Nannie the children and the Laird, I brought up the subject of what we might do next, my children and me. Telling the Laird that I had it in mind to return to Sandbourne, which would mean closing up Kirriemuir Castle, which would also mean laying off the staff!

'We could take them with us, we still need staff down at the manor house,' Grace suggested.

'But most of these people have families close by, they wouldn't want to travel so far from them,' I insisted. 'Anyway, don't you worry about it, I'll think of something,' I smiled.

Nannie took the children away then for their lessons leaving myself and the Laird alone; 'Listen, lass, will you take a ride with me over to my estate on the other side of the highlands,' he asked.

'Right now?' I asked, a little bewildered.

He nodded, 'yes right now, lass,' he insisted.

I knew his estate of course and it was less than 30 minutes away, not another castle like he'd given over to his son and me, on Rory's coming of age, but a big grand house just the same.

'I think you'll like what I'm about to show you, my dear,' he smiled as we drove onto his grounds.

The big house was already in sight and the changes took my breath away as we pulled into the courtyard; 'Oh my, it's a hospital!' I gasped. He laughed; 'It certainly is, my dear, a rehabilitation hospital to give it it's full name. Come let me show you around.'

As we climbed from the car, I could see patients on crutches, some with only one leg or one arm, or with their heads heavily bandaged, hobbling along the paths and across the grass, with the aid of nurses and doctors, for a moment I just stood in wonder, until the Laird took my arm leading me on. If I thought the outside was good, the inside was spectacular, there was just bed after bed after bed, all full of patients attended by nurses and doctors, in long white coats... and there was a dining room and a kitchen, with cooks, and servers to alleviate the work of the nursing staff. Nothing it would seem had been over looked, it was wonderful. But why had the Laird brought me here? I frowned, 'what was he up to?' He came to stand at my side, then waved a hand towards the hospital.

'The trouble with this place, lass, is that it's too small, oh, it's great for the patients to recover in, but what we really need is somewhere where operations can be performed, we have one surgery room here, but we need more... and I was thinking that maybe, if you're in agreement, you might like to turn Kirriemuir Castle into a full-scale hospital... operations, the lot.' He suggested. I had to smile; The crafty old devil, he'd planned this all the time! It was a brilliant idea though, and it would solve my problems of what to do with the place when I went back to Sandboune. It could even mean that the staff I leave behind might be able to retrain and still have a job. As we went back outside the two giants who had come to our rescue at the wake came from the hospital and gave us a warm wave; 'Ralph and Barry were our first two patients, both having been sent to us after being almost burnt to death when the oil tanker they were on was torpedoed. Being so badly injured they were both invalided out of the navy, which suits me fine.' He grinned. 'There is plenty for them to do here.'

I watched as they headed for, what appeared to be a garden shed; 'Come on my dear, let me show you what's in there,' the Laird smiled, striding on ahead.

I was astonished as we entered; It was not at all what I'd expected; there were men in various states of recovery, some with legs or arms in plaster others swathed in bandages all enjoying a peaceful recovery; playing chess or cards, there was even a ping-pong table and a darts board, but many were simply sat quietly reading. All being cared for by nurses and doctors in whiter than white coats, moving constantly around the room, it was quite a sight, and it stayed with me all the way back to Kirriemuir Castle... 'I'll do it Lord Andrew, or rather I'd like you to do it for me, turn this place into a military hospital; it's so what Rory would wish us to do... I just know it is.'

He put his arm around me; 'Aye, lassie it is that, my boy would be proud indeed,' he agreed.

Over the next two days, between us we put the wheels in motion, or the Laird did, for I knew little about the process, but by the time my children and I were ready to leave, I had high hopes of our plan being recognised. Despite the dreadful nature of our visit here, at least we had accomplished something good, and even the children were pleased when I broke the news to them, all agreeing that it was the perfect thing to do to honour their father. I was so proud of them, that they could put aside their obvious sorrow, to applaud this project was special indeed.

It was hard to leave Kirriemuir Castle knowing that we might never return, for most of the children's lives it had been their home, mine too for that matter, but it was time to leave the past behind us... Rory would want that, want us to get on with our lives. Still, it took all of my will power not to break down crying as we drove through the great gates, perhaps for the last time! We took a more leisurely root back to Sandbourne, stopping not twice but three times, but not in any of the big cities, but in backwater villages where there was less chance of being bombed.

In spite of our less hurried return, we arrived back at our Manor house with two days to spare before Ruby's 13th birthday, an event, I knew my children were desperate to attend. Nothing seemed amiss as we arrived back at the manor house, but there was a sadness about the place now and it was something I couldn't shake off; and I had a feeling that perhaps I never would, after all this place was supposed to be a respite where Rory would return to, and where we would be a family again. I felt the tears welling up and forced them away... No! I would not go there, not today... this was our new beginning... it had to be!

As I entered the house, I could hear the children arguing with Nannie and so went to find out what it was all about, for they never fought with her.

'But why aren't they here?' I heard Crispen demand.

'They should be here, Jane in the kitchen and Ruby in the playroom!' Grace insisted.

'Yes, I want Ruby to tell me some stories,' little Florence added.

I stepped in then; 'We closed the house up before we left and sent everyone home, don't you remember? But they'll be back, I promise,' I told them.

'But it's Ruby's birthday soon, can't we send her a message so that she knows we're back?' Crispen insisted.

'I thought we might keep it a secret and surprise her on the day, what do you think?' I smiled.

It took a moment for what I'd said to sink in but when it did, they were happy with the idea. Little Florence giggled and the others went along with it, now I only hoped that we could keep that we were back a secret, for I know how people gossip in small community like ours. The difficulty was going to be how to let Iris know without alerting the rest of her family. In the end I decided the best thing was not to even tell her, which made me feel a little guilty, but that couldn't be helped, it was the only thing to do.

The skeleton staff of Mrs Brown, the cook, Wendy the new maid and the old stable hand who looked after the horses were pleased to see us back and it was one of them... Mrs Brown, the cook, who brought me the startling news of just where Ruby's party was going to be held!

'On our island!' Crispen and Grace, cried out with delight... 'on our treasure island, will Jake the pirate be there?' Grace enthused.

'Oh my! Firstly, it's not a treasure island, my dear, it's just an island, and secondly, I don't know who will be there,' I sighed.

'Our treasure island, how wonderful,' Crispen sighed... 'our treasure island and with a pirate! Wow!' he sighed completely ignoring me!

I gave up; 'but the important thing is that we don't let anyone know that we are back! Just think what a lovely surprise it will be for Ruby when we turn up,' I smiled.

The children chuckled with delight and swore each other to silence, while cook and the maid nodded their agreement, although just how we were going to prevent the gossips I had no idea. We would just have to keep our heads down and hope for the best.

Chapter 12

Janie and me are at loggerheads over something very silly, and it isn't the first time in the last few weeks that we've had a falling out, but this is by far the most ridiculous. I don't believe in fate or destiny or karma, or any of that stuff, I just think we walk are own path and what happens, happens! Now that is how I see life, nice and simple! But my sister argues that, for instance, if you gave a hitchhiker a lift in your car and it breaks down and he happens to be a mechanic, now that would be karma. Although I would call it payback for a good deed done. But then my big sister points towards Lady Seymour and of our family's interaction with her, reminding me of how it had all begun with her applying for a job at the Manor House, a chance meeting that ended with our families becoming close friends. Destiny, she calls it, well, let her think that if she chooses, I'm just pleased that we are all friends... or were,' I thought sadly.

I longed to have Lady Seymour and her family back in our lives, although I was getting used to the fact that it would probably never happen. Still, there was no harm in hoping that one day they would return, but sadly it was not likely to happen. Their loss and so their grief was much too great at the moment. It's my birthday tomorrow and sadly the last I'd heard from the villagers was that the Manor house was still empty, and so I was forced to accept that they really wouldn't be here. Everything seemed spoiled now, somehow, less fun! Damn! I shouldn't think like that. I quickly shook the thoughts away, mum, dad and many others had put a lot of work into my party; if Lady Seymour were here, she'd be angry at my negative attitude.

Come the morning of my great birthday party I was helping mum with the little-ones and despite my negativity about the party, I was excited, but so nervous too, that something might go wrong and spoil it, but fingers crossed all would be well!

'Are you all ready for school, Ruby, farmer Drake has offered to drive you in today, the Davis twins too if they're ready when you reach their place... hurry your brothers and sisters up, girl, quickly now, I can hear his van on the yard!' Mum shouted. Our Jack and Danny were messing around as usual and I dearly wished that Janie was here to help me with them, but with the Manor house closed, and having no idea when or if it might reopen, mum had found her a part time job in a café on Poole harbour.

School was simply buzzing with excitement when we got there, everyone eager to talk about my birthday party on the island, it seems as if most of the village were going to be there! Even our teacher, Mrs Hardington commented on it, after she did the register, telling us all to be sure to enjoy every moment. Declaring that she certainly would, although I had no idea she'd been invited. After the lunchbreak, I discovered that neither my brothers or the Davis twins were anywhere to be seen; knowing they would be up to no good, I reported them missing to Mrs Hardington.

'Can you think where they might have gone?' she asked angrily.
I could only shrug, as they could be anywhere, the little beggars.
'Well go and find them, Ruby, if you would, please,' she sighed.
At my side Becky raised her hand; 'Very well, you go with her Rebecca,' Mrs Hardington said, waving us away.
'Where to start?' Becky asked as we went out into the playground.

I was at a loss to know just where to begin the search and so Becky took control; 'Why don't we start up along the clifftop, after all we'll be able to see for miles up there, we might spot them!' she suggested.

As I had no better ideas that's where we began our search. It had been a long time since I'd been up along this way and I saw a lot of changes; there were now pillboxes, and machine gun posts, as well as, observation bunkers and large gun emplacements, mostly manned by the Canadian Soldiers, who'd helped to build them. After a few failed attempts to shoo us away, when we told them why we were there, they allowed us to go to the very end of the track where there was a view down to the beach. We could see as far as the middle beach, festooned with barbed wire, trenches and dragons' teeth to prevent enemy tanks from going any further. But there was no sign of my brothers.

'Let's go down for a better look,' Becky suggested.

I nodded in agreement, but as we started down the track, a Canadian Sergeant stopped us; 'Sorry girls, but you're not allowed, it's far too dangerous, you best go back the way you came,' he ordered. I quickly told him why we were there and he pointed us in the direction of one of the machine gunners, saying he thought he'd seen him talking to some young boys earlier.

Racing across to the young man we asked him about the boys he'd seen and did he know which way they'd gone; 'Ah! I remember them alright,' he growled; 'They asked about my gun, wanting to have a go with it, said that their dad had guns so they were used to them,' he told us. I was silently raging, neither of my brothers had ever been allowed anywhere near dad's guns!

'What did you do?' I asked him.

'Showed 'um the toe end of my boot, girls, that's what I did,' he grinned.

But do you know where they went?' Becky pleaded.

'Yes, I do, as it happens, first, they cadged a fag off one of my mates, then they went down into that small stand of trees, off to the right of the path down to the beach,' he pointed.

'They're in the blue bell coppice' Becky confirmed, as a local who knew her way around.

'Lead the way then Becks,' I grinned, 'Let's get the little devils.'

We smelt them long before we saw them, the cigarette smoke coming to us on the breeze, and there they were, sitting in a circle taking it in turns to have a drag on the dwindling fag, which I quickly snatched away as I jumped in amongst them.

'Well, well, boys, now this is a silly thing to be doing don't you think, not only will you all most certainly be facing a caning from, Mrs Hardington, and your fathers... I will be very surprised if any of you will be going to my birthday party,' I growled.

It was plain by the look on their faces that they hadn't thought of that; 'Do you have to tell, Sis,' our Jack pleaded.

'Of, course I do, anyway, Mrs Hardington will, even if I don't,' I snapped, angrily. This was all I needed so close to my birthday, they might be little devils, but they were my brothers and I wanted them at my party.

Together Becky and me marched them back to school, where, as I predicted they were given the cane in front of the whole class and then sent home, under the watchful eyes of myself and Becky. While my friend took the Davis twins on to their home, I took my brothers to face the wrath of mother, who was the one who usually delt out the punishment, not because dad was too weak or afraid to punish us himself, but for the simple reason that he was seldom at home. In spite of being in the bad books, everyone, including mum and dad were interested in what they and I had discovered on our journey out across the clifftop?

'Sounds ta me, mother, that we're diggin' in fer the bloody invasion,' Dad tutted.

'Mind you, the Canadians have been yur, since way back,' mum reminded everyone.

'True the Canadians being 'ere don't mean much, but tank traps and land mines, mother! I ask you?' dad said shaking his head. 'Trust me, my dear the bloody Jerries are coming,' he insisted.

'But not just yet, father,' mum said seeing the look on my face, 'we're all going to enjoy a lively party first, and bugger the bloody Germans,' she swore.

There were a few giggles from the younger ones that I soon quashed with a threatening glare, I might not carry the same menace as our Janie, but I would not stand any nonsense, and they all knew it. I had worried that part of my brother's punishment would lead to them missing my birthday party out on the island, but as much as they deserved to be punished, I really didn't want anything to mar this very special occasion. And so, I was pleased when mum ordered them back to cleaning out farmer Drake's pig styes for a month as penance for what they'd done.

'A month? That's a bit much, mum' our Jack complained, in a huff!

'I'm sorry, did I say a month... I meant two months,' she corrected, sternly.

I could see that my brother was wishing that he'd kept his mouth shut, and almost laughed at the sight of his complete and absolute misery. 'Serves him right,' our Janet muttered in my ear. Yes, it did, but I wasn't about to dwell on the subject, our Janie was due home soon and I was eager to speak with her about the party and whether she had a decent dress that I might borrow, as mine were old, Jumble sale bought ones.

'What makes you think mine are any better?' she sighed, when I corralled her as soon as she stepped through the door. 'But you're welcome to see for yourself, sis,' she offered.

I was desperate and so I looked through her wardrobe, but she'd been telling the truth sadly, there were none there any better than my own. I started to feel a little panicky, I needed a dress, and not just any dress, a pretty, birthday dress; but I had nothing, and neither it seemed did Janie. I ran to find mum in the kitchen who tutted when I told her my worries; 'With all that we have to organise you're worried about a frock? Whatever next.' I tried to explain, that as it was my birthday party, I should look nice, especially as many of my school friends would be there.

Mum shook her head; 'What a vain child you are,' she sighed. 'Come with me.'

We went upstairs to her and dad's bedroom and from the top of the wardrobe she pulled an old suitcase; 'I have an early present for you, from Lady Seymour, now I know it's not new, but it is lovely just the same,' she said. Eagerly I threw open the case, and inside was a beautiful milky white, lace gown.' I gasped; it was the prettiest dress I'd ever seen.

'It belonged to Grace and as she is just a year younger than you it should fit,' mum smiled. 'Go on then, try it on.'
Quickly I pulled it over my head, it fitted me perfectly.
Mum clapped her hands; 'Look in the mirror,' she encouraged.
I raced across the bedroom, almost stumbling to my knees in doing so... 'Oh! Very lady like, I must say,' mum chuckled. I ignored her as I stood before the old, slightly murky looking glass.
'I look like a Princess... like Cinderella!' I gasped.
'Father, Janie... everyone, come and see this,' mum called down the stairs.

Before I knew it, I was surrounded by siblings and then dad drew me to him and bowed; 'My little Princess,' he smiled. 'Can I have the first dance?' I smiled, dad loved music and would often have us stand on his feet and dance us around the room to whatever was playing on the wireless. I blushed and the others all laughed and we had such a good night, although I couldn't help thinking about poor Grace whose dress this was and how sad she must be right now.
'It's the price of war,' mum sighed, sadly, guessing my mood.

I knew she was right it was happening all over Europe. People were being killed or displaced everywhere. All anyone could do was pray that it didn't happen to them. In the meanwhile, we just had to live our lives the best we could and enjoy every moment of normality that came our way.

My thoughts turned to the Seymour family and the sorrow they must be feeling, and realised how lucky we were that dad had not been called up to fight, after all he was not yet 40. Thankfully his reserved occupation and his health issues were what kept him from. Perhaps my sister Janie was right and it is all about luck and Karma! I mean, how fortunate we were to be living out here on this heath, where the war for the most part has passed us by. Oh! We have had our moments; like when the heath-land caught fire; and then the time when mum caught the two German airmen hiding out near the house, but all in all things could have been worse... so perhaps providence is indeed on our side and keeping us safe. I took a deep breath, trying to remain positive, especially in front of my siblings, the angry hurt inside of me threatening to erupt and spoil everything. Although it was my birthday, I felt so sad knowing Lady Seymour and her family wouldn't be here to celebrate it with me, once more I cursed the bloodiness of war.

The night before looking from my bedroom window, I had seen that all along the coast, everything seemed ablaze, with ragged waves of fire reaching up seemingly to ignite the sky itself... how could we plan a birthday party in the wake of all this... how could we? And yet, here we were in the aftermath of all that terror, doing just that, planning a birthday party! it, was crazy! Just crazy! Of course, to add to our fears, we all wondered if this air raid might be the beginning of their planned invasion, that, ever since Dunkirk we'd been expecting! But once the bombing finally stopped and with no sign of an invasion in its wake, life returned once more to its strangely unstable self.

Now I could again worry about petty things like my birthday, wondering if in fact we should go ahead with it, as there was talk of some of the cottages in the village being hit. 'Yes, some of the cottages in the village were hit last night,' mum confirmed at breakfast. 'Thankfully though, there were no casualties as everyone was safe in their shelters.'

That was good news at least, but I wondered if the villagers would be willing to leave their homes so soon after the raid? Still, the preparations for the coming party continued in earnest; mum was busy baking, and I had no doubt, so to were most of the ladies in the district. While dad and the rest of the men, during every minute of their spare time prepared the boats and saw to the tents on the island.

Whenever he found time to return home, I demanded an up-date, and was surprised and delighted by all he told me! Apparently, some of the stalls from the fair were still in the village and they had now been transported to the island, along with their owners... it was all very exciting. All of this just for me? It seems unreal, I thought, as I scrubbed the sleep from my eyes... and they've let me sleep in too, I smiled, well that made a change!

'It's your birthday!' I told the image in the mirror as I tried to see if I looked any older, I was a little disappointed, it was the same me... but not quite, for now I was 13, I smiled at the thought. It was about then I realised something. The house was very quiet, usually the little-ones would be wailing for their breakfast and my siblings would be noisily squabbling at the kitchen table, but today there was just an eerie silence. To my surprise when I walked into the kitchen there was only dad there, drinking a cup of tea, which was very peculiar because by this time he had usually gone off to work.

'Happy Birthday maid,' he smiled on seeing me.
'Where is everyone?' I frowned.
'On the island of course,' he grinned.
I looked at the old mantle clock and saw that it was only 7:00 am, 'What already?'
'It's going to be a strange old day, and that's a fact, daughter,' he laughed.
'It's only a birthday, only my birthday, and not a very important one,' I said shaking my head.

'You're, wrong maid, for starters every single one of your birthdays are important, if not to you, they are to mother and me. And this one matters because it's a bit of sanity in a mad, bad world. What's more you get ta share it with all our neighbours. Now if that don't make it important, well, I'll eat my ol' trilby,' he said, ruffling my bed-hair.

I nodded and gave him a hug.

'Besides,' he grinned, 'Here be some others who think tis very special.'

At his words; a group of people trooped out of the living-room; I gasped in disbelief; It was Lady Seymour, along with her children, Grace, Crispen and little Florence, who rushed into my arms as soon as she saw me, followed closely by the older ones.

'My Lady, this is such a lovely surprise,' I cried.

She looked heavy eyed, but she gave me a smile; 'The children insisted we got back for your birthday, and I was pleased to do so.'

'Do you like the dress, does it fit... I do hope it fits?' Grace worried.

I gave her a hug; 'It's perfect, and thank you... Oh dear!' I suddenly realised what a mess I must look, I was still in my nightdress and I hadn't yet washed or combed my hair! I was about to run off when dad, caught my arm; 'Sit, maid, eat your breakfast, then you can see to yourself; Her Ladyship just called in, to have a quiet word with you alone,' he said.

Lady Seymour smiled; 'The children and I will wait with your father in the other room,' be assured, we're in no hurry, so, please take your time, and if you should need assistance getting ready, I'd be pleased to help.' I watched in astonishment as she went with dad into the living-room with children tagging, reluctantly on behind. I don't believe I have ever eaten hot porridge so quickly in my life, I simply woofed it down in a matter of minutes then grabbed the kettle of ready boiled hot water from the range and ran up the stairs to my bedroom.

Filling my wash basin to the brim I set about washing the wrinkles of sleep off myself and was sat on the bed in my undergarments when there was a gentle tap on the door. It was Lady Seymour. 'Come let me brush your hair,' she offered, reaching for the brush on the bedside cabinet; I blushed as I noticed that her hands were shaking.

'Are you alright,' my Lady?' I asked bending my head towards her to make it easier for her to brush my hair.

She reached around to squeeze my hand; 'I will be, my dear, we all will be... in time!'

My dad and the children were waiting as we came down the stairs and I only wished my own siblings could have been here, especially our Janie, she'd have laughed herself silly to see me looking so haughty. But she'd have been so proud too. The carriage to take us down to the jetty where the boats were moored was already at the door, I hoped dad would be coming with us but he said he'd see us later as he had things to do. At the jetty, a large boat was waiting to take us over to the island, where I could see, even from where I was that much had been transformed. There were large tents and other structures and more people milling about than I thought possible to fit onto such a small piece of land. Even as we set off, I could see figures waiting at the water's edge and quickly recognised them as my very own brothers and sisters, they were all waving frantically and jumping up and down, I only hoped that none of the little-ones would fall in!

As we pulled alongside the tiny berth, I stepped aside for Lady Seymour to go ashore first, but she refused, insisting that I go ahead of her; 'This is all for you, Ruby, enjoy it,' she whispered.   Blushing profusely, I went on ahead of her, and was instantly swarmed by my dearest family, who all fussed around me like bees around a pot of honey.

'Happy Birthday, our Rube', Janie smiled coming to kiss me on the cheek, and then she whispered, you'd better make sure I get as good a party when it comes to my birthday, Sis... or else!' She winked and laughed, before making room for the rest of the family to greet me.

As I looked around, I could see just about everyone that I knew from the village along with school friends and dozens more that I didn't know at all, or at least didn't recognise. Finally, Mum came forward carrying a birthday cake, complete with 13 candles and everyone cheered as I blew them out... it was the most perfect day. 'It's not real,' Mum whispered as we embraced, 'it's made of cardboard, ' she confessed.

I burst out laughing and gave her a hug; 'It's perfect mum... just perfect.'
And it was, all of it, just about as perfect as it could be, as a chorus of; 'Happy birthday to you,' rang out across the island, and I was lifted aloft by none other than dad, who'd arrived on the very next boat and Mr, Drake, who seemed a little sad. I prayed that he'd not had any bad news about his son, Robbo! But no! I would surely have heard if anything had happened to him, being that our families were such good friends, with that I put the idea from my head.

After the last boat arrived from the mainland and all the fuss died down and everyone was either eating or playing games, mum took me aside; 'This isn't just for you daughter, take a look around, some of these good people have had very little cause to smile of late, never mind let their hair down... no, this is for everyone, even her Ladyship and her young family.' I reached up and kissed her on the cheek; 'And you made it all possible mum, thank you.' She smiled; 'Your father too, I'd never have managed without him organising the boats and the tents and getting the fairground people to go along with it all.'

'Where is dad? I should thank him too,' I insisted.

'He was over by the coconut shie... or rather, the turnip shie, should I say,' mum laughed.

Leaving her to see to the food, I went to find dad. He wasn't where we thought, he was with Janie, trying to shoot down tin cups with a pellet gun... and he wasn't very good at it!

'You should stick to rabbits,' I heard Janie tease. 'You haven't hit anything yet?'

With that dad picked her up, put her over his knee and slapped her backside; 'I reckon I have now, don't you maid,' He laughed.

'Oh! dad, I'm not one of the little-ones you know,' Janie blushed, looking around to see if anyone had witnessed her embarrassment. On seeing me her blush turned to a scowl.

'Well, I don't know about you, girls, but I'm off to find a hot potato and a few beans, and maybe a glass of beer too,' dad grinned. Even before he was out of sight our Janie had hold of me threatening all kinds of punishment should I tell the others what dad had done to her... I just laughed, if she thought I wasn't going to share this with all of our siblings she was fooling herself, and no amount of threats would stop me.

I was on cloud nine, this was the best birthday ever, for a moment I stood absolutely still, taking everything in; music was playing, people were dancing and laughing and eating and drinking, just having fun. It was just a moment in time though; I realised that if I looked too deep into the faces behind the masks many of the guests were wearing, I would find tragedy and sorrow, for like, her Ladyship, many here had lost loved ones to this bloody war.

Despite that the party continued at a pace, until finally with the approaching darkness and with the blackout about to be enforced it was decided that it was time to call it a day. Slowly, one by one the people came to wish me well and to thank mum for all she'd done, before they climbed aboard the waiting boats and headed back to the mainland. Finally, there was just us, my family and me, and Lady Seymour and her three children. They were standing by the last of the boats as I approached and seeing me; Grace, Crispin and Florence came running over to say their goodbyes, all of them close to tears, as was I.

'There, there, we'll see Ruby soon, I'm sure we will,' Lady Seymour promised them.

I took that to mean that she'd be wanting me back at the Manor house to entertain her children, and that just made the day that little bit more special. I watched their boat cross the water to the mainland and saw them climb into their carriage all waving franticly as it pulled away, taking them back to the Manor house.

Now, with everyone else gone and the boat having returned for us, we took one last look around at the empty tents and the ghostly silent fairground booths, before setting off for home.

'Your father and the men will be back tomorrow to clear everything away,' mum reassured me.

It was hard trying to return to normal after that, for weeks, all the people in the village and just about everyone talked about was the party on the island. Strangely we heard not a peep from the manor house, and I was all for going down to make sure all was well with them, but mum said no! 'Grief can come in stages,' she explained; 'And in different ways to different people, we must let them heal, they'll let us know when they want us back in their lives,' she insisted. I understood, despite her Ladyship's outward show of normality, I had witnessed the sadness behind her eyes and behind each smile; the children too were still much troubled, and needing time to heal. Although I believed I could help in that cause I obeyed mum to the letter, knowing her to be wise in such things, wiser than me anyway. With that in mind I gave the Manor house a wide berth, even though I longed to go back to how it had been before Lord Seymour's untimely death.

It wasn't until weeks later when we heard rumours of big changes happening down at the Manor that we had cause for concern, although mother was adamant that we stay away, saying that if Lady Seymour wanted our help, then she would ask for it.   But I wasn't so sure, a lot had changed since she'd lost her husband... she'd changed, and it was no good mum saying otherwise, why, her Ladyship had even left the committee... after all their achievements too. That to me said it all, something was very seriously wrong, and regardless of what mum said, I was determined to discover what!

Just how to go about that however I had no idea and so I turned to our Janie, who had just come in from working in the café on Poole Harbour and was very cranky indeed.

'Why ask me?' She snapped, impatiently. 'I thought you were her best friend?'

'Oh, don't be like that, Janie, help me,' I pleaded.

She sighed and gave a tired yawn. 'Ok, here's what I suggest... Go and ask her to her face, just what's going on... that way sis, you'll be getting it, from the horse's mouth, as they say!' she yawned.

She was right! I went to bed that night with a new resolve, tomorrow I would go down to the manor house and confront Lady Seymour, after all we'd once been so friendly and she'd been so lovely at my party. Why would she suddenly cut off all contact with our family... with everyone, her committee ladies too, it just didn't make any sense, unless her grieving bent towards their being alone! But that was not the Lady Seymour that I had come to know, she would never cut off all contacts with her friends and colleagues without a very good reason, and I meant to get to the bottom of this in spite of mum telling me not to.

Chapter 13

As the Lady of the Manor, I have responsibilities, I know this, but I can't simply turn the page and carry on as if nothing has happened. I've lost my husband, my soul mate, and nothing will ever be the same again, and yet I have to find a way to move forward, for the sake of my children if nothing else! And I do have a plan, or rather an idea of how to do that, but first I have to know if it is feasible, or simply a silly scheme born out of desperation. I know how my friends and fellow committee members must be taking all of this, they must be in no doubt that my grief is in control of my life. How can I tell them that they are wrong, without betraying the new plans I have for myself and for my children? If I should tell them, would they even understand, or put it all down to my heartache.

Sometimes life has a way of repairing itself, of undoing... well, perhaps not undoing, but showing you a new way, a different path that you need to take if you are ever to overcome great loss and bereavement, and take your next step towards a more acceptable future. God knows it's what I want, and more importantly it is what my children need now in their lives. Like myself they will never get over the loss of Rory, their father and my beloved husband, but we must somehow carry on.

I have to admit to being lost and rudderless for a while, after hearing of my husband's death, drifting on a tidal-wave of grief, wanting the world to go away, to leave me alone with my darling children. I'd even contemplated shutting us all away, up on our highland estate, to take no further part in the cruelty of this bloody awful war we are in the midst of, but that will not do, there has to be another way... and then I had an idea. Ever since my return from Scotland there has only been one thing on my mind, could I repeat what the Laird has done to his grand house, and is already in the process of doing with mine and Rory's castle at Kirriemuir... can I turn Sandbourne Manor house into a hospital?

There is no doubt in my mind that it's what I want, but will the authorities allow me to do it, that's my major concern. However, I do have Laird Andrew on my side, and rightly or wrongly he has clout, and so I pitched my plan to him. He thought it a splendid idea and began using all of his many contacts to make sure that I would be successful in my endeavour. But I have to say, right now it seems a rather long process, or perhaps it isn't, and it's just me being impatient, either way it's a worrying time, especially without my friends to share the burden with.

I have thought about telling the Miller family, as Iris is such a wise woman and would I'm sure help me carry the load, but in the end, I thought better of it, though I know not why. With every day that passes however the secret that I've only shared with Nannie, lies ever heavier on my mind. Not even the children have any idea of my crazy plans, neither do any of my committee friends. They surely by now must be thinking that the party on the island was but a respite for me, and that in truth I am still drowning in grief and that is why I cut off all contact with them. To my shame I have allowed them carry on believing that while I make my plans. Even when I severed my links with the committee, I gave them no reason why. But it had to be done, for the good of my future plans, which I am in no doubt will be all consuming once I set them in motion.

I promised myself that once everything is agreed with the department of Heath people and my Manor house is given the status of being a new hospital, I will tell everyone. The trouble is it seems to be taking rather longer than I hoped it would! So impatient am I that yesterday I rang the Laird to get his opinion on why they are keeping me waiting. He simply laughed down the phone and told me it was always like this, that bureaucrats are notorious for the time they take over such matters.
'Just wait, Lassie,' he chuckled; 'just wait!'

Despite my impatience though, a few days later, and things began to come together. I received a letter! And now, today, hopefully, will be a big step forward! A man from the board of hospitals is on his way to access whether my Manor House can indeed be turned into a hospital. Over the past few weeks, I have been in constant contact with my father-in-law, the Laird of Kirriemuir, who has been busy pulling strings on my behalf.

'He's here my Lady,' Nannie, called from the hall. I sat nervously waiting for the maid to show him in, going over in my head all the Laird had warned me to expect.

Rising, as the gentleman was shown in, I crossed to welcome him; 'Please, take a seat, sir, would you care for some tea and perhaps a biscuit?' I offered.

'No, Madam, I would rather we start if you don't mind… not that it should take very long, this is rather a small manor house to be turned into a hospital, if you don't mind me saying.' He sniffed.

What a rude man! I thought. How dare he. Biting back an equally nasty retort, I forced a smile; 'It really is much bigger than it looks, sir, would you like a tour,' I offered.

'Yes, but shortly, if you don't mind, first I have some questions; 'Do you have anyone in mind to run this hospital? Should we allow it to become one, of course,' he asked; 'Obviously you can't run it yourself, after all, you have zero experience,' he tutted.

I was in two minds whether to have him shown the door, but I held my temper in check, although only just, he was such an irritating little man!

'I will have a fully trained nursing staff along with doctors and specialists to deal with the patients of course, but I would expect to supervise the running of the house,' I insisted.

He raised his eyebrows at that; 'Perhaps you would show me around then?' He said, getting to his feet. I have to admit to being very angry by the end of our tour as he was not satisfied with anything, picking fault with the bedrooms, the hallways, the stairs, the Lounge and the Drawing room, and just about every other room I showed him, not to mention that he felt the kitchen to be too small!

As I watched him climb into his car, his weasel like face set in a scowl, I was in two minds whether to continue with the project or not, but after sitting down with my children to have tea, I calmed down and decided to call Laird Andrew and tell him of my experience.

To my surprise he laughed; 'That'll be Ratty Morgan; Now don't you worry, my dear, we'll see you get your hospital,' he assured me.

As he sounded so sure, I decided it was time I broke the news of my plans to my children and then to my friends, especially my friends, after all, dropping out of the committee the way I had was just not done. I owed them all an explanation... but perhaps I should wait just a little longer, to be sure.

The following day however, much to my delight, I was asked to send an outline of how the hospital would look once all the rooms had been finished and that was something the Laird had prepared me for by sending me his very own Architect to draw up the plans, which I had ready for just this occasion, along with a list of the number of nurses, doctors, surgeons and other staff, to run the hospital, with myself as supervisor. It all seemed perfectly straightforward to my mind, until I had a phone call from the hospital board, firstly with the good news that my plans had been excepted and that we could begin the change of use, but secondly that a fear had been raised about my qualifications to oversee a hospital. In spite of my anger at the latter argument, I decided for the time being to ignore it and begin the laborious task of turning my home into a hospital.

I thought my children might be unhappy with the change but instead they were thrilled, saying that of all the things we'd done for the war effort, this was by far the best. Which put my mind to rest. Now all that remained was to call a committee meeting, even though, officially I was no longer a member and let them all know just what was going on?

As usual, Iris was late, and Amber, Betty and Stella, by the time she finally arrived, were on tender hooks, waiting to hear what it was all about.

When I told them, they were shocked into silence, until Amber queried; 'Where on earth did all of this come from?' I told them of the Laird and all that he had accomplished in Scotland and how he was at this very minute changing my and Rory's old castle into an operating hospital and of how that had inspired me to want to follow in his footsteps.

'With Sandbourne being where it is, I imagine a hospital so close to the front will be a welcome addition for the care and well-being of our injured military men, be they soldiers, sailors or airmen.' I explained.

'Yes, yes I can see that,' Amber agreed, enthusiastically.

'But where do we come in to it?' Stella frowned.

I sighed; 'I don't really know yet, but I think I might need a lot of help with this project... if, that is I'm allowed to be a part of it myself.'

'What do you mean, my Lady?' Betty asked.

'Well to tell you the truth, one of the men from the hospital board in London, thinks that I am not qualified to be in charge of the hospital when it's finished?' I told them.

'Well, bugger that, my Lady,' Iris barked. 'This will still be your home, I take it?'

I nodded, and led them up the stairs and onto the long gallery, off of which were the rooms that myself and the children would use, all of which were separate from the main hospital. While we were there, I got out the plans to show them what my house would look like when it was finished, every inch of it was mapped out, with a diagram showing just where the beds would be, and how many would be in each room, also where the surgery was to go and a list of how many nurses and doctors we'd need. It was all finely mapped out and they gave a general nod of approval.

'The trouble is, ladies, I fear that this unspeakable man might be right! Perhaps it is too much for me to supervise this hospital once it's up and running, I might be experienced in running staff, but not on such a scale... and should I even try,' I sighed.

'Now none of that, My Lady, and anyway, you're not alone, you have us! I take it that's why you asked us here... and I have an idea,' Iris smiled.

Everyone's eyes were on our heroine of the Heath; 'It's simple really, you just make each of us responsible for a couple of wings of the hospital, nothing to do with the patients, just to make sure of the hygiene and to the food side of things. If we can keep on top of all of that it will take the weight off the doctors and nurses... we would of course need to work with one of the sisters on each ward, and they would tell us just what they wanted us to do... but it would save them having to do it themselves.' It was simple, but it was perfect and I decided to write it up in my next report to the Hospital Board and hope that they think the same. In the mean while we could at least get on with changing my home into a hospital. To begin with there was a lot of clearing out and storing to be done, and so I hired a removal company, recommended to me by Laird Andrew, for their careful diligence when it comes to handling antiques. Many of the valuable item were rehoused in the attic and squeezed along the sides of the long gallery, but the bulkier furnishings and the many family portraits were taken away to secret storage facilities, that only I knew of, although in case anything happened to me, I told the children.

With the house cleared of unnecessary clutter, I gave the go ahead for the builders and decorators to come in. We had a date of the 20th of October for the hospital to be ready for inspection and so it was with great urgency that we pushed the workers to complete their tasks. To my great relief everything was finished with a day to spare, and now all we needed was the beds and the equipment to be delivered and all would be ready.

'Are you going to sit in on the interviews for the nursing staff,' Amber asked as we were watching the painters finishing the whitewash on the walls.

I shook my head; 'I'll leave that to the sisters, they'll know what they're looking for, I'm sure.'

A few days earlier two sisters had been sent to us by the hospital board and they were just the perfect fit, understanding and approving of all we'd put in place, and I had every confidence in them.

'Right now, I need to inspect the beds they've sent us, while you all return to your wards and make sure everything that's needed is there, if not chase it up, and report to the sisters.' I advised.

Three doctors were expected today and I was on the alert for them so that I might be there to welcome them aboard their brand-new hospital, I just prayed that they'd approve of all we'd done. So far everything was looking good, until that is, I saw a big black car out of which climbed my nemesis, 'Ratty Morgan,' as the Laird had named him, his face set in its usual scowl!

I walked out to meet him with a feeling of trepidation; this could all go terribly wrong. He grunted an acknowledgement in passing, as he marched through the front door, with me trailing in his wake, given no time to say a word to the other occupant who stepped from the car behind him! Unlike his companion though he did smile and bow his head courteously, before following his companion into the hospital. From his very first steps along the hallway; Ratty Morgan began tutting, and scribbling notes in his little black book, causing me to feel very nervous, it seems, despite all our hard work, he was unimpressed. And as we reached each ward where I had ladies of the committee stationed, his tutting grew ever louder, and I feared for the worst. In my heart I felt that he was not going to approve it, and that, with not a sign of remorse, was what he declared as we returned to the front door.'

'Not at all acceptable,' he said, passing me his little book of complaints. 'Untrained people in charge of hospital wards, what on earth are you thinking, Madam,' he glowered at me.

I was too shocked and angry to reply; but there was no way I was going to take this after all our hard work, and was about to respond when the other gentleman spoke.

'Mr Morgan, she is not a Madam, she is Lady Seymour; and what she has here is a first-rate hospital that any nurse, doctor or surgeon would be proud to work in, so I suggest you go out and wait in the car... oh! And take this with you,' he took the note book from me and passed it back to him.

I watched in utter astonishment as the little man went sheepishly out of the door.   'But... surely, he's, the man from the Hospital Board and has the final say?' I questioned.

He smiled, 'well actually, my Lady, I have the last say, you see, I am to be the head surgeon here,' he explained.

I could have kissed him, but I stopped myself, not so my committee ladies though, each in turn pecking him on the cheek, Iris, embarrassingly giving him a great big bear hug. But while I blushed, he simply laughed. And so, it looks as if we have ourselves a hospital. The only thing missing is a Matron to be in charge of the whole of the nursing staff, but unsurprisingly, our new head of the hospital already had one in mind.

'Her name is Evelyn Chase, I've worked with her in London and not only is she excellent at her job, she is not afraid to call it as she sees it, and so I feel would fit in perfectly with the rest of your, um! ladies,' he smiled.

It was the way that he smiled that got me thinking that I'd met him before somewhere, but I couldn't quite think where that might have been.

'I'm sorry, sir, but I don't think I know your name?' I said, a little embarrassed.

He smiled, that funny crooked smile that I'd recognised; 'Actually, we did meet once, my Lady, but it was a long time ago, at a gymkhana, I believe, you beat my sister to the first prize, as I remember. My name is, Sir Edmond Bruce.'

The name didn't ring any bells to me but it was nice that he remembered me after all this time.

'Don't worry my Lady, we were just children, but it will be nice to get to know you again, I have a feeling that I am going to enjoy working with you and your committee ladies.'

Suddenly, I felt so much lighter, as if a great weight had been lifted from my shoulders; Ratty was gone, our new head of hospital is an old acquaintance of mine, even if I can't remember him! If I felt more at ease, that really didn't last longer than a day or so, as now that we were on the map, our beds started filling up very quickly, until we were so busy there was hardly time to think.

But it was a good feeling, for in some way I felt that I was helping to secure the memory of my dearest husband Rory. The pain of losing him would never leave us, but this grand endeavour I was embarking on, might help a little... just a very little! The fact that I was still in contact with his father the Laird, also helped, as we have a good understanding between us. We even swap patients if ever we have any from his neck of the woods and he has any from down our way. It's a nice arrangement and it keeps Rory firmly in my heart, for he would love all of this.

Not so long ago I would never have dreamt that this was possible? I wasn't even sure if the idea of Amber, Betty and Stella, controlling the wards, would work! But it does and it is taking so much off the shoulders of the nursing staff. It is all running just perfectly. And with Iris having an important role in the kitchen, ordering the hospital food, under cook's close supervision! All is well, and I even have her daughter Jane back working for me. Despite all the positives I knew there were bound to be the odd bump in the road, there always is! Our bump came in the form of a dreaded telegram that arrived for our brand-new Matron! Thankfully it was not one of the worst telegrams, not like the one I'd received, no one had died on this occasion. But I was disappointed by her news when she told Sir Edmond and myself, as we sat in his office going over the daily time-table; 'I'm so sorry,' she sighed; 'Only I've been called back to London, with immediate effect,' she said handing me the telegraph. Something about this just didn't feel right, but no matter who he spoke to over the phone, Sir Edmond could not get to the bottom of it, and so Matron was duty bound to follow orders, and leave.

Stranger still was the arrival of her replacement the following day; a, Miss Vera Trench, she was a burly sour faced woman, who wore a scowl throughout Sir Edmonds morning briefing, and looked at my committee ladies as if they had no business even being in the hospital.

I would have taken her aside and asked what her problem was; but today of all days we had a hospital ship dock across at Poole harbour, and were told to expect up to 60 new patients and we had beds for only 10, it was quite a dilemma.

'We will just have to refuse to take them,' our new Matron snapped, when she heard the news.

'But we can't just turn them away!' Amber argued. 'We could be killing them?'

'That's the trouble with untrained people like you and your... committee friends, you think we can save everyone, when the truth is, we should only concentrate on the one's worth saving, the strong ones, who once healed can be sent back out to fight again!'

When Amber told me what had been said, I was all for confronting her, but Sir Edmond intervened; 'Let's wait awhile and see what she's really up to,' he suggested. 'In the meantime, we need about 50 beds and somewhere to put them... any ideas?'

'Well, we could try the Poole storage warehouse for the beds and equipment. As for where to put them, if you give me a few minutes to speak to Iris, we might have the solution to that as well,' I smiled.

While I went to find Iris in the kitchen, Sir Edmond contacted the warehouse, before hurrying after me with the good news that we could have up to 70 beds if we need them. Meanwhile when I finally reached the kitchen there was pandemonium, and there was no sign of either Iris or her daughter Jane; and cook, was fuming; as she told me that our new Matron had dismissed them both! Now I too was fuming. But there was no time to find and deal with Miss Trench, that would have to wait, I had something more important to ask of my old friend Iris when I found her, if she'd still help me now!

I drove like my friend Amber would have, given the circumstances, like a bat out of hell, pulling into the yard of the house on the heath with a screech of brakes, before leaping from the car almost before it had stopped, bringing my friend Iris rushing out to see what was wrong.

'She sacked me, she did, that bitch... sacked me... I felt like smackin' 'er senseless,' Iris barked.

'I know my dear, and trust me you are not sacked, but right now I need to know something... does Pirate Jake still have his big tents?'

'Aye! He does, my Fred helped 'im store 'em away for the winter, in one of farmer Drakes barns... but why, are you thinkin' of putting on another show of some sort, my Lady?' she asked.

I smiled and told her my idea; 'I thought we'd put them up on the side lawn next to the house, between them I'm sure they'll hold at least 50 beds... what do you think?' I asked.

'And I suppose you'd like my Fred and his friends to deliver 'um and stick um up?' she sighed.

'Right away, if possible, my dear, we've 50 or 60 patients to find room for, patients that our new Matron says we should turn away... she's up to something, Iris, I can feel it in every fibre of my body... and you're not fired,' I called as I got into the car. 'Just watch your back... and watch her for me, will you?' I pleaded as I pulled out of her yard.

I drove more slowly back to the hospital needing time to think... and to wonder just what our new Matron was planning, for it was clear that she did have a plan.

Sir Edmond was pleased when I told him my idea of using the two borrowed marquees, and showed him exactly where they were going to be put.

'That's perfect Lady Seymour, why, the nursing staff would hardly need to go outside at all, simply through the French windows and walk into the tents.'

'Hardly a good environment, for the patients, I would have thought?' Miss Trench sniffed, eavesdropping on our plan.

'But much better than leaving them to die, don't you agree, Matron,' I said, desperately trying not to show my anger. Without answering, she turned angrily away, and as I watched her go, I knew I just had to be rid of her, and the sooner the better, for it was clear she meant mischief here!

To my delight however; when I walked around the ward's I saw that the nursing staff were all coping well, still using the blueprint that my committee had put in place, when we first opened the hospital.

It was a pleasure to see it still working so well. But when I questioned them, I discovered that not everything was running so smoothly, and once again the problems seemed to emanate from the kitchen. The complaint being of the poor standard of food of late. How was that possible when cook has been with me for years, I wondered as I went to check for myself. As I walked into the kitchen, I was confronted by a woman I'd never seen before.

'Is cook here yet?' I asked her.

'That's me, I'm the cook!' she replied confidently.

'No... no, you are not, I mean the real cook, Mrs Brown,' I snapped angrily.

'Mrs Brown's gone, she was caught stealing I believe and so Matron fired her... um! Who are you anyway?' she asked irritably.

Over in the corner of the kitchen, I heard Amber draw in a deep breath, in anticipation of the fury that must have been clear by just looking at my face. That was it, rather rougher than I'd intended I ripped the apron off her waist; 'I am Lady Seymour, now get out, and if you see the Matron tell her... no, no need, she's here! You! Get out!' On seeing me the new Matron made to turn back the way she'd come, but I caught her arm; 'Would you please explain why you took it upon yourself to fire a member of my staff, without first consulting me?' I was fuming and ready to take matters into my own hands and simply sack her on the spot.   Iris came hurrying in just then, along with the local constable, who to my astonishment, promptly, placed his handcuffs on Matron, before leading her away! It was all most peculiar.

'What on earth is going on, Iris?' I asked my friend.

She smiled; 'When you asked me earlier to keep an eye on Matron, there was actually no need, as I've been watchin' her from day one, and it's a good thing I 'ave, for I discovered that along with an accomplice, she's been buying black market food for the hospital, and none of it any good.'

'So, that's why she wanted you out of the way then Iris, she must have suspected that you were watching her, the nerve of the woman... and did they catch whoever it was helping her?' I asked.

She grinned; 'now you're not going ta believe this, my Lady... it was non-other than your favourite man from the hospital board, Mr, bloody, Ratty Morgan, yes, it's true, my Lady, I saw the two of them meetin' up, it was him alright.'

I could scarce believe what she was telling me; true I didn't like the man, but this! Really? I took a deep breath; 'Well then, we'll not have to worry about him anymore, as he's facing a long stretch in prison as well as a hefty £500 fine or more.' I watched with an air of disbelief as Miss Trench was taken away no doubt to join her friend in the local police cell. After that, things began to return to normal, all be it that we would soon have two marquees out on the side lawn, each with at least 30 patients, and now with no Matron to over-see them.

Seeing my look of despair, Sir Edmond said; 'Have no fear, my Lady, I have contacted the hospital board and told them the full story, and even as we speak; Matron Chase is winging her way back to us,' Sir Edmond, smiled. 'It would seem that it was Mr Morgan's doing to have her removed from here and have his own cohort replace her. A plan, no doubt, he'd had in mind from the very beginning, hence all the aggravation he gave you, my Lady.' I could scarce believe that there were people out there so cunning and artful that they would stop at nothing to further their own ends. It was quite sickening and I thanked the Lord for the goodness of the people that I'd found since coming here. Not just the Miller family but my committee friends too; Amber, Stella and Betty had proved to be a boon, and had not failed to help me no matter what the cause... if I called, they came running as true friends always do, and they are all true friends.

It was Sir Edmond who brought me from my revery with a timely reminder; 'Please don't forget, my Lady that we are expecting the 50 or 60 new patients by this time tomorrow,' he reminded me. Smiling I assured him that it was all in hand, confident that indeed it was, I had asked and was promised two large tents.

Everything was down to Iris and her Fred now, if they didn't come through then all was lost, we'd have all the beds and patients but nowhere to put them? But Fred and Iris hadn't let me down yet and we'd planned fairs and fetes and a dance together, and so a couple of hospital wards would be a piece of cake... wouldn't they?

Despite a little doubt, mainly due to the shortness of time that we had, I somehow knew that we'd succeed in the end, we always did! And when, a little later that day a column of tractors and trailers came trundling over the brow of the long driveway, I knew I was right to have faith in my friends and fellow committee members. Now all we had to do was assemble them and fill them with beds and all the rest of the equipment needed and that, as they say, would be that!

For most of the afternoon and into the gathering dusk, I watched as Fred and Pirate Jake and their men put the tents up, ready for the nursing staff to tell them where the beds and the side cabinets should be placed.

As there was no time to run electricity to the tents it was decided to use Tilly lamps, one to every other bed. It was agreed that doing it that way it would save the nurses having to carry one themselves. By the following morning everything was ready for inspection and I was pleased that Sir Edmond thought that we'd done a good job and that the tents were fit for purpose. It was getting on for late in the afternoon when the ambulances and trucks began to arrive with the wounded, some badly injured needing surgery, others hurt, but on the mend, yet still in need of convalescing. Then there was the shellshocked ones, more in need of mental care than a bed in the hospital, but in need of some care just the same. And so, I had my hospital and it was all I'd hoped for, and now I meant to make it the best damn hospital in the country, in the name of my Rory, God rest him!

Chapter 14

'Ruby Miller, give it time!' I told myself as I brushed my hair in front of the long mirror, before going down to see to the breakfast. It's often difficult to accept change, and often we fight it tooth and nail as if it is the very worst thing in the world, but sometimes, despite our worst fears it can be uplifting too, and that, more than anything else is what I see going on down at the Manor House. I was sceptical at first and not a little put out when mum told me the truth about Lady Seymour turning her house into a hospital... what about the children? What about me... would I ever again be called upon to read to them or play with them? I was disappointed to say the least and a little angry too, our Janie was back working for her Ladyship, but no mention had been made about myself, surely the children still needed entertaining? I'd known something was going on, ever since her return from Scotland, Lady Seymour has been a different person.

Not made whole again, yet... mum had said at first, before it had come out about her hospital idea. But now, there is no doubt in my mind that things for her are looking brighter, and that's good, it might open the door for me to go back to my old role of reading for the children. To my delight, of late Nannie has taken to bringing, Grace, Crispen and Florence up to our house on the heath to keep them out from under everyone's feet. It's an arrangement set up by our mum to give her Ladyship time to concentrate on the hospital. With Nannie giving Crispen, Grace and Florence home school lessons, out in our kitchen, away from the hustle and bustle going on down at the hospital makes us all feel as if we were doing our bit.

Sometimes my siblings would join in, and I was surprised at how many of them actually enjoyed being taught by a posh Nannie. In return, they repaid her kindness by taking her and Lady Seymour's children off across the heath through the tangled woods, and across boggy ground, which the children just loved, and Nannie barely tolerated.

With Janie mostly at work, I find myself more and more in charge of our siblings now, but thankfully Nannie is my saving grace and even she is partial to my stories and so I am able to keep everyone amused before they return back to the Manor house. Although one of the tales I told, I realised at once that I should not have told. I could see by the look on Nannie's face that it disturbed her. It was the true story of when my siblings and me went hunting for the Germen airmen, before mum and I found them the following day near the house. It was a tale that no one knew about, we had all made a pact, not to say a word about our adventure in the woods, and now I'd broken that pact.

'You went out on your own to track down those Germans?' She gasped, drawing her charges closer to her side. 'Wasn't that a little reckless, Ruby?' she said. 'You could all have been hurt, or even worse, killed!' she shivered.

What a fool I was, not even mum knew the truth of that day. Janie will slaughter me for giving our little secret away, but it was too late now to take it back, Nannie knew it all, and she didn't look in the least pleased.

'I do hope you'll spare Lady Seymour's children such trauma,' she implored, drawing them closer about her still.

'Oh! I'd love to capture some Germans!' Crispen said quite seriously.

'It sounds so exciting,' Grace sighed. 'I wish we could have been with you.'

When, finally it was time for them to go home I knew that Nannie would tell Lady Seymour about what we'd done and that she might decide her children were not safe in our care and it was a worry I carried with me, until a few days later, when her Ladyship asked to meet with me. I realised at once how worried she must be, if she was interrupting her work schedule to speak with me, especially as her new hospital had just received a huge influx of patients.

'Well, Ruby' she sighed as I met with her in the great hall. 'You must promise me that you will never put my children in harm's way... hunting for Germans indeed,' she tutted.

I felt myself blushing, it did sound rather foolish coming from someone else; 'You could all have been killed, child... does your mother know what you did?'

I shook my head; 'Please don't tell her, my Lady, she will think it's all her fault, that she has failed us in some way, or set us a bad-examples perhaps, which is so not the case, Janie and me just wanted to protect our home and our siblings.' I tried to explain. But even as I said it, it sounded ridiculous.

'But that's not your job, my dear, keeping the family safe and protected is for your dear mother and father, your job is to see to your siblings needs, nothing more.'

I stood in front of her dreading the worst, believing that my time as a companion to her children was over and who could blame her, what me and my siblings did that day in the woods was stupid to say the least.

'Alright now, I've said enough, Ruby. Although Nannie has her doubts about whether or not you are a suitable companion for my children, I believe you have learned a lesson here, now run along, you'll find Grace and Crispen in the playroom, Florence is with Nannie, exploring the hospital.' She smiled. Before seeking out Grace and Crispen I went to apologise to Nannie for my silly actions on the day we'd hunted the Germans, promising her that it would never happen again, and that I would never put her charges in any danger. I think she believed me, but I knew that from now on she would be watching my every move around Grace, Crispen and little Florence. But I didn't mind, for I truly had no intention of repeating my foolishness and could only reflect on how idiotic it had been.

'Ruby!' Nannie mused, a little later; 'Have you ever given a thought to telling some of your stories to the patients... not the very sick one's of course, but perhaps those relaxing in the library or out on the veranda, I'm sure there are many in need of being taken out of themselves for a while,' she suggested.

It made me think... 'but what stories would I tell them, they're grown men after all?' I asked.

Nannie didn't hesitate, 'Take them back to their childhood; read them; Peter Pan or Robinson Crusoe perhaps... after all, I've always found that men are just little boys at heart.' She smiled.

After having a word with the new Matron, Evelyn Chase, who got the sisters on the wards to pass the word it was agreed that I would be in the library tomorrow, Wednesday, after tea to read to anyone who was interested. To my surprise when I arrived the room was full for my first reading; and I'd chosen the story of Robinson Crusoe. The reason I chose that particular story was because it still reminded me so very much of my own life out on the heath, where we could go days without seeing a single soul. By the end of my first reading, it was clear that it was very popular and it was suggested by Matron to make it a regular after tea event and so I roped our Janet into helping me, as she was as good at reading as I was, and so we took it in turns. It was while I was handing over to my sister one day that I first caught sight of my two troublesome brothers, lurking about in the great gallery.

'What the hell are you doing here?' I demanded, grabbing them tight before they had the chance to make a break for it.
'Ouch! Get off, we work here!' Danny whined.
'Work here! You two... who on earth would employ you, and anyway you're both too young, so out with it, what are you really up to?' I demanded.
I'm sure Danny was about to tell me until our Jack shook his head in a warning for him to keep quiet, and so he refused to say another word.
'Alright boys have it your way, but be prepared to answer some questions when me and Janie come home, now clear off, the both of you before I get our big sister up from the kitchen to interrogate the pair of you... go on, scoot!' I barked, shooing them towards the door.
'And they actually said that they worked at the hospital... the cheeky little beggar's,' Janie growled as we were walking home from the hospital after our shifts had finished.

On entering the kitchen, it was suspiciously quiet with not even the little-ones crying out; but our brothers were around somewhere and we'd find them! It was Bella who gave their whereabouts away, poor Bella, she could never keep a secret!

'Come on Bella, we know you're covering for them... so, where are they?' Janie insisted, standing threatening over her.

'They're in their room and the doors shut and they won't let anyone in, and I don't know anything else, they just told me to go away,' she shrugged.

'The little devils are up to something, Sis,' Janie mused... 'but what? And where are the little-ones... Bella, where are the little-ones?' She demanded to know now that we realised, they were missing.

'Oh! It's alright, mum has them with her down at the farm, I don't think she wanted to leave them here without you or Jane being around.' She shrugged.

We both gave a sigh of relief, our Bella was very nice, but she was not able to see to the little-ones on her own yet, and the boys certainly couldn't.

'I think we should creep up to see what our darling brothers are up to,' Janie said, leading the way up the wooden stairs. The door to their bedroom wasn't locked but it was firmly shut and we had to push hard to open it, still there seemed like there was nothing to see when we did get in, the boys were just perched on the end of the bed, talking, although they stopped speaking as we entered.

'Alright, little brothers, out with it, our Ruby tells me that you told her you both have jobs in the new hospital, is that true?' Janie demanded to know.

Jack and Danny simply hung their heads refusing to answer her; 'Hah! I knew it was a lie,' Janie snapped. And for lying to us you get to do chores; there's logs to chop and coal to bring in, and the water needs fetching up from the well, and when you've done that the air-raid shelter needs reinforcing,' she ordered.

'But it's too hot for wood and coal and the shelter looked fine the last time we were in it,' Jack argued. I could see out of the corner of my eye our Danny nodding in agreement, the silly boy!

'Now let me see... did mum suddenly put you in charge... did dad fall off his tractor, bang his head and declare that you were now head of the family... well did he?' she screamed at him. He shuffled his feet and shook his head.

'Well get on with it then,' Janie snapped, clipping them both around the ear.

'I wish everyone would leave my ears alone,' Jack whined. 'I swear one of these days one or the other of them is going to drop right off,' he groaned.

'Perhaps that will be today, brother, if you're not careful,' Janie threatened.

We watched as he and Danny slunk out through the kitchen door onto the yard, despondent at first, but not for long; 'Whoopee!' I heard Jack cry out. 'We've got a job!' It was all I could do to stop Janie from rushing out after them.

'Can you believe it!' she barked, angrily.

I shook my head afraid to reply, when our Janie is in this sort of mood it's wise to say very little, just nod and agree with her, which is what I did as she grabbed my hand and led me into the kitchen. 'We should box their ears until they tell us what they've been up to?' she raged.

I was more cautious 'Perhaps we should wait and ask mum Sis,' I suggested. 'I'm sure she'll know what's going on down at the hospital.'

For a moment I thought she was going to erupt all over me, instead she went quiet, then nodded; 'I'm still going to make the little devils pay though,' she insisted, striding out into the yard. I turned back into the house to begin our evening meal, which was my job today. Beyond the noise of the pots and pans I was using in the kitchen I could hear our Janie bellowing orders to Jack and Danny... I smiled; 'my, was she going to make them pay for their cheek!'

It was the very next day when mum called Janie and me aside; 'I thought you both should know that Jack and Danny have been asked to help around the hospital, the Davis twins too...' Both my sister and me gasped at that.

Before we could comment however mum continued; 'They will be helping the staff with the patients, nothing technical, just running errands, you know, buying items the patients might want from the village shop... like chocolate, cigarettes, newspapers, and that sort of thing... she laughed then... 'Girls, did you really think that they actually did have a real job at the hospital?'

I felt myself blushing and glance at Janie who was also red faced.

'No, of course not, I mean, who would give those two a job,' I laughed half-heartedly.

I looked at Janie and she smiled; 'mum!' Do our Jack and Danny know that it's not a real job?'

Mum laughed; 'Not yet, I'm about to tell them;' she said.

The boys had been joined out across the yard by the Davis twins, and were kicking an old ball around. They stopped when mum approached them, I was half expecting to hear a cry of protest at the news she gave them, but instead they whooped with joy, all four of them?

As mum came back, she shrugged; 'Boys! I'll never understand them, your brothers are perfectly happy to work for free at the hospital... it's doing their bit, they said!' With that she went back inside leaving Janie and me shaking our heads, wondering just what our brothers and their friends were up to, because, we were both convinced, they had some dastardly plan! But for the time being all we could do was wait and hope that whatever it was, it wasn't going to backfire and bring shame on the rest of us.

Three days later while cleaning the boy's rooms I found an old sweet tin, it was full, not of sweets but of all sorts of odd things, and had been secreted away under Jack and Danny's bed. With as little fuss as possible I took Janie up to see it.

'Oh my God! The little devils have been stealing from the patients,' Janie gasped.

That had been my own first thought, but as awful as they sometimes where, our Jack and Danny had never struck me as being thieves, and I said as much.

'Then where did it all come from?' Janie insisted, angrily.

I shrugged and sorted through the items again; there was a French cigarette lighter, also a long cigarette holder, two penknives, a handful of coins, mostly halfpennies and farthings, a wad of foreign stamps and several hat badges, along with the only thing I was sure actually belonged to our Danny; a pair of wire-framed reading glasses complete with the blue case that we all knew so well! So damning was the evidence that we knew we had to tackle them about it, as we knew mum and dad would be heartbroken to think that their sons could do such a thing.

Stealing from injured service men was about as low as it could get.

'It's not what you think,' Jack protested, when we finally confronted them.

'Oh! Really, then just how is it?' Janie challenged aggressively.

I quickly stepped between them to calm everything down.

'You stole it didn't you? You should be ashamed of yourselves, the pair of you... I've a good mind to set the police on you... I would if it wasn't for the shame it brings to our family.' Janie shouted.

I'd never seen our Janie so mad; she was raging, and it was all I could do to stop her from beating the pair of them. Suddenly, Jack turned on her; 'It's not stolen... none of it, mostly it's gifts, given to us by the patients we run errands for, we don't steal them, we don't even ask for them. The men we help simply want to thank us, that's all', he protested angrily. Both Janie and me were rendered speechless by his outburst; 'Some of the things I can understand, but why would they give you a lighter and the cigarette holder,' I asked at length.

'Can I tell them?' Danny asked his brother.

Jack nodded, shuffling his feet nervously.

'One of the Doctors heard about our Jacks fear of the bombing and recommended he should start smoking to steady his nerves.' Danny explained.

Jack immediately punched him on the arm; 'I'm not scared of the German bombing, alright,' he snapped. 'It's just the noise, you know our Rube, I'm the same as you,' he said.

I could relate to that only too well, I hated loud noises... all loud noises! Although no-one had ever suggested that I should take up smoking.

Janie sighed; 'Sorry, Jack, I guess I got it wrong, tell us about it.'

'There's not much to tell, really, mum was there, and...'

'What... mum was there, she knows all about this,' I interrupted.

Jack nodded; 'It was her who told the Doc of my... well you know, that's when he said I might try smoking to steady my nerves, he even gave me a pack of cigarettes and the holder... he said, using the long holder was healthier!'

'What about the lighter, did he give you that too?' I asked.

'No, that's French, I was given it by a French pilot in the burns unit when I was running errands for him, he said it was something to remember him by.'

Janie and I looked at one another before moving as one to give our troublesome young brother a huge hug, ignoring completely his howl of protest and his demands for an apology.

'Ah! If only we could apologise, little brother,' Janie sighed, but you're such a little rogue; nine times out of ten, you're guilty as charged.'

He started to object but I pulled him up short; 'Um! What about the rest, the money, the stamps and the penknives?' I asked.

I saw him glance towards our Danny; 'Ah meeting!' I pounced. 'Come on, spill it,' I demanded.

'Alright, I admit, we might have taken the penknives... but they were in the lost property bin, and no-one claimed them, so after asking around to find their owners we kept them... the coins and stamps were gifts though, I swear it,' Jack said.

As we left our two brothers, I think we were both relieved that there was nothing to worry mum and dad about. For as good as our lives were out here on the heath, we were still living on the edge of an area the Germans meant to flatten and that was worry enough.

With the mild weather, it was no effort to have to cross the heath every day to catch the bus to school. And at the weekends, we would go down to the backwater and row over to our island, knowing that soon the winter weather would catch up to us and so prevent us from going. Now and then mum would pack us up a bit of food and we'd sleep over, reliving our previous times there, and we'd tell stories and play games or generally just fool around. There were still nights however when we found ourselves huddled together in the shelter as the Germans tried to bomb us into oblivion and also nights when we found ourselves trapped on our island unable to make it back home. Strangely though, we were never really frightened by the experience, as to us the war, although close to us, was all happening in a different world, far removed from ours, even if the ground beneath us shook with the explosions out across the bay.

Often, we would lie quite still on the edge of the water, counting the bombers as they swept along the coast. Sometimes we would pray aloud that they'd used up their bombs before they reached us, on Portland or Weymouth! Hoping that they didn't have any left for us! Which was a cruel, awful thing to wish for, and my only excuse is, we were so very frightened! But regardless of our wishes, of course, they always did have enough bombs for us, and the sky above our heads would burn blood red as fingers of fire from the burning ships and cottages leapt high, turning our world into a kind of living nightmare!

Through all of this however, I remained strangely confident, if not for our chances of winning the war, then for my families, ability to survive whatever is thrown at us. Having our island retreat helps a lot, for as silly as it might sound, we felt strangely safe there, even though it was closer to Poole Harbour that the Germans tend to target a lot! My siblings liken it to Never, Never, land, in the story of Peter Pan, somewhere beyond this world, untouched and untouchable by the events playing out all around us, and it was good that they thought that way, for it gave both them and us peace of mind.

One night, as I held tight to Janie's hand on one side and Janet's on the other, while we lay flat out on our backs on the grass on our island, I was convinced that nothing short of death would ever come between them and me. My sisters were my stalwarts, my rocks and I would give my life to keep them safe! I had tears in my eyes as finally the all clear sounded, and the drone of the enemy planes faded into the distance... once more we'd survived. For myself spending what little spare time I had across on our island was a pleasant change from school and the hectic life down at the hospital. Helping to entertain Lady Seymour's children and, reading stories to the patients, which was becoming ever more popular and keeping me and our Janet very busy, and was very tiring, for we still had our chores to do at home!

I wasn't alone in thinking that life at the hospital was becoming unbelievably hectic, with all the extra beds full and a shocking lack of nursing staff, both Janie and me were being called upon to do far more than we should; besides working in the kitchen, Janie was also helping on the wards, taking the food out to the servicemen, even feeding those unable to feed themselves. While I, as well as keeping the patients spirits up with my stories; saved the nurses a job by making sure the water jugs are always full, and by emptying chamber pots, which was a never-ending task. Non-the-less I do it willingly, without complaining for these brave men were here because they fought for our freedom and for the freedom of others, all across the world.

It was during one of my spells of fetching clean chamber pots for one of the wards that my two brothers came hurrying to find me; a look of worry on their faces.

'What on earth is wrong now?' I asked with trepidation hanging heavily on my words.

For a moment they hesitated looking at one another, neither it would seem wanting to say what the problem was; 'For goodness' sake!' I snapped, impatiently.

Our Jack finally broke the silence; 'It's our friend Robbo... we've found him... he's here,' he finally blurted out.

'What? Robbo is here, in this hospital, where did you see him... is he badly hurt?' I asked, all in one breath as I pinned my brother to the wall so that he couldn't escape my questioning.

'Ouch! Lay off sis,' he yelped, wriggling from my grasp.

'Well, where is he?' I demanded.

Jack shrugged; 'He was being carried from a truck when I saw him, you need to ask one of the nurses on the front line, sis, or Matron,' he suggested.

Leaving them to finish running whatever errand they were on, I hurried off in search of our friend, praying that he wasn't too badly injured.

Knowing that most of the new arrivals were destined for the two big tents on the side lawn, I made my way there.

'Hello my dear, you've heard then?'

I was studying the list of new arrivals on the front desk, and lifted my head, recognising the voice; It was farmer Drake! 'Yes, sir, how is he?' I asked, a little afraid of the answer to my question.

'Well, he's alive and that's good, he's lost an arm mind, has my poor lad,' he grunted, trying desperately not to shed a tear in front of me.

'Oh! That's so sad; But he will he be alright?' I stammered, tears welling up unbidden, to run down my cheeks and onto my white blouse.

Farmer Drake placed a hand on my shoulder; 'He'll pull though, my dear, he's a strong boy, though he'll not be able ta row you and your sister to the island anymore,' he sighed sadly.

'Is he in there?' I asked, pointing at the first of the two tents.

Farmer Drake shook his head; 'No, he's in tuther one, next to the operating theatre, in case they need ta do any more work on his arm.' He sighed, 'but he's sleeping peacefully enough now, so I'll be leavin' im ta rest for a bit, I just needed to know that he was truly alive... and he is.' I watched him go through into the main hospital, then followed on behind knowing it was pointless to try and see Robbo yet, after what his father had said, instead I headed down to the kitchen.

Our Janie was as upset as me on hearing the news of our friend, wanting to go at once to check on him, but in the end decided, just as I had, to wait.

'So, what happened to him, do you know, sis?' Janie asked as we strolled out into the garden to be by ourselves for a while.

Picking absentmindedly at the hedgerow as we walked, I shrugged; 'Your guess is as good as mine sis, all I know is that he was in the merchant navy.'

'Ouch!' I cried out as a thorn from the rose bush stabbed into my finger.

'Don't you ever learn, sis?' Janie tutted.

I sighed, sucking on my finger to numb the pain; 'I guess not, but enough of me, we should be talking about Robbo and making plans to keep an eye on him,' I insisted. Janie nodded her agreement, but added; 'I won't be able to help you though sis, the kitchen is so busy at the moment, in fact I should be getting back, rope our brothers in or even our Janet,' she suggested, taking her leave of me.

That evening, when we were all at home and sat around the big kitchen table, I brought up the subject of Robbo and was not surprised that news of him being at the hospital was already known by mum and dad and the majority of my siblings.

'Once Mr Drake says it's alright, we should take it in turns to go and see Robbo when he's up to having visitors' Jack suggested, stealing my thunder.

Despite my disappointment at not being the one to have said it first, I worked out a plan with the rest of them so that our friend would be well looked after by us all.

Almost a week passed before I was told by Mr Drake that it was now okay to visit Robbo, but it was with trepidation that I approached his bedside, as I was to be his first visitor, apart from his mum and dad, and I was pleased about that. But much to my annoyance when I arrived at his bedside, our Janie was already there!

'Hi sis, I just thought I'd pop in before we got busy in the kitchen,' she smiled, through my anger.

Ignoring her one-upmanship, which clearly this was, I went to say hello to Robbo. It was plain to see that this wasn't the same young man who had taught Janie and me how to row the boat! His face was shallow, and gaunt, his cheekbones sharp and protruding through sea weathered, leathery skin that bore no resemblance to the healthy tanned look of the farmer's son that we all knew so well... and his eyes that had once danced with the sheer pleasure for life, now looked right through us as if we were not even there. I felt myself welling up and so turned away.

'Please, Ruby, don't,' he pleaded softly.

Janie gave me such a look and I felt myself blushing; 'I'm sorry Robbo,' I said, trying to pull myself together. He gave my fingers a gentle squeeze and held on to me; 'I will come back from this, girls, I promise,' he sighed. 'And one day, I'll even let you row me across to your Island,' he sighed; 'as I fear my own rowing days are over,' he said looking down at his missing left arm.

Janie gave me a look that said; don't you dare cry! And so, I bit down hard on my bottom lip, as she leaned in and smiling, assured our friend that one day soon we'd be pleased to row him to our island.

'When you do, as I know how you like telling stories on your island, perhaps I'll tell you everything that happened to me, but that's for then, right now, I'm just pleased to be home and I'm pleased to see you both.' He added, before closing his eyes and drifting to sleep. Janie and I crept away then both teary eyed but also grateful that our friend had come home, knowing only too well that many other young men hadn't and never would.

It was looking to continue being mild for the rest of October, and the patients in the hospital were enjoying the spell of warm weather, even those out in the tents, in spite of the fact that everyone worried that they might not be warm enough.

As it happens it wasn't the weather that was the worry, it was the lighting in the tents, bought with what little money was left by the disgraced former Matron and her crony. Many of the cut price Tilley lamps were proving to be faulty and in need of replacing. Mum and Lady Seymour, were seething but there was nothing to be done about it as the culprits were already in prison.

Day upon day we visited Robbo, our siblings too, when they were allowed, and farmer Drake and his wife were grateful to us all for that, as they did still have a farm to run, and quotas to stick to, and the people from the government brooked no excuses, not even a badly wounded son. After all there were many of them across the land, but the nation still had to be fed. Talk like that made me so mad! The bloody Government officials, sometimes, in my opinion, pushed too much, of course people had to be fed, but those of us who worked on the land had lives that were equally affected by the war… not that you'd know it, listening to them. Mum said for us to ignore all that nonsense and just do what would be best for our friend Robbo and his family, and so we arranged a timetable with the Drake's, so that their son was never short of visitors, and it was while Janie and me were there together that, Sir Edmond Bruce, the head of the hospital, paid Robbo a visit; 'Jane, Ruby, can you give us a minute?' he asked. He sounded serious and I was a bit worried that something was wrong with Robbo? None-the-less, Janie and me left them to talk, while we went for a stroll through the grounds, where in summer the foxgloves, carnations, roses and Begonias and a host of wild English flowers, filled the air with their fragrant perfumes, alas all were withered now. Still the nurses with patients, or patients on their own, never seemed to mind the lack of flowers. They all appeared to be enjoying a rare moment of tranquillity in a world gone quite mad.

Later, when we returned to our friend's bedside it was to find him deep in thought; 'You look a little confused, is anything wrong?' I asked him

'Thick doctor, said, they want to order me an artificial arm from Chard town?' Robbo told us as Janie and me gathered by his bed.

I looked at Janie and she looked at me; both of us a little confused, as Robbo didn't seem very happy with the news. 'Well, Chard Town is not that far from here, you know.' Janie tried to reassure him. I went to sit on the bottom of his bed; 'Don't you want one, Robbo?' I asked him.

He shrugged; 'I don't know, I feel that I'll be a bit of a freak, that's all,' he sighed. 'That people will point and stare!'

'What nonsense!' Janie snapped, angrily.

I knew what was coming and thought about trying to steer things in a different direction, but there was no stopping my big sister when she got going.

'And do you think they'll not stop and stare at a one-armed man?' she fumed. 'Of course, they will, people are the same the world over, the truth is they'll stop and stare all the more, the way you are now.'

'Oh! Janie, how can you say such a thing?' I cried.

'No, she's right, thank you Jane, at least with an artificial arm I'll be able to do more to help dad around the farm, and who knows, I might even be able to row the two of you out to the island,' he smiled.

Despite what he said, I was not happy with our Janie, how could she be so cruel, this was something Robbo would have to live with forever, and if he was unsure about it, that was perfectly understandable. 'I should go,' Janie sighed, seemingly oblivious to her hurtful words. I nodded, not trusting myself to speak; How dare she treat our friend so badly, practically calling him a fool for not immediately jumping at the chance to have a synthetic arm!

'Stop that now, Ruby, your sister is just telling it as it is, as she always does,' he smiled. Although I nodded in agreement, I couldn't forgive my big sister so easily as that. She spoke as if having an artificial limb was an everyday option that everyone had to make, but it's not, it's an alien thing really, an unthinkable choice to have to contemplate. But Robbo was right about one thing, for someone as practical as our Janie, it's straightforward; you either have one or you live without the use of an arm!

I shook my head, it really isn't that cut and dried, it's about having to live with it for the rest of your life. Oh, I know there are many things we might have to live with; like, ginger hair for instance or freckles, or big ears or a big nose, or being born black or brown! But none of those things are of our own choosing and I guarantee if asked, everyone, of the; ginger haired, freckle faced, big eared, big nosed, black and brown people would rather be like they are than have an artificial limb... So there Janie! Despite my annoyance however, later, when the surgeon came to see him, Robbo agreed to be fitted for a new arm and, as it was a good month since he'd lost his real arm, it was agreed that the procedure could start at once. He was a brave lad, was our friend and the only thing he asked for while he was waiting was that me and our Janet to tell him some of our stories, and for me to make mine as scary as I like, which suited me just fine, although one or two of Robbo's fellow patients looked suitably disturbed by my ghostly tales, when I began to tell them.

It was approaching the end of October, and already one or two of the patients were talking about Christmas, and asking if the hospital had any plans for it. In truth I can scarce believe that almost a year has passed already! And what a year it's been. Sometimes I think that this must be a magical place. How can we possibly have gone through so much in such a short amount of time? I set my mind back to the beginning... our arrival onto the heath, seeing our white-walled cottage for the very first time... rowing to our island with Robbo, sleeping over with my siblings... oh! Also helping mum capture those Germans, and finally, meeting and getting to know Lady Seymour and her family, which was yet another adventure, what with the fair and the fete and the grand dance at the manor house... and the sad news of Lord Seymour's death.

Now, that was a heck of a lot to cram into a year and a bit, but we'd done just that. Having arrived here in September 1940, which looking back, seemed like a whole other time now, when we were different people, just a simple family of farmhand refugees, doing as the Ministry of Agriculture instructed.

'You alright, Ruby?' Robbo asked, breaking into my thoughts, as the pause in the story I was telling grew a little to long for his liking.

'Sorry, just thinking,' I sighed.

'Well, save that till you get home, girl, and get on with the tale!' the patient in the next bed complained.

I laughed and Robbo gave me a cheeky wink; 'It seems yore in great demand, Rube', best do as our friend says... and get on with it, I guess,' he chuckled.

It was good to see him so cheerful after all he'd been through, and tomorrow he was expecting the delivery of his new arm from Chard town, and with that he was hoping to finally go home, I sighed, I would miss him... miss this, my reading to him, but at least he was on the mend. I made sure I was there the next day, when they came to take him to have his new arm fitted and laughed when he came back and showed off with a clumsy wave. Farmer Drake came then to take him home, and along with some of the nursing staff and Lady Seymour and Sir Edmond Bruce, I waved him goodbye, although he and I had already arranged to meet up one day soon, and along with our Janie, celebrate his return home with a trip out to our island... if the weather permitted and he was up to it.

With the end of October, we were halfway through Autumn and still the weather was holding up well, so that there was still a window of opportunity left for our promised excursion over to our beloved island with Robbo. Although Mr and Mrs Drake were against the idea, along with our own mum and dad, who all said it was too early after him coming out of hospital. And so, Janie and me decided to leave it up to Robbo, and we asked him, standing, at the backdoor of his home, down on his father's farm, and with a cheeky grin he said; 'Okay girls let's go!' As Janie rowed us across the bay, I saw that our passenger was close to tears and I realised what a momentous occasion this was for him. Many of his shipmates had not made it home; I let my eyes travel beyond the bay, out across the mighty ocean; unlike our dear friend, they were lost out there somewhere, their bodies just flotsam now! Reaching out I held on to him as we docked and then climbed out of the boat and onto our island.

His eyes were dancing here and there, as if he were remembering all the times, we'd rowed here together and walked out across our island, just the three of us, as we were doing now. This was just as I'd pictured it, from the moment of his return back into our lives, and I began to cry, as I never truly believed we ever would make it to this wonderful moment. As we strolled along, Robbo was full of himself, laughing and joking about our early days, when, he confessed, he had serious doubts whether Janie and me would ever master rowing!

'Oh! Robbo... did you really? You mean you thought we were rubbish?' Janie glowered... 'Now you should be careful how you answer that,' she warned him. 'Unless you can swim back with only one arm!'

'Janie,' I blushed. 'You can't say things like that!'

Robbo laughed; 'I think she just did... and, no I don't want to swim back with one arm, thank you very much, and so I apologise for calling your rowing rubbish... even if it was,' he added quietly.

Both Janie and me laughed aloud, hooking up with him as we walked, although I was conscious that I was on the side with his false arm and worried about it coming off if I tugged too hard.

Glancing across, I could tell that our Janie knew exactly what I was thinking and I blushed, hoping that she wouldn't say anything, which she didn't, but Robbo did! 'You go careful there, girl, you're holdin' on a little too tight and I'd hate for my arm to... um! Come off!' he grinned.

I immediately let go, and both Robbo and Janie laughed; 'I was only kidding, Rube, it's perfectly safe, I promise,' he chuckled.

I blushed, again, and Janie came to swap sides with me; 'There, is that better Sis?' she teased.

In a bit of a huff, I went to fetch the picnic from the rowing boat, although it was far beyond the picnic season, we'd thought it would be nice just the same. As we sat down by the grey, soft rolling sea, we ate the sandwiches mum had made for us, and drank the cold bottle of tea, from tin cups, enjoying every moment, as we told Robbo all about the party, we'd had here for my 13th birthday.

'Your folks brought a fete all the way over 'ere? Wow! Now tha's what I call's special... and all the villagers came too, you must 'ave felt like royalty itself, Rube,' he grinned.

'And she's not let any of us forget it!' Janie growled.

'And I don't blame her,' Robbo sighed... 'and to think I missed all of that... I'm sorry Rube, but, happy birthday for then, anyway,' he apologised.

We talked then and Janie and me told him all about what he'd missed by being off at sea.

'And you didn't even save me a slice of the cake!' Robbo pouted; feigning hurt feelings.

I laughed, 'Well even if we had, it was made of cardboard, so it wouldn't have tasted very nice.'

We all chuckled at that, before getting ready to call it a day; the tide was coming in bringing with it a cold grey sea mist, which already cut off the view of the mainland. We found our way easily enough though and after pulling the rowing boat ashore for the winter, we all walked back to the farm where Robbo's mum was waiting with a hot drink and a piece of her home- made sponge cake, half of which she gave Janie and me to take home for our siblings.

'When you give them the cake, tell them it's a thank you for them visiting my boy in hospital,' Mrs Drake smiled warmly. 'And thank you, girls, what you did today will help my son no-end, now perhaps we can go back to something close to normal,' she said with a tear in her eye.

As Janie and me walked up through the heath on our way home a dog began to howl somewhere in the distance and I had the strangest feeling come over me. According to mum and dad, to hear a dog howling like that is a sign of a death in the family! A load of old nonsense I'm sure and as we reached the yard, I tried to shake the thought away, but for some reason it simply would not go!

Chapter 15

With all that was going on it was easy to forget that I was the Lady of the Manor and so had responsibilities to the community to contend with. Things like cutting the ribbon to open the new town hall in Dorchester, something that had completely slipped my mind until the mayor rang to remind me. Because of that near catastrophe, I decided to ask Nannie to check my daily time table for me, so that in future I didn't miss any important meetings. As pleased as I was with the progress of the hospital, I knew I had achieved it only by standing on the shoulders of giants; or so the quote goes. In my case standing on the shoulders of my father-in-law, Laird Andrew Seymour, of Kirriemuir, without whose guidance I knew, I would still be floundering in grief and misery. I vowed, that before the day was out, I'd give him a call and invite him to come down on the visit he'd promised myself and the children.

I felt that we were ready for his inspection now, although we did still have teething problems, thanks mainly to the bogus Matron and the cheating man from the hospital board. But somehow, we're coping and all of that was behind us now, and we'd even managed the emergency influx of 60 or more new patients, not to mention the one needing a new arm!

'So, if I come down, it will have to be for the whole of Christmas mind, for I'll not make the long journey for an overnight stay, daughter-in-law,' the Laird insisted when I called him.

'The children will just love to have you here for Christmas, Laird Andrew, as would I, and we'll do our very best to give you a wonderful Hogmanay,' I assured him.

'A good Hogmanay you say, do you English even know what that is, lass?' he joked. He was the replica of his son, my Rory, right down to his wicked sense of humour.

'We'll give it a go, I promise you,' I laughed. 'Just let me know when to expect you, my Lord?' I asked before he hung up.

When I told the children, they were ecstatic at the thought of having their grandfather visit us for Christmas, now all I had to do was arrange something special for him and for that I needed help! Since the early days of the hospital all of my committee ladies had been busy doing their bit to keep the wards going, leaving no time for fund raising or anything else. But now I needed them to come to my rescue. I had a plan to not only entertain my father-in-law on his visit to us from Scotland, but to entertain the hospital patients too. First though I needed to call a committee meeting, the first for many months, but as my ladies were to be found mostly close by, it didn't take much organising, although as they gathered in the grand Gallery it was clear by the puzzled expressions on their faces that they had no idea why they were there.

Even Iris was on time and that was unusual, although in fairness she'd only come up from the kitchen, and she like the rest was eager to hear why I'd called this committee meeting.
'Alright, then ladies, here's the thing; 'My father-in-law, the Laird Andrew, without whose help we would never have got this hospital off the ground is coming down from Scotland to spend Christmas with me and the children!' And of course, he will want to inspect our hospital and to meet my ladies of the committee, of whom he has heard so much about, from me...'
'All good, I hope, my Lady?' Iris piped up.
Everyone giggled and I was grateful to my friend for lightening the atmosphere.
'The thing is, I would like to put on some form of entertainment for him while he's here, and I was thinking that we might repeat what we did a year ago; a Pantomime and the Nativity.'
'As it happens, Reverent Clancy has already approached me about putting on the Nativity, which this year, we both agree, will be put on, both at the church and at the hospital.' But prior to that I want us to put on another Pantomime, for all the patients in recovery this time, who are, as you all know, in need of cheering up.

We could, I thought, put it on in the grand Gallery. As that is a part of mine and the children's living space, it will not interfere with the hospital, and once it's cleared, it has ample room for an audience as well as room for the players.'

All the Committee members agreed that it was indeed a good idea and so we settled down in my lounge to discuss how to go about it?

'So, then, my Lady, what? When? And Where?' Iris said coming straight to the point.

I smiled, 'Well, ladies, I've not really got that far, to tell you the truth. I wanted only to show off, I think, to invite the Laird down here, so that he'll see that we can more than match his efforts up in Scotland. But then, when he joked over the phone that he hoped we'd entertain him while he was here, another Pantomime came to mind!' I smiled.

'Ah! I see,' Iris said, 'we're all in this then, because you want to show off to the Laird?' my Lady, she asked, with a twinkle in her eye.

Amber and the others giggled and I blushed, cursing myself for ever having admitted to showing off in the first place.

I took a deep breath, 'I want us to put on another Panto, that's all, but not as a fund-raiser, this time for the patients here in the hospital… what do you think?' I asked, seriously.

'Well, speaking for my own ward, it would be a welcome relief and will help take their minds off the war, if only for a little while,' Amber said.

The others nodded in agreement as I led them through to my living quarters and rang for the maid, asking her, when she arrived to bring us the light buffet, I had asked cook to prepare for us.

'So, is it to be Aladdin again?' Betty asked, making herself comfortable on my chaise longue.

'Well, that's what we're here to discuss, my dear,' I smiled.

'Cinderella, I love Cinderella;' Amber shouted cheerfully.

Everyone chuckled at her enthusiasm and were quite taken with her idea, and so it was accepted without further ado.

'Well, that was easy,' I chuckled, 'now all we have to do is put it on!' I said as the maid arrived with our light snack.

As the ladies nibbled on finger sandwiches and sipped their tea, I began writing a list of the characters along with who might play them.

'I do believe we might have to call on one or more of your daughters,' Iris,' I said.

She sighed; 'Oh dear, that might cause a bit of trouble and I would have to leave it up to you, my Lady, to choose who will be Cinderella and who will be the ugly sisters!'

'Oh! Yes, I see your concern, Iris, I really do, um! Amber, what do you think?' I asked desperately.

My fellow committee member held up her hands in protest; 'Oh no my Lady, I think I'll leave this one for you, if you don't mind... telling one young woman that she's ugly, while her sister is a beautiful princess, is not something I would like to do, but good luck with that,' Amber chuckled. The others laughed including Iris, all of them refusing my pleas for help, but then I had an idea and it made me smile... 'let's forget about your daughters, then Iris: 'Amber, you will be the evil step-mother; Betty, you and Stella will be the ugly sisters; Clorinda and Tisbe, while Iris will be the Fairy Godmother and I will find another to play Cinderella,' I told them in no uncertain terms. There was the usual moment of silence before the protests began, but smiling I dismissed their arguments; 'You left me to decide, ladies, and this is what I would like.

'What about Prince Charming?' Iris grinned, obviously liking my cheeky plan.

'Well for that role, perhaps we could involve the patients, or at least one of them; I am thinking of asking your daughters friend, Iris, you know, the young man who lost his arm... um! Robbo, I believe he's called.'

'As I've said before, my Lady, you do come up with things very quickly, and they usually work,' Iris smiled, giving her approval to my spur of the moment idea.

'Me, the evil stepmother! Oh no! My Lady, please reconsider,' Amber pleaded.

I chuckled, 'No, sorry Amber; the roles are decided; and, Betty, Stella, you'd better choose which of the ugly sisters you want to be; either, Tisbe, who I believe is very evil or Clorinda who is not quite so evil.'

The rest of us laughed and we all had another pot of tea as we began to plan the event, discussing where the seats would be and how many people would be able to come to each performance; planning for there to be four shows in all over the period of the week beginning the 28th of November 1941. Although I hadn't included any of Iris's children in the Pantomime, I was hoping instead to ask for their help behind the scenes, and getting everything ready for the big event, and that's the message I sent home with their mother, Iris. I could have rounded up Jane and Ruby here at the hospital, as most days they were around, helping in some capacity, but I didn't want to interrupt the good work they were doing.

When I bumped into Iris the following day, she said, although her children were disappointed not having roles in the Pantomime, they would of course help out behind the scenes. Well, that took care of that! Now, as it was my idea to cast Mr Drakes son Robbo as Prince Charming, I took it upon myself to go and see if he would be prepared to take on the role.

'If'n 'ee don't want ta do it, my Lady, you come back and tell I, an' I'll step in,' Iris's Fred grinned, when I stopped off on my way to ask the young man if he was willing to take part. 'Specially if'n yor ta be Cinderella,' he chuckled.

'You hush, now father!' Iris snapped. 'Don't you take any notice of Fred, my Lady, Robbo won't let you down,' she assured me.

I couldn't help but smile at Fred's cheeky comment, my Rory would have liked Fred, of that I was sure, he did like a good sense of humour, did my husband.

As I continued my journey down across the heath, I was struck again by its rugged beauty, a beauty that not everyone would see this time of the year, half hidden as it was beneath the hoary long grass and under wilting clumps of heather and dying gorse bushes.

Although the Drake farm was a part of my estate, it was the first time I'd had cause to visit the place in all my years, and I was pleasantly surprised. The wonderful redbrick Victorian house was easily a match for my own Manor house, prettier even, I'm sure, some might say. The very person I'd come to see, greeted me as I stepped from my car, and despite of all he'd been through he seemed hale and in good spirits.

'You are looking well, young man,' I smiled.

He bowed his head, a slight reddish hue touching his cheeks; 'Thanks mainly to your hospital, my Lady,' he smiled.

It was a genuine smile too, I noted, full of gratitude, although it was not I, deserving of such a smile, it was the wonderful staff of my hospital, and hopefully I had a way that he might thank them himself, should he so choose. Mrs Drake came hurrying out just then, nudging her son aside, she invited me to take tea with them, eager of course to know why I was there, her face a little lined with worry, for I was her landlord after all! 'My husband won't be home till late, I'm afraid, my Lady as he's gone off ta market,' she apologised.

I smiled; 'It's not your husband, nor even yourself, that I've come to see, Mrs Drake, I'm here to ask something of your son?' I said, hoping to reassure her.

Out of the corner of my eye I saw Robbo flinch and glance at his new limb; 'Is something wrong with my arm?' he asked hesitantly.

'No, oh no, I'm sorry, your arm is fine as far as I know, Robbo, um! I have a favour to ask... and... look, don't be afraid to say no, I'll quite understand if you do... and...'

'Please, my Lady, won't you just tell us?' Mrs Drake pleaded.

I blushed, realising the tension my hesitancy was causing.

'Robbo, the committee and I have decided to put on a Pantomime for the patients at the hospital, Cinderella, in fact, and we would like you to play Prince Charming,' I blurted out.

He and his mother looked at one another and then burst out laughing and I joined in, so relieved to have finally found the courage to ask him.

'You're serious, aren't you, my Lady?' he said in disbelief.

I nodded, sipping my tea in the hope that I might appear more relaxed than I felt, and then I told them my plans, explaining on what day and whereabouts it would be held. 'And, my maid, Wendy has agreed to be your Cinderella!' I added... 'or she will, I'm sure when I ask her,' I added quickly.

Thankfully both mother and son laughed; 'so she's ta be shanghaied too,' Mrs Drake chuckled.

'Oh dear, it does sound like that doesn't it, but it's really not, she can say no, as can you, master Drake, with no offence taken on my side,' I assured him.

Mrs Drake made us another pot of tea while we talked about the Pantomime; 'It's just my idea to help the patients along their road to recovery, to perhaps, even if it is for a little while, take their minds off what they've been through.'

There was that dreadful moment of silence that always preceded something as completely off the wall as this... it was a moment when anything was possible, a yes, I'll do it, or, a don't be so ridicules my Lady!' I waited with bated breath for what seemed an age.

'Course, I'll do it, my Lady. I know's better than most just what this will bring ta the men on the wards, and I'll help any way I can.' Robbo agreed, much to my delight.

'Thank you, Robbo, I'll let you know when the rehearsals start, right now I have to get back and talk my maid into playing the part of Cinderella,' I sighed.

I started back then, very pleased with myself, now all we had to do was decide on the rest of the cast and agree on the right time and date for our latest grand adventure. I smiled to myself, for adventure it truly was, just like our fair and fete idea. I just hoped it worked out as well as that had!

The very next day, with the help of some of the recovering patients and members of my own staff, we began preparing the Grand Gallery by getting rid of all the stored furniture; the statues and paintings from along the walls, before putting in place row up on row of chairs, all taken out of storage for the week. At the end of the Grand Gallery, I had Fred and one of his friends, who was a carpenter, build a slightly raised stage for the actors to perform the Pantomime on. We began the preparations on November 5th, Guy Fawkes Day; a, time that was usually full of joy and fun, with exploding bangers and glittering cascades of beautiful fireworks, and rockets lighting up the night sky... and great big bonfires with burning effigies of the man himself sitting at the top. All of which were sadly not happening anymore, and hadn't been since this damned war started.

I smiled; If nothing else, what we were doing would help to bring a little cheer back to everyone's lives, God knows we were all in need of that! Once again, I roped Jane in to help design the posters to advertise the event and had the nurses and one or two of the older Miller children go around the wards putting them up anywhere they could. Even though I'd suspected that it would be well received, I was astounded by the wave of excitement that swept through the hospital. Not just that, but the offers of help we got from the patients themselves, two of which I was more than pleased to accept, as they were both amateur thespians! Michael Walsh and Derek Mason, airmen, from the burn's unit. They came to see me brandishing one of janes posters, despite their faces being swathed in bandages, I couldn't refuse them, so eager were they to get involved.

It was on our very first day of rehearsing when I realised that I'd made the right decision, as my two young thespians took over the running of the Pantomime with complete and utter confidence. Watching them working with the cast was a pleasure, they knew exactly what they were doing and better still knew what they wanted everyone else to do.

With such experts overseeing things I was able to turn my mind to other matters; Reverent Clancy was already pushing me to help him with this year's Nativity, wanting me to play the church organ again, like I'd done last Christmas... I just wasn't sure I'd be able to, not this year.

As I watch the rehearsal for our Pantomime, I could scarce believe that more than a year had passed already, since our arrival at our Manor House, here at Sandbourne. So much has happened, including us losing our beloved Rory. I shook my head, still unable to believe that he was gone! Tears ran down my cheeks and I quickly wiped them away, finding a smile from somewhere; My dear husband would be so proud of what we'd achieved in our short time here. As I walked my rounds through the hospital, that night, I could almost feel him by my side, walking stride for stride with me. 'This is quite magnificent,' he leaned in to say, and I felt the closeness of him, and I knew he was here, watching over us, as he always had and always would.

'My Lady... my Lady!' It was Robbo, dear sweet Robbo.

'Um! I'm trying to find the grand Gallery,' he blushed at being lost in a place he knew so well.

Turning, I took his arm and led him back the way I'd just come, and there the two newly appointed thespians took over, although I could tell by the look on his face that Robbo didn't quite know what to make of them, for farmers they most definitely were not! I left him there, feeling a little guilty for doing so, as he was clearly uncomfortable, but I'd gotten to know Michael and Derek over the last few days and they were both gentlemen and more important than that, they were nice people. As I walked away, Robbo was being introduced to his Cinderella, my maid, Wendy, who, reluctantly had agreed to play the role, but only after I'd promised her a rise in salary for doing so.

It was pleasing to see everything running so smoothly; the hospital, the play, even the plans for the Nativity with Reverent Clancy, but I was just waiting for the bubble to burst... something was bound to go wrong, that is the way of life, one minute you're up, the next you're down! I shook the thought away, perhaps this time it will be up all the way! I smiled.

I decided not to visit the grand Gallery for a day or two; 'let them get on with things,' I thought. When I did finally return there was but two days until the first performance and I was pleasantly surprised at the progress as I watched a full rehearsal of the Pantomime, and apart from Robbo botching his lines on one occasion everything was terrific. My maid, Wendy, was, to my surprise, word perfect and she and Robbo were getting on very well, in fact I'm sure I noticed a spark between them! Well good for them, I thought as I walked away, it is a love story after all. Getting all the patients who wanted to go to the Pantomime up to the Gallery was our next headache, as many of them, we knew, would struggle with the stairs, and there seemed no answer to the problem. But thankfully Derek, one of our thespians had the solution; 'We'll just have to take one or two of the performances down to the ground floor,' he suggested. 'The ballroom would be just perfect, I know It will mean moving beds and relocating patients to other wards, but it could work.'

The first thing I did was to ask for a meeting with Sir Edmond Bruce, Matron and my Committee ladies, where I told them of our problem and of our proposed solution; after mulling it over for an hour or so, it was agreed that it could work, it was just a matter of finding room for all the displaced patients! At first, because of the extra 60 patients we'd taken in, it was a struggle to fit any more into the wards, but then Iris, once again came to my rescue; 'Farmer Drake still 'as one big tent left in 'is barn, my Lady, we could throw tha' up on the front lawn, and put some of the patients there... or, better still, hold the Pantomime there, I'm sure my Fred and his friend could rehouse the stage in no time at all.'

It was a brilliant idea, there was nothing to say that we had to use the grand gallery, bringing it down to ground level made perfect sense, that would allow access to even those who couldn't manage the long climb up the stairs. So, it was agreed, and I drove Iris to ask Fred and his gang to assist us one more time and bring the tent to my Manor house and erect it on my front lawn, which they duly did, that very day. They also relocated the stage from the grand gallery to the tent. Once that was done, a host of helpers brought the chairs down and lined them up facing the stage, and finally, all was ready. Although it wasn't a fundraiser like last year's Pantomime, I believe we all took more pleasure from this one, just by seeing the looks on the faces of our patients. Many of them were close to tears, enjoying at last a true taste of the crazy Britain that they had fought for and which some of their friends had died for... including my own darling Rory... but they'd not fought and died just for our right to have pantomimes, no, their sacrifice has been to preserve a way of life... our way of life. The only disappointment to our main event was that the Laird could not come down for it, as, like my own hospital his was overrun by patients and he couldn't be spared.

After our pantomime though, there was a definite air of wellbeing everywhere, the patients seemed cheerier and more able to cope with their injuries and the staff too were more upbeat, whilst I was quick to notice the growing relationship between my maid, Wendy and Robbo... and it warmed my heart, although I'm not sure that Ruby or Jane felt the same.

As we moved into December, with the days racing by, I began preparing for the Nativity with Reverent Clancy, and was ready once again to play the organ for him, but then something quite out of the blue happened, I had a phone call from my father-in-law, asking, as he couldn't come to us, could we travel up and spend Christmas with him at Kirriemuir Castle. It was not an invite I'd expected, but it was one that I could not refuse, not after all of his help to change my manor house into a hospital; and anyway, the children and I would love to see him again.

I also could not resist the chance to check up on our old home to see what it was like now as a hospital in its own right. But there was a lot to think about. It would mean disappointing Reverend Clancy, and I'd already agreed to play for him! It was a worry, but once again I was rescued, not by a friend this time but by a patient. One of the thespians, Michael, offered to play the organ in my place, although I didn't take him up on his offer until I, along with the Reverent, heard him play. To my delight, he was wonderful, far better than myself, and so it was settled.

I thought my three children would be over the moon at the idea of spending Christmas with their grandfather, but instead they were unhappy at not being here to play with the Miller children. On this occasion there was of course no shutting the house up while we were away, it was a hospital now, and so it was never closed, besides there were plenty of staff to keep it going whilst we were away... still I couldn't pretend, that like my children, I would miss being here for Christmas. To my surprise Nannie too was a little reluctant to leave Sandbourne Manor, or Sandbourne hospital as it was now. I would have thought returning to the home where she had helped to bring Rory up, would have appealed to her, but it seems the world has moved on now, even for her. We knew our route well by now and our journey seemed not so far as before, still it was tiring and even with two drivers, it took us a good 10hrs or more.

The Laird was there to meet us as we pulled through the great iron gates and it was all I could do to stop the children from jumping from the car before it had stopped.
'Grandpa, Grandpa!' they cried, rushing into his arms.
He swept them up as if they were rag dolls, weighing nothing at all, swinging them around and around, and as they laughed so I cried, remembering how their father, my Rory used to do the very same to them, and to me too.
'A tour of the hospital first, I think!' he grinned. 'I do hope you don't mind the changes we've made to your home, my dears?'

The layout was almost identical to my manor house only on a bigger scale, but then, as I'd used the same architects as my father-in-law, I shouldn't have been surprised.

'Your rooms are at the top of the castle, well away from the patients, although I fear you'll all see plenty of them as I've said that you'll help decorate the place ready for Christmas,' he said.

It was December 22nd 1941 and we were in the middle of the Scottish Highlands, seemingly a million miles away from the war and yet I still felt as if at any moment the bombing would begin and we'd be diving for cover. But the Laird assured me that Kirriemuir was considered so safe that children from England were being sent here. I felt better on hearing that and along with the Laird and Nannie and the Laird's Gillie, I led the children out across the highland in search of a Christmas tree, it brought back such good memories as hunting for the right pine tree for the house was always one of Rory's favourite things to do... and I so felt him nearby as we searched the woodlands.

It was a tradition that the Laird insisted on year upon year, even though according to the rules of the Kirk, Christmas was not to be celebrated in Scotland as it was a part of the Catholic faith.

Strange? And I made up my mind to ask him about it the first chance I got.

'Here's a nice one!' Grace called, interrupting my thoughts.

With the Laird leading, we all went to see what she'd found, 'Ah! That'll do lass, that'll do nicely,' he beamed, unloading the axe from his backpack.

We all stepped away giving him room to swing his axe, and in no time at all he'd chopped it down. 'Right then, one more to go, keep looking,' he ordered as the gillie picked up the felled tree.

'But why do we need another one?' Crispen asked.

'One for the hospital and its patients, and one for the house, and us!' Nannie, explained.

'Over here!' Little Florence shouted excitedly.

'Well done, sweetheart, this one will be perfect for the house, stand back now,' the Laird warned.

Once again, he had it down in no time, and soon the children and I were carrying it home, side by side with the gillie and his tree. Dropping the one for us off by the front door, the Laird rang the bell for the hospital staff, and soon a nurse and two burly men, whom I recognised from my time here at Rory's wake, when they came to my rescue against the nasty Irish side of Rory's family. They both smiled and dipped their heads, 'My Lady!' they acknowledged cheerfully.

I smiled back; it was indeed a pleasure to see them again.

'Just put them in place, if you would, guy's, we'll let the children help with the decorations,' the Laird instructed.

As they walked off with the gillie and his tree, for the hospital, the Laird took hold of the other tree himself; 'Well, come on then, this thing will not decorate itself you know,' he grinned. We all helped to carry it to a wooden tub, in our drawing room, where the gardener was waiting to prepare it ready for us to decorate. For most of the time I stood back and watched the Laird and Nannie and my children hanging the tree with silver bells, paper trimmings, pretty lights and finally placing a fairy on the top... and I wanted to cry, this was how it used to be with Rory... just how it used to be. I watched my children closely, they were remembering it too, and I was pleased to see the look of joy on their faces. Nannie however seemed sad, no doubt, recalling my husband Rory as a child, doing all these self-same things... how hard must this be for her too, for Rory had been almost a son to her. Reaching out I made to touch her hand, but the Laird beat me to it, giving her fingers a reassuring squeeze, as if in recognition for all she'd been to his family and to his boy. It was quite the most beautiful thing I'd ever seen, and testimony to the fact that the Laird and my Rory were both wonderful caring people and a tribute to their clan.

Suddenly my thoughts were full of my Rory; of his laughter, his soft voice, and of his ability to make even the dullest of days, brighter, somehow!

For a moment I stood looking out of the window; lost in memories; the weather out across the Highlands was bleak, overhung with dark threatening clouds that promised snow, sleet and ice, and yet, I knew, if Rory were here, he would simply laugh and say something like... 'Hey, better break out the sledge, I think there's snow on the way!' However, thankfully, this time he would have been wrong as the snow held its peace, and I was pleased; as much as the children might have enjoyed us all fooling around in it, we had a long journey to make soon, so I'm glad it stayed away.

Christmas day was a day when, after the children finished opening their presents from their grandfather, Nannie and myself, we all went around the wards making sure the patients were alright, helping those who needed it to open their own gifts, either from family or from the hospital staff. It was a busy day, broken only by Christmas dinner, shared with some of the patients well enough to eat up at the long table, the rest we visited at their bedside, just to wish them a merry Xmas.

As hectic as it was, we all enjoyed every moment of it, the look of sheer joy on the faces of most of the men well worth the 10hr Journey we'd made and would have to make again soon to go home. We left the day after boxing day under the same threatening sky, that thankfully had come to nothing. On our departure, I made my father-in-law promise to come down and see for himself the progress we'd made on our own hospital. With his word given that he would do just that, we set off on our long journey home, determined not to miss the celebrations to see in the New Year, for we all had high hopes that 1942 might well herald the end of the war, not that I held such beliefs... but I could hope and pray that it would.

The weather held good for most of journey with the scenery ahead constantly changing as we made our way out of the northern lands and into the milder climes of the Southwest, settling our minds and our bodies, enabling us all to sleep for the first time. As pleased as we'd all been to visit with the Laird in our old home, way out on the Scottish Highlands, we were all so very pleased to be heading back to Sandbourne.

Like myself, the children felt closer to Rory there now, and of course it was where our friends were. I took a moment to digest that, for in truth, the ladies of the committee and the Miller family aside there was no-one else I would call friends! Where-as I had grown up in the northern lands, my family's farm was there, it was where my father had been born and raised and where he had met and married my mother! I glanced across at my children all huddled next to Nannie, Scotland and the north of England should be a big part of them, I smiled; but as much as they loved their old home and their grandfather in Scotland, Sandbourne down in the depths of the southwest had stolen their hearts... and mine too.

With that in mind I settled down, all my thoughts on my hospital and how the staff and patients were doing without me.

Chapter 16

'Ruby Miller, get a grip of yourself,' I muttered, all alone on the yard of our house on the heath. Lady Seymour will be back... she will, she'd have said otherwise, but still, I couldn't convince myself. I blamed that bloody dog; I'd been wearing a frown ever since I first heard it howling out across the way! Once more, under my breath I cursed Grandma Miller and my father for their silly superstitions.

'It's all nonsense,' mum had tutted, on seeing my worried face. Still, I couldn't shake the feeling of disaster from my head and so I searched my mind for one of mum's sayings to counter grandma Miller's tales of gloom and doom.

The only one I could think of was; 'The wind of change can be scary and foreboding, or it can be a sudden surge towards a better outcome and a steady walk away from trouble and strife, a path that we all should strive to take.' I'm sure I heard mum say it once and of course as always, she was right. When I thought about what Lady Seymour had been through of late; the loss of her husband and the upheaval of her home, it brought tears to my eyes. Although lately, it might not have been a surge towards better times, her Ladyship had taken, but it surely was a slow walk back towards easier days. Even so, the question I asked myself over and over as we celebrated Christmas at home on the heath and also with the patients down at the hospital... was, would she want to come back... would she?

When finally, I heard from mum of her return, I, unashamedly broke down and cried and cried, so convinced as I'd been that she wouldn't come back! It took all of our Janie's big sister bullying to set my mind right and despite the bruises, I thanked her.

We had all missed Lady Seymour and her children over Christmas, although thanks to her Ladyships wonderful organisation the hospital ran as smoothly as ever it did... and as for the Nativity it had also succeeded well without her.

In truth, her replacement, Michael, one of the hospital patients had done a wonderful job playing the organ in her stead. Despite all of that, it was not the same without her and her family, we all felt the loss of them, even the little-ones, who had all become used, like the rest of us, to having them around.

To welcome them back, mum and Mrs Drake were busy organising a New Year's Eve get together up at our place, it was not to be a big affair this time though, just our family, the Drakes and Lady Seymour and her children, plus, Amber, Betty and Stella, the committee ladies, oh, and of course, the Davis twins and their folks.

'You know, I can scarce believe that more than a year has passed us by already,' Mrs Drake smiled, skinning a poached rabbit that she was helping to prepare for the big day.

'Aye, I know what you mean, my dear,' mum replied... 'I swear we've packed at least two years into one, what with everything we've done and all the friends we've made down in the village and across the heath.'

I grinned; 'Not to mention Jake the Pirate with his toffee apples and Fairy Floss!'

Mum and Mrs Drake chuckled; 'That silly man could have got us all into trouble... but it was all a lot of fun;' mum declared, much to my surprised. I had to agree with her, it really had been a lot of fun, especially for us kids, as Pirate Jake seemed like a character out of our comic books, his fairground people too. But I have to say, comic book hero's or not, they were the making of the Fair and Fete and we couldn't have done it without them,'

Mum smiled; 'You know, when your father first took me to see them, I had my doubts, considering them just Gypsies, but I quickly learned that they are so much more, and now we are friends, good friends, why, how many would set up a funfair for a child's 13th birthday who was not even their own.' she said shaking her head.

The more I thought about it the more unlikely it seemed, who on earth would do such a thing and why... the answer of course was in what was happening all around us... it was the war, doing the exact opposite of what the Germans hoped for; instead of breaking us apart, it was pulling us all together, making us more reliant on one another and more tolerant too. I suddenly felt a tinge of guilt; 'We should have invited Pirate Jake, to celebrate the coming New Year, with us, the fairground people as well,' I said to mum, disappointed that I hadn't thought of it before.

'It's too late, Ruby, they're gone, my dear,' mum sighed. 'Your father went to find them but the ground they'd been staying at was empty.'

'Oh! But couldn't he have asked around, they can't have gone far?' I protested.

'They're travellers, my dear, they could be anywhere?' Mum shrugged.

As disappointed as I was, I concentrated on getting ready for the coming feast tomorrow knowing there was still a lot to do.

Later, as I helped our Janie and Janet with the little-ones, I couldn't help but wonder where all the days had gone. It seems like only yesterday that we'd first arrived out here on the heath, a place that had once filled me with fear, but that had quickly become something special. Somewhere even better than my favourite; Home Farm, back in Somerset. For a moment or two I stood in the yard looking down across the heath, seeing the winter heather in all its glorious red, purple and yellow grandeur swaying in the afternoon breeze. Thinking back to when we first arrived, I shook my head, how could I ever have missed the splendour of this beautiful place, but I had, calling it evil looking, if I remember!

The New Year's Eve party this year, was not going to be outside in the yard as there could be no lights showing and so a barbecue was not possible. Instead, all the food was being cooked on the kitchen range, and then served on tables in the living-room.

Despite the tension, it was all so exciting working to be ready for our guests to arrive, it was a bit manic though and despite all of mine and Janie's mad rushing around, dealing with the food, mum still expected us to see to the little-ones! But fed up, my big sister came down hard on our younger siblings Janet and Bella, screaming at them to do something, to help us out, which seeing the look on Janie's face they finally did.

'Take the little-ones upstairs, and keep them amused,' Janie ordered, our younger sisters, 'once they've settled, you'll be able to come down and join in the party,' she told them. With that Janie and me hurried to set the drinks out alongside all the food on the kitchen table, as already we could hear the sound of a car engine in the distance!

First to come was Amber, racing up across the wintery heath in her big black car, before screeching to a stop in our yard with Stella and Betty on the back seat, looking, as they stepped out, as white as the ground beneath their feet.

'For a while during our journey, I wasn't sure if we'd actually live to see the New Year in,' Stella growled, giving Amber an accusing glare.

'Here, here!' Betty agreed, climbing a little shaken and dishevelled from the car.

'Oh please, don't be such worry warts, ladies, I'm a great driver,' Amber insisted.

'But not a racing driver, my dear,' mum said, wagging a finger at her, as she went to greet them.

Amber grinned; 'But I could be, Iris, if they'd give a woman the chance'.

Even I chuckled at that.

Lady Seymour and her children came next and must have been thrilled by the reception they got, not only from the ladies and myself but from my siblings too, who would have rushed to greet them had Janie and me not stood in their path.

'So nice of you to invite us, Iris,' she smiled genuinely. 'Grace, Crispen and Florence are so excited, Nannie and I have had our work cut out trying to control them; isn't that, right?' she asked, as Nannie stepped from the car. The elderly childminder, smiled in agreement as she ushered the children from the car.

'Come this way, come with me,' our Bella urged, taking Florence by the hand.

Giggling, Lady Seymour's youngest followed our Bella up the stairs, closely followed by Grace and Crispen, hurrying up to find the rest of our siblings somewhere in the bedrooms.

'I hear the Nativity went well; Matron tells me the patients are still talking about how much they enjoyed it,' Lady Seymour smiled.

I wasn't sure whether she was speaking to me or mum and so I left it to mum to reply.

'Well, who would have believed anyone could play the organ as well as you my Lady, but that actor, he's very good too,' mum said.

I blushed; how could mum be so tactless!

But Lady Seymour simply smiled; 'After seeing how well those actors ran the Pantomime, I'm not a bit surprised, and I think, even if I do say so myself, I deserve a pat on the back for finding such talented young men.'

'You do that, my Lady, and not ta mention, how you got Robbo and your maid, Wendy, together for the main roles. 'If I'm not mistaken, they might be keepin' the love story going, or so I've been told,' mum winked, cheekily.

Everyone laughed, but Janie and myself had little time for merriment as we hurried about our duties, determined to keep everyone happy.

The Davis twins and their mum and dad came next and then with the arrival of our own dad and Farmer Drake we were all here and the festivities began for real. Robbo it seems chose to bring in the new year with Wendy and her family down in the village, Janie and me were a little disappointed, but we understood. Although it was early evening, the light across the heath quickly gave way to an all-consuming darkness, against which we dared not show any form of light, not even with the smallest of bonfires, which was what we all wanted, to dance and sing around.

Instead, we made do with music from the wireless and made merry around the hearth in the living-room. Songs were sung; gay music from the wireless echoed across the heath, and then stories were told and we all had a wonderful time. And then at midnight we sang Auld Lang Syne, just the perfect song for Lady Seymour and her children, what with their strong Scottish ties. I held hands with Grace on one side and Crispen on the other and we danced until the mantle clock struck twelve, and we all wished each other a very; 'Happy New Year!'

It was a wonderful night, all friends together, we sang and danced as if it were the last time we'd ever be together! With that thought, once again, my fears came to the fore and the old folklores of my family's past broke like bubbles all around me, and the voice of our Grannie Miller, back in Yeovil found its way to my subconscious, filling me with dread!

'Good fortune and bad, run hand in hand, child, when you are in the favour of one then expect the other to follow close on its heels, for that is the nature of all things in the world.' Her voice echoed insistently inside my head.

'Still in the land of dreams, then Ruby?' Lady Seymour, chuckled coming over to chat with me. Shaking away my silly thoughts I smiled. 'I was thinking how good it is to have you and your children back, my Lady... I wasn't sure if you'd stay up in Scotland or not,' I said, quite surprised at my own frankness. I frowned; Something of our Janie seems to be rubbing off on me?

'I did have thoughts about staying up there, I have to admit, Ruby, after all it was our home, with Rory, and it holds many wonderful memories. But in truth, this is our home now and myself and the children have grown to love it,' she smiled.

'I'm glad, my Lady, Sandbourne wouldn't be the same without you, and I've come to think of Grace, Crispen and little Florence as a part of my own family, if you don't mind me saying.'

There it was again... our Janie's voice coming out of my mouth, I clamped it shut, hoping that it hadn't caused too much trouble, as my big sister tended to do at times!

Lady Seymour laughed; 'You really are becoming your mother, my dear, the very image!'

'Not like my big sister then?' I questioned.

'No! Your mother, I would say, to the point, but not so blunt and prickly as Jane,' she insisted.

I grinned at that and was about to agree with her but didn't. 'The thing is, my Lady, without our Janie, we'd fall apart, my siblings and me, she holds us all together, when mum and dad's not around,' I countered.

'I didn't mean your sister any disrespect, Ruby, I simply meant that you and she are not alike, but, are a good team, she moulds your siblings into shape while you give them the final polish,' she smiled.

I liked that way of looking at things, for it was exactly right, Janie and me were the perfect team, even if we did fall out now and then, a bit like mum and dad really! That dog started howling again then, out across the heath and it made me feel uneasy; 'Do they have any silly superstitions in Scotland my Lady?' I asked with a shiver.

'Oh yes, lots; black cats crossing your path is a sign of a death in the family, black-faced sheep are supposed to be a sign of evil, while white heather is deemed to be a good omen,' she explained.

'Nothing about howling dogs?' I asked nervously.

'Well, I did spend a lot of time in England, so I have heard the lore that a howling dog brings death in its wake, should you hear it howling nearby, although I don't believe in such things myself,' Lady Seymour insisted.

Despite her words of doubt, I had grown up with such stories, amidst a family full of deep-rooted beliefs in ghosts and ghouls and other supernatural beings! And so, hearing a howling dog out across the dark gloomy heathland, spoke to me of unworldly things... things Dad and Grandma Miller told us stories about... dark, scary ghost stories, that they swore to be true! Even as the howling faded, I could feel a shiver creeping up my spine and hear a quiet voice deep inside, asking just who the Grim-Reaper might be coming for. Unbidden names started popping into my head; starting with the old-ones, like Grandma Miller back in Yeovil and the rest of the elderly family members, including mum and dad!

Although neither of them could really be called old, mum being 39 or so and dad not yet 42... they just seemed old that's all! I cursed dad then, for all the ghost stories he and I shared; and then my mind turned towards the hospital and all the poorly souls in there, some of them very close to death, the truth be known. Again, I shook the thought away, this was silly, just because I'd heard a dog howling!

'Come along Ruby, lets join the celebrations, we have just entered a brand-new year,' Lady Seymour said, taking my arm and leading me back to the festivities.

'About time to,' our Janie growled as I joined her in the kitchen, leaving Lady Seymour to go over to talk with mum.

'Where are Grace, Crispen and Florence?' I asked Nannie, who was sat across from us, obviously preferring the company of children, whether we were hers to look after or not.

She smiled; 'playing upstairs with your siblings, and at least I can be sure they'll not come to any harm up there!'

I knew she was hinting at the time we'd taken them out across the heath, putting their little lives in danger, as she saw it, even though they were perfectly safe... as safe in fact as they are now!

Still, I thought to check on them and was pleased to find them curled up on the big bed listening to our Janet telling stories. Crispen and my two brothers, Jack and Danny too, and even the Davis twins. I had to smile, if this was what the New Year of 1942 had in store for us then it would be a good year indeed, I decided. One by one our guests left, and mum called us all together in the kitchen, where she thanked us all for all we'd done since we'd arrived here, before finally we all went off to bed... although I couldn't go without standing in the doorway and listening into the night one last time, praying not to hear that dog again!

January is always a hard month and halfway through this one came such a frost that once again we had icicles creeping down the insides of the windows and a feathering of snow all across the heathland, but thankfully this year it didn't turn any worse than that, and so we were able to continue on with our lives as normal.

Lady Seymour and the doctors and nurses down at the hospital sighed with relief, all of them like the rest of us thinking that we were in for a nasty spell of freezing weather, which would have caused lots of problems for all the patients in the outside tents! There simply was not enough warmth, and if the weather turned, the old gypsy stoves would not be good enough to heat the tents; sadly, as despite the Tilly lamps giving off a good glow, they provided no extra warmth, so everyone prayed for a mild winter. The hospital staff took no chances though, piling on more bedclothes and asking patients to wear extra clothes to bed, even nightcaps and woollen gloves whenever possible.

Our Janet and me dressed as if we were going on a trip across the North Pole, which drew a lot of laughs from the patients as we sat and read to them in the afternoons, but we didn't care what we looked like as long as we were warm. Even the books we chose to read from were of a warm nature, such as; The Adventures of Huckleberry Finn, and my favourite, Treasure Island, both stories set in hot places, to warm the souls of both the patients and ourselves. Thankfully, although it did get colder, we had no more snow, which was good for all of us who had to make it back and forward across the heathland, although the bright crisp days seem to suit the Germans too, as the bombing all along the coast increased alarmingly! Twice we had near misses, one bomb landing up where the fair had once been and the other in the stable yard, although thankfully her Lady's two white stallions had gone off to stud and so were saved. It was a stark reminder however of the danger that we all still faced, for sometimes, given the tranquillity of our surroundings, and despite having the injured patients to remind us, we tended to forget, believing, for some silly reason that this was our safe place, our sanctuary!

Being complacent, Lady Seymour called it, and warned us all of the consequences of becoming too easy with our soft way of life in and outside of the hospital. 'Be vigilant', was her watch word, with a warning not to be afraid to use the bomb shelters when we were under attack. Although that was a problem for not all the patients were mobile enough to retreat to them. But none the less, we were to take the able bodied to the shelters and pray that the Germans obeyed the Geneva code of conduct, that prohibited the bombing of hospitals and the like. Of course, most of us didn't believe that they would, still it was all we could hope for, while doing our best to keep everyone safe.

Despite the bombing there was a general sense of hope now, as all across the hospital news of the first American troops arriving in the village began to spread. Janie and I were among the first to see them as we came off the heath on our way to work one day. I was not sure I liked them though, they seemed rather brash and too cocky by half, whistling and calling out to us as they passed in their trucks. Janie liked them, dad too, claiming that their attitude was just what we needed if we were to beat the Germans, who thought themselves the chosen race! 'The Yanks,' as dad called them, were here and raring to fight after what the German's allies, Japan, had done at Pearl Harbour. 'Trust me, girls,' dad told Janie and me; 'The bloody, Huns and the Japs will be sorry they ever brought the Americans into this war, and we'll be glad they did too. Cocky they might be, but fighters is what they are, girls,' he sighed.

I knew dad was right and so I couldn't argue with him. Even I had heard the terrible news of what the Japanese had done, at Pearl Harbour. Although it was being said that, prime minister Winston Churchill was secretly pleased by the event, as it gave us an important ally. Despite dad's enthusiasm over our latest war buddies, I still didn't like their over confident, flashy manners... although, as I told my big sister as we sat discussing it one night on our bed, some of them were quite good-looking.

With that she dug me in the ribs and we had a pillow fight, ending with us both vowing to get to know at least one of our new hero's. Of course, they were here to help us fight the Germans, but it was clear from the very start that they also wanted a taste of this strange old country that they'd ended up in. So, it was no surprise that one of the first things they did was to advertise a dance at their base, inviting the locals, so that they might get to know them.

At first mum wouldn't hear of me and our Janie going to such a thing, claiming that we were too young, but when dad came in from work, he had his own news on the subject.

'What do you know, Iris, we've been invited ta this dance at the Yanks base,' he declared.

'You and me... but why?' mum frowned.

Dad shrugged; 'it beats me, Iris, they're just trying ta be friendly is my guess, but the thing is, if that's the case, why are they not allowing the other half of their troops to take part in this dance?'

Janie and I looked at one another; 'what other half?' Janie asked for the both of us.

'The blacks, girls, on tuther side of the heath,' he tutted, as if we should know!

Seeing that we were at a loss, at what on earth he was talking about, with a sigh at our ignorance he spelt it out for us! 'There are two kinds of yanks, girls, the white ones and the black ones...

'Wait! Are you saying there are black Americans here on our heath? That's exciting, I've never seen a black man before,' I enthused.

Janie shut me up with a glare as dad continued talking; 'Not many have my dear, I know's em of course frum my time out in India, though they were a different kind of black people, many of them are already fighting for us in this war, as part of our Commonwealth forces,' he explained.

This was all news to me and our Janie looked a little confused too; 'Well I expect we'll get to see these black soldiers for ourselves pretty soon,' I said, the excitement of going to a real dance catching up with me.

'Oh no, the black Americans won't be asked to the dance, girls, it will be a white only affair,' dad said shaking his head. 'I saw this sort of thing going on in India while I was there, by my own British Officers, who thought the locals beneath them... and I'm afraid the Yanks are even worse towards their black people,' he said shaking his head.

'But surely not, dad, after all we're all fighting the same war,' Janie protested.

'Aye, you'd think that would make a difference, girls, but not with the Yanks, and what's more, bloody Winston Churchill has agreed to change our equal rights laws, and ban all black American troops from mingling with white troops, though they can mix with locals like us!' Dad said.

I could see that our Janie was as confused by all of this as I was. 'So, then, does that mean the black troops are all confined to their camps?' she asked.

Dad shook his head; 'No, from what my friend Farmer Drake tells me, Sandbourne will become what they call, a black and white village!'

'And what's that supposed to mean?' I asked, completely confused.

'Well, it's something that will be happening wherever the yanks are, to keep their white soldiers apart from their black soldiers, they will not be allowed into the village at the same time,' dad explained, or tried to, although I could see by the look on our Janie's face that he wasn't succeeding.

'It simply means that the powers ta be, will divide the week into black and white days so that the American troops are always apart... though God knows how they'll manage that when they're fighting side by side against the Germans, who I'm sure won't give a damn about the colour of their skin while they're killing them.' Dad was getting angry; 'Silly Buggers!' he swore.

Despite all the restrictions and the silly rules and regulations Janie and me went to bed both very excited by the thought of the coming dance and also the prospect of meeting black men! Neither of us had ever met any, not in all our lives, we'd only ever heard tales of them from father.

Although according to him these American black men were of African origins and nothing like the one's from India that he'd met during his time in the army back in 1918. We were bubbling with excitement as we took to our beds that night, not just because of going to the dance in a few days' time, but of meeting new people! I mean, real new people, foreigners from across the ocean. It was quite a thing to get to grips with, even if they did have strange customs that I found quite unacceptable. I was of course hoping to like them and hoping that they would like me, but this strange thing they had about their fellow soldiers, was beginning to put me off them!

I did my best to keep an open mind, as did our Janie, but then one day while we were walking through the village on our way to the hospital, we witnessed something that threatened to put us off our newest allies completely! Two white American soldiers stopped a black soldier and began cursing him, and demanding to know what he was doing in the village today, as it was a white only day. Janie and I were disgusted by their attitude as we stopped to listen to the poor black soldier trying to explain that he had a message to deliver to their officer on the other side of the village. But the white Americans didn't care and were getting ever more, angry and abusive towards him when he refused to show them the message.

'Sorry but it's for Major Coles eyes only,' the black soldier insisted, as they badgered him, forcing him off the pavement and into the road.

'Don't you talk back to me, boy!' one of them bellowed at him.

I felt Janie start forward and tried to stop her, but was too slow; 'Hey, you, Yank! Leave him alone, or I'll tell your Major... whatever his name is, that you tried to read his private mail,' she shouted at one of the white soldiers.

'You just run along home little missy, this ain't none of yore affair,' he growled in Janie's face.

Oh dear, this wasn't going to be good! I thought as I watched my big sisters face turning an angry shade of red. 'Well now, this is my country and my village, and you're just a trespasser, so I guess it is my business,' Janie barked back at him... 'And what's more you are on Lady Seymour's land who happens to be a very good friend of ours, and if she knows that you tried to bully us, I'm sure she'll have a word with your commanding officer about it.' Janie threatened. 'Now be on your way and if I hear that you've done anything like this again, I'll not bother telling your Major or Lady Seymour, I'll set our mother on you and believe me you really wouldn't want that... and if you don't believe me, just ask around about Mrs Miller and the two Germans she captured single handed out on the heath!'

I saw him blanch and realised that he'd already heard the story and knew our mother would stop at nothing to protect us, her children, even if it meant fighting our own so-called allies.

'Better, go back ta base, Yank,' a voice called over my shoulder, it was Mr Briggs the pub owner, and as I looked around, I noticed quite a few had stopped to listen to what was going on, including our friend Becky and her mother and two of their neighbours. The black soldier had already taken his leave, hurrying on to deliver his message; 'Now there goes a real soldier, duty first and foremost, despite the likes of you, trying ta stop him!' Mr Briggs snorted in disgust. 'And as for you my lad, one hint of that sort of thing if you visit my pub and you'll be out on your ear, and you can spread that around your barracks... you tell your buddies that they are welcome here, as are you, providing you all behave yourselves.'

'They'll not stand for any blacks in your bar while we're there, Mr, I can assure you of that,' he sniffed loudly, trying to have the last word.

'I know the law, young man and I'll abide by it, even if it is against everything I believe in as an Englishman, but you can't blame me if the black days turn out to be fun days, of music and dance,' Mr Briggs grinned, 'and the white days boring as hell!'

Even the guy's buddies had to hide a smirk of admiration for the pub owners gall. The crowd broke up then all going its different ways, with Janie, Becky, who now worked alongside her in the hospital kitchen, and myself making our way through the village and down the long drive, passing through the newly erected tented wards to our work places.

Some of the patients were already a little irritated by the time I arrived to read to them, but they soon settled down as I began my story, although the goings on earlier in the village had already reached their ears and so I had to explain that first.

'Bloody Yanks, one of the patients grumbled, if we didn't need um so bad, I'd say ship the buggers back home.'

By the time our Janet came to take over from me, I was tired and wanted only to return home and be with the little-ones for a while, to sit and play with them or push them out across the yard in the pram that was usually reserved for our piglet and not the little-ones at all!

Later as I stood gazing out across the wild heathland I was in a world of my own, my thoughts drifting away with the breeze. It was a cold but beautifully clear end of January afternoon, with just a hint of snow hanging on the breeze, threatening a storm in the very near future. But the weather was the last thing that concerned me. That kind of storm I could easily cope with. It was the other sort of storm that frightened me, the one that our newest allies had brought across the seas to us, a frightening tempest of narrow-minded bigotry and hate! Although in truth, it's little more than we ourselves first took out to the world beyond our shores... and now it has returned to bite our backsides! I thought about the incident with the black soldier earlier and it made me sick to my stomach and had me wondering just why we were fighting this war, because to my mind it was to create a better world, and to stop bullies treating others as inferiors, obviously the Yanks didn't get that?

Although I spoke of it later to our Janie, I never mentioned it to anyone else, especially mother, for fear of her taking it any further, after all, our own Prime Minister had agreed to the Americans introducing their own form of segregation, even though it was hostile to our own way of life.

A few days later, I don't know what I expected when we went to the dance at the white American base. Some sort of heavily constricted event, I think, given my first impression of them. But in truth it was wonderful. Far removed from our own dull, staid dances, where there was usually, some old lady playing a piano, another with a violin and finally one with a big double bass tucked rather unladylike, between her legs, playing the songs of Vera Lynn, The Andrew sisters and Judy Garland, all very nice, but quite boring for us youngsters. Whereas here they had a proper band, playing Blues, boogie-woogie and jazz, much like the music of Glen Miller that we got to hear on the wireless now and then, when mum allowed. In spite of my reluctance to admit it, given Janie and my run in with one of them in the village, we all had a great time, mum and dad included, along with many of our friends from the village and those who lived and worked out across the heath, which included, of course, the Davis twins. I was a little worried about them and my brothers, Jack and Danny getting up to mischief around the base, and in fact they did sneak off at one point during the dance, but were soon found and returned by the military police with a warning not to stray again, or else! Which I was pleased to note they took seriously and remained in the dance hall for the remainder of the afternoon.

On our way out we fell in step with Lady Seymour, who I have to admit to not even knowing that she was there; 'As a return gesture, I think we should throw a dance of our own in the village hall,' she announced. I have already cleared it with the Americans here, although, of course, they will not sanction a dance with the black soldiers' present… but you know me girls, I brokered a deal,' she laughed. 'We will run the dance in two parts,' The black Americans will come first and stay until the church bells chime at 3pm and then the white American troops will come, until curfew at 6pm.'

We were all astounded; 'How on earth did you manage to get them to agree to that, my Lady?' Mum queried as we walked away together.

'Well, a little birdie told me of some racial bullying that went on in the village, earlier in the week and I told the authorities that I would not stand for that on my land, that despite Mr Churchill agreeing to segregation I did not, and either there was a middle road that we all could travel amicably or I would close my land off completely to all but the locals,' she said.

'And do you have the power to do that, my Lady?' Janie asked.

She smiled; 'Probably not, my dear, but the Americans don't know that, now do they!' We all laughed and mum, much to my surprise, gave her a hug; well done, my dear, well done indeed,' she chuckled.

The next dance... or the black and white dance, as we called it was arranged for the following weekend, and because of its status it was being looked forward to with both excitement and apprehension, with police from both camps on standby, along with the village copper, for all he would be worth, if push came to shove!

In spite of the danger of there being trouble, neither mum or dad could come, dad being too busy working and mum because she was called back to Yeovil, in Somerset, as Grandma Miller was very poorly, which meant Janie and me going to the dance alone.

'You watch out fer one another, mind,' dad advised as we started out on our great adventure, for an adventure it surely was, as neither of us, despite our Janie being almost 16, had ventured out to such an event on our own before! The one good thing was that none of our siblings were with us and so we only had ourselves to look after and we were both more than capable to do that.   It was a little scary though when we first walked into the hall, despite Lady Seymour being there to welcome us in... 'Look at all the black faces,' Janie whispered as we took our coats off.

'What did you expect, sis?' I whispered back, 'Ginger hair and freckles?'

She stifled a laugh and dug me in the ribs; 'no, of course not,' she sniggered.

With the hall filling up the all-black band started to play, mostly jazz and what they called soul music, unlike anything we were used to, but simply wonderful just the same.

Over in the corner a group of villagers stood drinking, seemingly mesmerized by the wonderful music, among them was Mr Briggs the pub owner's young daughter, Peggy, who on seeing us came over for a chat.

'Have you ever heard the likes of this?' she smiled; 'Beats our Vera Lynn, don't you think?'

'I'm not so sure, I love Vera Lynn, as do our mum and dad!' our Janie hesitated.

'Oh no, give me this music every day,' I countered, tapping my foot to the rhythm of the beat.

A young black soldier came then, to beg a dance with me, much to everyone's alarm; he was, I noticed the same man that Janie and me had stopped from being bullied a few days ago, but even so I have to admit to being a little nervous, but I smiled and accepted his hand. Although me and our Janie had practiced swing and the jive in our kitchen at home, we'd never ever done it for real and when the young man started to swing me to the beat of the music it was like something completely different, it was so smooth, and so perfectly in sync with the music... and nothing like dancing with my dad, I thought to myself, smothering a smile.

He changed partners after our second dance much to my annoyance, but as it was with my sister Janie I didn't complain, and she seemed to be having as much fun as me, and everyone around us seemed in such good spirits, as we took it in turns to jive, and jitterbug and swing around the floor, laughing and having fun with any of the soldiers who cared to ask us, some of them were such good dancers that they could spin two of us around the floor together, it was quite wonderful. But then for seemingly no reason, the music ground to a halt and there was a nervous buzz in the air, I looked at Janie and she nodded for me to look across the hall where a group of white soldiers stood glaring right at us, I have never seen such anger or such hatred in all my life!

There was going to be trouble, that was obvious, but even as I thought it, I noticed the white military policemen disappearing from view, leaving their friends to do as they pleased, and I'm sure they would have had not Lady Seymour stepped forward to stop them.

'You gentlemen will leave this minute or suffer the consequence, it is not your time yet and I will not hesitate to send for your commanding officer, and what's more, because of your actions here today, there will be no dance for anyone from your base, not now or at any time in the future unless you apologise here and now', she demanded. The men from the village gathered around her, daring the white soldiers to try anything, but it seems there was no need for their help as a white Major came striding into the hall and all the trouble makers stood to attention, their anger silenced without so much as a word from their commanding officer. A burly sergeant came in then to join his Major and barked orders at the guilty party, sending them to wait outside until they could be properly dealt with.

The young officer apologised to Lady Seymour then, on behalf of the American forces, and vowed that nothing like this would be allowed to happen again. Despite his obvious embarrassment, Lady Seymour was not about to leave it at that, I could see it in her eyes, what had just happened had upset her to the core; 'My husband fought and died for the freedom that both of our countries believe in, that's a freedom for all, not just for a chosen few, you tell that to your men major, and to your government too, if they'll listen, as I will tell it to my own people, given the platform and the right time. Because, Major, if your President and my Prime Minister fail to understand that, then what is the point of all this?' With a stiff salute the American officer turned on his heels and followed his men outside and all those of us remaining in the hall started cheering and Lady Seymour blushed as she wiped a tear away. Having to bring her beloved husbands name into the argument must have been difficult, but, I thought, she's right, neither he, nor the thousands of others who had given their lives in this conflict have done so for the benefit of any particular political party.

No, they have died for the sake of freedom... for the right everyone has to choose their own destiny, be they rich or poor, white or black. That is the point I knew, my Lady was putting across, the same idea that my mum and dad has always taught me to abide by, all be it in a much humbler setting, but it is the same message, over and over again, that we are all born equal!

As the white American officer left a huge cheer went up and the band struck up again and the dancing continued and Janie and me had our choice of village lads and black American soldiers, I even managed a dance with Robbo, when I finally prised him away from his Cinderella; Lady Seymour's maid, Wendy.

'Yore, chance'n it then, Rube' taken my arm, I mean, you know's it might come off, dun'ee? He grinned.

I laughed; 'Or Wendy might kill me!'

He blushed, and it was good to see him once more back to normal; 'So what of, 'er then, Rube, is she right for me, she 'as no farmin' knowledge you know,' he sighed.

'Robbo Drake! If you don't snatch her up and wed her then yore a fool,' I told him. 'No farmin' knowledge indeed! The only question is, do you love 'er and do she love ee back?' I sighed.

He whirled me around with his good arm and then let me fall to the floor; 'whoops, sorry,' he said with a grin, 'but all girls are prone ta trip over themselves now and then,' he chuckled. He helped me to my feet and we both giggled as he returned me to our Janie's side and went back to spooning with his girl, who has no farming knowledge! I told Janie what he'd said and we both had a good laugh. All the village and everyone across the heath knew they were bound to marry, well everyone except Robbo, it would seem!

In spite of one or two of these light moments 1942 was not going to be, as we all hoped and prayed for, the beginning of the end of the war, although dad was convinced that invading Russia was a big mistake for the Germans; pointing out what had happened to the French general, Bonaparte in the past. Something that neither Janie or I knew the slightest thing about, which made mum smile; 'It seems father is better learned than the two of you,' she chuckled.

With that dad went on to say that this Bonaparte chap had underestimated the Russians and that the Germans were now doing the same, 'keep your fingers crossed girls, that old Hitler will fall into the same trap!' he said. We soon began to doubt dad's wisdom though that the Russians would make a difference, as the air raid sirens blared out yet again, sending us scurrying to gather up the little-ones and take them across the yard to the shelter. It seemed things were getting worse despite the Yanks and the Russians. Seeing my look of despair, dad pointed towards the heavens; 'look up maid, see, they've not broken our air force,' he insisted as a squadron of Spitfires swept overhead to engage the enemy. 'That silly bugger Mr Hitler has chosen to go after our towns and cities and leave our airfields alone.'

'But why, dad?' I asked as we all huddled together in the shelter.

'Oh, that's easy, he think's it'll break our spirit, girl, that's what he's after doing, but he don't know us Brits, if he thinks that, the truth is, if anything it's making us stronger, more determined.'

Well, I couldn't argue with that, I could see that all around me, in the way people rallied to help one another whenever there was a need.

'Hitler will need ta march over every heath and moor in the land ta beat us, maid,' dad added.

By the time the air raid had finished dad had me convinced that we would win this war, no matter what, Heir Hitler did.

'We just 'ave ta be patient, I know's a lot of people might 'ave thought the war might be over soon, maid, but it 'as a long way ta go yet,' dad said, as we started back across the yard after the raid.

'But folk said it would be over by next Christmas?' I continued to argue.

He laughed, 'They've been sayin' that every year since it started! Well, it'll do no good ta argue about it, we'll just have ta wait and see, girl… but changin' the subject, 'ave you heard old Gypsy of late, why 'ee's been, howlin' his fool head off fer weeks now?' dad frowned.

I knew just what he was getting at. 'Come off it dad, you're just trying ta scare me, we both know what they say about a howling dog? But it's an old wives' tale and you know it,' I accused, as we went inside the house. As soon as the little-ones were settled I went to help our Janie lay the table in the kitchen ready for our tea; while mum and dad relaxed, to share a few minutes alone in the living room, while our Janet and Bella challenged Jack and Danny to a game of tiddlywinks.

In spite of mum and dad wanting to be alone to rest for a while, I just had to tackle dad again about old Gypsy's howling out across the heath, more to put my own mind at peace that anything else!

'Could it be he's just ailing dad; after all, this other stuff is just rubbish... or like I said; an old wives' tale!' I insisted.

He grinned; 'Old wives' tales have been known ta come true, girl, I bet you'd agree if Grandma Miller back in Yeovil told 'ee so?'

'Grandma Miller!' She was the hub of all the supernatural tales told in the family, it was because of her that both dad and me were so keen on telling ghost stories. Many a time we'd gathered about the fire at her home while she and dad took it in turns to see who could tell the most frightening tale, and it was Grandma who always won... she really could be a scary old lady at times.

'Maybe we should 'ave a ghost story tellin' contest tonight, maid,' he suggested, stretching his long legs out with a tired yawn, reckon I could best you,' he grinned.

'Our Janie won't go for that, dad, you know what she's like, frightened of her own shadow, she is,' I whispered softly, so that only mum and dad could hear. 'Although best not to tell her I said that', I added quickly.

'Afraid of getting' yer ears boxed, are you?' he chuckled.

Opposite him in her chair by the hearth, mum smiled knowingly.

'Something like that,' I laughed, before leaving them alone once more as I returned back to the kitchen to prepare a couple of dads recently poached rabbits. They needed eating up before anyone saw them, as it was of course still against the law to steal game from the landlord's fields. And what's more on closer inspection I saw that they were the ones Janie's and I had caught! Then I realised something that brought a smile to my lips and I laughed cheekily; we'd served rabbit to Lady Seymour the other night at the New Year eve party, and as she's our Landlady, she was in fact eating her own rabbits!

Chapter 17

I rarely thought of myself as Lady Seymour anymore. Walking through the hospital and out into my gardens I felt a little sad about that. But then I passed Reverend Clancy in a deep conversation with two recovering soldiers. All three of them seemed agitated and I slowed in case I could be of any help, not that I had any idea what it was all about. A few minutes later however the good reverend caught up with me, and he was on his own, looking back I was in time to see the two soldiers he'd been talking to disappear back into the hospital.

'Is everything alright?' I asked, seeing the worried look on his face.

'I hope so my Lady,' he sighed, looking back over his shoulder. 'Those two men have gone through so much; they were the rear-guard, ordered to lay down their lives to stop the Germans getting to the thousands of troops stranded at Dunkirk. Most of their platoon either died or were captured and they were among the last to be rescued off the beach. Brave, brave men indeed, but now that they are physically well, or deemed to be, they have been ordered to report for duty, to be shipped goodness knows where, and the trouble is my Lady, rather than return to their unit, they speak of deserting!

'Deserting! No, oh no, don't they realise that they'll be shot?' I gasped.

'They know only too well, my Lady... but to tell you the truth, they just don't care, better that, they say than face the hell of the war again, with all its atrocities.'

I felt a little angry at this, after all it wasn't their place to question orders, only to obey, just as thousands of others had, my Rory included. He had given his life in the end following orders. I felt suddenly sad and very bitter that these men should dare to think this way, it was their duty damn it!

I was about to tell the Reverend what I thought, when he spoke softly to me; 'I know these men, and they are the bravest, truest men I've ever met... so I ask myself, my Lady, could it be their minds that bear the wounds and not their bodies? It has been known, and thank goodness finally now it is being recognised as battle fatigue and can be treated as such." Of course, why had I not seen it myself? I felt a little ashamed of my uncharitable thoughts, I'd heard of battle fatigue of course, I'd just never come across a case of it, let alone two, and in my hospital!

'I think I need to speak with Sir Edmond, as head of the hospital he will know what to do, much more so than I do, in the meanwhile could you speak with the two young men concerned and let them know that I am looking into it, and that they will be going nowhere until I say so.' I affirmed.

The reverend smiled, 'I knew you would understand my Lady, now all we have to do is persuade those two that it's alright to feel as they do, that it's natural to hate and fear all that war is.'

With that he left to find the two men, while I went to find my head of the hospital, Sir Edmond Bruce, to pick his brains on how to handle the situation without the soldiers concerned being arrested and charged with cowardice and desertion.

I found my man coming out of the surgery wing, looking very tired, which wasn't a surprise as we'd had two lorries full of injured sailors arrive late last night, all in need of attention, many having to have surgery of some kind or other, so it was no wonder Sir Edmond looked all in! I could see the frown on his forehead deepen as I approached and felt a twinge of guilt as it was obvious all he wanted was a hot drink, a bit of breakfast and a soft bed, none the less, I needed his advice, and it couldn't wait, not if I were going to intervene in a tragic mistake.

We walked along the corridor to his office, which had once been the children's play room, where he sat heavily down into his chair, waiting for me to speak. When I'd told him my tale of the two soldiers, he sighed; 'It's not a new story, Lady Seymour, we send these men… and women too, on occasions, off to war and ask unspeakable things of them and expect them to return the same people as before, but many of them don't, how can they be unchanged by the killing and torture they are asked to be part of?'

'What we need here is a better rehabilitation centre, and a good phycologist to run it, and I believe I know just the man, he happens to be working quite close to here at the moment as it happens; Dorchester, would you believe. I shouldn't think that he'll be able to come right away, but we can send our two soldiers down to him for the time being, and then, if he can't come here to work, I'm sure he'll be able to recommend someone for us.'

'Wonderful, Sir Edmond, I'll let Reverend Clancy know at once and he can inform the soldiers of our plans, I just pray that they have done nothing foolish in the meantime.'

He yawned; 'And now, I would very much like to catchup on a little sleep, Lady Seymour,' he said, eyeing the couch in the corner of the room.

Thanking him for his time I backed quietly from the room and went in search of the Reverent, wanting him to let the two soldiers know right away that they wouldn't be going back to the front any time soon, and that they were going to be transferred to Dorchester until we could treat them here.

After a search of the hospital and the grounds, I finally located my friend, where I should have looked for him in the first place, in his church, along with our two soldiers, both of whom looked like they were ready to jump at the slightest sound, and indeed leapt to their feet as I pushed the great big creaky door open on entering.

'Easy men!' I smiled, 'I have some good news for you... you will not be going back to the front anytime soon...' I then explained our plans for them and the younger of them couldn't hold back a tear and the other one let out a huge sigh of relief... 'We're not cowards, my Lady... it's just that... well I can't say what it is really, for my part, it just came on all of a sudden like, and I just froze, I couldn't fire my gun or march forward or even run away, I just sort of stood there trembling so hard that I couldn't stop!'

The younger soldier nodded in agreement, his limbs shaking, his powder blue eyes full of fear as he reached a hand to wipe the sweat from his brow. I reached out to touch his shoulder, feeling even more guilty for my uncharitable thoughts earlier about the two men; 'As soon as we have the right facilities here at Sandbourne we will bring you back from Dorchester, and I promise you both that you will not be sent back to the front until you are ready.' All four of us walked back to the hospital together then, each of us, I'm sure, deep in our own thoughts, for me I could not help but wonder if my husband Rory had suffered from the same fear that these two had. Just the thought of it brought a tear to my eye, that he should be so troubled and with no one to comfort him! It was not something I wanted my mind to dwell on after witnessing the fear and helplessness in the eyes of the two soldiers, for I'm sure they were as brave as my Rory.

I took a deep breath, If I have learned anything from the ruckus of this war, it is to live life with eager zealous and to help others do the same, and not to live life for tomorrow... for, who knows about tomorrow? Perhaps it will never come! Leaving the Reverend to see the two soldiers back to their ward I went to arrange the transfer of them across to our friends in Dorchester, but was unable to complete that as they needed Sir Edmond to confirm it, and he was still sleeping. I smiled, it could wait another hour or so, I wouldn't wake him. Thoughts of my Rory came to me then and I sniffed back a tear... 'you just never know,' I sighed softly.

Thinking of Rory, I decided it was time his father, the Laird came down to pay us a visit, after all he was the reason, I'd turned my home into a hospital, and so it was only right that he saw for himself the mischief his brain child has caused.

With that in mind I rang Kirriemuir castle and spoke to the Laird himself.

'So, you'll come then?'

He chuckled; 'How could I not, my dear, with you holding my grandchildren like a pistol to my head, saying how upset they'll be should I refuse.'

'Oh, no, please, I didn't mean it like that... only they truly would love to see you again, Lord Andrew, as would I and not only to seek your opinion on all we've done here, but for your good company too,' I assured him.

He laughed heartily, 'Nicely put my dear, how can I refuse such an offer, I've one or two things to do here first, but come, let us set a date, would the beginning of March suit you?'

I had no need to think about it or to ask anyone else and so it was agreed that the beginning of March it would be and I couldn't wait to tell the children.

But before he rang off, he had something else to tell me; 'I have a merchant seaman here at Kirriemuir, who would you believe belongs down your way; his name is Briggs, Toby Briggs, claims his uncle runs the public house in Sandbourne village, do you know of such a fellow?' the Laird asked.

'I do indeed, Mr Briggs was a great help to me when I was forced to put on a dance not so long ago... but that's another story, indeed, if this fellow is half the man his uncle is then he's more than welcome here. Will you send him on ahead or will you bring him down when you come?' I asked.

'I'll send him on ahead, I think, lassie, in case I should get held up, I'm sure the man must be impatient to be reunited with his family.'

'Thank you, my Lord, I'll be sure to inform Mr Briggs and we look forward to seeing you soon, the children will be thrilled when I break the news to them.' I assured him.

I couldn't wait to tell the children, but disappointingly they were out on a nature ramble with Nannie and so I decided to walk to the village and break the good news to Mr Briggs about his nephew. Once again however I was thwarted as he had gone off to Dorchester town to fetch some barrels of beer for the pub. His daughter Peggy was at home however and so I gave her the news about her cousin. To my surprise she turned pale and almost fainted and no doubt would have had I not caught her and steered her to a chair; 'What on earth is the matter my dear?' I asked her. She seemed suddenly full of tears, a strange way to react to such good tidings? But then she told me why she felt as she did. 'I'm so sorry, my Lady, but my cousin, Toby Briggs, is not a nice man,' she started to cry then and I was forced to comfort her, wondering just what this was all about.

'Toby lived with his mum and dad in Poole, mostly, but he was apt to coming over on the ferry two or three times a week, to spend time with us here in Sandbourne.'

'The trouble being, he was always after me, my Lady, trying it on, as dad would say, with not a care that we was so close related, in the end when he was called up, I was glad ta see the back of him.'

I was shocked by all I was hearing; 'What did your father say about his behaviour?' I asked her.

'I never did tell dad, for fear of what he might have done, my Lady, I'd hoped by the time Toby returned his nature might have changed for the better.'

'And maybe it has, my dear, war can change a person after all, but if it hasn't, then tell your father, or come to me, one of us will take care of the problem, I promise you,' I told her.

On my walk back to the hospital I had this very strong feeling that I'd made a mistake by inviting the young man to come here. I could of course ring the Laird and ask him not to send the man here, but in the end, none of us could prevent him from returning home; and as his home was but a ferry ride away from Sandbourne, well, there really was nothing we could do. By the time I made it back to the hospital

I was determined to find out as much as I could about this young man and so I called on my many navel connections. What I learnt was that he was not well liked, not even by his shipmates. It seems he is a bully and a braggard and prone to picking on the weakest young seamen around him, and what's more, there was a rumour of cowardly conduct on his last ship, The Foreigner, before it was sunk! The Foreigner? Something about the name rattled a memory, now where had I heard it before? But try as I may I couldn't remember for the life of me!

The children were back and as I hurried to meet them and give them the good news that their grandfather was coming for a visit, I suddenly recalled just where I'd heard the name of that ship. It was from our young, Prince Charming, our very own, Robbo. That had been his ship too! Now we were getting somewhere, with any luck he might recall this young Mr Briggs and be able to tell us something about him. Perhaps they'd been friends, now wouldn't that be nice. After telling the children the good news, about their grandfather coming I set off to speak with my young friend Robbo. if we were still friends after I'd shanghaied him into my Pantomime last Christmas... but at least he'd met Wendy, his Cinderella, now the love of his life, he owed me for that didn't he?

Once again, I stopped off at the Miller place on the way, although neither of them was at home, but Jane was in; I came upon her preparing to leave to go to work in my kitchen. Knowing what a resourceful young lady she was I told her my dilemma.

'Don't you worry my Lady, Robbo will help if he can, I'm sure of it, if he knows the man, he'll tell you all you want's ta know, his loyalty is ta us first, my Lady,' she smiled.

The warmth of her words, made me blush, she spoke of his loyalty to us as if we were all one big family and it felt nice somehow. It gave me a little more confidence as I started on down towards the Drakes farm. She waved a thank you and I went on my way quietly pleased with myself for finding someone who might not be, just Robbo's shipmate but perhaps a good friend too.

Nervously I knocked the door and was called to come in, I found him alone in the kitchen, and I was pleased that no-one else was in.

'Father's out across the woods with Mr Miller and mums walked into the village,' he apologised.

'Ah! Well, it's you I've come to see, Robbo,' I told him.

'Don't want I ta do any more Panto's do ee'?' he asked suspiciously, with a slight grin.

I smiled, 'No it's a little more serious than that I'm afraid, Robbo, I'm here after some information? Do you know someone by the name of Toby Briggs?'

His soft demeaner stiffened in an instant; 'Where did you hear that name from, my Lady?'

'I take it that you have heard of the man then, Robbo?' I sighed.

His jaw tightened; 'Aye, I know the worm, though I'd rather I didn't, I hoped to God that he'd met his end to tell you the truth of it, my Lady. But as you're askin' about 'im, I take it he still lives, but not for long if I get my hands on 'im, I swear I'll kill the monster myself!'

'Oh Robbo, no, no, what on earth did he do to make you want to do such a thing?' I cried.

'Killed a man, a fellow shipmate for a single lifejacket, that's what he did! I watched him do it with my own eyes as I struggled to save my arm that was trapped and broken under the weight of a munition box! He struck the man and pushed 'im under the water and drowned him, he did, I saw it all but could do nothing.'

'And did you report what you'd seen?' I asked him, shocked by all he'd told me.

'No, my Lady, it was chaos, the ship was burning, men were running every which way, many like myself, badly injured, some even worse, burnt and dying, screaming to be put out of their agony... it was every seaman's worse nightmare, with no time for a tale of murder... I prayed that the devil had gotten his just desert and lay floating among the dead, like the man he'd killed.'

'He survived, Robbo, he was picked up by a rescue boat off the Irish coast and ended up in my father-in-law's hospital in Scotland. Right now, he is being transferred to his home town of Poole.' I told him, and watched his face turn to thunder.

'I'll kill him, I swear, I will, my Lady, the man's a murderer, a cold-blooded murderer,' Robbo raged, slamming his fist down on the old kitchen table.

I put a hand on his shoulder, you're not the only one to be worried about this man, Mr Briggs...'

'What? Mr Briggs the pub landlord, is he a relative then, I should 'ave guessed by them 'avin' the same surname,' Robbo interrupted.

'Well, I can assure you he'll find no welcome there, Robbo,' I said, going on to tell him what the landlords daughter Peggy had told me.'

'Can't you do something, my Lady, stop the monster frum comin' back 'ere?' he pleaded.

I knew I had to do something, this man needed to be brought to justice, needed to pay for the grave crime he'd committed, but what to do?

'For starters my Lady, can't you ask your father-in-law to keep the man up there, until I've had time to report what I know?' Robbo pleaded.

'Of course, I'll ring the Laird, he'll know what to do, thank you Robbo, will your mother mind if I use her telephone, I'll pay her for the call of course,' I promised.

He waved me toward the telephone and I rang Kirriemuir Castle, but I was too late, the hospital matron said that the Laird was already on his way down to me and that Toby Briggs had been released from the hospital two days ago! Robbo leapt to his feet when I broke the news to him; 'That means that he could already be here, my Lady,' he barked angrily.

'We must get a message to the public house and Mr Briggs and his daughter, Robbo, come, you must do that, while I go back to the hospital to await the Laird,' I insisted.

Together we hurried back up across the heath to the Miller's place where we gathered up Jane, to take her to work but before that we stopped at the village public Inn, to warn them to be on the lookout for Toby Briggs. Old Mr Briggs was back at the pub now and looking very grave indeed, convincing me that his daughter had told him everything.

But not quite everything! I quickly outlined just what other crimes he was accused of. Neither Peggy or her father were the least bit surprised, saying that he was a rogue and always has been. But thankfully they had seen nothing of him, still I advised Mr Briggs to be on the lookout and to inform the local police constable about him, and how dangerous he was.

Leaving Robbo with them for added protection, Jane and me headed on down to the hospital where I was pleased to find the Laird being taken on a tour by Stella, one of my committee ladies, and they appeared to be getting along famously! Reluctant as I was to interrupt their amiable tour, I had to tell him about his former patient, let him know the sort of man he'd been treating, and discover if he'd given away where he might be going on leaving the hospital in Scotland. Stella gave us space when I caught up with them, rather reluctantly, I thought, but none the less I did manage to speak with my father-in-law alone.

'So, the man is a murderer then, worst still he killed a helpless shipmate... if only I'd known, I'd have willingly done for the man myself,' the Laird raged, his anger getting the better of him.

I placed a hand on his arm; 'No, you wouldn't, Sir, that is not your way, it's his way, this Toby Briggs, but it is not yours, you would endeavour to bring him to the justice he deserves.'

'And this Robbo saw it all, you say, saw him kill the other man in cold blood?' The Laird demanded. 'And is this witness a reliable man, can we trust his word on this?' he asked.

'He's as trustworthy as you or I, my Lord, I have come to know him well and his family too and I would trust them with my life and the lives of my children,' I declared.

'Then that's good enough for me, Lass, now all we have to do is catch the rogue, you have this Robbo inside the Inn and the Constable watching the place, so we must simply wait for him to make his next move, no matter how long that takes.' The Laird sighed.

For all of a week we were on the edge of our nerves, waiting for him to show himself, poor Peggy, the landlord's daughter beside herself with worry knowing his hankering for her.   All of us expected a night approach, with him creeping stealthily upon the Inn, looking for a door or window to prise open, instead he came at the busiest time, on market day, when the pub was heaving with farmers and farmhands, he was hoping no doubt not to be noticed in the throng of bodies. Unfortunately for him, Robbo recognized him and pointed him out to me, while I sat with Iris in the Snug taking my turn in keeping an eye on Peggy. The man was staring at her as she served behind the bar, watching her every move, obviously obsessed with her. I felt relieved and a little scared, but Robbo was here and the Laird, all watching out for the young woman. But then an argument broke out between two of the local farmers and for a moment we were all distracted and when we looked again our murderer was gone! We all rushed forward; 'Where's Peggy?' Robbo shouted at Mr Briggs who was behind the bar.

'Don't worry 'er's down in the cellar fetchin' up a crate of bottled beer,' he assured us, obviously having no idea that his evil nephew was, even as we stood there talking, hunting her down!   'Out of the way,' Robbo snapped almost sending poor Mr Briggs flying, as he barged passed, with myself close on his heels. As we clambered down into the cellar, I saw him first, he had his hands around the poor girl's throat, choking her to death, I screamed in my horror and as he spun toward us Robbo stepping passed me flattening him with a wicked punch to the jaw.

With all the noise we were soon joined by the village constable, several burly farmers and Mr Briggs, the Inn keeper, who rushed to his daughter's side as she struggled to her feet.
    'Oh my God, I didn't see him, I should have noticed him, I'm so sorry my dear,' he wept taking his daughter in his arms.
    'It's alright dad, I didn't see him come in the pub either, it's not your fault,' she said wrapping her arms about his neck and crying on his shoulder.

Robbo came to stand at my side then; 'Sorry you had ta see that side of me, my Lady, but I've been promising myself the pleasure of punching him ever since you told me he was alive. But it's over now, and hopefully he'll get what's coming to him,' he said taking a deep breath, as the Laird and the constable came to take the odorous man away. I was able to get a closer look at him as they dragged him away and he was a quite an ordinary sort, with nothing that spoke of murder about him. But then, it is never written on one's forehead for the world to see, it is always hidden away, usually behind a friendly façade. I shivered at the thought, then relaxed, for it is not an everyday occurrence to come across a murderer in our midst.

With the man taken into custody and the threat gone, we could once more relax, and despite the noise and smell of the animals, enjoy the coming together of the people from all corners of the district who were a huge part of market day. Mr Briggs and his daughter Peggy were finally able to relax now that the bad apple of their family was being carted off to prison and who would most certainly be hung in the end for his terrible crime. A sad and terrible climax for a man of the merchant navy, a man brave enough to risk his life out on the wild cruel seas, but who in the end could not find the courage to help another, indeed deciding that it was either him or the other chap, and so instead of helping, he killed him!

Finally returning to the hospital after all that had happened, I could relax and concentrate on the Laird and my children, who were already tugging at his hand, wanting to take him on a tour of their own, despite him already seeing all there was to see with Stella and myself. Still, they insisted and it took Nannie ringing the bell to announce that tea was ready to save him having to do it over again. Later, and before curfew we set off to explore a little slice of my estate as I wanted to introduce the Laird to some of my other friends; namely the Drakes, although he'd already met Robbo, but most of all, my very good friends the Miller family, who were about to take tea with the Davis twins and their mother and father, so we didn't stay, but I was glad that my father-in-law had met them.

On the way back to the hospital after our bout of visiting the Laird was unusually quiet and I thought I might have been wrong taking him to share his time with such lowly people. But I should have known better, should have judged him better, for he was not that sort of man, like his son Rory, my beloved husband, he judged people on merit not on wealth.

'You have something quite special here, you know, my dear,' he smiled. 'Rarely have I met such bonny people and every one of them ready to run to your aid should you call, it is a treat to see, and a weight off my mind that you are so well thought of and cared for.'

I sighed; 'So you agree with my own thinking, that Rory would like my new friends too, even though they are not full of airs and graces and so worldly as most of our old acquaintances?'

'Aye, that I do, lassie, my boy would just love these people as do I, and you've done well to gather their like about you in the short time you've been here.' The Laird complimented warmly.

'And the hospital, what do you think about how I've set it up, would you have done it any different... although it looks very much like Kirriemuir, as it should, given that I copied your own plans, my Lord, I smiled.

'If I spoke against it then I'd be speaking against my own architects,' he chuckled, 'and of course my own designs, given that I chose them... no my dear, your hospital like my own in Scotland is perfect.'

I felt terribly proud all at once, as well as very sad, that Rory was not here to see it all for himself, but of course he is here really, looking through my own eyes, his father's eyes and his children's too, and he always will be, as long as we all shall live.

To our delight the Laird stayed to see us through what remained of the winter and into the beginnings of Spring, seeing the heathland up around the Millers place blossom, just as sure as if he were back home in the Highlands.

He brokered a goodly friendship with Iris's Fred and farmer Drake, who took him out across the bay in one of the remaining boats to fish for Mackerel, they said, but to enjoy a bottle or two of beer and a quiet moment alone without women and children, is what we all thought it was about. Still, whatever it was for, it was good to see the Laird so happy, for like myself the hurt of losing Rory lay a yawning abyss within us, a never-ending canyon of grief that will run through us forever, something only people who have lost loved ones much too early, can relate to. But I repeat, it is so nice to see him carefree, if only for a little while.

It was the beginning of April when he took his leave of us on a bright Spring morning filled with the promise of things to come, one of which we all hoped might be the end of the war, but there was little sign of that yet... but as usual we dared to dream! It's fair to say that my father-in-law made a big impacted on our little community while he was here and so when he left the streets of the village were lined with people wishing him well. Having the Laird with us has been a rare treat, but all through his stay the hospital has been filling up fit to burst and it became clear that we needed to move the patients on quicker. The Laird had suggested that I should ask around my old, wealthy friends, as he'd done back in Kirriemuir, coming up with no fewer than 5 new rehabilitation homes! With that in mind I began a crusade among my old hunting, shooting and Oxford University set, plus anyone else with estates and big houses that might be up for giving us a helping hand. Once again, I turned to my committee ladies, although I did have to leave Iris out of this quest as sadly, she and her Fred did not move in those kinds of circles. Thankfully she understood and didn't take offence, instead, helped out by covering for me at the hospital while I was on my travels.

For a full week I telephoned everyone I knew within fifty miles or so of us, reaching down as far as the wild Cornish coast. The response, as I hoped it would, was heart-warming, resulting in twenty big houses across the southwest, opening their doors to us, it was all quite amazing.

With such great news I arranged with Sir Edmond, the head of our hospital to send envoys from the Ministry to talk with the owners of the large Estates, to explain exactly what they would need to do to be ready to receive patients. Thankfully quite a few of them were already in the process of turning large parts of their homes over to the military as part of the war effort, so we were able to start shipping our less serious cases to them almost immediately, and so freeing up the ever-growing number of patients being offloaded from the Poole ferries every day, mostly sailors, saved from torpedoed naval and merchant ships. But the worst were the soldiers rescued from the hospital ships after they'd been sunk by the German's submarines, already wounded and in pain they were traumatized yet again as they had to be dragged from the sea... many didn't survive their second brush with death and those that did were, in many cases, beyond normal hospital care. All the more reason then why I was so pleased, on my first foray down along the Southwest of England, to agree with three of my old friends to each take ten of our recovering patients, so freeing up thirty beds, it was beyond my expectations. No wonder then that I returned to Sandbourne a happy bunny!

Even before I stepped from the car on my return to the hospital, I was surprised by Stella, my fellow committee member coming to help me out, not that I needed helping out of the car!

'Um! I wanted to catch you on your own, my Lady...' she seemed very hesitant and that worried me; was something wrong in the hospital?

'Stella... out with it now, what's wrong?' I asked worriedly.

'Oh! No! Nothing is wrong my Lady, it's just that... well actually... to tell the truth... it's the Laird...

'The Laird, oh my, what's wrong, is he ill?' I demanded desperately.

She held up a hand to stop me; 'The Laird has invited me up to Kirriemuir, Lady Seymour, not alone of course, I will be taking my lady's maid. But I will not go if you disapprove my Lady.'

I have to confess to being very surprised, I had witnessed just how well the two of them seemed to get along during the Lairds stay with us, but never thought anymore about it. I smiled, well good luck to them, they were unattached and both were good people, so why not. Leaning in I kissed her on the cheek; 'Stella, if the Laird has invited you up to Kirriemuir then he likes you, and as I like you too, you have my blessing, not that you need it of course,' I added quickly.

As I stood watching her car disappear over the crest of the drive, I must admit to feeling quite emotional, and said a silent prayer for them both, they were good people, who like myself had lost the love of their lives, was it asking too much for them to find it again? Would I find it again? The thought dared to flash through my head, but quickly I blinked it aside, there was only Rory for me, now and forever more. I felt a tear trickle down my cheek and quickly brushed it away, I had to report my success to Sir Edmond and with his help choose which patients to send to our new hospitals.

When I finally caught up with him as he came out of surgery, he was as pleased as I'd hoped he'd be at the prospect of freeing up 30 beds. What with our hospital here at Sandbourne being on the front line and in great demand it was important that we moved patients on quickly.

'I still have 6 great manor houses to see this week, all of them belonging to old friends and acquaintances, so I am optimistic on that front too, Sir Edmond,' I announced proudly as we took tea in his office.

'There is no deigning it Lady Seymour, you are a wonder,' he smiled. 'I knew it even before I came here, from when I first picked up your letter and read what you had in mind, I knew I wanted to be a part of your plans... and now here we are!'

I knew I was blushing but I couldn't help it, to have such praise heaped upon me, by such a man as this was beyond belief, my Rory would be so pleased for me.

Later as I made plans to continue my journey down around Devon and Cornwall, I decided that it might be nice to have some company this time, Amber came to mind, but perhaps not, she did talk a lot and could be a little overwhelming at times, someone quieter then? One of the Miller girls... Ruby! Yes, Ruby would do nicely, she was quite well spoken and if necessary, could entertain me with one of her stories as we travelled along the narrow byways of the west country.

After running the idea passed Iris, who had no problems with her daughter missing a few school days by coming with me, I asked the girl herself and to my delight she was thrilled with the idea.
'No ghost stories mind,' I said, as we set off up the drive, with a lazy sun doing its best to break through the powdery white, cloudy sky, in an effort to add a sparkle to this early touch of Spring.
'Is that a new sticker on your windscreen?' Ruby asked as she settled into her seat next to me.
'Yes, it's a C sticker which allows us extra petrol for our work should we need it,' I smiled

Chapter 18

Life has a way of surprising you sometimes in ways that even I Ruby Miller, with my vivid imagination fail to see coming. What with all the books that I read and all the tales of adventures and spooky ghost stories I tell my siblings, nothing should astonish me... but yesterday mum did just that!

'Lady Seymour has asked if you might travel with her for a few days as she goes in search of big houses that might be turned into hospitals.' Mum explained after breakfast. At first, I couldn't believe my ears... Lady Seymour asking for me to travel with her!

'What about school?' I asked.

'Would you rather go to school?' mum asked. I shook my head. Even as she came in her big black car to pick me up the following day, I just could not believe what was happening. Why on earth would Lady Seymour ask me to accompany her on a trip, after all I only read to her children and keep them company.

I was so stunned that I was aware that I'd said hardly a word since we began our journey, and now I was sitting here at Lady Seymour's side and we were travelling through Cornwall, meandering down narrow country lanes.

'This is so beautiful my Lady,' I muttered looking along a road
 beset on both sides by beautiful vibrant hedgerows of fragrant Primroses, violets, bluebells and yellow cowslips, swaying majestically in the breeze.

'Found your voice then Ruby,' Lady Seymour chuckled.

'Sorry, my Lady, but I can scarce believe this is happening to me? It's like something out of one of the stories I tell the children, a fairy-tale come true!' I sighed.

She laughed, slowing the car to a crawl; 'Here we are then,' she said, awaking me from my daydreams.

We were just entering through a great stone arch that led us through to a driveway at the top of which a grand house stood and it was by far more splendid even than Sandbourne Manor. I could only sit and gape as we grew nearer.

'That is true Victorian architecture for you,' Lady Seymour said with just a hint of a smile. 'Never add two wings, if you can add five or six,' she tutted.

I was simply too speechless to answer, it wasn't just grand it was… well it was amazing! 'Wow!' was all that I could manage.

A group of people came out to welcome us as we pulled up at the front door, several of them servants, while it was clear to see that the others were the grand family who lived here. They consisted of an elderly couple and a young woman as far as I could tell, all of them friends of her Ladyship.

'Kathrine, my dear friend, how lovely to see you, welcome… Jenkins, the bags please,' the attractive young woman said, coming to greet us. I did know Lady Seymour's Christian name, although I don't believe I'd ever heard it called before, but I liked it, 'Kathrine' suited her perfectly.

'Hello Charlotte, it's been a long time, too long for my liking, how are you?' Lady Seymour asked embracing her warmly.

'Ruby, come here, I'd like you to meet my dear friend, Lady Court, of Landrake Hall, Lady Seymour said waving me forward. I was gobsmacked, to be travelling with a Lady and now to be introduced to another Lady, was beyond belief. I could hardly wait to get home to tell my family, although I was not sure they'd ever believe me, I know I wouldn't if the shoe was on the other foot.

Our hostess greeted me well enough although I thought that I sensed a hint of wonder in her voice at my being with her Ladyship! Out of the corner of my eye as I returned to my seat next to the door, I saw Lady Seymour lean towards her friend and say something and the woman, smiled and said; 'I see!' Before speaking to me.

'So, Ruby, are you hungry? I expect you must be after such a long drive.' Lady Court said. For a moment, by the look on her face I expected her to send me along to the kitchen, with the rest of the servants, after all it was my place.

But instead, knowing, no doubt that Lady Seymour was watching, she took my arm and guided me along with the rest of her family into the Parlour. A light lunch had been set out for us and it looked so delicious, that I couldn't wait to tuck in... as I sat down, I wondered just what my siblings would think if they could see me now. Glancing at our hostess, Lady Court I could tell that she was clearly uncomfortable! I could see it even if no-one else could, although I fancied the rest of her family felt the same, given how they were all looking down their Aristocratic noses at me. I could have been angry, but a little voice whispered in my ear that I shouldn't expect every one of the upper classes to be like Lady Seymour, she was an exception to the rules.

'So, Kathrine tells me that you are a story teller,' Lady Court said, breaking into my thoughts as she took her seat next to me.   Despite the showy weak smile, there was an air of frost in her voice, telling me that she was not used to sharing her table with the likes of me.

But her words sparked a warm response elsewhere, for no sooner had she said the words, story teller, than two children, whom I hadn't even noticed popped their heads up and eagerly hurried over to sit opposite me. Lady Seymour and everyone else laughed, including our hostess, while I blushed and gave them a smile.

'Nothing changes, does it, Ruby, always the centre of attraction,' Lady Seymour smiled. I knew I was blushing but taking a deep breath chose to ignore it and hope that everyone else did too, and thankfully they seemed to do just that, changing the subject to what we had travelled all this way for, to set up a new hospital wing here!

'Ruby, would you be a dear and keep the children company while we show Kathrine... sorry, Lady Seymour around, I could ring for nannie, but on this occasion, I think they might prefer you,' our hostess said, getting to her feet and sounding less stuffy. Everyone rose then and proceeded to move towards the door; 'the children will show you where their playroom is,' she said, over her shoulder, her voice flat and matter-a-fact.

Suddenly the children and me were on our own, and I didn't even know their names, although that was soon put right as the little girl took my hand; 'I'm Sofia and I'm 8,' she said confidently. The little boy tugged at the fingers of my other hand; 'I'm Albert and I'm 6,' he muttered a little less sure of himself, than his sister.

'And my name is Ruby, in case you didn't hear,' I replied. 'Now how about showing me your play-room before the grownups return and spoil our fun.' I winked, and they laughed. By the time the others returned I'd told them two short stories and was on a third that the children were desperate for me to finish, shooing the grownup's away from the playroom and back into the Morning room until I'd finished.

It's true to say that my head was in quite a spin as I was shown to a small room of my own in the servant's quarters, I'd never had a whole bedroom to myself before, I smiled; 'What do you think of this our Janie?' I muttered softly to myself.

'Well, you were certainly a big hit Ruby, I think I should take you with me all the time, not only did the children get what they wanted but so too did I; Lord Court has agreed to turn his west wing into a 20 bed, recuperation hospital.' Lady Seymour, smiled the next day as we began our journey home along the narrow twisty roads of Cornwall.

'Well done my Lady,' I grinned. I felt so pleased, as if I'd done my bit towards helping her precure it all, but of course it was all down to her Ladyship really, but just being at her side while she'd achieved her goal was good enough.

On our way back to Sandbourne we called in on three more of Lady Seymours old friends, two of whom were already doing their bit by sharing their grounds and grand house with the newly arrived American troops, while the third one joined our cause, offering rooms for a dozen or more beds. I have to say that I felt the same hostility, well perhaps not exactly hostility, but coolness as in the Courts fancy house. But I was alright with it now.

It somehow made my friendship with Lady Seymour and her family even more special. Anyway, all in all, our trip had been such a huge success that it had her Ladyship singing along with me, as we made our way back through the west country, both as happy as larks as mum would say.

It had been a long, long trip and Lady Seymour rued her decision not to stay over another night at one or other of her friend's houses, for they all had asked us to. But we didn't and so, as she dropped me off at home up on the heath, all I wanted was a good night's sleep. But there was little hope of that, my siblings swarmed to meet me even as I stepped from the car, and not even strong words from our Janie could stop them. But after a few minutes mum rescued me, ordering my siblings to their bedrooms while she and I and of course our Janie talked, or rather I talked while they listened to all I'd been through.

'Why is it that you get all the breaks, sis?' Janie sighed, later when we were alone.

'Because I'm me of course,' I chuckled.

I knew I shouldn't have said it almost as soon as it left my big mouth; our Janie was on me in a flash beating me silly with her hairbrush, until my backside was hurting and I begged her to stop.

'So, sis, not all the posh people are so nice then, not like our posh lot?' she added.

I shook my head, 'No nothing like our posh lot,' I grinned.

True to her word Lady Seymour took me with her on other sorties across the west country in search of rehabilitation hospitals. So far, she has managed to sign up no fewer than ten big houses to her cause. Mum said that I should be proud of myself, but really all I did was keep her company along the way.

'Never-the-less Lady Seymour is convinced that she wouldn't manage without you, Ruby. 'Goodness knows why, child?' Mum shrugged, winking at our Janie, who had a fit of the giggles... but I didn't care, I was travelling with someone I truly liked.

Today we were heading for South Devon and a place called Bigbury-on-sea, an odd sort of a name for a village, although it sounded simply wonderful to me. I couldn't stop talking as her Ladyship picked me up and we travelled on our way, both of us it seemed so full of excitement.

'I've a lovely treat for you today, Ruby,' Lady Seymour, smiled as we pulled into the village.

I wasn't really listening, my mind captured by the beauty of the place, my eyes ignoring the usual tank traps and barbed wire everywhere, saw only the island across the way. 'Have you heard of Agatha Christie?' Lady Seymour asked as she parked the car and we climbed out. The wind blowing a little stiffly off the sea, forced us to pull our coats a little tighter.

I nodded, 'she wrote a book called; 'And then there were none!' A very scary book it was, just the right sort of story for the likes of me and our dad.'

Lady Seymour smiled and said that she'd read the book too, but was surprised that my father had read it! I had to explain; 'Dad didn't actually read it himself, he doesn't read much, unless it's the sports pages in the Daily Mirror! But he enjoyed me reading it to him, and declared this Agatha Christie woman to be alright and that she told a good tale… almost as good as he did, although not quite as good, claiming that she could have thrown a few ghosts in. Lady Seymour laughed before striding away, forcing me to hurry to catch her up. I wondered what the hurry was, the tide was in and there seemed no way to get to the island just yet. Then I saw the sea tractor, in truth it was too big to miss, but until now I had somehow.

'Here's our transport to the island, Ruby, what do you think of it?' she smiled climbing aboard.

I stood back to take it in, it was huge, more like a tractor on stilts really, looking very unstable to my eyes, causing me to hesitate before following her Ladyship up the steps to the top.

The engine started with a splutter and a loud pop and then, very slowly we inched our way through the waves towards the island, seeing my nervousness Lady Seymour came to stand at my side; 'You might be interested to know that Agatha Christie wrote; 'And then there were none;' while staying on Burgh Island,' she said pointing on ahead. I felt even more intrigued as we approached the landing dock and so very lucky, what stories I would have to tell my brothers and sisters after this adventure; and the tales kept coming. First there was the ancient Pilchard Inn that we walked past on leaving the sea tractor, a spooky old place, that could easily have come out of one of dad's ghost stories, it gave me goosebumps just to be so close to it. But in truth, I couldn't take my eyes off the magnificent hotel standing proud at the top of the hill; 'this sort of design is called Art Deco,' Lady Seymour explained.

'It's beautiful,' I gasped.

'I believe it was once described as a shining white ocean liner surrounded by golden beaches and silver sea'. Her Ladyship sighed softly.

I could well believe that, looking up at the hotel as we made our way through the garden, it seemed every inch the fairy story that was painted inside my head, making me fear that I would never be able to capture its beauty as I told my siblings of it when we returned home.

'While I'm speaking with the owners perhaps, you'd like to explore the island?' Lady Seymour suggested as we reached the hotel.

Leaving her at the door I meandered on up through the garden before making my way down to a small bay, surprisingly unblemished by the trappings of war, where bluer than blue waves rode in to stroke gently upon golden yellow sands, a sight so pure and so very pretty that it brought a tear to my eye.

'Don't cry, my dear, such beauty can never be contained for long and so deserves a smile, don't you think?'

I was a little startled by the voice that seemed to come out of thin air! Then I saw her, a small, rather cheerful looking woman, perched on a rock dangling her feet in the sea.

'Isn't it a bit cold to be doing that?' I asked her.

She laughed, 'nonsense child, it is Spring after all and a good paddle doesn't hurt anyone, you should try it... come on... um, what's your name my dear?'

'Ruby,' I answered, 'my name is Ruby.'

'Well pleased to meet you Ruby, and may I say what a pretty little thing you are... now off with those shoes... that's it, kick them off, and join me,' she insisted.

I don't know what came over me, but such was the warmth of her smile that I felt obliged to do as she asked... but oh my, the water was bitter cold and I would have given up in a matter of seconds but for her... but if an old woman can stand the cold, then so can I, I told myself.

She smiled; 'the foolishness of the female mind, to persevere and not let anything beat us, you'll do my dear, you really will. I suspect that your mother is very proud of you... and how do I know that, us being strangers? Well, you have your feet in icy water don't you,' she pointed out. 'Don't you just love Spring, my dear, I swear it makes us all as mad as March hares and some people, like you and I are given to do the oddest things... how else can you explain us paddling in the freezing sea,' she chuckled.

I watched as she dried herself and slipped into her shoes before starting up the hill towards the hotel, turning to wave before disappearing from sight.

As I sat on a rock allowing my feet to dry in the weak Spring sunshine. I wondered at my encounter with the strange old woman, it ringing a bell somehow, reminding me a little of Alice in wonderland's encounter with the white rabbit, who led her such a merry dance. I smiled, yes indeed, Alice-in-wonderland! With my feet finally dry I put my shoes on and returned to the hotel in search of Lady Seymour, hoping that she might have finished her business here, not that I was in any hurry to leave, it was just that I thought it would be nice to explore the island together. As I came to the path that led to the hotel I spotted her in the doorway, she was in the process of shaking hands with a rather portly gentleman... the owner of the hotel as it happens. As he turned away, she saw me coming and beckoned for me to join her.

'Well, that went splendidly, Ruby, the owner; Mr Slater, already has permission to turn part of his hotel into a rehabilitation hospital. He has offered to help us in any way he can, by taking those patients we have from these parts, isn't that wonderful! I know for certain we have 5 who live but a short distance from here.' Lady Seymour said excitedly. It was so nice to see her like this, back to her old self again, it was still there though, the grief of losing her husband. Now and then I caught a glimpse of her sadness, in the tired turn of her head or a whispered long sigh; but day by day she was coping with it and I admired her for her strength, not sure that I could ever be as strong should I lose someone I loved.

The sea-tractor was waiting for us and we hurried down to the landing and climbed aboard. As we started away, I spotted the old woman I'd met on the beach, she was standing outside the hotel waving, both of us waved back as I told Lady Seymour of my strange encounter with the woman.

'Ah well that explains it then,' she smiled reaching into her handbag.

I had no idea what she was talking about and so stood there looking I'm sure like a fool, waiting for her to explain; her explanation came in the form of a book that she brought from her handbag. As she handed it to me, she couldn't hide her delight; 'You never said that you'd met Agatha Christie on your walk, my dear,' she said. I had no idea what she was talking about as I turned the book over in my hands, slowly reading the title on the front; 'Evil under the sun!' then I read the name of the author; by, Agatha Christie. I was dumfounded.

'Now look inside?' Lady Seymour said excitedly.
And so, I did.

'To my friend Ruby, who likes to paddle in icy water.'

Best wishes; Agatha Christie.

I was stunned as I made to hand the book back to her Ladyship... Agatha Christie... the old woman on the beach was Agatha Christie, and I'd met her!

'No, she meant the book for you, Ruby, keep it my dear, keep it forever to remember her by, I have to say, I'm quite envious, I'm a great admirer of hers.' Her Ladyship smiled.

'But why me? Why would someone like her even acknowledge someone like me, I'm nobody, just a poor nobody,' I said shaking my head.

Lady Seymour caught me roughly by the arm; 'Don't you dare to speak that way about yourself Ruby, it brings your whole family down, or do you consider them nobodies too... your dear mother, who has been my rock since Rory died, and your father who you love so very much, and your siblings, are they also nobodies?' she demanded angrily as we disembarked onto the beach at Bigbury-on-sea. I felt ashamed as we walked back to find the car and in truth would have burst out crying had her Ladyship not put her arm around me and drew me in close.

'Let me tell you something Ruby, not so very long ago I would not have dreamt of having a friendship with the likes of you... but, if anything good has come out of this war, it is this; that our families and many others like us across the country have been thrown together, forced to get to know one another, forgetting our differences, and long may it continue to be so, for I have had no better friends in all my life than you and those about you Ruby.'

As I climbed into the passenger's side of the car I lay Agatha Christies book in my lap, stroking the cover, before opening it and reading once again the words this famous author had penned just for me.

'To my friend Ruby, who likes to paddle in icy water.' I hugged the book to my chest.

Before she started the engine, Lady Seymour reached across and touched my arm; 'Keep that book forever Ruby, it's special.' She smiled.

I promised her that I would, that I would treasure it all my life. All I had to do was keep it safe from my nosy brothers and sisters and out of reach of the little-ones. I'd have to read it to them though and I looked forward to that, after I told them all about meeting the writer in person of course.

Now that was a tale even better than my Yeovil Town jumble sale stories... an island you could only reach at high tide by riding on a giant sea-tractor, and an ancient Inn as ghostly as anything out of one dad's grisly tales. And if that wasn't enough there was the magical wonder of the grand hotel, a vision of sheer beauty and elegance atop an island fit for the king himself.

As we neared Sandbourne something was niggling at the back of my mind; 'my Lady,' I asked, 'what will happen to Agatha Christie when they shut the hotel down and turn it into a hospital?'
She smiled; 'We thought about that, Ruby, and it's been agreed that her room will not be touched, it will not be a part of the hospital and will be set aside for whenever she chooses to use it.'

I felt relieved, after all it was part of her inspiration, helping her to write many of her classic novels and the world would be a poorer place without them. I hugged her book to me once again as we entered the outskirts of Sandbourne and Lady Seymour turned down the track that led to my home out on the heath. I was so excited to be back that I leapt from the car almost before it came to a rolling stop, calling back over my shoulder, a thank you and a goodbye to her Ladyship, who simply chuckled and waved as she turned to continue on her way to tell her committee ladies and her colleagues at the hospital the news of yet another recruit to their cause; the splendid, classical, Burgh Island hotel, down in south Devon. As I hurried across the yard my head was in a whirl over all that I had done or helped to do these past few weeks, if I hadn't been part of it, I would not have thought it possible. A girl like me, a mere farmhand's daughter, mingling with such fine people. It just didn't seem real! But it was, it really was, I was living my dream... living all young girls dreams I guess, wow! How was this even possible? I had my big sister to thank if truth be known, it was her that first got to know Lady Seymour... not that she'd ever let me forget.

I gave her a warm hug as she came to meet me at the front door, before I was swamped by the rest of my brothers and sisters all demanding to know everything I'd seen and done. I said I'd tell them later and went to find mum, deeming she be the first one to hear my great adventure. There was of course a bit of a hullabaloo but Janie soon sorted that out, ordering our sisters Janet and Bella to take charge while we sought mum, who was busy cooking dinner in the kitchen. Our Jack and Danny didn't like being ordered about by their sisters' mind, but with the added threat of a thick ear from Janie they slunk off across the yard to kick a ball about.

It was Saturday and so mum nor Janie were due to go off to work at the hospital and both were eager to hear my amazing tale, although when I'd finished telling them, I could see that neither of them believed half of it judging by the frowns they both wore, especially the bit about Agatha Christie! The look on their faces when I tugged her book from beneath my smock and let them read what she'd written, was worth all the money in the world.

'No! I don't believe it!' Janie gasped snatching the book from my hand.

'Well, there's the proof, child,' mum said, taking the book from her to read the words once again for herself. 'Who would believe such a thing, now don't you say another word more about your adventure to any of your brothers and sisters. When father gets home and after dinner; we'll have a proper sit down, story-telling hour in the living-room in front of the fire,' mum insisted.

Later with everyone present after a lovely rabbit stew dinner and the little-ones tucked up in their cribs we gathered about the range, the rain beating against the windows as the cold early Spring weather leant a rather eerie bent to the story, I began to tell them;

'When I first saw the great sea tractor on the sandy beach of Bigbury-on-sea, it was like nothing I'd ever seen before, the way it crawled its way through the high tide like some mechanical monster gave me goosebumps... and to think I was about to ride on its back!'

'Really... you rode on its back?' our Janet gasped.

I nodded, and continued, this was better than scaring them with made up ghost stories; 'Yes, all the way to the jetty, where the spooky old Inn stood all dark and mysterious, and as quiet as the grave, looking as if it had more than just the spirits in the bottles... but real spirits too!'

'No, now you're makin' it up Rube,' Janie accused, sliding a little closer to dad.

'Honest, it's true, but, oh Janie, you should see the Hotel at the top of the hill, it's, like something out of a children's storybook; like Cinderella's castle, a white glistening jewel, surrounded by the silver blue of the sea and the sky, a picture of sheer beauty... a place where royalty take holidays and where world famous authors dream up their next great story... and that's where I met my Agatha Christie.' I held up the book she'd given me for all to see, gaining a gasp from those who'd not seen it, which included dad. 'Read what she wrote,' Janie demanded. I hesitated not wanting to show off at all, but she dug me in the ribs and insisted.

'Alright, sis,' I sighed rubbing my sore side, as mum reached down and clipped Janie's ear.

Taking a deep breath, I read again the inscription inside; 'To my friend Ruby who likes to paddle in icy water, best wishes Agatha Christie.' There that's it,' I sighed, closing the book.

Although I hadn't expected them to be, even our Jack and Danny were impressed; 'So what's this book called then,' Jack asked, reaching across for it.

I slapped his hand away; 'You can look but no touching brother... it's called; Evil under the sun.'

'That sounds like good bedtime reading, what about it, sis?' Danny grinned.

'I've to read it myself first, brother, and then, if its suitable I'll read it to the rest of you,' I told him, expecting a cheeky reply, but all he said was, 'ok sis!' most odd!

Things returned to normal then for a while, and I went back to school and back to reading for Lady Seymour's children after school, while she returned to her duties around the hospital, although whenever we caught up with one another we both spoke of how much we'd enjoyed our little adventure. It would seem to have been a success in everything else too, as up to 15 men had so far been returned to the newly appointed hospitals nearer to where they lived in Devon.

I was halfway through Agatha Christie's book; Evil under the sun, and found it quite gripping although I thought the main character, the detective; Hercule Poirot quite odd, but he seemed very clever. But I did wonder why she chose that name for him or the reason he had to be Belgian and not English. Still the important thing was that I enjoyed the book, although I thought I'd need to break it down a little to read it to the family... not mum, she'd love it just as it was. The weather was warmer now and Spring was well and truly with us as we went on about our life out on the heath. Janie and me were once more rowing over to our island on a regular basis and I'd just heard from mum that grannie Miller was coming down from Yeovil to pay us a visit. I was so excited, it seemed ages since I'd seen her, dad said she'd be catching the train from Yeovil to Dorchester and then Mr Drake would pick her up from the station and bring her here.

'Can Janie and me go with him?' I asked mum.

'Well, you can, but as your grandmother is coming midweek, your sister will be working,' mum said.

Our Janie was a little disappointed when we spoke of it, but she understood and blamed it all on grannie for coming on a Wednesday instead of at the weekend.

'It will be lovely to see her again though,' she sighed after calming down, but it does mean we'll have to give up our bedroom, Sis, and shuffle the other rooms about a bit.'

I hadn't thought of that, but of course grannie would have to have our bedroom, it was the biggest and the best of rooms besides mum and dad's.

'I know!' Our Janie grinned; 'we'll shove our Jack and Danny in with the little-ones and we'll have their room... problem solved!'

I chuckled; 'Come on then let's go and break the news to them,' I said marching out into the yard where they were wrestling on the ground with the Davis twins.

'Hey, that's not fair,' they protested in unison; 'why should we be turfed out of our room, when it's your room she's having... why can't you move in with the little-ones?'

'Now that's a fair question, little brother,' Janie said, 'and the only answer I can give you is that I'm in charge and it's what I've decided on... but you're free to complain to mum if it'll make you feel any better,' she chuckled. Although my big sister was laughing, I could see the no nonsense glint in her eye, and so to could my brothers.... 'I suppose as it's for Grannie Miller, we'll do it,' Jack conceded reluctantly.

'So pleased you agree, lads, I'm so sick of having to tweak your ears. They're getting much too big for that now; don't you think our Rube?' She threw me a wink and we turned back into the house.

We were mid-way through April now and although the weather has improved, there was a hoary frost out across the heath in the early hours and the need for us still to wear our winter coats and hats and gloves. But Spring has already begun to soften things, for weeks now we've felt it in the air and have been able to see the changes it brings out across the way. Watch the wild flowers pushing themselves out of the ground, demanding to be seen, to be part of the blossoming season. Everywhere new life was yawning into existence, in a multitude of colours, from delicate Primrose to the beautiful bluebells set against the rugged prickly yellow gorse and the pinkness of the wild heather.

Grannie Miller would just love all of this, for although she lived in a town now, she was a country girl through and through. She'd been raised on a farm and had spent most of her life down muddy lanes in tied cottages. Dad says it's because she spent so much of her time in lonely places is why she has such a morbid outlook on life. It's also why and mum never seen eye to eye! But she's dad's mother and so mum does her best to be friendly, not that it's easy, for grannie could be difficult at times, and it's plain to see that there is no love lost between them.

Her husband, old grandpa Miller died a few years ago, an accident with a tractor we were told. He was a nice man, very much like his son, our dad, full of fun and mischief. I still miss him terribly. It was after his death that Grannie moved off the farm and into Yeovil town, needing to have the feel of people around her, she said. But whenever she comes to spend some time back in the country visiting us it's a boon to her, as it brings back so many wonderful memories, she says.

The road was heavy with military vehicles as I travelled along with farmer Drake on our way to Dorchester to pick grannie up from the train station causing us to arrive a little late. I feared the worst as I was well aware of grannie's bad temper when things didn't go as planned. Farmer Drake spotted her first, sitting in the empty station, her head cocked to one side as if she was listening to something, even as I stepped from the van and went to meet her, she didn't move, holding a hand up to silence me as I started to welcome her.

'Sh! Quiet child, did you hear that?' she asked, a frown deep across her wizened brow.

I shook my head as I bent to kiss her on the cheek; 'Come then grannie, let's not keep Mr Drake waiting, he's his farm to get back to.' I insisted bravely.

With a grunt she got to her feet and walked with me to the old van. Nothing about her seemed changed, she still had her grey hair up in a bun, pulled back off her wrinkled, weather worn face. A face that echoed years of worry and not a little grief, having lost brothers in the last great war and more recently her husband, grandfather Miller. Half way to the van that was parked in the car park, she slowed and came to a stop; shielding her eyes against a rare burst of sunlight, she looked out towards the hills surrounding Dorchester and clasped a hand to her holy cross that dangled beneath her throat.

'See those hills, child, they speak to me of death, over there is Maiden Castle where the locals resisted the Roman invasion, but at a terrible cost... so many lives lost, so very many!'

I shuddered and caught her arm leading her the last few steps to Mr Drakes rickety old van. 'Can you feel it child, can you hear them calling?'

I felt a shiver run down my spine; 'Not now gran,' I pleaded, helping her up the step and into the van. This was typical of her, only just arrived and already making up ghost stories... but as I glanced up towards the hill fort, I wondered how much of what she said was true... not the bit about the Roman soldiers, I knew about them from my history lessons... no the bit about her hearing voices calling!

Before I could introduce her to farmer Drake, she smiled and said; 'You feel it to Ruby. I can see it on your face, you are so much like your father and me!'

Changing the subject, I said; 'Grannie, this is Mr Drake, the farmer that dad works for.'

They shook hands and then we were on our way, but even as we left Dorchester behind us, I couldn't help but look again at the fort on the hill... how many had died there trying to protect our land from the Roman's, I wondered?

It was only a short journey back to our home on the heath and for most of it I was lost in my own thoughts, leaving Mr Drake to get to know grannie, realising at once that they really didn't need me as they could both talk, as mum would say, until the cows come home!

'Thank you, Mr Drake;' Grannie and I called to him as he dropped off us off before starting down across the heath to his farm. 'Now that's what I call a gentleman child, a real gentleman and you can't buy one of them for all the coin in the land... I hope your father realises that.'

'Of course he does, just as Mr Drake realises just how lucky he is to have father,' I answered a little defensively.

'Grannie... Grannie, it's Gran,' a chorus of voices echoed as my brothers and sisters all rushed from the house to greet her. Before they ushered her inside I managed to grab our Jacks arm; 'Take her suitcase up to her room,' I ordered. He gave me a frosty look but did as I asked, leaving me to go into the kitchen and put the kettle on the range so that I might offer grannie a cup of tea.

I had hoped mum or dad or even Janie would be here when we got back, but dad was out across the fields somewhere and mum and Janie were both working down at the hospital, and so it was all down to me to entertain grannie until they got back.

I was worried that we'd have nothing to talk about, but I was wrong, grannie told me of all that was going on in Yeovil and of how the helicopter factory had taken two big hits from German bombs just last week, losing four engineers and two wings of the factory. She also said that at least a dozen houses in the town itself had been destroyed with at least seven deaths and ten serious injuries. It was sad news, and in return for her information, all I could offer her were my travels with Lady Seymour, which shocked her to the core, for she was very much of the generation that tugged a forelock or curtsied at the mere sight of such people as her Ladyship.

Over a pot or two of tea I told her of our close relationship with Lady Seymour and of how it had all come about; of the Nativity and Pantomime in our first year here, and the dance, and mum joining the committee and helping to put on the fair and fete... and then of Lord Seymour's sad death and the resulting hospital that we were all so much a part of. By the time I'd finished, with mum's heroics out on the heath, capturing the two Germans, Gran was dumbstruck... 'and you've had tea with this Lady Seymour!' was all she could manage.

I smiled; 'Oh yes and much more, I would even dare to call her our friend now,' I answered.

Grannie sniffed; 'well, I've never heard the like... and your father, what does he say about all of this, he surely can't think it a good idea, I always taught him to respect his betters!' she said, stirring her tea with angry vigour.

'But he does, and she respects him right back, especially after all the help he's given her since we arrived here. Her Ladyship would not have been able to do all the things she's managed to do without dads help along the way.

I then gave her a list of all he and his farmhand friends had done for her. When I'd finished, she was left shaking her head. 'And he danced with her?' was all she said.

I laughed, an image of dad dancing toe to toe with her Ladyship at the ball, coming to mind; 'Yes dad danced with Lady Seymour,' I sighed, the memory still strong in my mind even after all these months... God how I love my dad and his unruly ways! Grannie Miller wasn't laughing though; 'Well I've never heard the like... my son dancing with a Lady of the Manor, what on earth is the world coming to... I blame the bloody Germans mind, it's all their fault... everything is changing and I don't understand my own world anymore! A tear trickled down her wrinkled face and I passed her the teacloth to dry her eyes.

Out across the heath old Gypsy began to howl and both grannie and myself looked toward the window just as a sparrow flew into it, stunning itself against the glass and dropping into the yard. Within seconds, much to my relief, it staggered to its feet and took to the air again, seemingly unharmed. I waited, a cold shiver running up my spine, for I knew what was coming, what grannie would say!

'How long has this been going on, child?' She asked getting to her feet and walking to the door and looking out across the heath.

'How long has what been going on, grannie?' I asked innocently, pretending not to understand the question.

Her face was suddenly an angry red; 'You know very well what, my girl... the dog howling and the bird crashing against the window, how long?' she demanded.

I really wasn't sure how long ago it was when I first heard the howling and I told her so, but saying that this was the first time a bird had flown into the window, and that was the truth. She frowned and went to stand in the doorway, the heath was quiet again now, quiet and still as it usually was... as peaceful as a graveyard, as mum would say. I shivered at the ghostly reference inside my head, knowing that grannie thought it just that, the voice of the spirits calling out to us!

We stood side by side staring out across the heath; 'I wish you would all return to Yeovil with me, my dear,' grannie sighed, taking me by the hand.

I squeezed her fingers; 'But we love it here gran, it's the nicest place we've ever been to, you just wait you'll come to love it too,' I smiled up at her. The heath was in full bloom now, a vibrant mass of floral beauty as Spring announced itself truly here, the bees were buzzing, the butterflies and the dragonflies taking wing, filling the air with life, just as the frogs filled our ears with their crocking melodies. To my ears, all was well with our world, but I could not deny the sound of the dog howling nor the bird crashing into the window, and I knew what grannie would make of it!

'It's a sign, child, you know that as surely as I do... someone you know is going to die!'. I felt sick, I knew the old wife's tales and superstitions, mostly I'd heard them from her, or from dad, who himself had heard them from her. But like mum I had always poo-pooed them... until now! I shook the thought away, this was daft; a dog howling and a silly bird banging into the window didn't mean a thing... only in the eyes of grannie Miller, who just loves to tell scary ghost stories... that was it, she was trying to scare me... well she wouldn't frighten me, I wasn't our Janie! Before I could say as much to her mum came in closely followed by dad; 'Sorry mother, meant ta be 'ere fer when you arrived but got caught up pullin' a stupid cow out of a bog, farmer Drake fetched I though, Iris too frum the hospital,' dad apologised, leaning in to peck her on the cheek.

Mum nodded her own apology from across the table as she poured her and dad a cup of tea each from the still hot pot, 'anyone else?' mum asked before putting the old teapot back under its floral knitted cosy to rest.

'Right then mother, I hope our Ruby has been entertaining you, and not boring you too much with her wild tales, I'd hate it if you thought we were letting them run amuck down here,' mum sighed.

'On the contrary my dear, I hear that it is you and my Fred who have run amuck... fairs and fetes and dances, not to mention making an alliance with people beyond your station, what on earth is that saying to the children, that they are the equal of such nobility?'

'Well, not the equal, perhaps, only we do exist in the same world and we are all fighting the same war after all,' mum said, her face blanched with anger.

Dad coughed loudly from across the kitchen table bringing everyone's attention to him; 'you know, perhaps you should take your grandmother for a walk down to the bay, girls, perhaps take her over to see your island,' he suggested.

'Do you think your mother capable of walking so far?' Mum intervened.

I saw grannie Miller flinch as she threw mum a wicked look; 'I am not yet a patient for your hospital, Iris, my dear, and quite capable of walking unaided you know,' she snapped.

For a moment or two I felt very uncomfortable and wished our Janie were here to help me, but in the end, I had to settle for our Janet, much to her delight.

'Thank you, Sis,' she whispered as we started out across the yard, with grannie Miller arm in arm between us.

'Now don't you girls walk too fast; I want your grandmother back in one piece,' mum called after us as we reached the path that led down to the bay.

'Is your mother always so bossy?' grannie grumbled digging her heals in a little so that we walked at a pace that suited her.

'Mostly always,' Janet agreed with a giggle.

I pinched her arm, giving her a Janie look, that should have been enough to shut her up, but I was not our big sister and so Janet rambled on regardless until we came in sight of the sea and grannie let out a sigh of disbelief. 'In all my days I have never seen the likes... it's beautiful,' she gasped. I was relieved and so pleased that she liked it, for grannie Miller was hard to please; 'Who's that?' she asked pointing on ahead.

At first, I couldn't see anyone, the sun in my eyes, but then I recognised, Robbo waiting down by the boat a grin a mile wide on his handsome face.

'How did you know we were coming?' I asked him as we stopped at his side.

'I didn't, although your mum told me to be on the lookout as she intended to point you in my direction, so I thought I'd hang around on the off chance,' he grinned.

'Grannie Miller, this is our friend Robbo, Robbo, this is grannie Miller,' I introduced.

'Pleased to meet you, my boy,' grannie smiled. 'And do you live on the heathland too?' she asked, shaking his hand, taking a long look at his false arm as she did.

'Yes Mam, I live with my ma and pa over yonder,' he said pointing to the old Victorian house up across the heath.

'You've been in the war, I see,' gran sighed, holding on to his good arm as he helped her into the boat. 'But you came out with your life, boy, that's the thing to always remember, so many others won't, so hang on to that thought.' Grannie said, taking her seat. Robbo nodded as he watched her settle into the rowing boat, leaving Janet and me to get ourselves aboard, which we did with ease, much to grannie's surprise.

'It's clear that you two have done this before,' she surmised.

I nodded, 'yes, it's our favourite pastime, although usually Janie and me come over on our own these days, since Robbo finished training us on how to row the boat.' I told her.

'So, where are we going?' she asked, settling herself down in the back of the boat.   I pointed to our island; 'Over there, it will only take a few minutes, gran,' I said. And true to my words a few minutes later we were out of the boat and striding across the island, although Robbo stayed with the boat leaving Janet and me to walk arm in arm with gran, as we told her of all our great adventures here, including my own birthday party, which judging by the look on her face she could scarce believe.

'Oh girls, how lucky you are to have such a place to call home,' she said with a smile.

But then she turned to me and the smile fell away for a second or two; 'But, Ruby, my dear, this dog. We really should discus him!'

Janet looked a little confused; 'Dog… what dog?' she asked.

'She's talking about the one that keeps howling all across the heath,' I reminded her.

'But that's just old Gypsy, Robbo's dad's dog,' Janet frowned.

'But why does he keep howling?' Grannie Miller asked.

'Oh, come on Gran, you're not trying to scare us with one of your old ghost stories,' Janet tutted, finally cottoning on to what granny Miller was saying.

'Don't poo-poo things that you don't understand child,' granny warned her.

I tweaked my sister's arm as I saw that she was about to get into an argument about superstitions and spooky stories, that our gran held to be true.

'I agree gran, it's all very odd, what with the howling and the birds crashing into the windows,' I said.

'What does your father say about all this?' she demanded.

'I've not spoken to him about it yet, although he did mention it to me a while ago and said he thought it a little odd!'

'A little odd! It's more than a little odd child! You mark my words, no good will come of it and that's for sure. I could tell you such tales of things like this that they would keep you from sleep a night or two.' grandma shivered.

'Oh, come off it, gran!' Janet interrupted rudely.

'Alright let's have no more talk of howling dogs and all that nonsense, we brought you here to show you the beauty of our little island...' I insisted.

I flinched expecting gran to object to being told off by a grandchild but in the end, she smiled and changed the subject, asking me to describe to her in detail the events of my birthday party on the island.

By the time I'd told her the full story it was time to return to the mainland and let Robbo get back to his duties on his father's farm.

'You're a good girl Ruby,' Granny sighed, taking my arm as we trudged back up across the heath... 'You're not so bad either maid,' she smiled at Janet.

Chapter 19

'Lady Seymour', I told myself, 'you were right to take Ruby with you on your last trip down to Cornwall.' Although it did feel a little unfair on my own children. However, Florence was not old enough yet for such adventures and Crispen made it quite clear that he didn't want to go touring around the countryside with a bunch of females! Which made me laugh and it also made me feel less guilty, but what of Grace, her and Ruby would be make excellent companions on my next journey. And so, it was decided.

You should have seen her face when I told her my decision, it was as happy as little Florence's was sad. Although my youngest daughter soon got over it when Nannie told her that she planned to take her exploring the heath with the Miller family. However, when she heard that her favourite Miller child, Ruby wouldn't be with them she almost revolted. But the last I saw of her, was with Janet holding one hand and Bella the other, swinging her through the undergrowth, and she seemed happy enough. Crispen, meanwhile, along with the Davis twins and Jack and Danny plus a member of the Canadian Army, went on an inspection of the newly built tank traps along the Sandbourne beach, and the gun turrets across the clifftops. Although I was a little reluctant to let them go, I was reassured by the company commander that he'd make sure they'd come to no harm.

With them all seemingly content we began our journey to seek more hospital outlets for our recovering patients, this time throughout Dorset and, Somerset, Ruby's home county. She and Grace chatted away like little monkeys in the back seat, whilst, sat alone in the front I began to wonder if I'd done the right thing inviting my daughter along? After all, I was the one who needed the company... wasn't I. A half an hour into our journey I pulled off the road on the pretext of needing Ruby to navigate as she knew where we were going. Feeling very guilty, I had her jump in the front seat next to me, much to Grace's annoyance, but she bore it well as she chattered away over Ruby's shoulder.

'So, Ruby, should we keep on the Yeovil, road? I asked her as we reached the outskirts of Dorchester.

'Stay on the Yeovil, road out of Dorchester then if we're going ta Sherborne and the Dyson Estate first, we needs ta turn up through Cerne Abbas, though you might want ta keep your eyes off the giant on the hill,' Ruby grinned.

'There's a giant!' Grace squawked. Ruby stretched back and whispered something that I couldn't quite catch, but whatever it was it had them in fits of laughter... 'well tell me then!' I said, feeling a little left out.

'Oh, you'll see my Lady,' Ruby giggled... you'll see.' They both started giggling then and I found it most annoying and almost missed the turning to Cerne Abbas, and would have had Ruby not cried out; 'here my Lady... turn here!'

It was a long climb to get up onto the right road to Sherborne and it took a lot longer than I'd expected to reach the top where the village of Cerne Abbas awaited us.

'Oh my!' I gasped as we levelled out below the huge chalk sculpture of the mighty naked giant on the hillside above the village... 'Don't look girls... don't look,' I pleaded.

'Is that his... wow! It's very big,' Grace said pointing up at him.

'Oh dear, did you know about this, Ruby,' I frowned.

'I'm sorry, I thought everyone knew of the Cerne Abbas Giant, my Lady,' she said fighting back a chuckle.

'I knew, Nannie did it in one of our history lessons,' Grace announced; 'It's been there for hundreds of years,' she seemed pleased as punch to tell us.

'I think I'll have a talk with nannie when we return, for clearly she has no idea what it is she's teaching you about.' I blushed. The two girls giggled again and I drove quickly away from the site, wishing that I'd never taken this way to our destination.

It was just a short drive from Cerne Abbas to the little town of Sherborne in the Dorset countryside and along the way I was enchanted by the scenery all around as we passed by old ruined castles and pretty honey coloured Hamstone hamlets, with freshly thatched roofs.

On reaching Sherborne itself I found it a picture of bygone times, with butchers and bakers and cobblers and even a wonderful old Abbey in the heart of the quaint little town. But it was the Dyson Estate that we were heading for on the other side of Sherborne, owned by friends of my father-in-law the Laird of Kirriemuir, who had informed me that they might be willing to turn a couple of wings of their manor house into a rehabilitation hospital.

As we pulled into the Estate through the stone entrance that should have had great iron gates attached to it, I knew we had come to the right place, for it was clear that this family were already doing their bit by giving up the big gates for the cause. Also, as I drove slowly up towards the manor house, I noticed that where there had been great lawns and swaths of flower beds, there was now row up on row of edible vegetation. Pulling up at the front door, even before I had one foot out of the car, a man in baggy trousers and an old wool jumper, looking the worse for wear, as if a host of moths had chewed on it came to greet us!

'Lady Seymour?' he asked with a broad smile.

Tentatively I offered him my hand, wondering why the gardener had been sent out to meet us?

'Um! Pleased to meet you… um?' I stuttered foolishly.

'Lord Dyson,' he smiled warmly, ignoring my blushes.

'Oh! Lord Dyson, I'm so sorry… I um, thought you were someone else, the um… gardener!' I felt so embarrassed and wished I could blow away like a maple seed on the wind and go spinning off into the distance, somewhere way beyond this awful moment.

He was already passed it though, opening the door for the girls to come out; 'Hello, and who might you two be?' he asked as Ruby and my Grace stepped from the car.

Introducing themselves they linked arms with him as merry as you please and he led them up the steps and into the manor house, chatting away as if they belonged, leaving me to follow on meekly in their wake.

'Oh, I do beg your pardon Lady Seymour, please, make yourself at home,' he smiled back at me, as we entered the great hall. 'Jackson, come and see to our guests,' he called to a well-dressed elderly gentleman who came hurrying to our aid.

'Go with Jackson, now... go... go!' he called back to us as he disappeared up a flight of stairs.

For a moment we stood not quite knowing what to do until Jackson took control; 'My Lady, young ladies, please, follow me,' he invited, walking away.

He took us into a small side room, like the one my children used as a playroom back at home, and I frowned, surely this wasn't where guests were entertained?

'You will have to excuse us my Lady, things are a little upside down at the moment, what with his Lordship wishing to use part of the main house as a rehabilitation ward.' He apologised.

Far from being put out I was thrilled that work on the project I'd come to speak to Lord Dyson was already underway. As Jackson left to see about getting some food for us, both Grace and Ruby started firing questions at me; 'Will we be sending some of our patients here?' Grace asked.

'Quite a few I shouldn't wonder, this house is bigger even than your place, my Lady,' Ruby said, daring to peep through a window into another part of the house.

I tutted; 'I can't answer any of your questions yet girls, like you I have only just arrived,' I sighed. 'Now find a seat and wait for Jackson or his Lordship to come back.' I ordered.

It was Lord Dyson who returned first, his gardener look gone, although he still appeared more the worker than the master. He grinned, rather cheekily, I thought, but light-heartedly too, reminding me of Ruby's father Fred, who always had a way of making me smile.

'As you see, Lady Seymour, I can be the Lord of the manor when it's called for, although, what with the lack of staff I have to muck in and do my bit to keep the old house together,' he admitted, wistfully. 'Still, we all have to do what we can in these trying times, don't we, my Lady?' he sighed.

'As you say my Lord and that is precisely why I'm here, and I thank you for agreeing to see me. I take it my father-in-law, the Laird of Kirriemuir explained what I am about'... he nodded and so I continued, Ruby and Grace fidgeting at my side... 'and so I would be very grateful for anything you might be willing to do to aid my cause,' I asked hopefully. Instead of answering me right away he turned to the girls, 'This must all be very tiresome for you two young ladies, why don't you go ahead and find Jackson, he'll have a spot of lunch prepared by now... through that door, in the dining room,' he motioned towards a heavily studded oak door.

They both looked pleadingly towards me and so I waved them on, telling them that we would join them directly, although I was a little annoyed that they couldn't wait just a little longer!

'So, shall we take a tour and I can show you just how much of my manor house I feel I want to offer up'. He sounded reluctant, and I was disappointed, as my father-in-law had assured me that his friend would be one hundred percent behind the project!

As we walked, through a part of the house that was already in the process of being changed, he waved a hand here and there... 'and we will use this room, and this room and down the great hall and the ballroom and of course the kitchen,' he concluded. I counted three wings of the house in all, which would be marvellous and would take a goodly number of beds, not all rehab beds though, for Lord Dyson explained that there would be an operating theatre too and so some of the beds would be for recovering patients. I had to admit I thought him a little ambitious there, but then I had not taken into account the true size of the great house. It was fully double the size of my own manor house, which I discovered for myself as we roamed on and on... indeed there was even scope for more, but now I was being greedy!

'Well, what do you think, Lady Seymour?' Lord Dyson asked as we strolled along the great hall.

'Impressive,' I smiled, 'very impressive.'

We regrouped with Grace and Ruby in the dining room and shared a delightful lunch, although it was clear the girls were eager to explore the rest of the Estate.

'Do stop fidgeting girls,' I sighed, trying to enjoy the lovely lunch put before us.

Lord Dyson chuckled and beckoned them to the window that overlooked the rear of the house and pointed out the zig zagging hedge that encircled all of the back garden.

'What is it?' I heard Grace ask, catching Ruby by the arm and propelling her to the window.

With them both standing looking out seemingly confused, I went to look at what all the fuss was about and immediately recognised it for what it was, having seen the like before; 'It's a labyrinth… a maze I chuckled. 'it's a long time since I've seen one of those, my father used to have one cut into his cornfield for the local village fete… but this is a real one, made to last forever and not just a season.'

'Oh! Can we go and use it?' Grace cried, grabbing for Ruby's hand.

Lord Dyson chuckled; Yes of course, and if you're not out within an hour I'll send Jackson in to retrieve you, off you go now,' he said shooing them out of the room.

He had a playful side did our Lord, but he could be serious too; 'I know you'd like to fill my wings with your overflow, my Lady, but I have to tell you there are other hospitals with the same idea… and so I will have to limit you to one wing only, I'm sorry,' he apologised.

I was a little disappointed but one wing in a place this size would hold twenty beds, so all in all I couldn't really complain, although I tried to look upset, but the smile on my face gave me away.

'So, you're happy with that then?' he surmised, as we walked to the window in time to see Grace and Ruby entering the maze. We waved as we witnessed them disappear into the entrance, both laughing happily, making me glad I'd asked my daughter along.

Over a glass of port while we waited for the girls to find their way out of the maze, we discussed just how our exchange of patients would work, for it wasn't just a one-way thing, it was agreed that if there were any of his patients who lived in our area, we would have them to recoup at Sandbourne hospital, a little nearer to where they lived.

'We will be ready to receive patients by the end of the month', Lord Dyson assured me as with the return of Grace and Ruby, he walked us out to the car. 'So, you had better start making a list of those you'd like to send to us, Lady Seymour,' he said as he stood to wave us off.

'Call me optimistic, girls, but I made that list before we left Sandbourne,' I chuckled as we started down the drive.

I could see by the look on her face that Ruby was excited as we started along the road to Yeovil, and I recalled the story she'd told myself and the children about how she would accompany her mother Iris there to go to something called a jumble sale!

It was a typical market town a little bit scruffy with a whiff of animals hanging in the air. We went through the heart of the town, through the borough, passing the 14th century John the Baptist church which Ruby pointed out, as we drove out the other side of the town onto a small road that Ruby said would lead us to our next Manor house. It was in fact owned by the Broadmead family who her father Fred used to work for before they were moved to Sandbourne she informed Grace and me.

'And down that road is where we used ta live,' Ruby pointed to a small track off the main road we were on, she sounded so melancholy that I decided to turn down the track so that we all might see it.

Stopping by a rather ramshackle cottage tucked away in the midst of a stand of hazel nut trees, across a mucky yard, both my daughter Grace and me stretched to see the home that Ruby and her family had shared before we knew them, in truth it was shabbier than I'd expected.

'Home Farm,' Ruby sighed, as if it were a grand castle. 'We had such lovely days here before the war. I know it might not look much my Lady... Grace... but down that lane beyond the house there is a stream where we all learnt to swim, and over there's where we built hideaways and tree houses, and in the field beyond we played on haystacks, and then ran wild through those ancient trees down in the thicket, much like we do now up on the heath when we take to the woods. She looked hard through the car window, clearly moved being back to this place that she loved, so engrossed was she that I hated to have to move us along, but it was getting late.

'Where do we go now, Ruby?' I asked her, settling back behind the wheel.

'Back up onto the main road and then sharp left, my Lady,' she said wiping a tear from her eye. In the car mirror I saw Grace reach over and gently squeeze her arm and I knew that no matter what, my enduring friendship with the Miller family was something none of us will ever regret or forget. As I have often said, some of my old friends might turn their noses up at our association with these people but seeing the empathy that my daughter Grace feels for Ruby, I don't care what anyone else might think.

The Broadmead estate was only a mile or so outside Yeovil on the road that Ruby said led up to Ham hill, where they quarried the beautiful golden-hamstone that many of the local cottages were made from. 'I can show you a whole village built of that stone', my Lady, it's called Montacute and when the sun strikes it... well, it's wonderful, all golden and shiny.' Ruby said, her smile lighting the car, causing both my daughter Grace and myself to smile with her.

'I'd like to see that, Ruby, perhaps on our way home... ah! Here we are, the Broadmead Estate,' I said as Ruby indicated that we should turn through a large arch off the main road that led down a long drive at the bottom of which stood a grand old house. In truth as I pulled up before it, I was disappointed, it wasn't as big as I'd hoped, not even the size of my own manor house. Seeing the look on my face, Ruby assured me that there were rooms that could be used for our purpose.

I wasn't about to argue with her even though to my eye it seemed, compared to many of the other houses we'd visited, tiny. But Ruby knew best, after all her father had worked for Lord Broadmead... 'I've been here a lot with our dad on farming business, the house is not very big, but trust me, my Lady it'll do,' she insisted.

The Lord and Lady of the manor came to meet us as we clambered out of the car, it was late afternoon and we were all feeling rather tired, we'd been on the road since early morning, and although we'd stopped off at the Dyson Estate at lunchtime, we were all a little car weary.

Lord Broadmead was a rather stout man, with a black greying beard in need of a trim as it bristled like an angry hedgehog, giving Grace and Ruby a case of the giggles, causing me to give them both a stern warning glare, to let them know that they were being rude, and that I wasn't amused by their behaviour. Thankfully they took heed and there was no more silliness. Lady Broadmead, older by some years to myself, but a most strikingly beautiful woman stepped forward, a welcoming smile on her face, I smiled back, at once feeling a warmth towards her and him too, as a broad toothy grin sprang from beneath his bristly beard.

'Welcome, welcome,' they chimed as one, ushering us on ahead of them into the hallway, where servants were waiting to steer us into the lounge, there a table of cakes and sandwiches and refreshing drinks were awaiting us.

As we sat together on a long sapphire blue sofa with a small table of food in front of us; Lord Broadmead asked, 'young lady don't I know you? He said, looking long and hard at Ruby.

Lady Broadmead leaned in close to her husband and whispered something to him, causing him to smile a smile that split his bristly beard in two.

'Of course, Ruby Miller, you're Ruby Miller, Fred's daughter... How is he, how is Fred... we miss him you know; you tell him that we want him back just as soon as those Ministry People stop buggering about,' He swore.

'Alfred, really, your language, please, we have guests,' Lady Broadmead blushed.

We all laughed; 'My mum and dad, calls um much worse than that, my Lady', Ruby grinned.

Lord Broadmead chuckled, 'I can imagine what your dear mother might say, she has a rough tongue on her when the needs must, came foul of it a time or two myself,' he recalled with a smile.

'Ah but there's a wisdom to her rough tongue wouldn't you agree, my Lord,' I insisted remembering all the times I'd turned to her for help since I'd gotten to know her.

'The salt of the earth, each and every one of them, are the Miller family and I include you in that young lady, don't think I never noticed the help you gave your father around the farm. Across the fields too, hey! Still got all his rabbit snares, has he?' he winked at Ruby.

I saw Ruby blush even though she tried to cover it up; 'I don't know what you mean, my Lord,' she stammered, clearly shaken.

He laughed; 'no need to be shy about it, Ruby, your father always shared his catch with me and the rest of the farmers, for milk, butter and the odd chicken and everyone was happy.'

'Well, I think I can safely say that Fred's poaching days are over now, he works on my Estate, you see and I think I'd know if... Ruby why are you smiling?'

'Do you remember that New Year eve party, at our place out on the heath...' Ruby grinned. I nodded. 'Well, you were eating your own rabbits my Lady!' she went into a fit of giggles and everyone joined in, including myself, when I got the funny side of it.

Finally, everyone settled down and we began our tour of the house, and I quickly found three places fit for use, rooms that could easily be turned into hospital wings; one was a gallery off of the small family church, the second being an old hothouse and thirdly and best of all, the ballroom.

'And you think they'll do, Lady Seymour?' Lord Broadmead frowned, obviously doubting the worthiness of his own great house.

I nodded; 'If you will allow me my Lord, my Lady Broadmead, I would like to send the Laird of Kirriemuir's architects to you so that they may access the work to be done, just as they did on my own manor house. Indeed, as you and he are such good friends the Laird might even come down with them,' I smiled.

It was late as we finally left the Broadmead Estate, but intrigued by Ruby's tale of the golden village of Montacute I decided on a detour so that we might all see it for ourselves. With Ruby directing me and Grace jumping about in the back seat like a demented grasshopper we drove, not to the village as I expected us to, but under Ruby's guidance to a place called Hamhill where they quarried the beautiful sandstone that the cottages were made from. Leaving the car in a small pull in we walked to a spot where we could see the village below us and as true as Ruby said, it was quite magical, the whole village aglow in the late afternoon sunshine, shining like a golden crown amid the green beauty of the countryside all around.

It was a sight I'll never forget, nor that my daughter Grace would easily forget as she stood spellbound at my side, her mouth agape. I swore then that one day I would bring my other children; Crispen and Florence to see this wonderful spectacle. Before we walked away, Ruby, who was surprising me more and more by the day, said; 'You know my Lady, they used stone from here to build the houses of Parliament. I learnt that when I was going to the school around here,' she informed me.
'Gosh! I wish I'd gone to that school,' Grace sighed.
I smiled; 'Wisdom can be found in many places, Grace, Nannie and I do our best to educate you but there will always be things that we miss, thank goodness then that we can call on our friends,' I said smiling at Ruby.
If she heard my complement to her at all it didn't show on her pretty face; 'How long will you go on searching for new hospitals, my Lady?' she asked as we retraced our footsteps to find the car.
'Are you getting fed up travelling with me Ruby?' I asked, a little surprised by her question.

'Oh no my Lady and having Grace along this time is even better... not that I haven't enjoyed being on my own with you,' she hastily added.

I laughed; 'Thank you for that Ruby, but I do know how nice it must be for you to have someone more your own age to talk to on our long trips. As for your question, I've decided that this is to be my last trip, that we have as many new hospitals as we can cope with... although in truth many of them are more convalescent homes than hospitals... places where the wounded might recoup a little closer to their homes, so that their loved ones might more easily visit them.'

It was early evening when we arrived back at Ruby's home out on the heath and we were greeted by a rush of her siblings all eager to ask questions, demanding to know what their sister had been up to. Despite the lateness of the day, I turned off the engine and we all stepped out of the car, as I was eager to share with Iris what news I had of all her daughter and I had been doing.

'So that's it then, My Lady, no more galivanting about the country, getting fat on cream teas and Cornish pasties,' Iris chuckled, looking directly at my tummy!

Defensively I put my hands on my stomach in an effort to cover it, then realising what I was doing I shook my head and laughed; 'Really, Iris, you are the cheeky one.'

On a more sombre note, she asked where the new hospitals were, and was thrilled when Ruby jumped in to explain that they were both close to their old haunt, that they were near Home Farm. Even Fred looked up from his newspaper when Ruby mentioned our visit to the Broadmead Estate and that Lord Alfred sends his regards to him and Iris.

'Aye, a good man is his Lordship,' Fred mumbled. 'Did he ask after when I'd be back? He and I got on well durin' my time there, encouraged my poachin' he did... as long as he got a share of the game,' he chuckled, winking at me.

'No good saying otherwise, my Lady, I knows the man well.'

I blushed; he was a rascal and no mistake was Fred Miller, but I couldn't help but admire how well matched he and Iris were, very much like my late husband, Rory and I had been. For that reason alone, I was bound to like him. For all his silliness, he could be serious when it was called for; catching my arm he stopped me. 'So, these new hospitals, all around 'er are so you can send patients to recover nearer home?' he surmised correctly. I nodded, taken aback by how well he understood what I was trying to do; 'That's good, my Lady, I think I would rather be close ta home, if'n I was hurt,' he sighed. 'So, what happens now?' he asked.

Before I could answer Iris jumped in; 'Once we know where the new hospitals are we check our own lists for patients from around that area and arrange to send them there,' Iris told her husband. I couldn't have explained it better myself and in fact I was eager to be on my way down to my own hospital so that we might sort out what patients to send where.

Ushering Grace back out to the car we set off across the heath, it was in full bloom now, a picture that any artist would find a joy to capture on canvas; the brilliant yellow gorse and the vibrant purple heather filling the senses with the joy of Spring, the air full of wonderful aromas and sounds; like the buzzing bees and dancing hum of the beautiful dragonflies on the wing.
'Stop mum... stop!' Grace suddenly cried.
I screeched to a halt and turned angrily to where she was perched in the seat at my side; 'Don't ever do that, while I'm driving,' I snapped, 'we might have had an accident.'
'But you were about to run over them,' she said pointing out of the windscreen.

At first, I couldn't see anything, then, almost from beneath my front wheels a family of ducks appeared, a mother and five ducklings, waddling on by, quite unperturbed it would seem, heading for a small pond across the track. I realised that but for my daughters warning I might indeed have run over them.

I got out of the car and beckoned Grace to join me as we trailed the ducks to their destination, watching the mother prod her little family one by one into the mildewed pond... 'it must be their first time in the water,' I whispered, squeezing Grace's hand. 'Thank you for stopping me, Grace, I would have been heartbroken had I killed them,' I sighed. Her fingers tightened on mine and looking down I could see tears in her eyes; 'I thought I'd warned you too late, that they were under the wheels, squashed,' she shivered. I put my arm around her; 'but you weren't too late and they are just fine, just look at them enjoying their first ever swim,' I pointed, hugging her close.

We left then, walking arm in arm back to the car, a soft warm breeze at our backs, the scent of the heath all around and over us, making me sure that we must smell of gorse bushes and purple heather and old mildewed pond... but for once I didn't care, Lady of the Manor or not! I looked across at Grace who's face I can honestly say I have never seen so flushed with happiness. If ever there comes a time when I doubt my husband Rory's decision to bring us here, I will think of the pleasure saving a gaggle of ducks brought to our daughter.

The sun broke from behind a cloud and it felt as if my Rory was smiling down on us, 'Well Grace lets go and tell of our adventure to your brother and sister, and who knows, perhaps tomorrow Ruby might come down and share a story with us about the old farm house we visited along the way.'
That was a nice thought to end our journey on, but even as we stepped from the car, on reaching the hospital I knew something was wrong and yet how could anything be wrong, I'd just spoken to Iris out on the heath, she would have said if there was a problem. And yet, Sir Edmond Bruce and matron were both hurrying out of the hospital to meet me. Sending Grace to catchup with Crispen and Florence I stood waiting for them to come to me, their sombre faces making me worry even more.

'What is it?' I demanded before either of them opened their mouths. I had just completed a long week or so of travelling the country and successfully too, I might add, but clearly that was not what was on their worried minds... so what was it?

'It's Robbo, we all know how close you are with the Miller family and how close they are to him, but he is in a bad way, his injured arm has somehow developed an infection and he will have to undergo another operation.' Matron sighed.

'What sort of operation, will he loose more of his arm?' I asked, praying that it wasn't that serious, but fearing the worst.

'All of it, or almost all of it I fear, Lady Seymour, but we will save as much as we can,' Sir Edmond said.

'Does he know... does his parents know?' I asked biting back my tears.

'He knows, my Lady, but no-one else does yet,' Sir Edmond informed me.

So that was the reason Iris didn't tell me, she nor anyone else knows yet!

'But his family... farmer Drake and his wife, they must be told right away, surely,' I insisted.

Both he and matron exchanged worried glances and I was annoyed; 'Come now, out with it, tell me,' I ordered, impatiently.

'The boy refuses to allow us to tell anyone, not his parents or even his fiancé,' matron sighed.

'Oh, does he now?' I was angry, very angry, and without another word to either of my colleagues I stormed off to find Robbo, which meant another trip out across the heath.

Once more I drove into the Millers yard, but could only tell them that I had a meeting with Robbo. Iris was curious as was Ruby and Jane, but they did not question me and I was pleased that they didn't. With a wave I set off down through the heath to the Drake farm below, where I found Robbo sitting in the yard looking very forlorn.

'I thought I might be seeing you my Lady, although you'd better know right now that I will not be letting them carve another piece off my arm... I will not... I'd rather die!' He barked angrily.

'Oh, you would, so you'd rather die, you, ungrateful little tyke! Never mind that you survived to return home to your family, when so many others didn't, my own husband among them. Now, just because there is a problem with your old wound you wish to be dead, even though as I understand, there is a good chance it can be made right again... what about your poor mother and father and the girl who loves you, and who you have promised to marry? Do none of these things matter to you?' I knew that I was close to tears, but I didn't care, I would not let this boy throw his life away.

'Lady Seymour! What's going on?' Mrs Drake asked coming out into the yard.

'Well, will you tell her or shall I, Robbo?' I demanded.

Reluctantly he told her all and when he'd done, she slapped him so hard that he staggered away from her. 'Mum!' he cried out, 'that bloody well hurt.'

'Good, now you listen to me, boy, I don't care how much more of you they cut off, just as long as they leave you alive, and I speak for your father too... and what about Wendy, does she know anything about this, I suspect not.'

Robbo shook his head; 'I can't ask her to go through with our wedding now, mother, how can I?' he sniffed, wiping a dirty sleeve across his nose.

'Think about it son, Wendy took you on because she loves you, even without one of your arms, she's a good maid and you will break her heart, so you will,' his mother said, wiping away a tear.

He wrapped his mother up in a warm hug, tears running freely down his face, letting her go he turned to me; 'Did the surgeon say how much more of my arm he'd have to cut off?' he asked.

'That's not something he would share with me, Robbo, but listen to your mother, she makes sense, like Wendy we all know you for the nice young man that you are, and as long as you are breathing that will always be the case, with or without one of your arms.' I assured him.

'Can I come back to the hospital with you, my Lady, I think I'd like another chat with the surgeon if it's possible,' he said nervously. I nodded, and saying goodbye to his mother we drove up through the heath back into the Millers yard. Ignoring their offers for us to stay a while, we set off at once for the hospital.

After taking Robbo to see Sir Edmond, I went to find my committee ladies, to have them start going through the list of patients and matching them against the new hospitals I had lined up to take them. To my delight there were twenty-five in all, giving us a little breathing space and the ability to take on more urgent cases of our own. With Lord Edmonds contacts within the chain of command, we were all very aware about the state of the war. Things were still not going as well as the news on the wireless would have us believe.

The enemy were still trying to bomb us into oblivion and gathering an invasion fleet along the coast of France, ready for the day that everyone knew was bound to happen sooner or later. So, it was vitally important that we got as many of our good men back up and ready to fight anew, God help them.

'So, we are all set,' Amber said as I updated the committee on all I'd been doing these past weeks.

'Yes, it's just a matter of sorting out who to send where, so I depend on all of you to check with the nursing staff which of the patients are fit enough to be moved on and where they should be sent.' I said, feeling rather proud of what I'd achieved.

Stella and Betty came forward next, 'We have every faith in you my Lady, so as soon as we have the whereabouts of these new Manor houses that you've coerced the owners into turning into hospital's we'll make our lists.' Betty grinned.

'Coerced! I did no such thing,' I blushed, stung by their insinuation; 'I merely asked that's all, and...' they were all chuckling, and I knew it was all a bit of fun on their part.

'Well really!' I protested, half-heartedly, before laughing along with them... 'although I'm not averse to applying a little pressure, if necessary,' I winked. 'Come, let's retire to my quarters so that we might go over your lists and see where best to send those fit enough to travel,' I suggested.

An hour later after a pot of tea and a plate of cooks best homemade tartlets we had thirty names ready to present to the matron who would then confer with Sir Edmond about the worthiness of our list, and whether the men were fit enough to travel. Later Sir Edmond asked me to meet him in his office; I have to admit to feeling a little nervous, despite this being my house, he was the man in charge of the hospital, and so he outranked me somewhat. But I was pleased to note that he was smiling as I entered and sat in the chair opposite him. 'Well; my Lady, you have done excellent work. Here, you will need this?' He passed me a revised list to the one we'd given him to check over, but to my delight there was only two changes.

'We had to take Collins and Peters off your list as they have both had a slight relapse, nothing serious but enough to prevent them from travelling just yet.' He smiled. 'As for what you've achieved these last few weeks, Lady Seymour, it has been nothing short of amazing.'

I felt rather pleased with myself as I started away from his office only to bump into Robbo, who approached me rather reluctantly; 'My Lady... um! I'm sorry, I panicked when they told me that they needed to operate on my arm... or what's left of it, I thought I was past all that, that I was on the mend, it, sort of hit me for six,' he apologised.

'I understand Robbo, I really do, but where there is life there is hope. When my Rory died, I thought I wanted to die too, such was the pain his passing brought to me, but that was wrong, my husband would not have wanted that, he would have wanted me to live on, to do what I am doing now, helping others in their hour of need.'

'I know it's easy for me to say, I'm not the one who has to lose a limb, if that is what it comes to, but think, boy, of your parents and of Wendy, of the sad dark days of mourning that might very well last a life time, just because you can't stand the thought of people seeing you like you are.'

'It's all right for you, my Lady, you won't have to put up with the pitying looks for the rest of your life... the pointing and whispering, and...

'Stop! Now stop this nonsense, tell me truthfully if it were me standing before you saying that I was going to lose one of my arms, would it make any difference to what you thought of me?'

'No, of course not, my Lady... but...

'No buts Robbo, you belittle me by thinking that I have not the grace to see past your injury, while you would accept it if the tables were turned and it was I who lost a limb'.

He hesitated and I pressed my point home; 'when it is a loved one or a friend as I believe we have become, you see past the negative things and see only the goodness that never changes no matter what. Everyone who knows you Robbo would miss you should you die and wouldn't give a damn how many limbs you had as long as you were still here among us.' He sighed a deep sigh, his eyes a little glassy seeming like he was close to tears; 'What about Wendy, how can I ask her to marry me now?' he pleaded.

I felt like slapping him hard, as his mother had done, the silly boy! 'If you think so little of her that you feel she will turn tail and run at the slightest problem then perhaps you shouldn't marry her, because you don't deserve her,' I snapped angrily.

He blanched but I kept at him, this boy was confused and frightened, but he was strong too, and gentle and kind and I refused to let him destroy his future and the happiness of his parents and the woman he loved and who loved him... not if I could help it! But why was I so interested in this boy? After all I hardly knew him... It was down to the Miller family again, he was their friend first and foremost.

Although the way he rallied to help me with the pantomime and cast down that murderer in the pub, and has been willing to help ever since shows his true nature. In truth, Robbo was not someone any of us could afford to lose, there were too few of the likes of him around anymore thanks to the war. It was for men like him that I'd been scouring the country for rehabilitation sites and I would not see him throw his life away... I would not, not as long as I had breath in my body,' I vowed.

'My Lady!' he clutched my hand. 'If I agree to this operation, would you be there beside me in the operating theatre, please,' he pleaded.

I squeezed his hand and smiled; 'I'll be there, I promise,' I assured him, my heart in my mouth, for I had never witnessed an operation close up.

For the next two days I went with him to have his arm assessed and to listen to the surgeon's diagnosis; 'Well fortunately we have managed to stop the spread of poison in your wound, but even so we will need to amputate most of what is left of your arm... I'm sorry lad,' Sir Edmond apologised.

Robbo nodded his consent and I held on tight to his hand, wishing that he hadn't chosen me to be with him that afternoon, but he had and I'd agreed and so that was that.

Once he'd been sedated, I could easily have slipped away, but I'd given my word and so I stayed holding on grimly to his good arm, trying desperately not to watch what the surgeon was doing on the other side. But finally when it was done I almost collapsed and would have, if Sir Edmond hadn't caught me.

'Well done, Lady Seymour,' he smiled helping me to a chair, 'that young man is fortunate to have a friend such as you.'

I waved away his complement; 'No, it is I who is the fortunate one, this boy, like so many others risked his life so that we might be free of tyranny. No, my Lord it's we who shall be in their dept until the end of our days; 'God bless them all!' I went then to find Robbo's parents to let them know that the operation had been a success and that he was now back on the ward under sedation.

Chapter 20

It seems an age since I went with Mr Drake to fetch grannie from Dorchester train station and later took her across the bay with Robbo and our Janet. But it was barely a week ago and I'd travelled the highways and byways with Lady Seymour since. I was shocked to hear of Robbo's troubles this morning at breakfast, he'd said nothing about it to us, when he'd taken us out in the rowing boat, and he'd seemed well enough, although thinking about it he did keep rubbing his arm a lot! I made a mental note to find out more from mum just as soon as she came in from the fields, in the meanwhile I had the little-ones to see to and my grandmother to keep happy.

Our Janie was busy working in the hospital kitchen, and it was our Janet's turn reading to the patients, although I dearly wanted to take her place and read them my Agatha Christie book, alas no number of bribes or threats could persuade her to swap with me. I had to make do with reading it to grannie Miller in front of the range in the living room, while our Bella took a turn seeing to the little-ones. I was interrupted though by old Gypsy again howling his fool head off out across the heath, which brought grannie to her feet!

'Tis a sure sign, you mark my words maid,' she insisted taking my hand and walking me to the open door... 'Someone close to this family is going ta die!'

I shivered and glanced around, thankfully there was just the two of us, Bella and the little-ones being in the kitchen, while my brothers were off across the heath somewhere with the Davis twins.

'Now come on Grannie, you really don't know that, and anyway you'll frighten us all if you're not careful, you know how our Janie hates such tales,' I said. My thoughts drifted automatically to Robbo and his medical problems... could it be him? Angrily I shook the thought away... bloody grannie Miller and her old wife's tales, I fumed.

Mum came trudging in then as usual looking very weary; 'Can you see to the tea today, Ruby, I'm not feeling so good... to be honest I just feel like curling up in bed, but I really must go down to the hospital to make sure everything is alright.'

She seemed agitated and was sweaty and flushed, not herself at all and I was worried about her, not that grannie Miller showed any concern at all; 'So now you're goin' out again? I don't know why I bothered to come all this way, I really don't,' she moaned.

'I'm sorry, grannie but needs must,' mum sighed.

'And old ladies like me have no needs, is that it,' grannie snapped, raging up the stairs to her bedroom.

Mum shook her head, 'Keep an eye on your grandmother Ruby, make sure she has enough to eat and drink and I'll see you later.' At the door she turned; 'Oh, and when your father comes home tell him I might be late,' she sighed.

I watched her all the way across the heath and felt very concerned, she was not well and the long walk into the village and then down to the hospital was going to be hard for her. Within minutes of her disappearing over the horizon Mr Drake drove up in his old van asking for her. When I told him he'd just missed her, he set off to catch her up. But before he left, he called back to me; 'Have you heard Ruby, there's a bit of a sickness bug down at the hospital, it seems, half of the staff are down with it, including your mothers committee members; Stella, Betty and Amber, who is, I'm told, the worst of them all'.

I watched him drive away; perhaps that's what mum has? I thought, she certainly doesn't look well! Trying not to worry I got on with making the dumplings for the chicken stew that mum had prepared for tea...

'That's not the way ta make dumplings, girl,' grannie Miller, sighed leaning over my shoulder, here let me show you!'

I bit down on my temper and stepped away giving her my space over the kitchen table, watching as expertly she made a dozen perfect dumplings.

'You see it's easy when you know how,' she smiled triumphantly.

'Yes, thank you grannie,' I breathed through gritted teeth.

'Would you like to help me set the cutlery out around the table?' I asked.

'Oh no, I'm sure you're capable of doing that by yourself maid,' she grunted. 'I think I'll go back up to my room for a lie down, call me when it's teatime, or when your father comes home,' she ordered from halfway up the stairs. I felt like throwing mum's ladle after her, but instead took a deep breath and continued with what I was doing.

By the time dad came home I had everything ready and sent our Bella up to wake grannie, who came down as moany as she'd gone up.

'I thought I told you to call me as soon as your father got home!' she fumed.

'But I did, grannie...' I started to say.

'Well clearly you didn't, as he already has his boots off and is in his evening slippers,' she scolded.

'The maids right, mother, I've just this minute walked through the door,' dad insisted.

'Nothing changes does it, Fred, still under the heel of yore daughters, they maids have you wrapped about their little fingers,' she growled, giving me such a dirty look.

He winked at me; 'I'm proud to say yes to that, mother and no mistake, for I couldn't wish for better daughters and you couldn't want for nicer granddaughters,' he insisted.

'Tea's ready,' I called, 'Bella fetch the little-ones, Grannie, Dad, take a seat please,' I insisted, holding grannies out for her to sit.

As I began to serve up the chicken stew, I was waiting for some comment from grannie but she kept quiet, much to my surprise and only spoke to confirm how nice it was.

'Now that didn't hurt you any, did it mother,' Dad chuckled.

Changing the subject grannie asked dad if he'd heard the dog howling earlier.

'Aye that I did mother, tis old Gypsy, and he's been on at that these past weeks or more, and I surely don't know just what ta make of it, dad said scratching his head.

'Well, I know what ta make of it, son, and so should you,' grannie declared, giving him such a look.

'Even so, there's a whole hospital down below, with poor souls meetin' their maker every single day, perhaps that's what the dog is howling for,' he surmised.

'You know better than that Fred, he's howlin' for someone close, for family or friends, God help them!' Grannie sighed.

I felt goosebumps running up my spine and shuddered, bringing a word of warning from dad; 'Now you hush yore nonsense mother, yore scaring the girls,' he snapped. With a glance in my direction, she got on with her tea and let the subject drop, but it was too late for that, it was all I could think about now and across from me our Bella was too afraid to even eat.

'Bella, see to the little-ones,' I called, bringing her back to reality.

'Dad! Have you noticed how poorly mum is looking at the moment, Mr Drake says there is a sickness bug going around the hospital, we should keep an eye on her,' I suggested. I wasn't worried about mum being the possible cause of the howling dog, that she was the one destined to die! She was much too strong to succumb to a simple sickness bug. But I was worried about some of the other people we know, the members of the committee for instance, and of course, Robbo? Then there were the patients we'd come to know quite well, the ones Janet and I read to, and the two actors who helped put on the Panto at Christmas and many others. Not to mention the staff, including Mrs Brown in the kitchen and our Janie. Also, the Seymour family themselves, I shook the horrible thought away, no not them, please don't let it be them.

'Damn Grannie Miller and her superstitions she had me thinking the worst, the very, very worst!

The one name that stuck in my head was Robbo, he was due to have surgery, the last I'd heard and what with the sickness bug and all he must be at risk.

I wanted to rush off down to the hospital to check on him but dad stopped me; 'you can't do any good down there, maid, we just have to wait, what will be will be,' he sighed.

To take my mind off of things I took the little-ones out across the yard and down to the wood where they could crawl and play in the dens we'd made there, and our Bella brought left over bread and butter from dinner for them to chew on.

After about an hour I heard someone calling; and making their way through the woods towards us, it was our Janie her shift in the hospital kitchen having finished.

'Dad told me what our daft grannie has been saying, just ignore it sis, a dog howling is just that... a dog howling, nothing more... you know I blame you and dad for all this nonsense, with your creepy ghost stories and all that... it damn well serves you right!'

I smiled; 'but it could be true, sis, all these superstitions must come from somewhere.'

She punched me hard on my arm; 'see, you're at it again, leave it be, sis, you're just scaring yourself... which is quite funny really,' she giggled.

'By the way, the doctors have tracked down the sickness bug to something called Salmonella, caught off a batch of bad eggs, and everyone who had it is on the mend,' Janie assured me.

Apart from my sore arm where she'd hit me, I suddenly felt much better, although there was still Robbo and a few others to worry about.

'Come on sis let's get this lot back up to the house, mum will be home soon, Lady Seymour is bringing her back herself.'

When we got back home, dad had already returned out across the fields and so we settled the little-one upstairs in their play pen and I put the kettle on ready for when mum and Lady Seymour arrived.

'How is Robbo,' was the first thing I asked as they entered, Janie thumped me on my other arm... 'Ouch!' I complained.

Ignoring my hurt she asked, what I should have asked; 'Would you like a pot of tea?' she smiled sweetly.

'Thank you Jane, that would be lovely,' mum said grinning at my discomfort.

'I'm sure that would have been your next question wouldn't it Ruby,' her Ladyship smiled.

I blushed seeing my big sisters look of satisfaction, mum laughed to make matters worse, and even Lady Seymour tittered.'

'Oh, I'm sure you will want to know that Robbo's operation went well and he is now recovering back out on the ward,' her Ladyship informed us.

'But Lady Seymour is not telling you everything girls. Robbo asked for her to stay with him during the operation and so she did, holding his hand to the finish,' mum said proudly.

'How could I not when our Prince Charming asked so nicely,' her Ladyship blushed.

She is magnificent, Janie and I agreed later alone in our bedroom, simply magnificent, a real true Lady of the Manor.

Things quietened down then for a while, the patients suffering from sickness got better, Robbo continued to improve and was announced fit to go home providing he rested, and reported back to the hospital once a week for a check-up.

'No rowing over to any island mind,' Lady Seymour joked as she watched him leave with his parents.

Janie and me were there to see him discharged and were both taken aback when on reaching the front door of the hospital where his fiancée Wendy was waiting, he turned, walked back to her Ladyship and kissed her on the cheek!

'Thank you very much my Lady,' he said, with a tear in his eye. 'I will be forever in your debt,' he smiled.

'No, it's I who owe you young man and always will,' she smiled. 'Now off with you, your young lady is waiting.'

Janie and me were hugging one another trying desperately not to cry, but cry we did, blubbing like two of our little-ones. With Robbo on the mend and the sickness bug under control everything seemed to settle down as we entered May and could enjoy warmer weather, but with the better weather came the Germans bombing and threatening an invasion again, setting us back on tender-hooks, fearing the worst. So much for the war ending in 1942, still it was rolling on, seemingly forever.

Chapter 21

As Lady of the Manor, I should be content with my lot, but with no more hospitals to seek out I feel a little starved of the adventure. Usually, one or other of the Miller family keep me amused, but with the six weeks school summer holidays loaming I'll not be seeing much of them. In fact, just how long I'll have their mother Iris to lean on I'm not sure as just last week she confided to me that she was expecting another child! I have to admit to being surprised thinking her too old for that sort of thing, but she's only 39! Still the news shocked me!

'Nannie,' I called feeling a little down in the dumps.

'Yes, my Lady what can I do for you,' she asked coming through the door, a bundle of books in her arms... 'sorry my Lady I was about to take these to the children's playroom!' she apologised.

I waved away her apology; 'Nannie I have decided a return to my Scottish roots is on the cards and what better time than now, during the children's summer holidays. I think my children should have the same break from lessons as everyone else.' So, pack up Nannie, we leave by the end of the week... Oh, and I think I'll ask my friend Stella to join us as she so enjoyed her visit to Kirriemuir a month or so ago.'

The children were excited to be going up to their old home and to meet their grandfather again as was I. Everything here was running smoothly and so there was nothing to prevent us having a jolly nice holiday together. I wondered what Sir Edmond would think of me dropping everything and disappearing for a few weeks, leaving him to run the hospital without me? Would he be mad at me for not giving him enough notice? But I need not have worried, he simply smiled when I told him; 'My Lady, if anyone deserves a break then it's you, go, enjoy your family... and wish the Laird well for me,' he said.

Stella was thrilled when I sought her out and invited her to come with us, although she did mention, rather sheepishly that the Laird had contacted her only last week, suggesting she and her maid come again to Kirriemuir for a visit.

She blushed profusely as she told me and I laughed; 'Well now's as good a time as any to take him up on his kind offer, don't you think Stella?'

She blushed anew; 'Are you sure you don't mind my Lady, I wouldn't want to step on any one's toes, or cause hurt.'

I wrapped her up in a warm embrace; 'We're friends are we not, Stella, and you and the Laird are grown-ups and free to choose your own destiny without a yea or a nay from me,' I smiled.

She hugged me back; 'The truth is my Lady, I like him so very much, he is the only man I've felt like this about since my husband died in 1918... I thought myself too old for such nonsense,' she sniffed.

I hugged her tighter; 'You're never too old for love,' my dear, I smiled, feeling close to tears.

On the Friday as we all clambered aboard the two big cars waiting outside the main doors on the drive, half the hospital, were there to wave us off, including, Jane, Ruby and Iris Miller. Friends who were the measure of just how far I had come in the short time I'd been here. But as we set off, I couldn't help but wonder if all would be the same on our return, this moment had the awful feeling of a permanent goodbye!

It took us all day to travel up to Kirriemuir as the roads were heavy with military vehicles all heading towards one coast or another, to protect us from the possibility of invasion. In one rather long traffic jam I ventured to ask the driver what he thought of the chances of a German invasion any time soon? He smiled confidently; 'They won't come now, my Lady, not now they've invaded Russia, not even the mighty German army can wage war on two fronts,' he assured us. He was of course no expert but his words gave us all confidence, even the children sat a little taller in their seats and I patted him on the shoulder to show my thanks.

Behind us in the second car Nannie and Stella rode together and I did wonder how they might be getting along; my husband had been Nannies favourite child and the Laird was some-what God-like to her! I could only hope they were not at logger-heads, although they might be. As I recall Nannie had not thought it proper that Stella should visit the Laird alone when she had... having a maid along didn't really count as far as she was concerned! The more I thought about it the more I worried and found myself looking out of the rear car window more and more.

As soon as we stopped for a toilet break, I hurried to check on them, but found nothing amiss, in fact they seemed very amiable with one another. While we stretched our legs and Nannie checked on the children, I took Stella aside; 'is everything alright Stella, Nannie is not being difficult, I hope? I know she can be very possessive at times, especially when it comes to my Rory or the Laird.'

Stella smiled, 'on the contrary my Lady, she is being very nice and so understanding, why she has even given me tips about his likes and dislikes, she is such a lovely woman.'

I felt so relieved and so pleased, obviously, like myself Nannie had noticed the special way that Stella talked about him, recognising that there could be something beautiful happening between them. The thought warmed my heart for they were both lovely people who deserved another chance at happiness.

When we finally arrived at Kirriemuir castle the Laird came out to greet us a wide smile across his still handsome face, made bigger still when Stella stepped from the second car... the way they looked at one another brought a tear of sheer joy to my face.

'Stella, my dear, how wonderful it is to see you again,' he smiled. Almost ignoring the rest of us until the children swarmed all over him. Finally, then, he bade us all welcome and ushered us on ahead of him into the castle.

Once nannie had taken the children to their old playroom and Stella had gone up to refresh herself after our journey, the Laird and me settled in the lounge, where he told me some startling news... news that could change my life forever!

'Kathrine, my dear, my doctors have informed me that I must slow down, that I cannot keep going at the same rate as I am for much longer... I was bent on ignoring them first off, but you have brought with you a reason for me to listen to them... Stella is that reason my dear. I would like to spend what time I have left with her! I do hope you understand, I never thought I would find the love I shared with Rory's mother again, but I have...' there were tears in his eyes and I put an arm around him.

'What can I do to help?' I asked.

He got to his feet and paced across the room, clearly disturbed by what he was about to say, I rose to stand in front of him... 'just tell me,' I begged him.

'I would like you to come back, to take over the running of the castle and the estate, after all it is by rights, yours.'

I was stunned, how could he ask this of me, I had my own hospital to take care of. I collapsed to the sofa my mind in a whirl, my head every which-way... was he serious, really serious? He came to sit with me and took my hand, 'this was always going to happen lass, you surely must have realised that. After all you are since Rory's demise, the Lady of Kirriemuir and responsible for the whole of Kirriemuir's highland estate.'

'But I gave it to you my Lord,' I protested.

'You gave the castle over to me to turn into a hospital, nothing more lass, the estate still belongs to you, my dear,' the Laird insisted.

I was lost for words, he was right of course, but what to do now? The Lairds illness must be of a serious nature otherwise he would carry on as before?

'Have you no-one who can manage your hospital down in Sandbourne, lass?' the Laird asked hopefully.

I shook my head, my brain disengaged for the moment, Stella came in then but started out of the room again on hearing the seriousness of our discussion. 'No, please stay,' I begged her. 'I might need your voice on this conundrum,' I sighed.

She sat quietly listening, then said; 'why don't you donate the hospital to the committee and the village of Sandbourne,' let them run it for you,' she suggested. Of course, it was such a wonderful idea that I could have kissed her. Instead of returning it back to a manor house when the war is over, let it be forever; The Sandbourne Hospital!

Stella went to sit with the Laird, holding on tightly to his hand and I realised she must have known about his condition from her last visit, but obviously the Laird had asked her not to say anything. I felt a little annoyed at that, but despite his illness they seemed happy and content together and that made me feel happy too.

When to break the news to the children though, that was the next problem, they were happy down at Sandbourne, they had friends… they had the Miller family, as did I. What a shame that I couldn't just wrap them up and take them with us. Now I was sad, really sad, together that family and me had achieved so much and my children had come to love them. I set my jaw against the painful nature of saying goodbye to all of that, determined to carve out a future equally as good up in the highlands, where, if truth be told was where we truly belonged. It was Rory's home and so would in time become our home again too.

The children, Nannie and I left the next day, leaving Stella behind to help the Laird run the hospital until our return. The children were so quiet as we retraced our way back down to Sandbourne. I'd broken the news to them of our pending move back up to the highlands and they were not at all happy.

'Well, I won't go, so there!' Grace pouted.

'Neither will I,' Crispen shouted, kicking the back of the driver's seat not once but twice.

'I want to stay with Ruby,' little Florence cried bitterly.

'So, you all want to leave your grandfather sick and alone up at the castle, do you,' I snapped, losing my temper with the lot of them.

There was silence for a while and then both Crispen and Grace said; 'No I suppose not!' Although little Florence still insisted that she wanted to stay with her Ruby!

I don't think I've felt this sad since my Rory died, it was going to be a great wrench leaving Sandbourne and the many friends we'd made there, especially the Millers, for I counted them among the best of my friends now. Just how I was going to break the news of our leaving to everyone I just didn't know... and who to tell first, that was another big question? I knew I had to take action right away before my children or Nannie spilled the beans and so I called a meeting within hours of getting back, asking not only the committee members but Sir Edmond and Matron too for I would be leaving the hospital in their charge.

As they began to gather in my quarters up in the long gallery, Sir Edmond and Matron, along with Reverent Clancy and the rest of the Ladies of the committee looked a little worried and confused! Especially as I'd asked Jane and Ruby to come along with their mother Iris.

'So, what's going on, my Lady?' Amber demanded, the first to react as usual.

I waved her back to her seat, and began my explanation, hardly able to keep the tremor of sadness under control. When I had finished, at first no-one spoke or budged from their seats and I was close to tears. And then Iris came to wrap me in her arms and one by one the others followed and I broke down completely.

'So, you wish us to carry on, my Lady, to keep the hospital going,' Sir Edmond clarified.

'Yes, of course, and I could not wish for it to be in better hands... I am so very proud of what we have accomplished here and would hate to see it fall asunder just because of me,' I said.

'Just because of you indeed! Without you none of this would even exist,' Sir Edmond insisted... 'And we all know the contribution your father-in-law, the Laird made and so it is fitting that you should rescue him now in his hour of need.'

There was a general nodding of heads and I was so proud of the friends me and my children had made here and we would sorely miss each and every one of them.

As the meeting began to break up, Jane and Ruby asked if they could go and sit with my children in their playroom and it warmed my heart to know how much they cared.

It was a balmy day as I drove one last time up across the heath to say goodbye to our friends the Millers. Typically, with the school holidays half over the sunshine decided to show itself bringing the spiders out of hiding to spin their shiny gossamer webs across the heather and prickly gorse. Although Crispen, Grace and little Florence seemed oblivious to its beauty as sad as they were.

Tomorrow was our moving day and I was determined for them to spend a little longer with their friends before we left. We had nannie with us as she was eager to wish the Millers goodbye too, for despite their lowly stature compared to our family she too had grown to like them.

'I never counted on this, my Lady, on feeling so sad to be leaving such folk as these behind,' she sniffed. 'But in truth, the master, our Rory, would have loved them so dearly,' she insisted.

I sighed knowing the truth of her wise words, my Rory would have taken to them, he surely would have. As we pulled into their yard, I was pleased to see Robbo and Wendy his wife there, along with the Mr and Mrs Drake and the Davis boys and their parents. Now I could tell them all goodbye and wish them well.

Stepping from the car; Fred and Iris came from the house to greet us, along with their children, including the little-ones, and an old woman whom I took to be Fred's mother from Somerset. I was quite taken aback by the look she gave me, as if I had no right to be mingling with her family, indeed she touched her forelock and did a little curtsy, as if to apologise for her kin!

His mother's standoffish attitude had no bearing on Fred though taking my hand he twirled me into the house as if we were on a dance floor. His mother tutted, Iris tweaked his ear and the children all blushed with the shamelessness of him, but Fred simply grinned; 'Just wants ta send her Ladyship off, happy,' he chuckled. He warmed my heart did this tender man, for there was not an ounce of harm in him, just a host of mischief, and I'd miss him as much as all of his wonderful family.

'Be off with you Fred,' Iris said coming to my rescue,' start up the barbecue and let's make merry,' she ordered.

For the rest of the afternoon, we ate grilled chicken and rabbit and drank homemade wine and mead and danced about the yard to songs playing on the wireless. As the shadows began to spread across the yard, we all became a little melancholy and a bit teary and so we knew it was time to call it a day… a sad day in the end, for it was our last day.

The children cried and so too did I, unable to stop hugging Jane and Ruby and their mother Iris, knowing I'd not likely see their like again, not in the world that I was returning to, where all the niceties would be adhered to at all times… which had been fine once, but down here I had experienced a different world, and I liked it.

Everyone was crying as the driver started the car down across the heath with the Millers and the Davis twins chasing on behind waving like mad. Crispen, Grace and little Florence were all crying, calling back to them, urging them to run faster, to catch us up, but sadly they fell away as we came off the heath on the other side.

Now it was time to concentrate on Scotland and our old castle in Kirriemuir, where a new life was waiting for us.

Chapter 22

It had been a week since Lady Seymour and her children left, heralding in a new era. I sighed, still desperately sad as I saw to the little-ones, washing and dressing them and getting their porridge ready. The school holidays were almost spent, although I would not be returning to school myself as I would soon be 14 with a job lined up in the same café as our Janie on Poole harbour. After Lady Seymour had left neither of us could stand being down at the hospital anymore, and so Jane had left the kitchen and taken a job in the café, and now I was looking forward to once more working with her.

Grannie Miller interrupted my thoughts as she came shuffling into the kitchen, as irritable as usual, demanding her cup of tea and a piece of toast... 'not too burnt mind, like the last one 'she grumbled. I ordered our Janet to see to it while I finished feeding the little-ones and seeing to everyone else's breakfast.

'When on earth are you going back to Yeovil?' I muttered under my breath.

'Did you say something child?' Grannie snapped angrily.

I sighed; 'No, Gran!' I lied.

Just then old Gypsy started his howling again out across the heath, bringing grannie to her feet in an instant; 'Oh no! This is not good girls, not good at all. I thought the danger had passed but clearly whatever it is that dog is howling about hasn't yet happened. Just listen to him will you, he's calling death down to the heath!' Several of the little-ones started crying alarmed by the tone of her voice, while our Janet and Bella looked scared out of their wits! Even Jack and Danny looked a little frightened although they tried to hide it in front of us girls. As much as I loved grannie Miller, I decided to ask mum just how much longer she'd be with us, praying she'd say she'd be going soon, after all she'd been with us for weeks and weeks now.

'You'd better ask your father, Ruby, she's his mother, though I do hope it's sooner rather than later,' she sighed.

I felt torn, I'd often wanted my gran here to celebrate the important times in my life, but I wasn't really sure that was the case anymore. In fact, I found myself hoping that she would not be staying for my birthday on September the 12th! Having thought it I immediately regretted it, what an awful thing to wish for! And anyway, it was still a couple of weeks or so away yet, surely, she'd be gone by then? As if granting my wish grannie decided it was time she returned to Yeovil and just like that she was gone. Mr Drake took her back to Dorchester railway station where we'd first collected her from and I think everyone was relieved, including dad.

Now I could look forward to my birthday, although it seemed no time at all since my magical 13th birthday on the island last year. I was beginning to feel truly grown up, especially as I was about to get my first real job. Helping her Ladyship with her children had been really nice, but it hadn't been a real job as such.

I still had a hurdle to climb though as dad wasn't keen on Janie and me working across on the harbour, because of all the air raids. I knew he had a point, although the Germans seemed to be concentrating more on the big cities if you believed what they said on the wireless? And certainly, we'd seen less of them.

'Have you been told?' Janie whispered as we sat on the edge of my bed staring out across the darkening heath a week before we were going to start our new jobs.

'Been told what?' I asked, a little concerned by her tone.

'Well, as you know mum's expecting again!'

'I sighed, that means another little-one to look after, sis.'

'I'm sorry to have to tell you Rube, but it also means that, mum will be taking the job I got for you at the cafe and you'll be looking after the kids, for the remainder of the summer holidays at least.'

'What... no! But that's just not fair!' I groaned.'

'Dad says that looking after the little-ones is hard enough for her in her state, let alone having to see to the older ones too during the holidays, so that's that I'm afraid.'

We fell into silence, and I felt so angry, not that I blamed our Janie this sort of thing had happened to her often enough. Now it was my turn and that was all there was to it.

Despite understanding, why it had to be done, I couldn't help but feel upset about having to remain home to look after my younger siblings, and that evening I dared to say as much to mum.

'I'm sorry Ruby, but needs must,' she insisted. 'In any case, are you sure it's not the young soldiers, sailors and airmen, you were hoping to meet in the café,' she asked with a smile.

I saw her wink at Father; 'If it is, you can rest assured there will be plenty more passing through in the next few months or so, enough even for the whole of Sandbourne to ogle,' she chuckled.

Father laughed as I turned a bright red and slunk off out into the kitchen; 'I don't ogle anyone,' I protested to Janie as she came to join me.

She sniggered; 'Bigger fool you then Rube.'

With August well underway my siblings wanted one last celebration before going back to school, and so they asked me to row them over to our island. To keep the peace I agreed, although it wasn't the same without our Janie and Robbo, but I just about managed, forcing our Janet to row us back, which to my surprise she did, and did well, making me wonder if she hadn't been secretly practising. In spite of my early reluctance, we ended up having a wonderful day, some of the little-ones experiencing it for the very first time.

By now, mum was getting bigger, but still working at the cafe in my place, whilst we saw very little of dad, as he was working harder than ever down on the farm. Farmer Drake did spare him what time he could, although it wasn't much at this busy time of the year. And that's why it was odd to see him arrive home in the middle of the day, looking very agitated and out of sorts.

'Is anything wrong Dad?' I asked, seeing how distressed he seemed.

'I've just heard some bad news!' he sniffed, taking my hand.

'What bad news?' I asked desperately.

'Young Robbo's arm, it got worse an' he died from blood poisoning just this morning.' He wiped away a tear and drew a deep breath.

My own breath caught in my throat for a second; 'Are you sure dad?' I couldn't believe that Robbo, our dearest friend, who Lady Seymour had personally watched over during his operation was dead! I began to weep bitterly, uncontrollable tears and dad gave me a hug, and I prayed that he didn't say again that; it's the price of war! Thankfully he didn't, he just held me while I cried and cried and cried.

Later, in the backyard, when Janie returned from work, we cried our eyes red over the young man who had done so much for us, and for his new wife Wendy in her moment of grief.

In church the following Sunday Reverent Clancy read a beautiful eulogy to our dearest friend that had us all in tears again, until Farmer Drake stood by the side of his son's new bride and said that Robbo wouldn't want to see us like this, that he'd rather we all wore a smile and remember him wearing one too. I found that hard to do in the following days, Janie did too, although we both tried, just for him, just for our rowing instructor! But everything now had suddenly changed, the war seemed to be forcing its way ever deeper into our lives, and the heath was no longer the sanctuary I thought it to be, somewhere for us to hide away from the real world!

Despite all the drama though we still had to get on with things; dad worked the fields, mum and Janie went off to work each day and I saw to the children, though there was scarcely a moment when I didn't think of poor Robbo. We'd all thought he'd come through the worst, even the operation to rid him of gangrene had, we thought, been a success, but it had come back to steal his life.

I was in the living-room thinking of our dear friend and of old Gypsy too, thinking that perhaps grannie Miller had been right all along about his howling heralding a death! And old Gypsy was Robbo's family dog too! But before I had time to dwell on it, there was a huge explosion that shook the house! It was like nothing we'd ever experienced before! I ran out to check on the children who were playing in the yard. They seemed startled but no worse than that, like myself to them it was just another explosion. Still, I counted heads wanting to be sure, to reassure myself that it was just another army thing... but surely their practice day is tomorrow! A flash of panic rushed through me and I fought to stay calm! 'Perhaps the army changed their routine, yes, of course, they must have. I told myself. Taking a deep breath, I set about seeing to the little-ones, putting the whole thing behind me, I had enough to do without scaring myself with silly fantasies. But just then as I picked the last of the little-ones up off the rug they'd been playing on in the yard, dad stumbled through the gate and collapsed in a heap!

I ran to help him yelling for our Janet and Bella to see to the others. When I reached him, he didn't move, he just lay there sobbing like a baby... and then I noticed the blood, he was covered in it!

'Oh my God! Dad, oh dad, you're hurt, you're bleeding,' I screamed.

He gripped my arm and pulled me to him; 'It's not my blood maid, it's... its, he was weeping again, and suddenly I felt so afraid, I'd never seen a man cry before... not ever, especially not father.   I wrapped my arms around him so tight it hurt, but I didn't care.

'Dad... dad, what happened? Whose blood, is it?' I pleaded, wiping his face with my sleeve. He tried to stand, but couldn't his legs refusing to support him and I was of no help he was too heavy, all I could do was cry with him.

He pushed away from me; 'It's your brothers... its Jack and Danny, it's their blood, they're gone, maid... dead!' he wept.

I couldn't believe it; 'No! No! No! 'They're here, I saw them, I saw them,' I screamed. Jumping to my feet I ran franticly about the yard... I thought they were here... I was sure they were, it was a mistake, it has to be.

'What happened?' I asked father as I finally found my wits.

He sucked in a deep breath; I was working out across the heath when I heard the explosion and feared the worst as I'd seen the boys earlier going in the direction the blast came from, but being as the army weren't using the place today, I thought no more on it.'

He was shaking and I put my arms around him hugging him to me in spite of all the blood.

'I ran like the wind girl... like the wind... On the way I found one of the Davis boys, he was badly hurt, he told me that his brother and our Jack were dead, but that Danny was still alive. I just left him there on the ground and ran on ignoring his pleas for me to help him. Tears were streaming down his face again and I cried alongside him... our Jack and Danny both dead... why hadn't I realised they were missing... why? If mum had been here, she'd have missed them, gone after them, made sure they were safe. I collapsed next to dad and cried and cried, and everyone came to join us, only a few of the older ones seeing our grief for what it was.

'Farmer Drake's sent one of the hands with a message for mother and our Jane, they should be back on the next ferry... I should clean myself up... can't let 'um see me like this,' he sniffed.

I helped him to his feet and watched as he staggered inside, it all seemed so unreal, like something out of a nightmare, our Jack and Danny dead! How was that even possible, they were too young, only 11 and 8 years old, it couldn't be real, it just couldn't. So, grannie Miller had been right all along the dog had been howling for us, and it was to our family that death had paid a call. It was all of 2 hours before mum and Janie came hurrying across the Heath. I saw them coming from a long way off, but my legs felt so weak that I couldn't run and meet them, all I could do was wait in the yard. Mum swept by me as if I were a ghost, paying me no mind at all as she hurried on into the house.

'Are you alright Rube?' Janie asked, putting her arm around my shoulders. I looked at her and shook my head, unable to find my voice.

'It's not your fault, it's not,' she said, stroking my hair.

'They were in my care and I failed them, and now our brothers are gone... they're gone Janie, gone!' I cried.

'No, now you stop that, we all of us play out across the heath, it could have happened to any of us.'

From inside the house came an awful wail and I wanted to run in, but Janie held onto me; 'Gather the little-ones,' she ordered gently. Across the yard I saw that our Janet had them all in a huddle and was trying desperately to keep them calm even as she tried to remain so herself. As I reached her, she squeezed my hand... 'I didn't know they'd left the yard either,' she sobbed. It seemed like hours before mum came to call us in, as I passed her in the doorway, she caught me by the arm. 'Why didn't you see that your brothers were gone? Daydreaming again no doubt,' she accused savagely, her red rimmed eyes blazing. Across the kitchen dad sat motionless, staring at his feet, a mug of tea growing cold on the table at his side, if I hoped for his help, I knew that it wasn't coming... 'Well Girl? They were in your charge,' mum yelled at me her spittle soaking my blouse.

I began to cry again. 'Stop that, and don't look to your father, he'll not be of any help this time,' she raged... 'what happened... what happened?' she screamed, shaking me as if I were a rag doll. What happened next was like a pantomime; First the army came skidding into the yard followed closely by the police and then Reverend Clancy, all of them firing questions at dad, questions that he clearly couldn't answer.

He just sat with his head in his hands. I wanted to tell them all to leave him alone...but in the end mum did.

'Get out! All of you! Now. Do you hear me?' She screamed at them.

Seeing her anger, they all backed out of the door, but she wasn't done yet... 'you,' she screamed at the army captain, how many times have we complained about your lot using live ammunition on the heath... how many times? She raged. 'And you, call yourself the home guard, just whose homes are you guarding, not mine that's for sure... get away from here... all of you... yes you too Reverent and don't you ever again preach to me about the goodness of your God... there is nothing good about this. If he is all you say he is, why does he take innocent children... my innocent children, when there are so many evil people he could take? What about Adolf bloody Hitler and the whole bloody German race, why doesn't he take them... oh no, your so called, benevolent God would rather take little children! Benevolent you say... evil is what I call him, as evil as the devil himself. Now get out Reverend you and your God are no longer welcome in my home.' she raged.

The poor man! He, didn't try to reason with her or to defend his faith, he simply turned on his heel and left, patting me gently on the head in passing; 'Stay strong Ruby,' he muttered. I watched him cross the yard to begin his long walk back to the village and felt a little sorry for him... he'd been a good friend to us ever since we'd arrived here and none of this was his fault. If anyone was to blame then it was me, they were in my charge after all... mum had said so and I knew it was so, and when the truth be told I'm sure everyone would agree. I felt a shiver run down my spine; 'Jack and Danny are dead!'

The thought echoed and echoed in my head. But no matter how many times I told myself it was true, I still couldn't believe it. They were my brothers! How could they be dead? We'd had breakfast together just a few hours ago... we'd talked of their work at the hospital, of how they enjoyed helping the patients, and... and now they were gone! Oh, how I wish it were me instead of them. Across the room I could hear mum wailing as she clutched at dad trying to comfort him and herself too. Not once did she look my way, she blamed me for everything, everything!

I tried to hold back more tears, for the sake of the little-ones, but failed. I ran to the bomb-shelter, to hide in its darkness, but even in its blackness my thoughts ran riot! 'You should have taken better care of them; you should have known they were not in the yard.' 'Should have... should... should... should!' 'What sort of a sister are you? Oh, you were there to clip their ears whenever they got up to mischief, but not there when they needed you most'. I tried to ignore the voice in my head, but it was persistent and I slumped to the ground and cried and cried.

It wasn't until dad spoke that I realised he was even there; 'Enough o this, maid, I'll not see you blamin, yer self. You couldn't 'ave know'd this would 'appen.' With that he lifted me up and held me close, his clothes had the familiar smell of the farm, and as I clung to him, I felt a little better, until he led me outside and I noticed traces of blood in his hair, and the horror came flooding back.

No-one said much for the rest of the day, and it seemed unreal for the most part, especially at meal times with two empty seats where our brothers would normally have sat. That, more than anything upset us, for it emphasised the fact that they were gone. As sad as it was, it was a blessing that we had little time to grieve, for we received notice that the funeral would take place two days later at St Nicholas Church in Sandbourne. I held my breath as mum was given the news, after her outburst at Reverend Clancy I feared she might explode again, but she didn't, even though he would be presiding over the funeral. It was a sad pilgrimage across the heath that day and the cloudless blue sky overhead seemed out of place somehow. Thankfully the little-ones in their prams had no idea what was happening, but even they seemed sombre, it was almost as if they knew.

In the church I was sat with Janie, Janet, and Bella and we all had a sibling on our laps. I tried to catch mum's eye once or twice for she hadn't spoken a word to me since it had happened, but still she avoided looking my way... 'She blames me, I know she does,' I whispered to Janie.

'Sh! Of, course she doesn't. Hush now and listen to the service,' she sighed.

'You think it's my fault too, don't you?' I accused.

'No of course not, now just shut up, will you,' she snapped angrily.

I stared down at the stone floor beneath my feet my mind in a turmoil. She does, she thinks I'm to blame, I can tell by the tone in her voice, I convinced myself.

Later, at the graveside, I stood back, away from the others, looking out across the fields to where the sea sparkled silvery blue in the distance. I barely heard the Reverends eulogy. I was thinking about my brothers and how they would love this view. It seemed like only yesterday that we'd arrived here as strangers and fallen head over heel in love with the wildness of the place, our only worry then had been how long would we be able to stay. And now our Jack and Danny would be here forever!

At first the thought threatened to overwhelm me, to think of us one day leaving them behind, but then I glanced again at the wonderful panoramic view and knew it was right for them.

'Right for them!' No! Being alive, being my brothers, that was what was right for them. Tears were streaming down my cheeks and I looked about desperately for somewhere to escape to.

'Come maid, walk with me,' dad interrupted my thoughts as he took my arm and led me away. It was only then that I noticed most of the others had already left, with one last glance over my shoulder I allowed him to steer me up the path and away from my dearest brother's grave. We stopped again as we reached the gate leading out of the graveyard.

'None of this is down to you Ruby, I'm only sorry that the burden of looking after the family fell to you on such a terrible day. It could have been anyone of us,' dad insisted, shaking his head, his wise eyes threatening to overflow again and let him down. I cuddled into him, the warmth of him giving me strength as he held me close.

'They'll have a headstone soon,' he said, as we turned for one last look to where they were buried. Reverend Clancy gave me a copy of what it'll say, here see fer yourself Maid.' My hands shook as I took the piece of paper and read it aloud;
In
Loving memory of
our two dear boys
Jack and Danny Miller
Died August 28th 1942
Aged 11 and 8 years
Gone but not forgotten.
Also, in memory of
Rupert Davis aged 10
Played together
Died together
Pals to the end.

The tears just choked me up and I had to hang on to dad to prevent myself collapsing in a heap. 'That's lovely, dad, just lovely,' I said.

He took a deep breath, 'Your ma wrote it,' he told me.

We walked on in silence for a while, until we came to the path back cross the heath-land, up ahead a posse of people were waiting beside an old horse-n-cart.

'Come on now Fred,' Farmer Drake, smiled, handing dad the reins, 'you take yer family back in this'un and I'll walk back we' tuthers.'

'But I'd rather some o the women, rode in my place,' dad argued.

'We won't hear of it, Mr Miller', one of the village ladies said. 'So off you go now, you dear man.'

So off we went, with an assembly of villagers and neighbours trailing on behind, it wasn't at all what we wanted, but such was the affection for our family that we could scarce refuse without causing upset. And so, we had a wake!

Chapter 23

As it turned out it was the last thing we did on the heath-land. A day later the man from the Ministry came knocking on the door and we were ordered back to our old home in Somerset. When mother told our friends at the hospital and in the village, there was a lot of sadness and not a few tears were shed at the thought of us leaving their lives. I wondered if Sandbourne village would ever be the same again. First they had lost Lady Seymour and now us, not that I compared our family with hers! But between us both we had contributed a great deal to the community. I managed a smile as I thought of all our families had given since arriving here... including our Jack and Danny in the end! Unbidden tears welled up in my eyes again, tinged with guilt as I thought of the times Janie and myself had mistrusted them out of hand. Always assuming that they were up to no good, even when they had only been helping! I forced a smile, but they'd never held it against us, as they had always owned their bad behaviour and the consequences of it.

Although for months now we'd been dreading the coming of the Ministry man, none of us were unhappy about seeing him this time, as we all knew that if we stayed our Jack and Danny would haunt us all of our days. Much better that we carry them with us in our hearts than forever be looking out across the heath expecting them to come in for dinner. In spite of that I felt a great deal of sadness at leaving our magical white-walled cottage on the heath and all of the many friends we'd made here... mostly though my thoughts were for our dear brothers whom we were about to leave behind.

Janie and me were the last to leave and it was with great sadness that we walked hand in hand through the front door to the removal van. All the others were aboard. The sky was a brilliant azure blue, lit by a golden sun that sent a shimmering heatwave cascading over the yard and dancing on the window panes. And as I looked teary-eyed out across the heath, I swear I could see our Jack and Danny standing there with that same mischievous twinkle in their eyes watching us leave.

'Goodbye my darling brothers,' I whispered softly, as I climbed up into the back of the old removal van.

As we started up through the heath, I was sure at any minute to hear them calling after us; 'where are you going? Wait, wait for us!' Mum... Dad... our Janie... Ruby... please don't leave us behind!'

I was shaking, tears streaming down my cheeks... 'No! No! We can't go, not without our dear brothers, we just can't!' The words unspoken, screamed through my head, and I wanted only to jump from the old van and run across the heath to find them! Seeing how distressed I was Janie came to sit by my side gripping my hand tightly, her face as distraught as my own. She didn't speak, neither of us did, we just sat stony faced and sad, staring off into the distance, as if we expected to see them again, although we both knew we never would, not ever!

The terrible sound of silence was deafening as we travelled back towards Home Farm in Somerset, even the little-ones never as much as let out a whimper and I was glad for I wasn't sure I wanted to see to them anymore! Everything seemed so very familiar as we finally pulled into the mucky old yard back at Home Farm, although nothing was the same now and never would be ever again. Janie squeezed my hand; 'We just have to carry on!' she sighed sadly. 'It's all we can do, Rube.' She was crying, right there in front of the little-ones, something I'd never seen her do before, I hugged her to me, ignoring mums angry glare. With a loud sniff she got control of herself and helped me off load our siblings, ordering our Janet and Bella to see to the little-ones while we helped mum and dad to unload the van.

Nothing seemed real anymore and time passed so slowly, as we struggled to come to terms with being back in Somerset, a county that we knew so well and yet now struggled to call home. My 14th birthday, which should have been so special, passed by almost unnoticed, as we settled back into our old cottage. Still, I really didn't mind, this was no time for celebrations. But I was now old enough to go out to work and our Janie had got me a job in a bakery with her.

Although I was still living at home, mainly for father's sake and slowly building bridges with mother, our Janie was now living with grannie Miller in Yeovil and had a boyfriend named Ian... how I envied her and nothing seemed the same without her.

Oh, how I missed her... and my devilish little brothers, Jack and Danny, I bit back a tear, I missed them terribly too. Was it them who had added the soul to wherever we were and now that they were gone, would nothing be the same ever again? I found myself walking alone down the lane, to the ancient woods where we had all played and to the stream where we learnt to swim and to the old dens my brothers had built among the trees, that they now would never again share with us. They were still there, a little overgrown with weeds and brambles but good enough to play in just the same, bringing lovely memories flooding back.

Down by the mildewed pond where we'd spent many a happy hour splashing about in, I sat and dangled my feet in the icy water, dreaming of days gone by, and would have stayed longer but for feeling a hand on my shoulder; 'So there you are, Sis!' It was Janie, come to fetch me home. I was a little surprised to see her as she didn't usually visit mid-week.

'Mum's gone into labour,' she said; 'We'd best get back, dads with her, waiting for the midwife to come, and he'll need us.'

'Where did he find a midwife?' I asked as we hurried back to the cottage.

Janie, smiled; 'One of the Gypsies down the lane sis,' she said.

'What! There really are Gypsies down the lane?' I frowned.

'Yes, really, and they're not us,' she grinned.

Hurrying across the mucky yard, we were just in time for the birth of our newest little brother David, who mum immediately passed into the arms of Janie and when she got him back, didn't pass to me! I felt gutted, but didn't say anything, not until Janie and me were alone; 'She is never going to forgive me, sis,' I sighed.

Janie put her hand on my shoulder; 'Give it time Rube, she'll come round,' she assured me. But I wasn't so sure, everything in our lives seemed different now without Jack and Danny, although with the little- ones growing fast and mum having our new little brother David, there was no less to cope with. But not for me, mostly now that was our Janet and Bella's job. With mum still not trusting me with my siblings, and Janie not living with us now, my two younger sisters were forced to step up. Because of my strained relationship with mum, I knew I would leave if not for dad, but I felt he still needed me. It was obvious he'd not gotten over losing his sons although he, unlike mum didn't blame me! Even though he'd held our Danny in his arms as he died!

No! I decided, I would not leave until I thought dad was alright. I truly wished I could feel as close to mum as I had been out on the heath, but it was clear she didn't trust me anymore. She never actually said as much, but I could tell!

'Don't be silly, Rube!' Janie, said, when I complained to her again on one of her rare visits. 'She's just a bit sour, and out of sorts what with just giving birth to our David and all,'

'Um! I suppose.' I grunted.

Our newest little brother, did tend to cry all night long keeping mum up till the early hours almost every night. However, despite that I still believed I'd not been forgiven for what happened to our Jack and Danny back on the heath. Still the war was rumbling on, most of the talk had been that it would be over by 1942 and here we were nearing the end of that year and still there was no sign of it ending!

Yeovil town was filling up now, with troops, mainly Americans and I dearly wanted to join our Janie in Grannie Millers home, so that I might chance to get a glimpse of them. Our Janie had already teased me about her and her Ian going to a dance at the Americans base camp, telling me how wonderfully they could dance.

Despite my envy I still felt that I couldn't leave dad, he needed me, as despite working in the bakery in Yeovil I still helped him out across the farm now and then. Lord Broadmead was grateful and would often come over to where ever I was lending a hand to ask about Lady Seymour, and to reminisce about us coming to see him, those long months ago. 'Come and visit the hospital wing, when you get the chance, Ruby, my dear, after all you helped create it,' he smiled as he walked away with dad.

In spite of my feud with mum, life down the lane on Home Farm, although not as it once was, still had its moments. Now and then our Janie would come back to sleep over and we'd go out across the fields poaching with dad like we used to. Those nights warmed my heart and stopped me from running away... which was what I truly wanted to do at times.

Grannie Miller and our Janie came to us for Christmas and New Year celebrations and for a while it was like old times.

'Happy New Year,' we all shouted.' 'May 1943 be a lucky year for all of us,' grannie cried, raising a glass of port, and drunkenly spilling half of it across the kitchen floor.

'Steady there, mother,' dad chuckled taking her arm.

Mum scowled, and I laughed along with dad earning a stern glance from her which I ignored. I was getting tired of mum's nasty attitude towards me, and I was pretty close to packing my bags.

'You can't,' Janie said, when I spoke to her later, 'you're only 14 and not old enough to leave home yet, besides, what about dad?'

'Well, you're only 15, and you've left home,' I argued.

'But soon I'll be 16 and anyway I've moved in with Grannie so, in fact I'm still living with family,' she grinned.

I couldn't argue with that and anyway I could never leave dad, the moment of that terrible day seemed to still be haunting him, as most days now he wore a deep frown, his normally bright sparkling eyes glazed with sadness.

'Yore time will come maid,' he smiled, one day when I was helping him in the milking parlour; 'but I'm glad it's not yet, I don't know that I could manage without yore pretty face of a morning,' he sighed. I was so touched and so deeply surprised by his words that I had to beg a short break so that I could go outside and dry my eyes. He never commented on my leaving the milking shed and, on my return, we simply carried on as before, but I had a new resolve now, in spite of my own wishes to leave Home Farm I would remain, for his sake, if for nothing else.

It was my job in the bakery with our Janie that kept my spirits up, that and mum being a little more friendly of late; I put that down to our David settling down better, giving her less restless nights, but whatever the cause, I was pleased.

As the months rolled by our Janie came to see us less and less, she was now almost 17yrs old and madly in love with Ian. I was pleased for her, but I couldn't help but feel a little jealous, her life was moving on, while mine was at a standstill, or so it seemed. The war was going better though since the yanks came on board and there was talk that we might be on the verge of retaking France. But none of us were holding our breaths, as it was clear the Germans, if you believed the wireless reports, were still dug-in along the coastline across the channel. Although it was plain that we had won the battle in the air, for apart from the buzzing bombs, as dad called them, the days of the German Luftwaffa seemed to be over and we rarely saw them anymore.

The Ministry people had left us alone for a while and I hoped we'd seen the last of them. But just after my 15th birthday they came again and we were moved again. This time to a place called Burley, a village in the New Forest. I'd been reluctant to go, especially as our Janie was to remain behind and continue working at the old bakery in Yeovil.

For the first time I wouldn't have her to share my thoughts with and that made me sad, although knowing how happy she was with Ian, stemmed the hurt a little.

Chapter 24

Surprisingly, arriving at our new home cheered me even further, for it was in the centre of the village and as much as I'd always enjoyed living in the back of beyond, right now I felt the need to be close to other people. Things felt so much different than they'd been on the heath, and not in a bad way. As much as I'd enjoyed our time there, here I was no longer a silly school girl expected to stay at home and look after the little-ones, instead I was being allowed to go out on my own in search of a job. I thought for sure that mum would insist on finding something for me, but she didn't interfere at all, leaving me to get on with it. I could have done with a few words of comfort however when I went for my first interview, for I couldn't stop my legs from shaking.

The job was as a waitress, a job I knew well from my days working in the café on Poole harbour, a very busy place what with it being close to the ferry. I glanced about, this place could be equally as busy being in the heart of the village, I decided. I just hoped that the owner liked me, for I knew nothing of her or of the cafe. I'd discovered her advert in the window of the local post office on our first day in the village, which was just two days ago. I'd rang her from the telephone box on the village green and arranged a meeting. God! I felt so nervous! And so excited too. I stole a peek through the window into the little cafe, it looked great, so neat and tidy and much bigger than it seemed. Like a nosy busybody, I counted at least a dozen tables all covered in white linen, with four chairs to each table. I smiled to myself, it was just lovely, now all I had to do was get the job!

I never saw her coming and so when the door opened, I was quite taken aback, standing before me was the most beautiful woman I'd ever seen, more beautiful even than Lady Seymour.
'You must be Ruby,' she smiled, ushering me inside.
I could only nod and half curtsy;
She smiled the most glorious smile and I followed her into the cafe.

'Have you done this sort of work before Ruby,' she asked as we sat at one of the many tables.

'Only part time at the cafe on Poole harbour. In Yeovil, near where I come from, I have been working in a bakery,' I added quickly, that it was my first real job, since leaving school.

She looked so tall and willowy and so beautiful as she rose... why was she getting up, was the interview over already? Had I failed, what had I said that was wrong?

'When can you start?'

I was a little tongue-tied at first... 'I've got the job?' I gasped finally.

'If you want it?' she laughed. Her laugh suited her, it was soft and musical and it sent a tingle up my spine.

'Yes... yes, I do, thank you... um, Mrs,' I was so stunned I couldn't even remember her name.

'Granger,' she reminded me, 'and it's not Mrs, its Miss Granger, but you can call me Darcy,' she said reaching to shake my hand.

'So then, you haven't told me when you can start,' she prompted.

I blushed; 'No, oh, sorry, tomorrow... or today, if, if you need me?' I stammered.

She chuckled; 'Why don't we say Monday, that will give you a few more days to settle into the village and find your way around.'

As I walked to the other end of the village to the house we were staying in, I felt like I was walking on air, and I couldn't wait to tell everyone the news. But first I remembered mum had asked me to call in the village shop to buy a bar of soap.

'You're new!' the woman behind the counter, growled.

She wore her mousy hair up in a bun and had on thick lens glasses that made her eyes look huge, 'like an owl's eyes,' I thought to myself.

'Well!' Her forehead wrinkled into deep furls and her eyes widened even more.

'Yes, we're new, we've just moved into the old farmhouse,' I finally answered.

'Well then this is your lucky day young lady, I happen to have a job going and you can start tomorrow,' she offered.

'Thank you but I already have a job at the cafe, I just want a bar of soap, please,' I smiled.

Her face wrinkled into deep cavernous angry lines; 'You'd do well to stay clear of that place my dear, the owner... well... let's just say she's not all she seems?' she winked slyly.

I bit back an angry response; 'Well she seemed very nice to me,' I answered as politely as I could.

I could see that my tone stung the woman, her face was like thunder as she banged the bar of soap down on the counter.

'But then you don't know her do you?' she sniffed. 'It's rumoured that she's twice married and on the lookout for husband number three! Although why she should want another one is a mystery to the whole village. After all, it's not as if she takes their names, she stands by her maiden name; Miss Darcy Granger, now what do you think of that?' she ranted. I didn't answer, I simply paid for the soap and left, I didn't care what that bitter woman said, I liked Miss Granger and that was that. Or was it? What if Mum knew of the rumours and stopped me from working with her.

That worried me as I hurried home. What if more of the villagers thought my future employer a bit of a harlot? I took a deep breath, so what if she wouldn't use one or either of her former husband's surnames? Why should a woman have to change her name anyway?

I mulled it over as I walked the rest of the way home; would I want to change my name? I thought about it... did it really matter, for I would always be Ruby Miller on the inside, wouldn't I? I smiled, and that was exactly how my future employer viewed it. My brief meeting with her had me convinced that she didn't care what any of them thought. Which made me like her even more. But my worry as I hurried home was whether I could convince mum that Miss Granger was not as bad as some of the villagers painted her... but that might be difficult in light of our current relationship!

I tried to choose the right time to bring up the subject, it was no good trying to talk to her while the little-ones were running about the place, so I waited until they were all in bed and our Janet and Bella were busy in the kitchen.

'Mum... I began, 'I've something to tell you!' She stopped knitting waiting for me to say more, but for a moment I lost my nerve, and my voice too.

'Well?' She sighed. 'Get on with it, girl, I've not got all night, your father will be home soon wanting his supper.'

I took a deep breath; 'I've been offered the job in the cafe,' I said, hoping that would be enough. But it wasn't!

'I see, well that's good, isn't it?'

I took an even deeper breath; 'Miss Granger, the owner, doesn't seem to be much liked in the village.'

She looked at me and I waited for the outburst, but it never came; 'Just be sure you work hard and don't let yourself down,' was all she said.

As I walked away, I wondered if perhaps mum hadn't heard the gossip about Miss Granger, but I doubted that, even though we'd only been here a few days, she'd visited the shop at least two or three times, and that vile woman would, I'm sure, have whispered her poison in Mum's ear. I longed to have my big sister here to tell my good news to, but Janie was of course still in Yeovil and so I chose to tell our Janet the good news, and although she was thrilled for me it just wasn't the same somehow.

'Make sure you behave yourself, my girl,' mum said as I was leaving for my first day's work on Monday morning. I sighed; here I was off to work and she was still treating me like a child!

'You off then maid,' dad grinned, as I met him going out the door. I'd forgot he always came home for breakfast. He ruffled my hair and gave me a hug; I tried to push him away, as he smelled of hay and a lot worse, and now I needed to do my hair again. I felt like screaming; as I would be late on my first day. I turned ready to berate him for being so thoughtless, but he just stood there, smiling, with a look of absolute pride on his big, silly face, and so I hugged him instead. It was so good to see the change in him of late.

Miss Granger was already busy polishing the cutlery as I came hurrying in; 'You're late!' she barked, 'Go on through to my private room at the back.'

I went bright red, and wondered if I should even bother to take my coat off. I'd not seen this side of her during the interview and I was not sure I liked it.

'There are one or two things you should know Ruby if we are to get along,' she said, ushering me to sit on her rather plush divan. 'I will not tolerate; lateness, rudeness, or idleness.'

'I'm sorry,' I said, lamely.

'Don't be sorry, be on time, and bear in mind what I said regarding, rudeness and idleness,' she warned.

Even as I sat there being told off, I couldn't help but admire her stunning beauty and wondered why she had not yet found husband number three. While I was busy wondering about her, she'd continued talking!

'Ruby! Ruby! Are you even listening to me?'

I hung my head; 'Um! Sorry Miss Granger... I... I'

She sighed, 'never mind, I'll tell you again... I was talking about the Yanks... the American troops!'

I frowned for I'd heard nothing of any troops, American or not!

'Burley,' she began again, 'is a Black and White village... it...

I held my hand up to stop her; 'I know what a black and white village is, Sandbourne, where we once lived was one.'

'Good, so you know there are two American camps, one on either side of the village. One is full of white troops, the other of black troops who are not allowed to mingle.' She sighed.

I nodded, still bemused by the whole black and white divide idea, which still seemed absolutely crazy in light of the war we were fighting.

'So, then you'll know that for part of the week, the white GI's will come here, and the rest of the week the black GIs are allowed here.' she explained.

I nodded, but still didn't get it; 'And why can't they all come together?' I asked as confused as ever.

Suddenly she looked angry; 'Because the white Americans hate the black Americans and believe themselves superior to them... and our bloody Mr Churchill has thrown our equal rights bill out of the window just to curry favour with them,' she snapped. Having met black soldiers back in Sandbourne and discovered how nice they were, it did seem very unfair. Miss Granger took a deep breath and calmed down; 'Anyway, it's not likely that you'll encounter any of the black GI's here, as you'll only be working the white shift,' she confirmed. I nodded and started my very first day in the café.

It wasn't a difficult job for I had more than enough experience, and it was much easier than looking after half a dozen siblings. For the first time in quite a while life began to feel a little better. If only Janie were here to share it with me. The thought had me feeling a little sad. My sister had chosen to stay down in Somerset with Granny Miller, although in truth it was to be close to her new boyfriend, Ian. I forced a smile; for I didn't blame her at all, but I did miss her so. Still, there was enough going on in Burley to distract me, and I wrote it all in a letter to Janie and couldn't wait for her reply! I wrote;

'Dear Janie,

'Yesterday I saw my first black man since Sandbourne! It brought back so many memories, some good and some bad, but mostly good. And oh Janie, you should have seen this one bloke, he was beautiful. I honestly don't think I've ever seen such a handsome man. Sadly, I probably won't see him again as the Yanks here have even stricter rules about white girls meeting black GI's than our last place and there's no Lady Seymour to come to the rescue.

But changing the subject, will you be coming for a visit over Christmas? Please say you will Janie, I miss you so much. Janet and Bella are lovely of course but I can't talk to them like I do with you. I'm sure Granny and your Ian can spare you for a few days, or they could always come with you, I'm sure we could find room for them.

Oh, and I haven't told you about my new job... yes, I have a job, isn't that great; its only waitressing in the village cafe, but oh, Janie, you should see my boss, she is quite the loveliest woman I've ever seen. Miss Darcy Granger is her name, even though it's said she has two previous husbands, she refuses to be called Mrs! I think you'd like her, sis, she speaks her mind without a care for what others might say... she reminds me very much of you!

I'm sorry, I know I've not mentioned our dear brothers, Jack and Danny. It's not as if I'm trying to forget them or anything, it just that I get melancholy whenever I think of them... and still feel so very guilty. They would have loved it here Sis, among all these cheery Yanks. God knows what mischief they'd have got up to with two camps to play off against one another. They would probably have started a war of their own, setting the Black GI's off against the White GI's. Now wouldn't that have been fun? Perhaps I should do it for them... in their honour... now that would be something.

Remember all the times we had to clip their ears or tweak them so hard it made them yelp... I wish we could still, although now I think I'd just hug them, no matter what. So sorry Sis, here comes the melancholy, so I'll stop now. Be sure to write back at once to let me know about Christmas as I'll not be able to sleep until I hear from you.'

All my love Ruby.

The days seemed to pass more quickly in Burley, unlike our time on the heath which was more languid somehow; perhaps it was the Americans that make the difference, they being so lively and full of themselves.

'Arrogant,' mum still calls them, although dad still likes them well enough.

I agree with dad, but hold my tongue; so far mum has been fine about my new job and I want to keep it that way.

As the days passed, I was starting to really enjoy life in the café. Miss Granger and I got on well as long as I followed her rules of; being on time, being polite to the customers and of never being idle. As for the customers, who are mostly Yanks, they are pleasant, well behaved and extremely well-mannered, with their; 'Thank you mame, or thank you Honey and; 'have a good day.' It is hard then to believe that these same soldiers can be so nasty to their own people! But unfortunately, I know it's true, as I witnessed it first-hand.

As I was walking home one evening, a few steps behind me, two White GI's who I'd only just served in the cafe and who were both so very nice, hurried to pass me! I soon saw why, coming towards us was a lone black GI', and what happened next was hard to believe!

'Get off the side-walk nigger,' one of the white Americans barked, can't you see there's a white girl, a comin' this way?' I felt my face go red. The black GI' stepped aside and I went on by, but the sniggering from the two white Americans angered me and I just had to turn on them. 'How dare you?' I raged in their faces. 'This is not your country, it's ours, and we don't treat people like that, especially people who might die fighting for us... you should be ashamed of yourselves.'

I could see the anger in their eyes but I refused to be afraid and stood my ground forcing them to step off the pavement to go around me; 'excuse me Mam, never took you for a nigger lover.' One of them said spitting at my feet.' I was shaking with anger by the time I got home and although I didn't want to speak about it, mum forced it out of me.

'Right! Janet, Bella, see to the little-ones, you, come with me!' she snapped grabbing my arm.

I tried to protest as she marched me the half a mile to the White American camp, and I stood dumbfounded as she demanded to speak to the officer in charge. It took a while but finally someone came and we were taken into a small office where mum made me tell what had happened.

'Now, if you think I'm going to stand for my daughter being spat at and called names by some lout, whether he be black or white you'd better think again,' she raged.

The officer looked flustered as he asked me to repeat what had happened, but in the end, he agreed to get to the bottom of it and find the guilty parties.

Two days later he turned up at the cafe with the two GIs in question and they were made to apologise, and they did, even if it was half-heartedly. Miss Granger came over to see what was going on as I hadn't told her anything about it, and she listened quietly until the officer had finished then she promptly barred the two GIs from her cafe.

'Mam, this might cause you a lot of trouble,' one of the GI's,' growled.

'So be it, now you get out, I don't like bullies who spit at members of my staff... did it make you feel good treating a young girl like that... well did it?' she snapped.

'No Mam,' the younger of the two muttered, shuffling uncomfortably.

With that the officer marched them away and we returned to normality, although it was noticeable that not so many white GI's came to the cafe after that, but Miss Granger didn't seem to mind. Besides there was a big increase in black troops to make up for that.

'If anything like that ever happens again, Ruby, you be sure to let me know, I'll not stand for it, the very notion that you should be treated so!' I thanked her. What with mum standing up for me, which if I'm honest, I hadn't expected, and now her, I felt a lot better about my life in the village.

Chapter 25

All I wanted now was for our Janie to reply to my letter, hopefully in a positive way by agreeing to come, with or without her Ian or grandma Miller for a Xmas visit.
As if in answer to my prayer, two days later a letter arrived to say she was coming. I could scarce hide my excitement as I danced a jig around the kitchen with my siblings, all of whom were as excited as myself. Even mother couldn't hide the smile she started wearing from the moment the letter arrived and father too was over the moon. For a while we'd be a family again, it felt so good. We weren't sure how many were coming so mum had me make up the spare bedroom and sort out the sleeping arrangements, in case they all came. But there was no need in the end as Janie came on her own. Although it would have been nice to see her Ian and grandmother Miller, it was lovely to have her here alone, it was more like old times, just us and the little ones, along with mum and dad of course. It felt an age since we'd all been together like this and there was so much, I wanted too catch-up on!

Once all the furore had died down and our siblings were all sleeping, Janie and me sat on my bed and chatted into the early hours and it was as endless as time, just like it always was.
'I'm engaged, Rube,' Janie whispered quite out of the blue.
'What!' I squealed. 'When? Did he get down on one knee?' I demanded to know.
She put a finger to my lips; 'Sh! It's not official yet, he needs to speak to dad first,' she giggled. 'And no, he didn't get down on one knee, that's a bit old fashioned sis.'
I gave her a hug, 'Still, it's nice that someone loves you enough to want to marry you,' I sighed.
She hugged me back; 'Your time will come Rube, you're so pretty, how could it not.'
I smiled, 'Well who knows, there's a dance at the village hall on Saturday, perhaps I'll meet him there. Do you think your Ian would mind if you went with me?'
'He wouldn't mind at all Rube, he trust's me as much as I trust him,' Janie sighed.

'Oh! Not at all then?' I giggled.

She gave me a slap across the thigh that tingled a bit.

'Ouch! What was that for?' I yelped.

'For your cheek,' she laughed as she pushed me off the edge of the bed.

For a moment we were kids again belting each other with pillows, enjoying each other's company, until the door sprang open and mum came in.

'If you two want to play silly buggers, play outside, you'll have the little-ones awake in a minute,' she barked.

'I see she's still as cheery as ever,' Janie said as mum left.

I sighed; 'We don't seem to talk much anymore, in truth I just don't know what to say to her, or what to do to change things... any ideas?' I pleaded.

'Just bide your time, she'll come around, after all she did come to your defence against those horrible GI's, that's shows how much she cares for you Sis.' Janie smiled. I'd forgotten I'd told her about that.

'I suppose that's something,' I muttered.

'Of course, it is... now come here and tell me all about the dozens of handsome, nice Yanks that must be falling over each other to take you out.'

I laughed; 'that'll be the day, Sis!'

As we walked through the village on Saturday night, I pointed out the village shop where the grumpy woman lived and also the café where I worked. Although both were closed and sheathed in darkness we stood awhile and peeked in.

The hall was teeming when we arrived for the Christmas dance, mainly with black GI's! 'Oh goodness,' Janie, said as we hung up our coats and sat down alongside the dance-floor. 'I'd forgotten just how black they are Rube, but every bit as handsome,' she giggled. I felt myself blushing, our Janie had no idea just how loud her voice was; 'Sh! Janie, they'll hear you!' I protested. She simply laughed and continued speaking loudly. On the opposite side, a row of black faces beamed at us through teeth as white as snow and one of them I recognised right away.

'See the one, second from the left, Janie, well, that's the one who was forced off the pavement to let me pass,' I whispered.

'He looks nice Rube, you should ask him for a dance,' Janie said, rather to loud.

I felt myself blushing; 'The dance hasn't even started yet, Sis,' I muttered, 'and please, keep your voice down!'

But she didn't reply and when I turned towards her, I saw that she was already chatting to a man who'd crossed the room to talk to her... he was white and a local by the look of him. I was about to remind her that she was engaged, when the music began and he asked her to dance.

I sighed, that was just like her, stealing my thunder. I was the one in need of a partner, in need of cheering up, she had Ian after all. I was still pouting when I felt a tap on the shoulder. I almost fell out of my seat in surprise!

'Sorry Mam!' Didn't mean ta scare ya!'

At first, I thought it was the GI from the other day, but quickly realised it wasn't, this guy was a little younger and if it was possible even more handsome.

'Will ya do me the honor, Miss,' he smiled warmly.

I took the hand he held out to me and joined him on the dance-floor.

The band were all black GI's from the camp, and after the start up number they began to play a Jitterbug. Janie and I loved this dance; I tried to catch her eye as she swirled passed me, we'd often practised this in the kitchen at home and we knew it well.

'Not too many Brits know's how ta do the bug,' my partner smiled.

I smiled back; 'Well here's one that does... and there's another,' I laughed as Janie spun on by. 'Although I'm not sure her partner can dance at all,' I giggled, as Janie's man tripped over his own feet; 'Whoops! Sorry!' I heard him apologise.

'That's my sister,' I explained, not wanting him to think I was being rude to a complete stranger.

'Ah! I see, well then I guess that's okay,' he laughed as he swung me off my feet, then whirled me through the air, it was exhilarating and nothing like the way Janie and I had practised doing it in our bedroom at home.

'Hey, yore not half bad for a Limey,' he said as he spun me again and again.

'And you're not too bad for a Yank!' I laughed.

Then to my disappointment the number stopped and he escorted me back to my seat, where Janie was already waiting; 'My name is James,' he smiled.

'And mine is Ruby,' I beamed... 'And this is Jane... my...'

'I got it; Hi Sis,' he laughed, kissing the back of her hand.

Across the room I felt as if everyone was watching us, and not in a nice way, there were looks of anger and disgust... and I couldn't understand why? In the corner I noticed the vile lady who ran the village shop, she was deep in conversation with several others, all gesturing in our direction.

'I think we might have upset one or two of your neighbours Sis,' Janie sighed.

'Take no notice, I don't think they like us being with black guys', I said.

'You going to see him again?' Janie asked.

I grinned. 'Of course!'

At 9pm there was a roll on the drums signalling all change, and the black GI's and the black band all left making way for the white band and the white GI's to take over. It was clear the locals were well used to it by now, but to Janie and me it all felt very strange. And a bit daft! How could they be like this with each other, then go off to war and fight side by side, it just didn't make sense. After another Jitterbug and a couple of lively Jives, we decided to call it an evening and head for home although not before we were confronted by one of the two white GI's I'd had trouble with.

'I hear you' al been dacin wi niggers,' he scowled.

Before I could stop her Janie punched him with all the power of years of heavy farmwork in the blow; I heard his nose crunch and knew it was broken even before he screamed as much himself. The local man Janie had been dancing with earlier might not have been able to Jive, but he knew how to handle himself when it came to troublesome Yanks. 'Ok buddy, out you go,' he ordered.

Several other GI's came rushing over but so too did the bulk of the men from the village, and it looked like getting ugly there for a while until a whistle was blown and a possee of military policemen arrived.
'You do know you broke his nose, Sis?' I said as we were walking home.
'Well I wasn't trying to shake his hand Rube, that's for sure,' she growled. 'He's a nasty piece of work if you ask me, perhaps someone should check his papers, he could be a Nazi in disguise.'
I laughed out loud at that as we sauntered on arm in arm. I was still a little shaken by all that had happened, but, oh so proud of my big sister, and so very pleased that she'd come for Christmas.

Awaking on Christmas morning with Janie in the bed opposite made my heart sing. And as the little-ones awoke to find the stockings they'd hung expectantly the night before now full of all sorts of goodies, took me back to Christmas on the heath! That thought for a moment made me heart sick as images of our Jack and Danny flashed through my mind... they should be here... would be here... if... if... Before I could finish that thought Janie came to give me a hug. 'None of that now Sis, here open your present.' With that, she pushed a very poorly wrapped parcel at me; I smiled as I took it; 'Will you never learn how to wrap presents Janie,' I teased.

I should have known better! In an instant she was tugging me out of bed and encouraging our siblings into giving me a ragging, it was rough, it was noisy, it was fun, and for the briefest of moments my dear brothers were pushed to the back of my mind. But then mum came in and the look she gave me stole all the joy from the room.

'Alright now, take your presents down-stairs,' she said to the little-ones... and, Jane, Ruby, I could use some help with breakfast as I've the dinner to prepare.'

Janie looked at me, shaking her head as mum left the room; 'I think it's a good job I'm not announcing my engagement this trip Sis, the times just not right.'
'She's not right you mean... and I'm beginning to wonder if she ever will be again,' I sighed.
Despite my reservations, we all had, a wonderful, few days, and by the time our Janie came to say goodbye even mum was in a better place. 'Now don't you go breaking any more noses,' I heard her whisper in my sister's ear; 'after all we need all the Yanks to fight the Germans!' she chuckled.   Our Janie went bright red before wagging a fist at me behind mum's back, as if to accuse me of tattle-tailing. I shrugged my shoulders and shook my head to indicate that mum had not found out from me, but the memory of that night still made me smile.

Later, as I walked Janie to the bus-stop we talked about her bloke, Ian. She told me that he was an RAF mechanic stationed just a stones-throw from the farm where we all grew up.
'But what about you Rube', do you think you might see that black guy again?' she asked.
I blushed; for he'd been on my mind all over Christmas; 'It's not very likely, but who knows,' I laughed, digging her in the ribs.
'You watch your step Sis,' she warned, suddenly getting serious; 'If you're not careful you really will start a war of your own.'
The bus came then and she scrambled aboard; 'You can't change the world Rube,' she called back as the bus trundled down the beat-up old road.
'But I can try Sis,' I yelled after her.
As it disappeared around a corner I started for home, a little sad at my big sisters going, not knowing when I might see her again?

The months rolled by oh so very slowly after that and sadly I never did get to see anything of James during that time, being on the white shift as I was.

Janie and me exchanged letters and she said how well her relationship with Ian was going and asked about James, wondering if I'd been in touch with him at all.

It was halfway through April before I could tell her anything positive, and that came about because one of the other waitresses took poorly and Miss Granger took me to one side. 'I need you to change shifts for a while, Daisy's off sick and I can't do the baking and serve too... so what do you say?'

'Yes, that's fine, when do you want me to start?' I tried to remain calm, this was a dream come true, I'd be working the black days. It was my chance to meet James again.

'Would Monday be too soon?' she asked.

'No, no, Monday will be just fine,' I replied, trying desperately to hide my excitement.

I'm sure Miss Granger suspected something but she didn't say, and I'm glad for I didn't want to lie, I liked her too much. For all my excitement though I saw nothing of James that week and desperately hoped that my co-worker Daisy would be sick at least another week or two... Janie called me wicked when I wrote and told her my thoughts, but I didn't care, I just wanted to see James.

It was half way through my third week when he finally came into the cafe and I was so excited I tripped and spilt a plate of sandwiches in his lap! It was so embarrassing, everyone started laughing and I went redder and redder, finally bursting into tears. Such was the commotion that Miss Granger came from the kitchen to see what was going on; 'Pull yourself together Ruby,' she snapped. 'Clear up the mess and reorder the sandwiches.'

'Here please allow me!' I looked up to see James standing over me, an empty plate in his hand.

'There really is no need, Sir,' Miss Granger smiled, reaching for the plate.

'But I insist Mam, there's no harm done, none at all I assure you,' he smiled back at her, his teeth set in the most dazzling smile I'd ever seen.

Finally, my employer retreated back to her kitchen leaving me to clear the mess; I knew I probably hadn't heard the last of it but with James standing right there in front of me I didn't care.

'I'm so sorry,' I said gathering up the last few crumbs. 'I'm not usually so clumsy.'

He simply smiled his glittering smile, then turned his attention back to his friends and I thought; Wow! What a clown I am... what must he think of me?

I stayed well away from his table after that unable to even look his way. When he and his buddies left I made it look as if I was too busy to notice. Thankfully one of the others paid and I took the money without even looking up from the till.

'Well Ruby, that was well enough done,' Miss Granger smiled, as she came to stand with me.

I was taken aback, expecting to be told off not smiled at.

'I take it you're quite smitten with our young American then,' she chuckled.

'Smitten out of my mind,' I blushed.

She put a hand on my shoulder; 'I thought so, well good luck to you my dear, just have a care, many unlike you and me will not think it a match made in heaven... made in hell more likely.'

I knew she was right and if he hadn't been waiting for me as I finished my shift I'm not sure I would have pursued my dreams... but he was waiting.

'So then, will you walk out with me? He asked, so full of himself, as he leaned nonchalantly against the café wall.

I almost said no, but then he smiled such a wonderful smile that I couldn't help but say yes, with no thought to the consequences that simple little word might bring about!

It was the beginning of everything! We tried to be discrete at first, meeting in out of the way places, going for walks along country lanes or through fields of wheat, whilst spooning in old barns or fragrant hayricks. Now and then, James drove us to one of the bigger towns where we went to the picture house or the dance hall.

It was handy that James had the use of a jeep as it enabled us to travel away from the village with its ever-wagging tongues. Sometimes we would go down to the coast where we could at least admire the sea even if we couldn't go anywhere near it.

'Do you think they'll ever take away the barbed wire and the tank traps?' I sighed, as we stood on the cliff looking down at the coastline.

'Maybe one day, Honey,' he said, stroking my hair.

I wasn't sure I believed him, but I prayed that he was right, after all this war must surely run its course soon, nothing lasts forever.

I felt so very happy and wished with all my heart that our Janie could see me now, for I knew she would wish me all the happiness in the world. But alas she was many miles away, I felt a tear run down my cheek and sniffed it away... I did so need her advice! It was clear that my relationship with James couldn't continue as it was for much longer, already people were starting to gossip, and a few angry white GIs were kicking up a storm fit to burst. But then it came to me. 'I think you should meet my family,' I suggested one day when we were strolling along our favourite clifftop walk.

He laughed his beautiful laugh; 'And there I was tryin ta be diplomatic, and you want me ta meet the folks, what a girl you are Ruby Miller.'

That evening as I tried to pluck up the nerve to speak to mum about it, our Janet spilt the beans before I had the chance.

'Someone at school says you're dating a black man,' she blurted out during supper.

I didn't know what to say, all I could do was sit there with a silly look on my face. For a moment there was silence, then mum turned from stirring a pot of stew on the range, and I thought, oh, oh, here we go! But to my surprise she simply said; 'If that's true girl you'd best invite him to tea so we can all take a look at him.'

I could feel everyone's eyes on me and I wasn't sure what to say...

'Well?' It was clear she was serious.

'I'll need to find out when he can come... and...'

'Saturdays best for us... ask him to come over then,' she insisted.

'Oh... right then, I'll see if he can come on Saturday, although he might be on duty.'

'He's not on duty, that's why I suggested it,' mum said.

'But... but... how do you know for sure?' I felt really flustered.

'Because I asked him of course,' she sighed.

Just then dad got in from his work; 'Do you know about Saturday?' I asked him.

He grinned, 'Aye and I can't wait ta meet the lad, maid.'

I couldn't quite believe what was going on, it would seem that James was to come to tea on Saturday, although neither he nor I had planned it!

'But how did you find out about us?' my head was in a spin.

'I heard it from the woman who runs the shop, and you must know that you're the talk of the village my girl,' she tutted. I was suddenly very angry, how dare they spy on us, what right did they have? I turned on mum and raved at her about my rights about our rights, James and mine. It took dad to calm me down; 'Easy now maid, blame the gossips if you must blame someone,' he said. I took a deep breath and suddenly felt very silly, of course, it was that stupid woman in the shop and her cronies. I made up my mind that the next time I went there I'd tell her just what I thought of her and her gossiping friends.

'I know what you're thinking girl and you'll stay well clear of that shop; and besides, what did you expect? Did you really believe that in a small village like this you could walk out with a black man and not have people talk about it? Well, did you?' mum snapped.

She was getting angry too now and once again it was dad who stepped in; 'Enough now, we'll talk to the boy when he comes fer tea, and see what's what; but now I'd like a bite ta eat,' he sighed.

Nothing more was said on the subject, at least not by mum or dad, our Janet and Bella however had plenty to say; 'So, come on, out with it Rube' what's he like... is he really black? Is it true he drives a jeep?

I've never even seen a jeep,' little Violet piped up. 'Do you think he'll take us for a ride in it?' she chirped gleefully.

'Oh, shut up Vi,' he'll not be taking you anywhere,' I growled.

She started to cry. 'There was no need to speak to our Vi like that,' Janet snapped going to comfort her.

'I'll speak to her how I like, I'm in charge here not you,' I barked. With that I slammed out of the house, going for a walk down through the village, it was getting late by this time and so there was not many people about.

Reaching the café I stopped, it was strange to see it empty and dark, although it was well past closing time. I lingered for a minute or two staring into darkness my mind a million miles away, until a loud rap on the window brought me back. On the other side of the glass Miss Granger was smiling and gesturing for me to come in; I tried the door to find that she'd unlocked it for me.

'What brings you here at this time of the day?' she asked as I entered.

'Just needed to get out for a while, get away from the family,' I sighed.

She frowned and I knew I'd said something she didn't approve of; 'Now we both know it's not family you're running away from don't we... go... go on through, I'll make a pot of tea.' She ushered me through the dark and empty cafe towards her personal space at the back. From my seat on the sofa I watched as she put the kettle on to boil and readied the cups and saucer, I did rise and offer to help but she waved me back to my seat.

'Now while we're waiting why don't you tell me what it is that has you walking the village this late at night?' she asked, perching on the other end of the divan.

So, I told her how mum had interfered by asking James for tea without telling me, and how my sisters now thought they had the right to have a say, as if it was anything to do with them. Before I could continue my rant she held up her hand to stop me; 'So you think this is nothing to do with your family, that it's only your business?' she said. I nodded.

'Well really! You start dating a black GI, against everything the white American army believes in, possibly starting a major commotion that could prove to be devastating, not only for you and James, but for everyone, and you say it's nobody else's business! I thought better of you Ruby,' she said shaking her head.

The kettle started to whistle then before I had the chance to reply giving me a moment to consider what to say; 'So you think I'm wrong to be dating a black man,' I finally asked.

'No of course not, but I do think it's very naïve of you to think that what you are doing is not going to affect your family... and so is nothing to do with them.'

'But it is nothing to do with them,' I insisted.

I felt so upset, this was about James and me, no one else! As she brought the tea things over and placed them on a small side-table, I could see that she was on the verge of becoming very angry.

'You just don't see it do you? This is not about the two of you, this is about deep-rooted prejudice, but you should know that you saw what it was like down at Sandbourne.

'Yes, I saw it and it was so unfair, you can't condone such a thing, it's... it's evil!' I was close to tears.

'Of course, I don't condone it, but it's a reality you both have to live with. James knows it better than you, in his own country he's not allowed to sit next to a white woman, let alone date one.'

'Surely that's not true, it can't be,' I said, shaking my head.

She poured the tea and handed me my cup; 'Not only is it true in the USA, our government has allowed it to happen over here to a lesser extent. That, as you know, is why the black and white GIs come into the village on different days. Across the country there are pubs, cafes, picture-houses, theatres and many other places where black GIs are segregated, they either have to accept it or are not allowed in. So now can you see just how big this is?' I sat for a moment quietly sipping my tea; trying to decide if this thing with James and me was serious enough to warrant all the trouble it was going to bring down upon our heads... and not just our heads it would seem, but my, families, heads too?

Finally, I spoke; 'Thank you, Miss...'

'Darcy, please, outside of work its Darcy,' she smiled.

'Thank you, Darcy,' I corrected as she walked with me to the door.

'So, what will you do now?' she asked, leaning to kiss my cheek.

'Ask him to tea on Saturday to meet the family, I guess,' I smiled, waving her goodnight.

There was a lot for me to think about on my way home that night. I wasn't sure what was the best thing to do. Perhaps dating James was not such a good idea, it could bring a lot of trouble to my family! By the time I reached the front door I'd as good as decided to call the whole thing off, but it was mum, to my surprise who set me right!

'No matter what, you must never let, gossips and racists, dictate to you how you run your life. Your father and I are the only ones who have the right to question what you do or who you do it with, just us and no-one else. Even then at the end of the day it's you who must plot your own course.'

It was such a surprise to hear her saying such things to me, I really didn't think she cared one way or another. I went up to my bedroom my head in a spin; clearly she does care!

On Saturday I was full of nerves as I waited with the rest of the family for James to arrive and it was all I could do to stop myself from throwing up, the butterflies in my stomach were going wild!

'He's really coming isn't he sis?' Janet asked, this isn't an April Fools thing, is it?'

I shook my head; 'April the 1st was ages ago, he's really coming, and...'

'He's here! He's here!' Bella cried, interrupting me as she came flying down the stairs, where she'd been looking out of her window wanting to be the first to see him.

'How do you know it's him?' Janet snapped, annoyed that she'd not seen him first.

Bella was beaming, 'Who else would it be, he's black and he pulled up in a jeep!'

'Right, all of you to the kitchen... away with you now... Janet, Bella, take the little-ones with you, and mind our David he might be in need of changing,' mum ordered. There was a lot of moaning and groaning but they all trooped off together, leaving just mum, dad, and me to welcome James to our home. Mum at least let me open the door when he knocked, but was close on my heels at all times.

'Come in lad, and welcome to ee,' dad said, coming to shake his hand. 'So, you must be James... or do they call you Jimmy or Jim,' he smiled.

I could have kissed him; I could tell by James face that he already felt at ease.

'Nice ta meet you Sir, some do call me Jim, but mostly it's James,' he grinned, his white teeth shining in the candlelight.

'Then James it'll be lad, and we'll ave no more of this Sir, its Fred,' dad insisted lightly.

'Thank you, Fred, that's mighty nice of ya, Oh, and here, Ruby tells me you smoke.' He handed over a pack of two hundred cigarettes and dad almost collapsed back into his chair.

'I don't know what ta say lad, but can you spare so many?' dad seemed bewildered.

James smiled, 'They're part of my rations sir... sorry, Fred, only as I don't partake, its usual for me to give them away.'

He turned to mum; 'Sorry mam, I know it should be ladies first but I didn't want ta walk thru the door with ma hands full, so if you'll pardon me for one minute...' with that he went back through the front door, leaving behind him a stunned silence.

So far he'd not said as much as a single word to me, nor as much as looked in my direction, which caused my cheeks to redden a little although I wasn't angry, just embarrassed. But his wide smile as he came back through the door arms laden with all manner of things; from coffee, which we'd never had; to sugar, tea, cookies and chocolate and much more, along with a bouquet of flowers, that I thought was for me, but that he gave to mum! With the formalities over the rest of the family were allowed back in and poor James had to endure a mountain of questions, many referring to the colour of his skin, all of which he answered with a smile, even laughing aloud as our Violet climbed up onto his knee and tried to rub his face clean with the edge of her dress. 'It won't come off,' she sighed. We all laughed at that.

After that day James became a regular visitor, he even took us all out for rides in his jeep, and even mum seemed to like him. It wasn't the same with many of the villagers though, and as for the white GI's they became openly aggressive, not just to me and James but to the rest of the family too. That was upsetting, but James had warned me what to expect, although I never believed it would get so bad! The woman at the shop along with most of the village looked at me as if I were dirt and she often refused to serve me things that I knew she had in stock. It was upsetting but we put up with it.

For as hurtful as all this was there was still a war going on, with much talk of us launching the greatest armada of ships ever, taking with them hundreds of thousands of men and tons upon tons of war machines. So, what went on in this little village really didn't amount to much! Already most of the units around the village had been shipped off to the coast, and all of the others, including James's outfit were on standby to follow them. It brought a kind of reality to it us all, focusing the minds of everyone, including the local hate mongers. Especially when the soldiers began to disappear from the streets, leaving behind a strange emptiness.

It was hard to believe that we'd been here at Burley almost a year, but we had and I was petrified that James would soon be shipped off, as his unit was now one of the last remaining here. We both knew that it was just a matter of time, and so that is why, for the first time he and I had sex! It wasn't planned and not at all how I'd thought it would be! In my dreams I'd pictured us sharing a bed in some beautiful little country cottage whilst on our honeymoon; but in truth it was just a half an hour in an old barn that stank of cow's shit! For all that, it was wonderful, and for a few weeks we used that old barn as our bedroom with the fear hanging over us that any day soon James might be going off to war.

Chapter 26

I knew after missing my period in July that I was expecting a baby and I was so scared that I couldn't sleep for a week. The first thing I did of course was to write to Janie, for if ever I needed her it was now, even though I knew she was busy planning her wedding. Within a week of my writing to her she came, turning up on the doorstep quite out of the blue with the pretence of needing my help to choose her wedding gown!

'So, who knows?' Was her first question.

We were once more perched on the edge of my bed; I shook my head, 'no-one!'

Janie was surprised, 'Not mum and dad? Not James?' she asked.

Again, I shook my head.

'Go and tell mum and dad now, I'm sure I've just heard them come in,' Janie said.

'No, not before I've told James'... I was sure that was how it should be.

'Well then when will you be seeing him, it had better be sooner rather than later, these things tend to get out you know!' Janie warned.

'Tomorrow, I'm seeing him tomorrow, I promise I'll tell him then,' I sighed.

I started to cry then and Janie held me, and cried too, stroking my hair and patting me gently on my back, and we were children again, sibling sisters as close as ever we were in the past and it gave me such strength to have her with me.

After a restless night where I slept barely a wink, I hurried off after breakfast to meet James. We were going out for the day in his army jeep, and after a silent journey down to the coast, we sat on the clifftop with the silence opening a chasm between us!

'What's wrong, honey?' he asked, his voice so full of concern it tore at my heart. 'Have I done something ta upset you?'

I sniffed back a tear and told him.

If it was possible for a black man to turn white, then he surely did! Oh My God! Oh my God!' was all he kept saying. Which of course did very little to help me.

'Have you told yer Ma and Pa?' James asked as we sat holding hands.

I shook my head; 'I wanted to speak to you first,' I said.

He went quiet for a while, then said; 'We need ta go back right away to see my captain an' ask fer a marriage licence.'

I was quite taken aback; I mean, could we even do something like that without mum and dad's consent? Despite my worries James was adamant and so off we went.

I'd never met his captain and so was surprised to discover that he was white. I had assumed that everyone on this side of the village was black... and they were, James explained later, apart from the officers.

The white captain listened patiently as James explained to him our circumstances, then he asked if my parents knew!

Um! 'No! Not yet Sir.' I blushed.

He shook his head in disbelief and rose to his feet ushering us out of his office. 'We'd best go and tell them don't you think young lady,' he sighed.

We all went in the same jeep we'd used to go down to the coast, with James and the captain in the front and me huddled, terrified in the back.

On our arrival, the first thing I saw was our Janie ushering our siblings up the stairs, leaving just mum and dad sitting in the kitchen drinking mugs of tea and eating homemade sponge cake. It was dad's favourite, that at least might be in my favour. But I knew it was a slender thread to cling too, with what I had to admit to them! I saw mum glance towards dad and then look my way and I knew that already she'd guessed! I felt my cheeks burning and choked back a flood of tears as I saw her shake her head, a knowing look written deep in that hard face of hers. It wasn't a surprise, it was all she expected of me... it was there, plain to see. I'd killed her sons, my brothers with my carelessness and now this, shaming the family in the eyes of all the village! ...and they want a marriage certificate...' was where I picked it up after being lost in my own dark thoughts! The captain, hesitated, and gave me such a look that it took me back to all the troubles I'd had with folks both local and military since my friendship with James was known... it was clear he didn't approve.

'Of course,' he continued, 'should you agree Mr Miller, and they go forward with the wedding, we, the American forces, will ship your daughter and the expected child back to the U.S. There they will be taken to stay with James's folks until his return.'

I was stunned, I didn't know that I'd have to go to America alone! I began to cry and James put his arm around me to comfort me.

'It's alright honey, my people will take good care of you and the baby,' he said.

'No! I'll be buggered if my maid's goin' tuther side o' the world ta live with strangers, how will we know what's become of her?' dad said, jumping to his feet.

I was shocked, I'd never heard dad so outspoken!

Mum hadn't said a word, and still she kept quiet, although I saw her nod in agreement at what dad said.

'So, there'll be no weddin...,' dad began...

I interrupted him before he could go any further; 'But me and James want to wed dad!' I implored him.

'No! If you love each other, then, tha' won't change, and you just as well wait fer un here, rather than in a strange country.' he insisted.

This was so unlike him, it was more like mum, but it wasn't her, it was dad and he meant every word of it.

In truth I couldn't argue with him, for I had no wish to be alone in the USA with a little baby without my family to turn too. And so that was how it was left. The officer gave James and me a minute to say goodbye and then they were gone.

I stood at the window watching them drive away up the cobbled road and out of the corner of my eye I could see mum looking at me her face so full of disenchantment. Whether dad noticed or not I wasn't sure but he came and gently placed his rough, work worn hand on my shoulder; 'Yer not the first an' you won't be the last, maid,' he sighed. At his kind words I thought mum was going to explode with anger, but she gritted her teeth and walked away without a single word to me about any of it. Janie returned back to Yeovil and as the months rolled by I felt ever more alone. I saw no sign of James, but with the war still raging across the channel it was only to be expected.

The weather was on the wintery side as I made my way once more up to the U.S. camp, but then it was November! It was obvious now that I was with child and not even my winter coat could hide it.

'Sorry Miss, but there's still no news,' the GI at the gate said.

I was devastated, that's what they always said! I wanted only to talk to James, to find a way that we could be together, but I couldn't even get to see him! For all I knew he might already be at the front fighting! I cried all the way home. To make matters worse I hadn't heard from our Janie for a while, although I wasn't surprised what with her wedding day looming, she did promise to return just as soon as she could however.

I threw myself into my work at the cafe for the next few days ignoring all the side glances and slyly whispered remarks. I wondered how long it would be before Miss Granger decided to let me go, being the size, I was. I wasn't surprised at the end of the week when she approached me as I was about to close up for the day.

'You can stay here until you decide you can't manage, you know,' she smiled. 'If you want to?' She added.

I turned and gave her a hug. 'Thank you, I will, I'm alright at the moment,' I smiled back.

Two weeks later Janie returned and as soon as we were alone, I collapsed into her arms sobbing my heart out. For the next few hours, we stayed in my bedroom and I caught her up with everything.

'What about mum... how is she taking it?' she asked.

I took a deep breath; 'Not well! I thought we were making progress; she likes James... but now... we're back to square one... hardly speaking again.'

'So, what about you and James?'

I started to cry again, 'I haven't seen him for ages, he could be fighting in France for all I know,' I sobbed.

'Well bugger this! Come on Sis, let's go find out,' she said, taking my hand.

We were down the stairs and out the door before anyone could as much as speak in our direction.

'Sorry Miss, but...'

'Enough of this bullshit, fetch the officer in charge,' Janie barked in his face.

The young GI went bright red before sending his guard buddy to fetch someone, a few minutes later the Captain I'd already met came out to see us. Before he could say anything, Janie spoke up; 'You'd best understand, my sister won't be going away unless you tell her where her James is.'

'I'm sorry, ladies but that's impossible, since we liberated Paris back in August his unit could be anywhere, but I am only allowed to tell you that Corporal James McKenzie is no longer on camp!' The captain insisted firmly.

It was odd to hear him called by his official title and not just James, but it didn't help me! I look at Janie and then at him,

'But what does that mean exactly?' was all I could manage.

The captain, sighed. 'It means that he is no longer on camp... and that ladies, is all I can say. Remember, we are still at war!' he reminded us.

There was nothing left to do but head back into the village, although I didn't really want to go home, not yet. 'Let's go to the cafe and get some coffee,' I suggested.

It was a black day and the cafe was full so Darcy took us through to her private lounge; 'Stay as long as you like,' she smiled... 'and Ruby don't even think about offering to lend a hand in the café. Enjoy spending some time with your sister, we can manage.' So, we sat and chatted and Janie caught me up on her wedding plans and all that was going on back in Yeovil where she worked and lived with our grandmother. It brought back so many happy memories of our time there before the war and I made a silent vow to return there one day, taking James's baby with me.

'How is Grandma Miller?' I asked as we sipped our coffee in the quiet of the back room.

'Missing everyone, and cursing this bloody war,' Janie sighed.

'And what about your Ian, how is he?' I asked.

Janie put her hand gently on my arm; 'Never mind my Ian or Grandma, what are we going to do about your James?'

I shrugged; 'I don't know! I'll just have to keep asking after him up at the camp until they give me an answer to where he is, someone must be able to tell me.' I dabbed away another tear.

'Bugger that! Janie snapped, getting to her feet.

I followed on behind her as she marched into the café and watched and listened in disbelief as she banged a tin tray down loudly on an empty table bring silence and all eyes turning her way.

'Right then, gentlemen,' she shouted; 'Now that I have your attention, my sister, here wants to know the whereabouts of Corporal James Mckenzie.'

There was a moment's stunned silence and then the sound of chairs being pushed back as customers, one by one rose to leave; 'wait… wait, it's a simple enough question,' Janie insisted, stepping in front of a bulky private before he could get to the door.

'I'm sorry mame, but you'd best ask the officers at the camp, we've not seen hide nor hair of James for a while now, some say he's been transferred, others say he was shipped off to France to join up with the rest of his unit… mostly though we believe it's because of your sister… and her condition,' he sighed.

'But that's nothing to do with anyone else, that's for Ruby and James to sort out,' Janie insisted.

As he pushed his way passed her, he muttered; 'If only we all lived in the same world Mame, then all would be well, but we don't and it aint. Good luck with finding James, he's a good man and if I hear a whisper of what's become of him I'll do my best ta let ya all know.' With that he went out the door followed by the remaining customers, leaving me to apologise to Darcy and drag Janie away back home.

'I'm sorry Rube, I truly am, it just got to me… after all someone must know what's happened to James, people don't just vanish off the face of the earth,' she sighed, as we reached the front door.

After Janie returned back to Yeovil and her Ian things took a surreal turn in Burley.

Almost overnight both the white GI camp and the black camp were gone... shipped off to fight, dad said. And now, where their camps had been there was just row upon row of empty wooden huts, all reminding me of my missing lover. Now there was no one to answer my questions, no one to say where James was.

There were rumours of course; some said he was sent back to the US, others that he'd simply gone to France to re-join his unit, which frightened me very much when I thought of the possibility of him being killed in action. But the rumour that scared me the most was the one that said he'd been arrested and put in prison for raping an underage white girl! This last one was the scariest of all because I'd heard of this happening, when a family discovers their daughter is pregnant by a black GI, it's been known for them to cry rape, with the deadliest of consequences. I could only hope that James had not fallen prey to that.

To my dismay, before I had any answers to my questions the bloody man from the Ministry came again to move us on. Dad was recalled to our old stomping place near Yeovil. Although I did my best to be allowed to stay in Burley with Miss Darcey, mum insisted, because of my condition that I go along with them.

It was a sad farewell on the day that we left, with Miss Darcey the only one to come and wish us good luck. It was a far cry from when we'd left the heath, most of the village had turned out to see us off then. But that wasn't what upset me the most, it was the thought of leaving James behind, just as I'd left my brothers behind out on the heathland that tore at my insides! That thought haunted me all the way to Home Farm. Despite my siblings treating me so warmly, all eager to know about my baby, the little-ones all coming to check out my belly, sitting next to me smoothing me gently I could have cried.

Once again back at home farm, Christmas came and went and I tried to be cheerful, doing my best not to spoil it for my siblings. And as we tiptoed through the early days of 1945 under a wintery sky, we all hoped above hope that this war would finally come to an end.

Chapter 27

Old Home Farm seemed less welcoming somehow on our return, and that upset me. It had always been such a tranquil place, a kind of sanctuary really, somewhere to hide, away from all the troubles of the world, but now, it felt as if we'd brought all those troubles back with us.

Standing in the yard looking down the leafy lane seeing the softness of the hedgerows and the beauty of the early flowers beneath was still a wonderful sight, but now somehow it lacks something. An image of our Jack and Danny framed my mind and I sighed, of course, without them here, nothing would ever be the same. But it's not just them who's missing, it's me. When I left here I was a child and soon I'll be a mother with a child of my own! What would my little brothers have made of that, I wondered?

'You alright Rube?'

She made me jump, I didn't know she was here, we hadn't been expecting her, not today, but I was pleased to see her none the less.

'Janie, Oh Janie, it's so good to see you.'

Reaching forward she touched my tummy. 'Have you heard anything from James, or anything telling you where he might be?' she asked, linking arms with me and starting us walking down the lane. I shook my head too afraid I might weep if I dared to speak about James, but finally I did answer her; 'I had a letter from Miss Darcy yesterday, there's still no word of him and to make matters worse, the few GI's left in the village are all new, and claim to know nothing of what went on before.'

'I'm sorry Sis, I don't suppose there's much more anyone can do,' Janie sighed.

'Maybe not, but I mean to keep trying to find him... I must... Oh Janie what am I to do?' I wept.

Janie held me close; 'You my little sister are going to be strong. You will have this baby and, with the help of us, your family, you will be a wonderful mother to, him, or her, she smiled.'

I wanted to believe her, but my relationship with our mother was still very strained and I sensed a growing hostility between us with every passing month.

'I'm sure mum feels that If I'd been more careful, I wouldn't have got pregnant, just like if I'd been more careful back on the heath, our two brothers would still be alive! I truly believe that's what mother thinks, and I also believe she's right.'

'Oh, really Ruby, come on now, stop all this self-pity, life's too short for that. Think of all the poor souls who died and who are still dying, fighting this awful war so that we might live in peace. It's so sad that our dearest brothers are gone, but gone they are, and nothing can bring them back. You're expecting, that's the true reality that you have to face up to,' she snapped. 'Think of the baby if nothing else,' she insisted. But still I was down in the dumps! 'What about James? Perhaps he'd still be around but for me. I'm convinced the Yanks have disappeared him. All because he's black and I'm white and I chose to ignore that fact, even though all the world told me it was wrong and now he's gone and it's all my fault!

She slapped me then, full across my face; 'Oh, for, goodness- sake! You can't keep on blaming yourself, Sis,' Janie said, angrily. With my face still tingling I could barely speak as she changed the subject. 'Look, tomorrow, why don't you come into town with me and help me find some wedding clothes?'

Damn! How selfish was I, prattling on like an old fishwife. I'd completely forgotten our Janie was getting married soon.

I forced a smile; 'You trust my judgement that much?'

She grinned; 'Of course not, you'd probably take me to one of your jumble sales... although, perhaps we could find you a bridesmaid's dress there, if we're lucky!' I jabbed her in the ribs and we both laughed aloud, and I realised that was the first time I'd laughed for a very long time.

Later, sat at the kitchen table we started speaking in earnest about the wedding. The ceremony was to be held in St Johns Church in the heart of Yeovil, close to Granny Miller house, which was nice. After seeing Janie on her way, I went off to bed.

The following day was warm and sunny as we strolled arm in arm through the streets of Yeovil. The threat of air raids was few and far between now as the allied forces pushed the Germans back so we could relax and enjoy the frosty but sunny day. There was talk that this year of 1945 would be the final days of Heir Hitler and his Nazi's party, but then, they'd said that last year, and still, it's not over. I shook the thought from my head, this was not about the war, this was all about our Janie's wedding plans.

'Well, what do think of this dress?' Janie asked, as if reading my thoughts.

We were in Mrs Barnet's second-hand wedding gown shop, the only place to be if you wanted something decent but cheap; I brought my mind to order; 'Um! Well... I'm not really sure... what do you think?' I fudged

'It's about what you think, Sis, it's why I brought you along,' she sighed.

I took a deep breath; her tone was a little aggressive, and I was doing her a favour after all; 'Okay! Well, why don't you try it on, then I'll let you know what I think,' I snapped. I spent the next few minutes looking fruitlessly around for something that might do for myself, but being 8mths pregnant that was an impossibility, and anyway, I told myself, as I stopped searching, the wedding was in May and by then I would have had the baby.

'Well, what do you think then?'

Janie looked beautiful in her second-hand white gown, but I was in too much of a mood to tell her that, instead I shrugged; 'It seems a little tight under the arms and across the tummy, I think you should try a bigger size.' I barked.

'Right! That's it... you, out! Go across the street to the café and order us a pot of tea and some scones, I'll be there as soon as I've changed,' she snapped. I knew I'd upset her but I just didn't care, I was totally pissed off. I'd thought I'd be alright with the whole wedding shopping thing, but I wasn't. It just got me thinking more and more about James and where he might be, and I couldn't help thinking that this should be us getting ready for our wedding? 'Oh James,' I muttered, 'where are you'? I wiped away a tear as I crossed the road to the café... How could he have seemingly dropped off the face of the earth... then the scary thoughts returned; he could have been shipped back to America in chains or be rotting in an English prison, or worse still, waiting to be hung for raping me!

I shook the terrible thoughts away, as I selected a table by the window and waited for Janie, she'd be mad as hell with me, I was sure. I know I would be on such a special day. But when at last she came to sit opposite me she took my hand and smiled.

'Sorry Sis, I know this must be hard for you. I should never have asked you to come with me, especially in your state,' she sighed.

'Me being so fat, you mean.' I snorted.

'No, of course I didn't mean...'

I started chuckling...'

'Oh, I see, so you think you're; Arthur bloody Askey now?' She raged.

I wasn't sure what she meant; I only knew him to be a small comedian on the wireless. 'Am I that funny, Sis, why he's about the funniest man in the country,' I giggled.

'I didn't mean you were as funny as him, more like you look like him... small and round!' she laughed. We both giggled at that as the waitress came to take our order. It was a nice treat to be able to get away from everything and everybody for a short while; just Janie and me, like it was in the old days. We seldom met up anymore, what with us both working and Janie still living with grandma Miller.

'Have you had any news from Miss Granger lately?' she asked as we waited for our tea and scones.

I shook my head, trying not to look her in the eye for fear of gushing again. 'No, not a word but I'm still hoping, mum did get a letter from the Yanks last week. Have you heard? The bastards are coming to take the baby when its born… or so they think… it'll be over my dead body Sis, I swear it will,' I ranted

'Don't worry dad will stand by you, after all you're his favourite 'little maid!' She teased.

I tossed the table napkin at her and laughed; 'Now you know dad doesn't play favourites, Sis, and if he did it would be you for sure, we all know that.'

The waitress gave me a dirty look as she came with our order, no doubt having seen me throw the napkin, but Janie and I just laughed, upsetting the poor girl even more.

'But seriously Rube' what's to be done about the Yanks, after all you're not yet seventeen, and sixteen in their eyes is too young to be a mother. Can they really take the baby from you?'

I nodded; 'Unless…' I paused, unable to find the words.

'Unless what?' Janie asked, sitting further forward in her seat.

'Unless I allow mum and dad to adopt the child!' I sighed.

Janie's face blanched; 'And you'd do that… give your baby away?'

I nodded; 'It's not as if my baby will be leaving the family, I'll still be able to see it and help look after it every day, just like I used to see to the little ones back on the heath.'

The words about the young ones and the heath were out of my mouth before I realised and I almost choked on them, remembering my failure to take care of my dear brothers. And our time on the heath was still a sore scab refusing to heal between mother and me.

After our tea we parted in the Borough, Janie heading to grandma Miller's, while I caught the old bus back to the farm, both of us promising to meet up again soon. It was an ill made promise for we were both far too busy getting on with our lives.

Janie with her wedding plans and myself taking another trip back to the village of Burley in search of my darling James. Nothing much had changed in Burley, the wild ponies still roamed the streets of the village, the old busybody still ran the store and miss Granger still had her café, although it wasn't nearly as busy now what with the troops having all moved out.

To my delight my old mentor greeted me with open arms and insisted I stay with her while I was in the village, which I have to admit is what I hoped would happen. After she closed the café for the day, we had tea in her private room and she filled me in on all the latest gossip. Sadly, nothing she'd heard was about James. Although there was a glimmer of hope as the Yanks before they left, reprimanded our nosy old busybody in the village store for falsely claiming James had been arrested and imprisoned on the charge of raping a minor. The yanks said that he'd simply gone about his duty and joined his unit in France. That, Darcy, said, was their final word on the subject, 'and there was no talk of either you or the baby.' As sad as I was that I knew no more of his whereabouts at least I knew James wasn't in prison because of me and that there was every chance he might survive the war and return to me and our baby.

Although I was disappointed at not finding him, two days later I rode the bus back to Home Farm feeling much more at ease... James would return... I was sure of it. But as time rolled on, I knew it was just false hope, that James was never coming back and I was going to have to cope alone.

On the 9th day of March 1945 after a lot of pain and awful lot of screaming on my part, I gave birth to a bonny baby boy, who although not as black as his father, being a rather soft chocolate shade, was the image of him just the same. I didn't argue when mother insisted on his middle names being Jack and Danny after the two boys we'd lost on the heath, although I did insist his first name be James, after his father. Ten days after his birth, mum and dad officially adopted him, and five days after that the Yanks came to take him, but they left empty handed and James became a part of the family.

With the coming of Spring 1945 the war in Europe was almost over and we were able, for the first time in six years to relax. Our days of travelling the high ways and by ways of South West England were over too. Now it was time for us as a family to settle somewhere permanently, and I prayed that it would be at Home Farm, just the perfect place for a little baby to grow up.

'You do know that you'll have to leave!' mum's words hit me like a bomb blast!

I was sat on the rug in the living-room bottle feeding James and I couldn't believe my ears; 'But why... I don't understand,' I pleaded.

Mum stood in front of me her arms folded across her chest; 'Not right away of course, but soon, little Jimmy is weaned off breast milk now and we both agreed he can only have one mother.'

'Yes but...'

'No, there are no buts Ruby!' Already you keep interfering about his feeding, his bedtime and everything else and we can't have that.' 'You're his sister now... his sister, and that's all, are we clear? I think it would be best if you went to live with grandma Miller, she'll have a spare room once Jane has moved out.'

I didn't know what else to say, yes I'd agreed to giving him up, but not like this, not completely like this! And his name is James, not Jimmy!'

I went to my room, my mind in a whirl, after all that had happened in Burley, I'd thought coming back to Home Farm would help to settle me. I believed that with or without James it would be my home forever. I never dreamed my life here would end so soon. No! No! I would not except this, it just wasn't fair, she had no right to send me away, no right at all. With a determination that I hadn't felt for a long time I went down to confront her again, although by the time I found her busily cooking in the kitchen, much of the bravado had gone. I loitered for a moment in the hallway, before taking a deep breath and going in to see her.

For a moment we just stood looking at one another and I steeled myself, waiting for her to erupt, but instead she sighed!

'Would you rather the Americans took him, child?'

I shook my head, 'No, I guess not!' I admitted sulkily.

'And we've already gone over the fact that if he's to grow up in the family, he can't have two mothers. He has to believe that I'm his mum and that you're his big sister, it's the only way. But clearly, it's too difficult for you to be under the same roof as him, and so you'll live with grandma Miller. You will be welcome here as often as you like, but little Jimmy will be my son... mine, as far as you and everyone else is concerned, agreed!'

I nodded, at least I'd see him grow up, and who knows one of these days his father might return and I'll be able to reclaim him.

I returned to my bedroom my head full to bursting with un-spilt tear, as one by one my siblings came to comfort me and we snuggled together on my bed. I would miss them dearly after all we'd been through together. Yes, I'd miss them all so very much! After they'd all crept back to their own rooms, I thought about dad. I hadn't seen much of him today and wondered if he was aware of all this. He surely wouldn't have agreed willingly to my being sent from the only home I'd ever known!

In spite of the lateness of the day I decided to walk out across the fields to where he was working. Even before I got close to him, the look on his face told me that, in fact he did know what was happening. Seeing that telling look I almost walked away without speaking, but he caught my arm and held me fast.

'Tis the only thing for it, maid, you love the boy as a mother should, but you can't do that, not now, deep down you know it.'

His gentle eyes were full of tears; 'As for you leaving Home Farm, maid, it's not just you, we're all leaving, we'll be moving into Yeovil, into a council house...' I was stunned! 'But what about your farm work, how will you do that from a council house in Yeovil? I asked.

'Ah well, I'm comin off the farm, see, I've been offered a job in the building trade. There's a lot of houses that need repairin and building now we're almost done with the war, maid,' he sighed.

'And,' he began before I could speak, 'If you think about it, we'll be a lot nearer you and grandma Miller, so you'll be able ta visit as much as you like.'

As I walked back across the fields, I tried to take it all in; dad was coming off the land, moving into a town, I'd never have believed it had I not heard it direct from him.

I thought my siblings would be sad at the thought of leaving the countryside but instead they were excited at the prospect of a new adventure. I couldn't really blame them, for the past 5 years, their lives had been all about travelling the highway, not knowing what the next place would be like. Now there was the surety of a modern house with gas and electricity and even running water and an inside toilet. It was practically luxurious compared to most places we'd called home. That thought brought me up short; did I really believe that? My mind was then filled with memories; of blue bell groves, golden fields of wheat and ancient woodlands, that we ran and played in, if not for ever and a day, then for many wonderful weeks and months.

I smiled, but nothing lasts forever, not even if you wish it would. In an instant, images of our Jack and Danny floated to the fore and I had to force away the sadness once more; 'James will live for you now, he has your names, you know, and I've given him to mum'… I whisper softly to my little brothers. Tears were streaming down my face… 'He's not here to replace you, no one could ever do that… he's just here, another member of the family.' Even as I thought it, I knew deep down that it was not exactly true; I did feel as if Jimmy, as mum insisted on calling him, was in some way a settlement for my part in her losing her two sons back on the heath. Now perhaps she might be able to forgive me.

Chapter 28

I thought Janie's wedding was going to be the next big event in my life but it wasn't, on the 8th of May it was announced that the war was officially over. Suddenly the whole of Yeovil it seemed were on the streets, dancing with strangers and just about anyone who came near and singing their hearts out in sheer joy, people were going mad, but all in a good way, many of them crying tears of joy. Finally, it was over, the bloody Germans were beaten... pubs were throwing their doors open offering free beer to everyone, cafes too, were offering free food and hot drinks and all the while the church bells were ringing out all across the land, proclaiming victory... finally!

I met our Janie in the Borough and we danced and sang along with everyone else, staying well into the night, without the worry of curfew anymore. We met up with our siblings after that and celebrated with mum and dad down on Home Farm along with some of the Gypsies down the lane, all of whom, strangely couldn't stop weeping. After I'd bottle fed James, Janie and I went back to share some time with grannie Miller and we raised a glass or two in honour of all the gallant men and women who had died to make this moment possible. Janie stayed over and we shared a bed and talked through the night, of our dear brothers and of Lady Seymour and her children, recounting the old times and of times yet to come.

May 20nd 1945! Janie's wedding! It was on us before we knew it and what with everyone preparing to leave Home Farm it came just in time. Mum had the food for the reception ready, along with a fresh made wedding cake, all of which was laid out across the kitchen and living room, down at Home Farm. Thankfully one of our neighbours offered to watch Jimmy and keep an eye on the food, allowing mum to come to the ceremony in Yeovil.

Our Janie looked beautiful as she walked arm in arm with dad down the aisle, it was all I could do to stop from crying, but as much as it was our Janie's day, I couldn't take my eyes off dad, he looked so very proud and happy. I couldn't help but feel a little envious and prayed that one day he would do the same for me. But I quickly snapped out of it, this was my sister's day not mine.

Later, with the ceremony over and with the photos being taken outside the church I found the chance to sidle up to Janie; 'You alright, Sis,' I whispered. She smiled and kissed my cheek before burrowing back into Ian her new husband's side.

'I can't tell you how wonderful I feel Rub, it's like a dream come true.'

I couldn't reply, as choked up as I was, and the tears that I shed were tears of joy at seeing my darling sister so happy.

It was one of the happiest days ever, there was about twenty people, both family and friends who followed us back to the farm for the reception, a reception that went on well into the evening and only stopped when Janie and Ian made their escape to go on their honeymoon.

'Where are they going?' I asked mum as they left in Ian's old ford car.

'Torquay, if his old car will make it that far,' mum sniffed, watching them judder up the lane. 'He calls himself a mechanic,' she grumbled, as the car popped and spluttered its way up to the main road.

'Oh my God!' I thought to myself, can't she be happy for anyone?

'You'd best stay over tonight; I'll be needing help to clear up as father's off to Yeovil market first thing and won't want to see this mess on getting up.' Dad had slipped away early during the reception, no doubt to fix something for one of his farmer friends. I smiled, even now with the war over he was still in demand, what would the farm owners do without him.

Things went forward at a pace after that; I finally left Home Farm to go and live with Granma Miller and then helped the family to move out too, which brought a tear to my eye as I recalled all the good time's we'd had there... but times move on, and so must we. The house they moved to in Yeovil wasn't a new one, but it did have four bedrooms, which was plenty big enough now that Janie and me were gone from home.

After their honeymoon our Janie and Ian moved into his cottage out in the country, of which I was very jealous of as it reminded me of our place out on the heath. Bella and Janet were now in charge of the little ones although they weren't so little anymore, they were growing up fast. Our Violet and Morgan were about to start school and Charlie would soon be following them, which was grossly unfair, Janie and me decided whenever we got together for a chat. 'Think of all the times we had to see to everyone, just about every hour of the day,' I grumbled. 'And our Bella and Jan only have them before and after school.'

'And I bet they complain at that!' Janie said shaking her head.

'Still, we did our share of moaning and clipping ears, don't you think?' I grinned.

I often think of those days when Janie and me were in charge of our siblings travelling the countryside in beat up old lorries, not knowing where our next stop might be. It was an adventure, like something out of a comic book, and it didn't seem real now, just a childhood fantasy that we've woken up from, something that never really happened at all.

Being away from the farm and in a new environment makes me feel more grown up somehow, Grandma Miller lets me do pretty much as I please as long as I don't have the wireless too loud or have rowdy friends around too often.

She's not much of a talker though, and I miss that, I was used to having Janie or one of my other sisters to air my troubles to, but Gran prefers silence. She does open up occasionally though, usually when she's had a nip of gin!

One night after supper she brought out a bottle from the kitchen and asked me to join her in a toast to the end of the war and all the good men and women who had fought for us. I hesitated, I would not be turning 17 until later in the year and in truth I'd never really drunk alcohol.

Grandma giggled; 'Mothers ruin! That's what they call this, but it's a bit late for it to be the ruin of us don't you think?' she tittered reaching to refill her glass and mine.   I refused any more and so she just topped up her own glass.

'I know about the baby,' she announced after another couple swigs of Gin.

'Is that why you're plying me with Gin then, Granny, because you think I'm a girl of easy virtue,' I snapped angrily.

'No, oh no, my pet, my knowing about the child and us drinking Gin together has nothing to do with that. If there is anyone here of easy virtue then it's me!' she sighed, setting the bottle down on the table.

'You? I don't understand,' I frowned.

She took my hand then and I couldn't believe the story she told me... it seems my gentle loving Grandma was at one time during the first world war, a prostitute!

'You're, mother knows, most of the family do too, although I'm not sure if my son, your, father does, even if he does, he won't believe it, he's that sort of man,' she said.

For the next hour or so we sat and drank and talked and she told me what had led her into that life. 'I had 16 children to feed, house, and clothe, and with my husband, your Grandfather away fighting in the great war, it was impossible. His army pay was always getting to me late and sometimes not at all and the children were starving, and so I did what I did, and I'm not ashamed of it. Your father and most of his brothers and sisters survived although some didn't!' she added sadly. She put her arm around me; 'So you see, I'll never judge you Ruby, not ever.'

Her words gave me strength and I was determined to do more to find my son's father. I would go one more time back to where it all began in the village of Burley. A good six months had passed since my last time there and perhaps with the war over, there might be some news of James. I left on the train from Yeovil Station the very next day, trying desperately not to expect too much, but with my hopes high just the same… maybe, just maybe this time it would be different, this time I would hear news of him! But the day did not start well!

As I arrived at the café, I found my friend Darcy closing it up!
'With the troops gone, sadly, the place isn't paying its way anymore,' she sighed.
'Oh dear, what will the villagers do without you?' I frowned.
She laughed, 'Well they'll have one less person to gossip about that's for sure.'
'But seriously, where will you go? I pressed.
She held out her hand, showing me the ring on her finger, 'his name is Henry and he owns a hotel in Cornwall, so you see, Ruby my dear, I'll not be alone. But you'll have to promise to visit, I couldn't bear the thought of us never seeing each other again.'
I gave her a hug; 'I'll miss you,' I sighed. 'And I promise I'll visit, and we'll write too, won't we?' I couldn't stop the tears as they streamed down my cheeks. She passed me a hankie and I dabbed my eyes, 'I thought I might try one last time to find out about James, I don't suppose you've heard anything?'

She shook her head, 'No, sorry, nothing, but then everything is chaos even though the war is over. All you can do Ruby is hope for the best but brace yourself for bad news, my darling girl.' She sighed sadly. I knew she was right but still I went up to the US base full of hope, after all, men believed to be lost were turning up all the time!

I found the camp almost empty, with just a skeleton crew manning it, and as I stood waiting to be seen, I was filled with despair, wondering, just what had become of all the brave soldiers that had been stationed there? When finally, an officer came, despite his weary, care worn image, he was kind and asked me into his office for a coffee, there we talked for a while, but alas to no avail. In the end he held up his hands and apologised, saying that very little news was coming back to Burley now, and very soon, he and what was left of his outfit would be moving out for good. And so, I left with still no news of James. Sadly, I had to concede that the chances were that I might never see him again.

As sad as that conclusion was, it felt as if my life had shifted somehow. I knew now that it was time to move on, time to put the trauma of the war behind me. But what now I wondered as I stepped off the train onto the platform at Yeovil Junction? My dream of going to America with my son in my arms and my lover James by my side, was now just that, a dream... a dream of a silly young girl!

'Yes, it's time to move on;' that little voice in my head repeated yet again! 'You can't keep going over old ground. That part of your life is done now; no more running back to Burley, he's not there, he'll never be there! Pick a new road, everyone else is, even dad's come off the land! As much as I wanted to ignore that silly annoying little voice I couldn't for it was only telling me what I already knew. It was time... no it was way past time, for me to move on.

Despite feeling sad at not finding James; I felt like a great weight had been lifted from my shoulders. Looking back, true we'd had some bad times, but we'd also shared some good times too my siblings and me. And good and bad is all part of the mix when it comes to life, especially farm life. One day your tip-toing through a yard full of cow shit and then dancing in a shady glade full of lovely bluebells.

Right now, it's the bluebell glade that is stuck in my head, and as I walked up the path to Grandma Millers front door, I find myself muttering; 'Beautiful!' simply, 'Beautiful!'

'You alright Ruby,' Grandma, called as I entered, no doubt a little concerned at my silly muttering. 'Any news of your man?'

'No! And now I have to forget him, Gran, I really must.' I could feel the tears welling up as she came to give me a hug.

'Somethings are just not meant to be child! It just means God has something else in mind for you that's all.' I gave in to her hug, but not her words. Like my own mother I had doubts about God! He'd played me false once too often... first my brothers on the heath and then my child and now the love of my life, James. Just how much more pain did he expect me to endure?

'Please don't blame God for all your troubles my dear, it won't help, and it really isn't his fault. He only created us, he doesn't control us', grannie said as if reading my thoughts. 'What we do with our lives is down to us in the end... all the wars and the cruelty it brings with it is our doing, not his.' I wondered at the words of wisdom of a confessed prostitute, as I moved through to the kitchen to put the kettle on. Had God forsaken her or had she forsaken him? In my own mother's defence, she blamed God for taking her two young sons from her. Grandma Miller on the other hand had not lost any of her children... 'Not true!' that nagging little voice, insisted, 'not only was she driven by poverty to do what she'd did to keep them alive, she too lost babies, you heard her say as much!' As I poured the water into the teapot, I watched Gran settling into her chair by the hearth, and my heart went out to her, she'd done everything in her power to save her loved ones, and there was no shame in that. It was me who felt ashamed now, for doubting her because of what she'd done. Now I could understand her praising God, by sinning she had saved her children, and the fact that most had survived was proof to her of God's forgiveness!

I decided, as I carried the tray with the tea things on it that I'd give God one last chance, but if he did me wrong again then I'd be done with him.

'So how are mum, dad and the family doing, Gran asked, as she dunked a biscuit in her tea, 'I've not seen them since the wedding.'

I frowned; 'but that was weeks ago, I've been to Burley and back since then, never mind I'll go over to see them later today.'

'You make sure you do maid, I expect yore father is missing you terribly,' she insisted.

I'd not given much thought to dad lately, he was always such a funny, jokey man, nothing much troubled him. Mum might be the matriarch of the family but he was the one who kept our spirits up when we were feeling low during our darkest days. I should take into account that the world was changing for him, with the war now over, all the men would be returning back to civilian life! But he was clever was my dad, that's why he had secured himself a new job away from the farm and found work in the building trade. He hadn't changed though, he still laughed and joked and told his silly ghost stories, and frightened us all half to death, and we still loved him for it. He was without doubt a man to be proud of, as unafraid of the future as he had been of the past when we'd travelled the countryside with no idea of what lay ahead. In my heart I just wanted to be like him to face the future and all that it held with my head up high and a smile on my lips.

I felt a little guilty as I made my way across the town to where the family now lived longing to see my darling, growing son. I'd not seen much of anyone since moving in with Gran. And even though I revelled in my new found freedom, a part of me yearned to be with them, back on the road again! To have mum berating me and our Janie big sistering me… but that was all gone now. I seldom saw anything of our Janie, and mum preferred, because of little James, not to invite me around so often.

And anyway, since their move into Yeovil nothing seemed the same anymore! Dad worked hard, but then he always did and yet somehow, he didn't seem to fit into a town, he's of the country, a true journeyman. But of course, he wouldn't complain, but then he never did, and he seemed happy enough working on building sites.

The truth is, everyone seemed happy apart from me! My sisters, Janet, Bella and even little Violet had settled into their new school, less than a mile from where the family now lived, leaving only three of the little-ones and my Jimmy for mum to see too. I did offer to help but she refused, saying I had my own life to lead now! If the family had still been on the farm and she'd had all her other chores to do, she might have been glad of my help, but they weren't and so she could cope on her own. It was a torment as I lay on my bed at grandma's that night, knowing that I was only searching for reasons to be around James! Helping mum was just an excuse, she and everyone else knew it, and I blushed at the thought. Casting it all aside, I sat up with a new conviction, to stop being sad and to stop blaming myself for everything.

'Goodbye Jack... Goodbye Danny,' I whispered softly, 'Rest in peace my dear brothers,' I sighed... with that, I let them go.

The next morning, I awoke to laughter coming from grandma's living-room, I looked at the clock on the bedroom wall, it was just past 7:30am, a little early for visitors. Rubbing the sleep from my eyes I went down to see who it was?
Mum was sat on the sofa with James on her lap. I ached to reach forward and take him in my arms, but I simply smiled and nodded. 'Nice to see you, mum, how's our little Ja... I mean Jimmy?' I corrected quickly.

'We're both well, thank you, maid, I was just saying to grannie that perhaps you could see to Jimmy for the day, only your father's off to the market, he's after a new hen and a rooster... but as you know, the last time I let him go alone he returned with a pair of bantams! The most useless birds ever bred, they lay eggs the size of marbles, and are too small to make a decent meal!' she sighed.

I was so pleased at the prospect of spending the day with James and silently blessed dad for his poor taste in chickens, for I agreed with mum, bantams were rubbish! It was a mystery to all of us just what dad saw in them... but for some strange reason, he loved them.

'So, you'll take him for the day then?' mum asked.

It had been a long time since I'd seen her so happy. 'I just thought that it's time you moved on maid, I know you went back in search of James again,' she sighed.
Before I could answer, Grandma Miller put a hand on my shoulder and glared at mother; 'I agree, it's time we all moved on my dears,' she smiled.

Later as I walked with mum to the bus stop, pushing our son on ahead of me, I could only hope that she understood that Grandma was saying she should move on as well. But regardless of whether she did or not, I knew that I had too! With that in mind as mum caught her bus leaving my son in my care, if only for the day, I suddenly felt free of the past. Then, the little voice whispered inside my head again, this is your time, your sweetheart James is never coming back and your son is safe and being taken care of. Now you must go forward, find a life for yourself, the whole world is changing now the war is over.

Up ahead, I saw people stop to read something pasted on the bus shelter. On reaching it I saw that it was advertising a dance in the town hall... I hadn't been to a dance since Burley! I smiled on remembering that time when I'd gone out dancing with our Janie and she'd punched a soldier and broke his nose! I found myself chuckling and had to put a hand to my mouth. For the first time since those days at Burley, I felt happy, really happy and even baby James was content as he slept peacefully in his pram.

'Hey Rube where are you going, I was on my way to visit you at Grannies?'

I turned to find our Janie standing there, trying to steal a peek at James. 'Just giving our boy a bit of fresh air Sis,' I smiled. I told her about my latest trip down to Burley as we walked and of my resolve to finally move on, she put her arm around me; 'It's time sis, it really is,' she sighed. I caught up her hand; 'It is alright isn't it, Sis, I mean it's not too early for me to be giving up my search, is it?'

She smiled; 'no, you can only keep searching for so long our Rube and you deserve to be happy.'

I sighed, 'At least he left me James to remember him by.'

'Yes, but I'll not call him James, our Ruby, he's in mum's charge now, you gave him to her, remember? If she wants us to call him Jim or Jimmy, or whatever, then that's what we'll call him,' Janie insisted.

She was being quite the big sister again and I could tell by the look in her eye that she was in no mood to be argued with.

'I guess so,' I sighed.

We'd reached grannie Miller's house. 'Alright then what about this cup of tea?' Janie grinned as we went inside. Grannie was pleased to have us back so soon and we enjoyed a nice natter before Janie took her leave of us. As she was leaving, she pressed a note into my hand then went on her way. But before I had the chance to read it James woke up. He needed changing, and so I put the note unread into my pocket, and promptly forgot all about it.

For the rest of the day, I stayed with grannie and little James, enjoying a rare long spell with him.

'Two bloody pairs, of bantams yore father bought,' mum swore as she came in, there was no stoppin the man, crazy for em, he is!'

Grandma and I both chuckled; 'I thought you'd gone to stop dad?' I laughed.

Mum reached to clip my ear, still as proficient at it as ever she was when I was small, and chuckling grannie, clipped her right back, and we all laughed. After she and Jim had gone, I remembered Janes note, so leaving grannie in the kitchen I went up to my bedroom where I could be alone. When I read it, I was astonished!

'Guess what Sis... I'm pregnant! I almost fell off my bed, wanting only to hurry to see her, I needed to give her a big hug and tweak her ear for not telling me in person. With no thought for anything else I hurried to catch the bus out to her village, which thankfully was but a mile or so from Yeovil.

'Oh my God, Sis! How long have you known... does mum and dad know? When's it due?' I hurled at her almost before the front door was open. 'Oh, and take that for not telling me sooner,' I said, tweaking her ear.

'Ouch! You little slut, I owe you one for that,' she threatened playfully.

'I suppose Ian knows?' I asked.

'Well of course he does, he's really pleased, we both are, just think our children will grow up together... perhaps they'll be friends, maybe best friends?' Janie grinned.

'So, it'll be James and... have you chosen any names yet, sis,' I asked.

She laughed; 'Cherry if it's a girl and Peter for a boy.'

'Oh perfect,' I clapped... and it'll be a boy, I'm sure it will... James and Peter, best friends,' I sighed.

Reaching across she dug me in the ribs... 'Jimmy and Peter, best friends,' she corrected with a smile.

We both laughed; 'unless it's Jimmy and Cherry,' best friends,' Janie chuckled.

....

But it was a boy and Jimmy and Peter did grow up together and become best friends... Sadly I never did hear any more of my lover James from Burley but I did find someone else and we married and had 4 children. We lived up north mainly so I didn't see much of my son James. But after Reg's death I returned to my roots, going back to live in Yeovil, where I could be close to James. He knew who I was by then, mum had told him in the year 1966 when he turned 21, but of course to him I was now forever his sister Ruby.

After first mum died and then dad, it was left to the rest of us to remember and try and retell the amazing adventures we'd experienced through the war years. But sadly, as the years rolled by one by one my siblings, even the little-ones died, until only Janet, Janie and myself were left. It was so hard to come to terms with, we had gone through so much together. I thought nothing could make me any sadder than I felt on losing them. But then our Janie was diagnosed with Alzheimer's and put in a care home by her loving son Peter, where he and my James were her constant visitors.

On her last day they summoned me in to sit with her and I held her hand to the last... my wonderful, magnificent Janie. She never spoke to me but near the end as I leaned in to kiss her cheek, she tweaked my ear, and then she was gone.

As I made to leave with my son James and her son Peter, to find our Janet and break the sad news, one of the nurses came and gave me something... it was a letter, gone brown with age... but I recognised it right away as the letter from the Ministry that had started our long journey down to the heath. I was transported back to Home Farm, a child again, trudging along the hallway once more to open the door to the odd-looking man in black standing there in the shitty yard...

I scowled, and in my head began again the journey that had taken us down to our magical white-walled house on the heath.

The End

Footnote by James Miller

When Ruby Miller finally passed away her last wish was that her ashes be laid to rest with her brothers Jack and Danny at the Cemetery, down in the village of Sandbourne.

Although Ruby failed to find out what had become of her James, years later I managed to trace him with the aid of DNA... he'd survived the war and returned to America where he married and had 2 daughters. He passed away in the 1990s before he could meet me... his son James.

But now a new chapter in our family's remarkable story has begun, as I get to know my two beautiful American sisters and their families.

IN
LOVING MEMORY OF
OUR TWO DEAR BOYS
JOHN AND DENNIS MITCHELL
DIED AUGUST 2ND 1941
AGED 11 AND 8 YEARS
GONE BUT NOT FORGOTTEN
ALSO RAYMOND RODDICK
OUR DEARLY LOVED SON
DIED AUGUST 2ND 1941 AGED 8
PLAYED TOGETHER
DIED TOGETHER
PALS TO THE END

ROY MICHAEL RODDICK
TWIN BROTHER TO RAYMOND
1932 - 2013
REUNITED